Black Country Orphan

Birmingham Rose
Birmingham Friends
Birmingham Blitz
Orphan of Angel Street
Poppy Day
The Narrowboat Girl
Chocolate Girls
Water Gypsies
Miss Purdy's Class
Family of Women
Where Earth Meets Sky
The Bells of Bournville Green
A Hopscotch Summer
Soldier Girl
All the Days of Our Lives
My Daughter, My Mother
The Women of Lilac Street
Meet Me Under the Clock
War Babies
Now the War Is Over
The Doorstep Child
Sisters of Gold
The Silversmith's Daughter
Mother and Child
Girls in Tin Hats

ANNIE MURRAY

Black Country Orphan

MACMILLAN

First published 2021 by Macmillan
an imprint of Pan Macmillan
The Smithson, 6 Briset Street, London EC1M 5NR
Associated companies throughout the world
www.panmacmillan.com

ISBN 978-1-5290-1179-1

1 3 5 7 9 8 6 4 2

A CIP catalogue record for this book is available from the British Library.

Typeset in Stempel Garamond by Jouve (UK), Milton Keynes
Printed and bound by CPI Group (UK) Ltd, Croydon, CR0 4YY

Visit **www.panmacmillan.com** to read more about all our books
and to buy them. You will also find features, author interviews and
news of any author events, and you can sign up for e-newsletters
so that you're always first to hear about our new releases.

Dedicated to the memory of
Mary Reid Macarthur, 1880–1921

We then visited Spinners End, near to the Five Ways, Cradley Heath, where we saw numbers of women and girls making 'American Swimmers', as they are called, or more properly, 'traces, cow bands, small twist link' etc.

This sight will not be easily effaced from our recollection. For while we boast in England of our Christianity, there are some things done which if the sun were made to shine upon them, would appal the heart . . .

Report from representatives of the
northern unions, 1859

My first glimpse of Cradley Heath was a dark November afternoon. The train stopped just outside the station and from the window of the carriage I looked down on a long, low shed. The iron gratings which served as windows, the red glow of the forge fires and the dim shadows of the toiling workers made me think of some torture chamber from the Middle Ages. Later, when I knew more of the life and labour of the district, that first fleeting impression returned and has never quite left me since.

Mary Macarthur, 1907

For an hour the pageant wound through the dejected street . . . till it came to a deserted slag heap, selected for speech making . . . As I watched, a strong fancy visited my brain. I seemed to see over every rugged head of these marching women a little yellow flame, a thin flickering gleam . . . a trick of the sunlight maybe? Or was it the life in their heads, the indistinguishable breath of happiness, had for a moment escaped prison, and was fluttering at the pleasure of the breeze?

It seemed to me that in these tattered, wistful figures, so still, so trustful, I was looking on such beauty as I never beheld.

> *John Galsworthy, reporting on the first day*
> *of the strike, Cradley Heath, 1910*

A Chainmaking Town

The town of Cradley Heath grew up on a rough heathland between the great city of Birmingham, situated to the east, and the lands bordering Wales to the west. North of this place, the town of Dudley, with its Lord and his castle, his mines and factories; to the south, Worcester with its cathedral tower looking over the River Severn and surrounded by rolling farmlands.

Cradley Heath lay in the south of the region known as the Black Country for its coal mines, its innumerable chimneys belching smoke, its manufacture in an array of specialist trades too various to list in full: tin-plating and japanning in Wolverhampton and saddlery in Walsall; optics for lighthouses at Smethwick, enamels at Bilston. Spread all over the region was the mining of shallow, abundant seams of coal, the smelting of iron and production of steel and, threading all through and about, the watery network of canals built expressly for the transportation of these materials and products. And – lying surrounded by its neighbouring villages of Cradley, Old Hill, Quarry Bank and Netherton – Cradley Heath, the clanging, filthy, impoverished centre of the world's production of chains.

It was a mean, soot-covered town for whose inhabitants, at the close of the nineteenth century, no civic authority had thought to furnish provision of a library, of public baths, or any parks. A town along whose shabby, functional streets, nailmakers, chain forgers and coal miners lived in clustered groups, upholding each other in their joys and sorrows.

The town was dominated by the hammering of chains of all weights and sizes, for the world's ships and industries, its farms and slave owners. The heaviest chains were forged in the larger works, such as Samuel Woodhouse & Sons and Richard Sykes & Son. Much of the lighter calibre chain was hand-hammered by outworkers in cramped, fume- and smoke-filled, backyard forges. Most of these outworkers, earning less than one fifth of what a man working in a factory could expect, were women.

For anyone not familiar with Black Country terms, there is a glossary at the back of the book. And if you are from the Black Country and you find anything that feels wrong – all I can do is apologize.

I
Cradley Heath, Staffordshire

One

1898

'Go on, little wench – you go with our John and our Clem and they'll tek care on yer.'

Lucy Butler, five years old and facing her first day of school, was so frit she thought she might bring back the watery sop she had just forced down into her belly. Go out from this yard, which she had seldom ever left in her life, and struggle all the way to the terrifying school with John and Clem Hipkiss! Boys who could run and play the way she never could. Lads who, most of the time, looked right through her. Could she be one of them – just for this once?

She stood in the yard, in a new dress for this special occasion, which Mom had sat up stitching during the candlelit hours. Over the top she wore a little white pinafore. And her mother, Ellen Butler, had cut her hair pudding-basin short, her mouse-brown fringe chopped in a dead straight line above her trusting blue eyes.

It was Mrs Hipkiss who had spoken – the boys' mother. Lucy squinted up into the dark-browed face of their neighbour. Bertha Hipkiss loomed before her in the rare beam of morning sunlight which had managed to force its way into the smoky yard. She wore a cap yanked down tight over her black hair like a man, but her chain-maker's apron – a rough length of hessian tied over her skirts riddled with scorch marks – was thrust out at the front, her most womanly childbed belly rounded as a heap of slag.

John and Clem Hipkiss, eight and a half and seven years old, also seemed like giants to Lucy. They stood in front of their mother, shirts tucked into their britches, cut-down weskits and caps on newly shorn heads. John was quiet, solemn as usual, Clem grinning like a Cheshire cat.

Lucy had known the Hipkiss lads all her life, seen them tearing about the yard, scrambling up the back wall to gaze over all that lay beyond – things she could never do though she longed to with all her heart. She could play marleys and jackstones and little games with the girls or her baby brother George – but when it came to tip-cat and tag, running and climbing, she was always the one watching in the shadows at the edge. The lads barely spared her a glance on any other day. Lucy, cripple girl, widow's child, had already learned not to expect much from anyone.

George, who was two, toddled over and clung to her, snivelling. They were inseparable most of the time, Lucy his playmate and protector.

'Dow go . . . Wanna come with yow . . .' He banged his head against Lucy's thigh, clinging to her good leg.

'Ow!' she said. 'That hurts, Georgie!'

'Pack it in, George – yow cor go to school . . .' Ellen Butler, Lucy's mother, scooped the sobbing little lad up on to her bony hip. 'I wish our Albert could tek 'er,' she said to Bertha Hipkiss, her face tight with anxiety. 'P'raps I should go with 'er, just this once.'

Ellen, a malnourished wisp next to Bertha Hipkiss, looked as though the wind might blow her over. She was also dressed for work at the chain hearth, her thinning brown hair scragged into a bun. Although her once pretty face now looked pinched by endless work, by fretting over every farthing and poor fittle, there was still a sweetness to her which she had passed on to Lucy. Already exhausted from a day at the hearth, she had sat up late last night to sew the little frock from a dusty-blue rag of a skirt, the very best she could manage for her one, precious girl.

Albert, Lucy's elder brother, was still allowed go to the foundry school because their father had worked at the foundry. Mom said it was too far for Lucy to walk. She would go to Lomey Town with the Hipkiss lads instead.

Lucy was glad of that in one respect – she never liked going anywhere with Albert. He was five years older than her, would lug her up resentfully on to his back, yanking her arms over his shoulders until it felt they would pop out of their sockets. He'd not a shred of patience in his nature. But how was she going to keep up with the Hipkiss lads on her crutches? Her belly clenched again with nerves.

''Er'll be all right, Ellen,' Bertha said. 'You go with them, Lucy.' She gave her boys a menacing look. 'Yow lads – mind the 'oss road and mind out for Lucy – mek sure yow wait for 'er, gorrit?'

'Yes, Mom,' they chorused.

No one of sound mind would contradict Bertha Hipkiss, gaffer of the yard, a tanker, a locomotive of a woman. Nor would anyone comment to her face on her being up the stick again at her age, even with a husband as sick as hers was. His only remaining pleasure, the women tittered behind Bertha's back, but there was no spite in it, for everyone sorrowed for poor Jonno Hipkiss.

'Goo on then – off with yer,' she waved a hand over them.

Pulling her crutches in close, pressing the worn leather tops up into her armpits, Lucy tucked back her scrawny shoulder blades and tried to stand straight on her one good leg. She was ready – she could do this!

'Bring 'er back with yow, lads!' Ellen Butler's eyes were fixed on Lucy as if she never wanted to let her go.

'Yow've gorra let 'er out of yower sight some time, Ellen,' Bertha said, turning away.

Lucy's heart was banging fit to match the hammers chinking in the smithy behind her. A sick feeling curdled the sop in her stomach, to which Mom had even added a rare drop of milk.

'Yow gunna need yower strength today,' she said, and stroked her scarred fingers over Lucy's head. In that touch, Lucy knew all her exhausted love.

But a shadow fell over that sunlit moment. *His* voice, rough and filthy as slack, boomed from the entry. Lucy saw the way her mother's jaw clenched. Loathing flared in her eyes.

'What's all this then, my wenches?'

Seth Dawson was the fogger for their employer, Ridley & Sons Ltd, the chain works half a mile up the road. He did that all the time, creeping up on them, rank as a fart. Lucy sometimes glimpsed him, his hat a shadow passing the window after creeping along the entry into their yard, snooping about as he did so.

The foggers, or middlemen – a few were women, though none the better for it – were the enforcers of the firm. Seth Dawson brought them their orders and the nine-foot iron rods for working into chains. Some of the foggers made the women fetch their own but they reckoned Dawson liked to bring them so he could have a good nose around and keep an eye on them. He took a quarter of the worth of everything they made and his main activity seemed to be beating down wages and crushing their souls – not to mention groping the unmentionables of any woman available if he got half a chance.

Seth Dawson had appeared as an incomer from Birmingham years back, unmarried, and even now had not so much as a whammel for company. Stranded somewhere in middle age, he was a stunted barrel of a man, swarthy of face with black stubble scattered like mould over the lower part of his bullying features. He wore a black billycock over black hair – both coated in filth and grease. His belly strained at his weskit buttons and his walk was crouching and bandy-legged.

'E cor stop a pig in an entry, that'un,' Bertha said of him.

Plenty of other remarks were made about what ugly fruit might be hanging down there between Seth Dawson's crooked thighs – or so he'd like you to think. Never be alone with him, that was the rule.

He liked to leave the buttons of his collarless shirt undone so that a pelt of black hair bristled out at the edges. And he had a way of standing, thumbs hooked into his weskit pockets, rocking as he spoke. He had a poor stock of words and none worth the time to listen to.

'I don't see much sign 'o work 'ere this mornin' . . .' he grunted, rocking on his heels.

The women did the only thing they could do so far as possible which was to ignore him. Mrs Gornall and Mrs Wilmott were already hammering away in the forge in any case, the usual *chink-chink* of hammer on metal filling the air. Lucy's mother cast her gaze to the ground where cinders glistened in the sunlight, as if to pretend he wasn't there. Bertha stared right back at him.

'. . . and you wenches always mitherin' over yer wages . . . I can't go on paying yer at this rate if yer doing nowt but idling . . . Yer tekkin' the coat off of my back . . .'

Coat off his back – at these sweated, starvation-level rates! But what could they say? This evil man had power over all their livelihoods. Refuse to work, and there was always someone would take your place.

A furious yell suddenly echoed round the yard.

'What d'yow want now, yow Brummy divil? Come to flay more of the skin off of our backs 'ave yow, yow filthy varmint?'

Lucy's grandfather, Old Man Walker, was standing propped in the doorway of their house, shaking his fist, his face contorted with rage. He had long white hair like an ancient prophet and was prematurely bent and stooped.

'Pa!' Ellen hurried over to him. 'Come back inside.' She hustled the old man into the house out of sight, shutting the door as she returned.

'The work'll be done.' Bertha Hipkiss had her hands on her hips. Lucy couldn't decide which of them was more terrifying, though she knew who was most evil by far. The sight of Seth Dawson made her feel queasier still. 'Goo on kids,' she waved them away. 'Get yower-selves off.'

The three of them had been as if turned to stone in those moments, but now Lucy set off gamely over the rough ground after the boys, swinging herself along on her crutches as fast as she could.

Clem immediately ran ahead, whooping to make his voice echo as he scampered along the entry between the Hipkisses' old cottage and the other yard houses. John, the elder of the two, was a quieter, stiffer kind of boy. Unlike Clem, who was always on the go, now and again, when there was nothing else doing, he even sat and joined in a game with Lucy.

They left the yard and set out along Hay Lane, the short track parallel to the railway embankment, which took them to the main road at one end and petered out into the fields at the other. The air was thick with smoke from myriad chimney stacks, and from the train that had just gone by, billowing a long black flag behind it.

'Does it hurt?' John asked as they headed for the main road.

Bravely, Lucy shook her head, pushing her chin up.

They had had to cut her right leg from her body, just below the knee, when she was only five months old.

Always, she might have said. And the crutches pushed up hard into her armpits. Her shoulders were strong by now, but she had never been this far before – she had to keep going!

Every night, however worn out she was, Mom always washed the end of her amputated leg with carbolic soap and dried it very carefully like the doctor advised. She washed the rag and hung it out every day, doing her best to keep everything clean. It worked a lot of the time, but regularly Lucy would feel a tingle begin at the end of the stump, a sore patch which would break out and take a time to heal. Mom would make poultices of bee balm or chamomile.

At the sight of her stump and the scars on her other leg, Albert would make gagging sounds and turn away, however much Mom scolded him for unkindness. Sometimes Lucy dreamt that she had two legs and could run free, on and on for ever.

Clem capered about the busy street. He was a sunny lad, swarthy-skinned and strong with a head of treacle-brown curls. At present he had a gappy grin because some of his milk teeth had come out. Beside him John, his older brother, seemed a shadow. He was pale and bony, with thin brown hair and a quiet, inward personality. Lucy knew though, that John would usually be kind where Clem was forever exciting.

'D'yow want me to carry yer?' John asked.

Lucy hesitated. She hated being lugged about like a sack of spuds and it hurt her arms. But walking was so painful and tiring – dot-and-carry-one she had passed under the railway bridge, the huge chimneys of the blast furnace looming behind them. They still had to go all the way between the houses and shops on Graingers Lane to Five Ways and Lomey Town. She was already flagging and her arms ached. John had asked kindly and he would be gentle, not like Albert.

'All right.'

She held a crutch in each hand and went to dangle them over in front of him the way she did with Albert, as John gathered her up into a piggyback.

'Clem, come 'ere and carry these crutches!' he instructed.

Clem ran back and took them, clowning around. It was so funny seeing him dodging round on them, annoying everyone who was trying to get along, that Lucy was soon giggling. Her nerves began to seep away, as well as the dark cloud of Seth Dawson. She felt safe with John – but Clem was so funny and naughty!

They heard the blare of a trumpet further along the street.

'It's the tat-mon!' Clem called, tearing on ahead.

The rag-and-bone man strode along the street, giving out his usual cry. His lad, of about twelve, led the big brown-and-white horse which clip-clopped along, pulling the cart.

Whether that was what distracted John, Lucy never knew, but it was then that his ankle turned and he suddenly plunged, face first.

Lucy gasped, clinging on as the ground rushed up at her and they crashed, she rolling off him at the last minute and slamming her shoulder on the cobbles. John groaned as if the wind had been knocked out of him.

A woman stopped to help him up, but after that, Clem's face, with its solid jaw and laughing brown eyes, was suddenly so close that he was all she could see; looking up to this big man of seven years old.

'Yow all right, Luce? Blimey, John – yow both went a right purler!'

'T'weren't my fault!' John snapped, his face red. 'My ankle got twisted – in that 'ole!'

'I'm all right.' Lucy took Clem's hand and was scrambling up, no blarting – she was used to pain. Her shoulder didn't hurt so very much.

John got up once he had his breath back and everyone faded away, seeing they were just kids who could fall and recover like pups. But Clem was still holding Lucy's hand, waiting to give her the crutches back. When she straightened up, he looked into her face and there again, full beam, were Clem Hipkiss's eyes, not laughing or teasing for once, but serious and intent.

And Lucy felt something in her give a little flip, silver-bright like a landed fish. There was she, five infant years to Clem's seven, in the mucky street by the rag-and-bone man's cart, and on that sunny September morning, before she even got to school for the first time, she had lost her heart to him.

Two

1893

'That's it – you 'ave a good feed, my little Lucy Ann . . .'

Ellen sat cross-legged on the straw mattress, a fragile, pretty young woman of thirty, with wide blue eyes, her child at her breast. The night was bitter and she was wearing all her clothes except for her cracked old boots which stood beside the mattress, shaped by the wear of many years by someone else, even before they came to her ownership. She cuddled the nursing child in the ends of her woollen shawl, which smelt of smoke and sweat and milk.

'And you, my little mon . . .' Ellen leaned down and for the umpteenth time that night, laid her hand on her young son's forehead. She had blown out the stub of candle so as not to waste it but she could feel that Albert, who was five, was burning up. His forehead was hot as new bread and he kept thrashing about, pained whimpers coming from him.

'You've got to fight it, son,' she murmured desperately, stroking his dark hair. 'You'll have to fight back . . .'

Late as it was – the church clock had struck midnight some time ago – she could still hear hammering coming from the forge across the yard. Aggie Robinson putting in her night's work. It suited her, she said. Get it done while the kids were asleep. She was a mardy cow any case,

14

so if she slept the morning away without them having to look at her squilty fizzog, no one was pining.

'You want to watch you don't find you-know-who turning up while you're out 'ere all alone,' some of the women warned her.

'If that bastard Dawson comes in 'ere trying it on, I'll tek this and knock 'im and 'is filthy *thing* to kingdom come!' Aggie would say, brandishing her hammer. ''E wants to try it.' They knew she meant it as well, what with her drunken rages.

Exhausted as she was from working at the hearth all day, feeding her child and tending to the family, Ellen's worry would not let her rest. She had never seen her boy as sick as this. At least Lucy, the babby, did not seem to be going down with it. She was five months old now, had been sucking heartily and was now contentedly asleep.

A dog barked out in the night. The men were asleep – she could hear the rattle of a snore through the house. That was not her James, asleep in the next room – he never made that much noise. It was the old man, downstairs in his chair, who snored fit to make the house fall down. She felt very alone, the only one left awake.

Ellen rubbed her cold feet with her free hand. The bones in her spine were sore from pressing against the wall. The baby's lips had relaxed on her nipple but hovered there, her little breaths giving her a pleasurable, tingling sensation. Like James, kissing her tit . . . His loving her, the making of her babbies . . .

'You're my wench – look at yer . . .' How he had always worshipped her slender body – too thin she always thought she was; scraggy after growing up the child of a poor nailmaker. James adored it when she was swollen with milk after a child, his handsome, blue-eyed face crinkling as he smiled at her.

15

James's father had been from Ireland and James had all the charm and dark-haired, blue-eyed looks. But it was not all blarney – he truly loved her. And his smile always moved her because his face had a serious set to it and she was the one who could light it up. She loved to see his eyes change when she unbuttoned her blouse, his muscular body, hard and urgent for her, saying she was his, his wench, that there could never be anyone else . . . Her lips turned up in the darkness, her mind taking refuge in her memories.

She and James had moved to number two, back of twelve, court three, Hay Street, when they married, six years ago. Ellen, small and wiry, was a skilled worker. As a youngster she was apprenticed to a firm in nearby Old Hill where she had learned her skills.

After marrying and having Albert, she left the factory and turned to outwork, joining the many other women slaving in the hot, smoky backyard chain forges with their younger children about them, trying to make ends meet. For those with a husband in work, their meagre wages supplemented his. But for a woman on her own . . . The Lord help her. In these brick hovels women worked side by side for most of the day's God-gifted hours – in between cooking, washing and tending to their families.

All day they stood at the hearths amid the terrible heat, the sparks flying. After the end of the rod had been heated until it glowed, a short section was cut off, bent and hammered into a loop to pass through the last completed link in the chain. The ends were hammered closed and welded together in the fire. The women were on piece work, earning by the yard, so it paid to be quick since it took many hours just to cover the rent.

There was hardly an hour of the day when the *chink-*

chink of a hammer was not heard from the brick forge at the end of the yard. Even working a fourteen-hour day, or more, it was hard to earn much more than five bob a week, once the foggers had taken their cut and they had paid for their fuel for the fire. When a batch of chain was done, unless Seth Dawson stirred himself to bring a dobbin to the yard, which was rare, the women hauled the lengths of chain, hung round their necks like workhorses, the half-mile back to the factory.

Ellen woke, heart pounding.

The boy was thrashing beside her, his body rigid. She could see nothing, hear only terrible little grunting whimpers like nothing she had heard before.

'Albert, what is it? Oh my babby, oh Lord above . . .'

She was across the tiny landing in seconds, jerking at her husband's shoulder.

'Wha'? What's up, woman?'

'It's Albert – there's summat wrong . . . He's really bad . . .'

'He'll be all right. You mollycoddle the lad, Ellen – that yer do!'

'Mollycoddle be damned – he's having a fit!' She was shrieking, pulling on his arm. 'Go and stay with him . . .' She was running back for her boots. 'I'm going for a doctor. I'll tek the babby . . .'

She lifted Lucy in her arms but even by the time she got down to the yard she felt impeded by the weight of her. How could she run like this? Hurrying across to the forge, where the glow of a fire was still showing through the window, she found Aggie Robinson bent over her hearth.

'Our Albert's been took bad – I'm frit 'e's going to die!

Mind this'un for me, will yow, while I go for the doctor? Keep 'er by yow 'til I get back.'

Coughing in the smoke, she laid Lucy, swaddled tightly, in the wooden box on the floor where they put the smaller babbies – she still just fitted. She tore out of the yard, too caught up in her fear and urgency to notice either Aggie swaying on her feet, or the miasma of drink about her.

It seemed to take a terrible long time to get to Dr Gaffney's. Her boots clattered on the blue bricks, the sky stained blood-orange by the glow of foundry furnaces all round town. And when she got to the house, the doctor's wife told her he was out on another call. She could wait for him or try going to another doctor? Later she could not even remember this part of the night because she felt half out of her wits, running here and there. In the end, the other side of town, she found a bad-tempered medical man who said he would follow on after her, if he must.

When she got back to the yard, the first thing on her mind was to go tearing up to her poor Albert.

Later that day she sat, still unable to stop shaking, at Bertha Hipkiss's table. It was before Jonno Hipkiss had his accident and he was working then, over at the lime kilns. Bertha sat – for once – with tea on the table, since something so serious had happened.

'It weren't like any other scream I'd heard on a babby.' Ellen put her pitted hands over her face for a moment, the horror of the sound still in her ears. 'I dunno if 'er were making a noise when I come back to the yard – I never heard anything. I was so set on Albert . . . Lord above . . .' She rocked back and forth in distress. 'But when I went down again . . . It wasn't like a hungry scream . . . It curdled my blood to 'ear it.'

She sat up, pulling her hands away and staring at them for a moment, as if they were someone else's, trembling in front of her. What had happened had still barely sunk in.

'When I ran in, Aggie was sat back against the wall, senseless. 'Er were so kalied 'er never heard my Lucy . . . The noise 'er was making – it was like a little rabbit in a trap.' She stared at Bertha for a second, her eyes stretched wide with the horror, reliving the moment. ''Er was down on the floor in the box, and there was a terrible stink in the place . . .'

Bertha's dark eyes never left Ellen's face. She brought a hand up to her throat, as if to protect herself from what she was about to hear.

'That sodden bitch was out cold. The sparks on her blanket had burned through. I'd swaddled her tight, see, and they must've been smouldering all that time. When I opened up the blanket – or what was left of it . . .' Ellen's head sank and her shoulders started to shake.

'God in heaven.' Bertha got to her feet and, leaning down, gently took the weeping young woman in her arms.

Three

The worst things were the ones she could not remember. At least, not in the way you recall things as if in full light of day, clear in front of you. Sometimes she felt a horror in her body, an agonizing echo of something reaching her, the way ripples eventually lap the edge of a pond after a stone has been dropped in. *The sawing of a tiny bone.* It left her sick and wretched, but she couldn't meet it head on.

She asked her mother, Ellen, about it when she was four. They sat at the table together and it was a moment she would always remember. Mom sitting. Something she hardly ever did, not just sitting, spending time. She was a widow by then, worn to the bone, cheeks pinched and dark shadows under her eyes, desperate to keep her head above water.

Ellen told her about that night when Albert was so sick. Lucy watched her mother's haggard face. Mom looked at her then, very closely, and Lucy could see all Mom's soul shining out of her eyes.

'God in heaven.' Her eyes overflowed as the tears – tears, Mom! – ran down her cheeks. Sniffing, she wiped her face, then reached out and with her bony fingers gently caressed Lucy's gammy leg, the flesh-capped stump with its scars of stitching. 'My little babby! I'll never know how they kept you alive.'

And Lucy knew that for all the bad things Mom had seen, this was the one that haunted her the most: the fire from the sparks from Aggie Robinson's hearth smouldering through her tightly wrapped legs, burning deep through her flesh to the bone on one side. They had to cut just below her knee, the scorch marks on her other thigh leaving it puckered and shiny like the shell of a wasps' nest.

'I thought I'd lose the both of yer that night – you and Albert. They took you to that Guest Hospital all the way over in Dudley and they kept you there a terrible long time. But yow lived, Lucy Butler. I don't know how, but yow'm a strong little wench, and dow yow forget it. Life'll be cruel 'ard for yow at times, but I know you ay the giving-up sort – I saw that right from the start.'

Mom smiled suddenly, her tear-filled eyes brimming with warmth, and she patted Lucy's hand.

'I can see yower dad each time I look in yower lovely blue eyes, babby.'

She picked up her cup again and heaved a deep sigh. 'We'll get by some'ow, eh?'

Mr Clark, who lived round at number fourteen, Hay Lane, made her crutches. He was a coffin maker, with a little workshop right at the end of the lane, abutting the wall of the last house. The front houses shared the facilities in the yard and now and again on passing along towards the lavs, he had eyed Lucy, hopping or sitting, or having to be carried to get about.

'It's time yow 'ad some crutches, little wench,' he said, when Lucy was three. He squatted down beside her as she sat at the side of the yard while the other children played about her. Mr Clark was a kindly man, sandy-haired, with a thin, serious face and a long wispy beard. He eyed her closely.

'I need yow to stand up for me a tick, babby.'

He helped her to stand and looked again.

21

'Right – put yower hand on my shoulder a minute – yow won't fall. And hold yower other arm out for me.'

She did as bidden and Mr Clark rested the back of one of his hands on the ground, the other under her out-stretched arm. He eyed the distance, seeming able to feel it without measuring.

'All right.' He helped her down again. 'Yow leave it with me, littl'un.'

A couple of days later he came back with two small crutches: each a length of wood with another curved piece fastened to the top, around which he had wrapped some sort of padding and nailed shammy leather over the top. He went to the forge to fetch Lucy's mother.

'Oh!' Ellen was tearful at the sight. 'Oh, that's marvel-lous, Mr Clark – yower so kind!'

Lucy was excited when she saw the crutches. He had made them so carefully! But they were a disappointment. As Mr Clark and her mother watched, she did her best to swing her way across the yard. But she was only little and it was hard. It hurt under her arms and she felt as if she was going to fall. Even though she didn't want to, she started to cry.

'Never mind, bab, it'll come to yer,' Mr Clark said. He and Mrs Clark had brought up six living children and he was a gentle sort of man. 'Just tek it a day at a time like and yow'll get used to it.'

He was right, of course. Bit by bit, with Mom's help, Lucy persevered. Her shoulders grew strong and before long she could move about quite speedily. As she grew, every so often Mr Clark made her a bigger pair of crutches.

'D'you know,' he told her one day, when she had gone to ask him to fix the top of one of them back on again, 'there used to be a landlord over at the Plough and

Harrow had lost 'is leg and someone'd made him an iron one. It were strapped on somehow, I believe. One of these days I'll 'ave a go at making one for you. Not out of iron, though, that's not my material.'

He turned to her, in the middle of sandpapering down the end of a piece of wood, and gave her a big wink.

The other thing she could not remember was her father. Her pa, who both her mother and Albert mourned every day. As he grew older, Albert became more and more angry and discontented. 'The lad needs a father,' Lucy sometimes heard Mom say to Bertha, or one of the other women. But there was no bringing Pa back again.

The yard – court three – where Lucy was born off Hay Lane, was right on the eastern edge of Cradley Heath, where the little jerry-built yards of houses gave out to the fields surrounding the town.

The entry into the yard led from Hay Lane, between the three back houses making up one side of the tumble-down yard, and the side wall of the cottage, an older dwelling than the rest of the houses around which the yard was built. The cottage still had some remaining bits of a broken-down wall enclosing a piece of ground which showed the outlines of old garden beds. These were now long gone and everything trodden down into a flat, cindery surface.

The three houses at the side of the yard backed on to three others on Hay Lane. The families in both front and back houses, and the Hipkiss family who lived in the old cottage, shared the two dry-pan lavs and the miskin or rubbish tip up at the end, each contributing to the rank stench pervading the yard. In summer it was overpowering and humming with clouds of flies.

Along the yard's long back wall, the forge stood in the

right-hand corner, facing the cottage. It was barely more than a hovel, with a leaking roof and iron grilles instead of windows. Inside, all in a row along the back wall, were five hearths for working chain. To the left of the forge was a brick wash house, known as the 'brewhouse', with its copper inside for heating water and the water pump outside.

The rest of the wall, abutting the lavs at the far end, separated their yard from fields. An adult could just see over it. Children tall enough would scramble up it, like the Hipkiss lads, to look out over the land stretching beyond. The fourth side of the yard was bounded by the wall shared with the yard next door.

Living at number two, in the earliest part of Lucy's life, were her mom and dad, Ellen and James Butler, along with Albert, already five years old when Lucy entered the world, and William Walker, her mother's father. Old Man Walker's body was bent and his soul embittered, decades of his life ground down on the endless toil of making nails, which had paid barely more than slavery itself. It had left him with only one living child, his daughter Ellen, to support him in his old age.

Lucy's young brother George came along later. But her pa was four months buried when this new son announced his screaming arrival into the world, in the bed his father had not long ago slept in upstairs.

Just three hours after birthing him, Ellen, newly widowed, had been back at the chain hearth. She worked long into the night, a rag diper staunching the blood between her legs and the new baby, swaddled and placed in that same box on the floor beside her, where Lucy had lain on that terrible night.

*

Lucy had never seen the men working at Corngreaves at the far end of the road, but she had been told about them; the shadowy figures who could sometimes be spotted, black as ants against the infernal glow of the blast furnace.

Her father had worked at Corngreaves as a puddler. All over the area there were mines, both of coal and iron ore. The iron ore was taken to be heated in the blast furnaces from which molten metal was poured into sandy moulds, its blinding orange fading to the brown 'sow' of pig iron. The puddlers worked the next stage of the smelting. The pig iron was reheated in a puddling furnace into a doughy 'bloom' which they would gather into a great fifty-pound ball on a rabbling bar and hook it out, to be pressed into blocks, or shingles of wrought iron.

Corngreaves, like the other big foundries, stained the night sky red. The furnaces were tapped every two hours, a hole drilled into the hottest depths to let air in. The brilliance of the molten iron pouring out would light the streets at night, so bright that they said you could see to read a newspaper in Graingers Lane.

As she got older, Lucy could only imagine her father having been one of those dark figures, the sweat pouring off them. Before she had even reached her second year, one icy afternoon, James Butler was carried vomiting from the foundry. Soon after, he sank into unconsciousness and died that same evening in his bed, a man of thirty-six. Something burst in his brain, they said. George was born four months later, after the turn of the year.

'He was a good man, my James.' Mom couldn't speak about him without tears. 'A kind, steadfast man.'

The life of a puddler was short. She had always hoped he would be the exception. And over her dead body would her sons go to the foundry to be carried off by the same work.

Lucy could remember him only as a presence, a voice somewhere in the air above her. She had an idea that her brother Albert had a look of Pa, the dark bristly hair, strong brows and loping walk, but maybe it was only because Mom said so. For Lucy, her father was a ghost who summoned the smell of faggots and peas – his favourite – a pair of big black boots, a voice, a cough. These impressions died with him, fading, as did anything remaining of her mother's youth or peace of mind.

Mom could scrape together five and six on a good week at the hearth and there she was, left with rent – three shillings – and her fuel to pay for, before she ever had any money for herself and her children. And there was the old man to be fittled.

'I dow want to move away,' she wept to Bertha Hipkiss, after James died. 'Everyone I know is here. I've got to keep us going somehow.'

They had got by well enough with her dad's foundry wage. Now, Old Man Walker, instead of sitting about being kept, bestirred himself and set to the hearth again as well. Aggie Robinson and her family left the yard soon after Lucy's burning, driven out by the scorn and anger of the neighbours, and Old Man Walker took over her hearth. A man who can make nails can soon learn to fashion chains. Much as he scowled and moaned about it, it was in his interest to earn his beer money – and it was either that or all of them starve on the street.

While bitter about his life, Lucy's grandfather was never unkind to her. Sometimes she sat by him, his gnarled hands restless on the arm of the chair, his voice hardening as he talked about starting work as a nailmaker in 1844, at the age of nine.

'Those foggers am bad now – and they was bad then,' he'd recount in his creaking voice. 'Factors, we called

26

'em, bought the nails off of us and sold 'em on – for a profit we'm was never gunna see. And they'd mek us tek our pay in goods instead of money. The "Trucking system" it were called and an evil system it were an' all. They'd pay yow out of they'm Tommy shops – at the pub or somewhere known to 'em – fittle a rat'd turn 'is snout up at, and for twice the regular price. Cheated us at every turn, they did – on the measures, on the pay . . .'

Lucy heard the story over and over again. Then sometimes the old man would shout, 'The death of our mother, they was! Ground her into an early grave – 'er were only thirty-eight when 'er passed on!' His whole body would turn rigid with hatred as he spoke.

'Starved my father out, that's what they did . . . And 'im left with five children and them growing fat on our sweat in their big 'ouses, meking us live on starvation levels. Men and women both – sweating and slaving for 'em! You just be glad, little Lucy, that yow weren't born in them days to a nailmaker's family . . . We was the cursed of the earth – proud workers we was, the nail-makers of Blackheath, but they ground us down so's we'd be thrown on the Parish, even when we was working . . .'

His rheumy eyes would turn on her and sometimes, in happier moods, he'd give her a wink. Once, he laid his hand on hers and said,

'Don't yow go working in a chain hearth, little wench. That's more slavery, that is. You find yowerself summat else . . .'

But mostly he would sink back into his own thoughts, his burning resentments.

Four

1898

Bertha Hipkiss opened her eyes into the deep blackness of the bedroom and at once knew two things.

By the unbroken silence, she could tell it was well on into the small hours of the morning. And by the hot, spreading sensation in the depths of her belly, she knew her time had come. Her sleep had been fitful, in a way she recognized from the warm, melting sensation in her belly – her body was gearing itself up.

'Here we go.' Her lips shaped the words. 'Oh Lord above, not again.' The very thought of trying to right herself in the bed, let alone the effort of bringing forth this child, exhausted her before she had begun. She was forty-eight and far too old for all this caper.

'I've gorra get up,' she murmured. 'I cor stay 'ere . . .'

With a groan she levered herself upright on the sunken mattress, rusty bedsprings creaking with every move. Breathing hard, she pulled her shawl round her shoulders, then sat listening for a moment. No sound came from Pauline, her fifteen-year-old daughter sleeping in the bed beside her. Pauline was the only girl left at home now Susannah and Aggie were wed.

The lads, John, Clem and her youngest, Freddie, just four, all slept in the other upstairs room in this mouldy old cottage with its low ceilings and damp stench.

Her old man, Jonno, bless his poor heart, stayed in the chair downstairs now – not for want of love but want of strength and ready breath.

She ought to wake Pauline, get her to run for Mrs Heath, but though the echo of the child's arrival had begun, her time was not quite yet. Pulling the shawl closer about her, she sat on the side of the bed, straightening her back to pull air inside her lungs.

How many times had she done this before? Eight – as well as three miscarried. And of the eight, her little Wilf dead at one month and Mary at only a few weeks more than that. Grief surged through her at the thought. Most days she tried never to think of those times, or of her dead little ones. But the state of birthing seemed to pick layers of skin off you, laying you bare.

And at this time, she always thought of her own mother, dying soon after she, Bertha, her latest daughter, took her own first breath. She had been born in Purser's Yard, or Anvil Yard as some called it, in Cradley. The place was its own world, enclosed on three sides, with seventeen houses in a filthy, broken-down jumble of buildings, scattered with the muck and mess of nail and chain workshops, teeming with kids and rife with disease. Typhoid carried off two of her cousins in the yard – but that was after she had left and moved down here to Cradley Heath with her miner husband, Jonno Hipkiss.

Her Jonno had come to the Midlands from Wales, to work the mines in his grandfather Hipkiss's part of the country. He would sometimes say, 'If you've survived Anvil Yard, *cariad*, you can survive anything.'

She smiled faintly, tears filling her eyes at the thought of her man, the man he had once been when they met and fell in love, and when they stood in front of the minister for God's blessing on the union of their hungering bodies.

29

Jonno, what a vigorous man he was, with his strong-boned face and ready grin – much as young Clem's was shaping into now. In those days she she could scarcely look at Jonno's stocky, muscular body without wanting to lay hands on him. And what a hunger he had had for her! Together they made their babbies . . .

Memories filled her mind as she sat in the darkness, the cold frame of the bed digging into the backs of her knees. The pains had not got started fully yet, but the glow, the stretching, had begun inside her and she knew she would not sleep.

She let the images drift – walked the lanes outside Cradley with Jonno, her coal miner sweetheart, muscles like rocks in his arms. She listened to the past, to his belting laugh, felt the pull of his arms round her, saw his grin, heard his jokes and songs . . . A man who never seemed tired, was never still. Not like now. My man, my love.

Grief pulsed through her like her blood. And now, this child – another little one that Jonno's eyes, scorched blind, would never see.

The pain came, pulling tight round the girth of her. Bertha sat up, gasping. It was beginning. She must wake Pauline . . . But immediately the urgency was of a different kind.

'Oh no . . .' A sudden burning pressure in her bowels. 'Not here, I can't, not here . . .'

Getting up she shuffled to the stairs, bent over with the pain, desperate to hold herself in. Not here – she had to get out to the privy. Every stair of the old cottage creaked at the weight of her body. Halfway down she had to sit, panting, so as not to disgrace herself, until she could manage to go on. She could hear the scrape of Jonno's breathing from the room below where he slept propped in his chair.

With a last desperate effort, she reached the bottom of the stairs and out into the gaslit yard. Bent over, she staggered, moaning as she began to lose control of herself. The two lavatories, shared between the inhabitants of the yard, were crude and foul. She pulled her way into the first and balanced, panting, on the wooden seat, whimpering with the force of her body emptying itself.

'God, dear God . . .' Sweat had broken out all over her and she held her head in her hands, feeling humiliated and helpless. Could she get back to the house? She had to wake Pauline, should have done it before . . .

When that spasm had passed, she sat up in a cold sweat, the stench of the place all about her. She had managed to get up, her hand on the rough door, ready to walk, when it happened, abruptly, with no warning. A spasm passed through her belly, an overwhelming force which buckled her into a squat, pressed between the wood of the lav and the door.

'Oh . . . No . . . No, no . . . Not here . . .' She had not even had time to light a candle and she was engulfed in darkness.

There was no stopping it. She was naked under her shift. Her body opened under this gigantic force like a storm hurling its way out of her. The urgency within her would not be stopped, the pressure of the head bearing down, so that the nails of her hand dragged across the splintery door, trying to cling to something. But then she had to move one hand to reach down below, feeling the sticky roundness forcing its way out, the slither of the body which she had to gather in both hands, gasping and sobbing.

'Oh Lord . . . God in heaven – help me, someone . . .!'

Cradling the limp little body, she forced herself up to grab at the latch, still trailing the child from within her,

31

and almost fell out into the yard. She knelt in the dim light from the lamp, feverishly wiping at the tiny creature's face, slipping her little finger into its mouth.

There was another convulsion of her body and she felt the liverish remains of the birth deliver itself between her thighs, her legs slick with blood.

'Come on . . .' She could pay no attention to herself. She had a desperate, primal task. 'Come on, little'un . . . Let's hear yer . . . Tommy – come on, my lad, that's your name . . .'

But even in her frantic state, she could tell. The baby's limbs were floppy, like a rag doll in her arms, not drawn up and kicking on the freedom of release. The mouth stayed shut. This tiny boy child had left the world without even beginning to draw a first breath or opening his eyes, just once, to see his mother's face.

She made herself get up, grimacing at the feel of the blood and mess between her legs, and went into the house for a knife to cut the cord. Then, wrapping the little boy in her shawl, she took him to the house and laid him bundled next to the range. There was nothing better she could think of doing.

Taking the ash can she went out again and scooped all her intimate mess into it with her hands, still feeling a faint warmth to it. She carried it round to the midden behind the lavs, burying it deep in the ash heap. She lifted handfuls of ash to scatter over the bloody mess in the yard.

Going to the pump by the brewhouse, she scrubbed herself, whimpering at the coldness of the water as she scraped at the rime of blood from her legs with her nails. Lastly, she pumped a bucket of water to soak her slip and carried it into the scullery.

Dawn was just breaking as she came downstairs at last,

dressed, a thick rag diper between her legs. She lit the range to boil water and make tea, while Jonno slept on in the chair that was now his bed. She sat beside him, waiting for the water. His head was tipped back, his skeletal form under the blanket seeming so small, so reduced. His sleeping face looked like that of a man twenty years more than his age and his lungs rattled and whined.

Bertha went to the scullery and uncorked the bottle which stood next to a pail under the stone sink, one of her stock of pungent home-made brews. She poured a good nip into a cup and returned to sit beside her husband, taking gulps of the pungent elderberry so that the liquid moved down like a flame inside her.

She watched the window for the first hint of day. She was not the woman she had been when it was last light. Another child, another death. Something in her had given way. She felt pooled in grief. But no. She must not show it. Not to Jonno.

'You know the dawn's come when you can tell a black thread from a white.' That's what her father had told her, all those years back, in Anvil Yard.

Dawn – when things came to light; when they had to be told. She knocked back the last of the country wine.

As the kettle got up steam, she reached over and took Jonno's hand. She didn't want to wake him, to bring him grief. But she craved his touch, his words, for comfort. She needed him to mourn with her. Each new child had been a joy to him, and he would grieve. Yet he would find it in him to be strong, as she would herself. The strength to stand against the force of another of the blows life dealt; they would stand together, as they always had. He would not blame her. Never that, she knew.

But now she would have to tell her Jonno about the death of another son.

Five

1901

'We brought nothing into this world, and it is certain we carry nothing out . . .'

The vicar's solemn voice sounded thin in the winter wind which kept scattering flurries of leaves across the rows of soot-blackened gravestones.

'Well, that's the truth,' Lucy's mother muttered as they stood huddled together, watching her father, Old Man Walker's, coffin – the cheapest possible – lowered into the ground. The dark outline of the church loomed to their right.

Lucy's stump ached in the icy day, tied into a kind of muslin sock. Her crutches pushed up into her armpits. Mr Clark was still trying to perfect some sort of leg for her, but his contraptions with wood pegs and straps to tie round her waist rubbed horribly on the stump and today she felt safer using her familiar crutches.

They were all frozen to the marrow, Lucy, Mom, her brothers – Albert, thirteen, and George who was five now and was leaning up against Mom, too cold even to cry. Albert kept his head down, not looking at anyone. Lucy wished she could go and cuddle up against George for comfort, but she had to hang on to her crutches and it was hard enough to wipe the tears from her own cheeks.

Mom had her hands huddled in the sleeves of a threadbare coat, lent to her by Mrs Clark for the occasion. Having a husband who made coffins, she kept a couple of such garments to lend out for funerals. It was the only coat they had to wear between them. Even so, Lucy could see that her mother's body was clenched up in the cold. All of them were shivering as if stricken with fever.

A few of the neighbours had come; people rallied round to offer a few coppers towards the rites. Once the brief ceremony was over, and the thud of shovelfuls of earth falling on the lid of the coffin began, other sounds seemed to reach them: the clop of hooves on the road in the distance, the clang of metal from a factory nearby.

'That's enough, let's go,' Ellen said, reaching down to pull on George's hand the moment the droning words had died to a final 'Amen'. 'I cor put up with any more o' this canting.'

Lucy, now eight, knew Mom had no time for the Lord and all his supposed blessings. Few seemed to have come in her direction. She could hear the utter desperation in her mother's voice.

William Walker, her grandfather and Mom's father, had not been an easy man. Lucy had sat many an afternoon being fed all his complaints. But he had rallied round, his already bent back becoming even more bowed from standing over a chain hearth day after day. He had worked slowly at his age, but he had brought in a few desperately needed shillings a week.

'You're the man of the house now,' Mom said to Albert as soon as the old man's last breath had faded. 'You're to go to Hoskins and ask to be taken on.'

Albert, cap at an angle over frowning eyebrows similar to those of his grandfather, looked up at her. 'I'll earn myself more than the old man,' he said fiercely. 'You'll see.'

Bertha Hipkiss came over, wrapped in a black knitted shawl which made her face look very pale in contrast. She laid a hand on Lucy's quivering shoulder. Bertha had aged suddenly, rapidly, everyone could see. It was since that last babby, the surprise that she was expecting at such a late age; then its arrival, without a breath in its body.

'Bearing 'em's one thing, but burying 'em's quite another,' Lucy had heard her say to Mom. 'There's been too many and this'un's been the worst of the lot. I thought 'e might be the comfort of my old age . . .' There was a silence. Then Bertha gave a sobbing sigh. 'You feel things different as yow get older. Thank God my days of childbearing are over.'

'Lucy?' Bertha said quietly, now, by the grave. 'Come away a minute.'

Lucy tried to control her chattering teeth as she swung herself along slowly beside Mrs Hipkiss, past the tilting stones, their engraved words encrusted with soot. She looked up to meet Bertha's strong gaze. Of all people in this world she had the most respect for this woman. Bertha glanced over towards Ellen.

'Yower mother's going to need yer.' She stared down at Lucy, as if trying to impress something on her, but Lucy could not understand what it was. 'Thing's 're gunna be cruel 'ard for 'er as a widow, with the old man gone.' She hesitated. 'We all help as best we can. But we all need to . . . Just keep an eye out, eh, Luce? Don't go leaving her on her own more than you can help?'

Lucy stared up into Bertha Hipkiss's face. Mom would be lonely, Lucy thought. That must be what Mrs Hipkiss meant.

'But – when I'm at school – and our Albert has to go to work . . .'

Bertha smiled. She patted Lucy's shoulder.

'I know that, bab. You can't stop home every minute. I just meant . . .' She looked as if she was regretting saying anything. 'Look – don't you fret about it, all right?'

Lucy spent her waking hours when she was not at school minding George, her little brother, while he played in the yard or in the forge. This was a long, narrow brick building that had no door and only a grille of iron bars the length of the window frames and wooden shutters outside. These were never closed, even in the depths of winter, so that the smoke and fumes could billow out into the yard.

The floor was brick and each of the five hearths along the back wall had its bucket of coal and bellows, its anvil and tools. On the ground lay bunches of iron rods waiting to be heated in the fire for cutting and bending into chain links.

They were not the huge, heavy ships' chains which would be made in the factory workshops. Lucy had seen some chains with links so enormous that lifting even one would be beyond her. The women made the lighter chains, some for farm ploughs and others for dog chains. The completed lengths were strewn and coiled about the floor.

There were always other children in here – George for one, who she usually had the job of watching and who was into everything. Their neighbour Mari Gornall had two young ones in with her. Mari was not an especially likeable person. She spoilt for a fight whenever she could arrange one, the more pointless the better. Her children were all deathly white with narrow, mean-looking eyes. The older two, Amy and Sid, thirteen and ten now, mocked Lucy for her lopsided walk, mimicking her in a nasty exaggerated way, making noises as if the injury was in her head and not just her leg. Lucy loathed them both and kept away from them. These days, what she wanted most was to help Mom.

''Er's a good wench, your Lucy is,' Mrs Wilmott would say, smiling over at her.

Of the four women working the hearths here at present, Edna Wilmott was the oldest, sixty-five or so. She had been widowed years ago and her one son Sidney still lived with her. Sidney got himself the odd job of work from time to time, but mostly Edna still kept him, to the disgust of the others.

Sidney was a lumbering simple-minded man, like a child even though he was knocking on forty and a lazy lump into the bargain, but he was the light of his mother's life.

Edna had a braid of salt-and-pepper hair pinned round her head. She always looked the same and Lucy had never seen her with her hair down. There were warts on her chin with black hairs bristling out of them. She hammered out chains with her gristly arms from dawn 'til dusk and had done already for 'over fifty years' as she would say proudly. She had never been anywhere further than the High Street in Cradley Heath. She was a stolid person, hardly seeming to look left or right, and of all of them remained the most cheerful. She was the one who would often start off a song in the workshop.

'No good being miserable, ar it?' she'd say with a wink.

Ellen Butler, Lucy's mother, and Bertha Hipkiss were the other two, with their kids. Lucy did what chainmakers' children did to start with, when they were little. She worked the bellows which stoked the fires in the hearth, keeping up a red-hot flame for Mom to heat the length of chain for cutting and hammering.

38

'You need to keep the iron hot,' Mom would instruct her. 'You 'ave to hammer a lot harder, else.'

All Lucy's life had been set against the sound of metal hammering on metal. Mom had started to teach her the work as well. It was very hard for her as she had to balance on a box to be tall enough to see.

'Yow've gorra be able to keep yowerself – you never know,' Ellen said, her tired eyes looking into Lucy's. These days Mom's face seemed strained and exhausted all the time. And these words frightened Lucy. 'Yower not one who's going to . . .' Mom trailed off, looking away.

But by now Lucy knew what had gone unsaid. *You're a cripple – you'll never marry because no one will want you for a wife, so you'll have to be sure to earn your keep yourself. Don't expect anything else.*

Mom was teaching her to hammer a cut length of rod into a U-shape after heating it in the fire. Ellen could do it fast, years of skill sharpening her every move.

'That's it, babby – like that. Then we 'ommer it on the skiddy . . . I'll learn yer everything yow need to know.'

Skiddy was the name they gave to the anvil. Lucy felt as if the hammer would soon drag her arm off, the weight of it causing her muscles to ache and twitch and the heat of the fire making her skin red and painful. Her hands came up in blisters and sores. And it was hard for her, having to stand for so long. When she worked the bellows she could move about more, adjusting her weight and throwing herself on to the handle. But standing at the hearth she was bearing all her weight on her one leg until it was trembling from the strain and her hip hurt.

I'm going to ask Mr Clark to have another go at making me a peg for my leg, Lucy thought. Somehow, she had to be able to stand better than this.

She felt oppressed and sad that day. Earlier on, Amy

Gornall decided to amuse herself by running up to her, dancing about in front of her to flaunt her two working legs, poking Lucy in the ribs and backing off before she could retaliate. Then Sid joined in. They were the two eldest of Gornall's five children: below them were Vic and little Maggie and the babby, Jo.

'Let's see yow run then!'

'Hop then, cripple!' Amy was giggling, Sid behind her. 'Let's see yow hopping with them crutches – I'll race yow!'

She kept coming back, like a wasp, circling and poking. Lucy hardly ever let herself get caught out in the yard alone with Amy and Sid Gornall if she could help it, especially the two of them together. Her stomach turned with dread. How could she get them to leave her alone?

While this was going on, suddenly, out of the corner of her eye, Lucy saw someone jump down from the wall and come hurtling across the yard. Clem Hipkiss threw himself on Sid and the two of them went down, wrestling on the ground.

''Ere – what'm yow doin'?' Sid bawled. 'Gerroff of me!'

Clem, older and stronger, soon had the upper hand. He ended up sitting on Sid, pinning him to the ground and landing a punch in his chest.

'Yower a bully, Sid!' he yelled at him. 'Yower yaller, that's what yow are!'

When he had finished with Sid, Clem went back to his perch on the wall without looking at anyone. Lucy's heart was beating like a drum. Clem had stood up for her! He seemed like a hero on a big white horse and she kept thinking about it after, the way he had rushed over and pummelled Sid Gornall on the ground.

But it was still humiliating that anyone had to rescue her. Over time, she had hardened herself to a lot of the jibes, but now, standing at the hearth, struggling to learn the work and plagued by thoughts of Amy Gornall with her shrewish, fish-white face and her nasty little sod of a brother, made her sink right down into misery.

'I'll never do it,' she said to Ellen, tears in her eyes. 'I'm no good.'

'What'm yow saying?' Mom squatted down beside her, a fierce expression on her face. She spoke quietly and urgently. 'Dow yow say that – yow'll soon get the 'ang like anyone. It teks time, that's all. Yow *will*. Yow just need to keep on.'

Lucy shook her head, staring down at the sooty brick floor. 'I'm no good for anything.'

Mom looked shocked. Lucy was not usually like this. She had learned to suffer in silence. She never bothered to mention how left out she felt, about the things the other children called her. What was the point? There was nothing to be done.

'None o' that!' Ellen's eyes blazed at her. 'Yower all right, Lucy Butler, and don't yow let anyone tell yow yow ay! Look at yow – yow can read, and that's more'un I've ever been able to do!'

She put her fingers gently under Lucy's chin and Lucy looked up at her, her eyes full of tears.

'No one keeps their brains in their legs, Luce. Yow keep up yower schoolwork and maybe yow won't spend your life sweating 'ere like yower mother. Yow could learn to do summat else, eh?'

'But Mom – I could stop going to school and come and help yow.'

Her mother was the one to have tears fill her eyes now. 'Oh, babby – I know yow could. But not yet. Yow keep up with that reading for longer – it might stand yow in good stead one day.'

Her worn face managed a watery smile. Lucy nodded, feeling a bit better, even though her own eyes were full of tears. She managed to raise a little smile back.

And she did feel a bit better, except that the sight of her mother's face these days worried her more and more. Up close, when Mom smiled, she could see the bones of her jaw moving under the skin. She was stick thin and since the old man's death she had changed. Every hour she could manage, she was in the forge working and working, and she wore a permanent frown of worry.

Albert, who was thirteen, had now started work at one of the other chain shops. It was a smaller factory where the 'blast' for the forges was still supplied by hand. Albert stood turning the wheel for the blast for twelve hours a day, for which he earned half a crown a week. He came home exhausted, bursting with anger and resentment. He hated it with a passion and Lucy could see how much Mom felt for him.

But even apart from this, on top of Mom's day-to-day worries, there was something else. Lucy could sense it, but she didn't know what it was.

It was some time before she began to get some inkling of the trouble her mother was in. And that was only because she caught a cold on her chest and had to stay home from school one winter day. She lay coughing on her mattress, feeling the icy air inside the room against her feverish cheeks. Her throat was so sore that even swallowing her own saliva made her face crease with pain. She drifted in and out of sleep, dreams coming and going, peculiar, broken shapes seeming to play on the backs of her eyelids. Sometimes she dreamt her dream that she had two proper legs and could run and climb and play like the others. She would toss and turn restlessly, only realizing, when she opened her eyes to see her crutches on the floor beside her, that it was not true.

But sometimes the dreams were just broken-up colours or smells, or scraps of the sound of voices. So that, one afternoon, half-awake with feverish images playing in her head, when she heard that voice downstairs, she thought it was a dream.

Six

1902

She hurried along the icy pavements of the High Street, her old cloth bag weighed down only by a swede and a couple of onions, banging against her leg. Resting on the top of them was tuppence worth of chitterlings in a twist of paper. The little piece of rag into which she tied her coins now held nothing save a couple of farthings.

'God in heaven,' Ellen prayed, moving as fast as her trembling legs would carry her. 'I wish I had someone to help me.'

She had to get home, to get on . . . She hadn't done nearly enough today. The hours raced by and Albert and George, who was now at school, would both be home, needing something in their bellies. At least today, thanks to Albert's wage, there would be something more for him than a slop of stale bread and water.

The street was busy, carts churning along the muddy road, manure fouling the tram tracks. Housewives bustled from shop to shop. Ellen glimpsed a woman, clammed scrawny as a cat, seated on a step, slumped in a faint against the side of the doorway. Ellen's innards turned. Her own body felt limp and drained from hunger, but pray God she never sink as low as that . . .

Her stomach tightened with dread even more at the sight of a burly figure coming towards her along the pavement. The woman was clad in a long black coat and wide black velvet-covered hat with a bouncing black feather. All the finery. An old woman, knocking on sixty with several chins and a face like a hatchet, so broad and square she was like a house on the move. Ellen, forced off the pavement, snatched at her skirt to keep it out of the mire. She was tempted to spit in the gutter as the woman passed.

Thirza Rudge, a fogger for one of the biggest chain firms in the town, was the scourge of outworkers in some of the other yards round this part of Cradley Heath. While Seth Dawson was renowned as one of the worst among the middlemen, Thirza Rudge was worse still. Hard and unyielding as an iron rod, that one, screwing every farthing from the outworkers under her. Everyone said Thirza Rudge was a woman with no soul. The sight of her made Ellen shudder with loathing and she saw another woman duck away as the vile, bullying harridan walked past, fattened by the fodder she had from keeping her workers close to starvation.

Ellen picked her way along the cindery mud of Hay Lane and turned down the entry into the yard. Her feet were so cold she could not feel them and she was desperate for a cup of tea. Pushing the door open, she listened. There was no sound from upstairs. Lucy was abed sick, sleeping.

The back kitchen was cold, the fire almost dead in the grate. She lay her humble groceries on the table and set to work struggling to breathe life into the fire. She nearly sent herself faint blowing on the damp coal until, in desperation, she threw the cloth bag on and set it burning, managing to spark some life into the coal. Wretched and exhausted, she was close to breaking down.

'Ay no use in blarting,' she muttered, clinging to the

45

table as she hauled herself up. Head bowed, she steadied herself until the blood stopped banging in her ears. 'That ay gunna bring my James back or get our dinner cooked, ar it?'

She had to get back to the chain hearth the second she could and put long hours in tonight. She put the chitterlings in a pan to fry with a bit of the onion later – at least she and Lucy might taste a bit of the leftover gravy. Meat was a rare thing in their house, but it was Albert's favourite and she had to improve the lad's temper somehow. She knew he missed his father with every bone of him. He was not a happy soul, her lad. She could not seem to breathe any joy into him and now he found his daily work an endless hell. Every evening he came home like a black cloud and he needed – demanded – more in his belly than a stale crust softened with stewed tea, even if that was what she survived on most of the time.

The kettle came to the boil and she poured hot water over the pinch of tea and spoonful of sugar. Standing at the table, her back to the door, Ellen started peeling the vegetables. The door to the yard was shut in the cold, the window streaming, as was her nose. Dizziness overcame her and she hung her head, leaning on the table, hearing the blood bang in her ears. Exhaustion washed over her. How could she go on, day after day . . . But she must, there was no choice . . .

Her thoughts lingered, troubled, on her eldest son. Since her father had died, the full burden of widowhood had fallen on her. Albert brought in his small wage now, which was better than nothing, but he was exhausted and like a caged animal, the work seeming to confine something in his already unhappy spirit. She hated to see her boy so oppressed and it was weighing on her. Not to mention some of the company he was getting into.

And, a couple of weeks back, that riffy bastard Seth Dawson had taken it into his head to cut their rate by a farthing a yard while his own belly swelled. However hard she toiled, from before dawn to well into the night – making a hundredweight of chain before the week's end – by the time she'd paid the rent there was precious little left to fill their bellies from one day to the next.

Her head throbbed. If only she could sit by the ailing fire and let herself sleep and sleep. But those lengths of chain were not going to make themselves . . . As she started to cut the purple skin from the swede, the knife slipped, slicing hard along her finger.

'Blast and damn it!' Throwing it down on the rough wood of the table, she stuck her finger in her mouth, blood and iron on her tongue, tears starting in her eyes.

'Not above a bit o' cussing then, wench.'

Every nerve of Ellen's body jangled. She could smell him, the metal-and-sweat stench of him. She whipped round. Seth Dawson, hat in one hand, was leaning casually up against the door frame, the back door closed behind him. He was *inside her house*!

Wildly, her gaze went to the handle of the door, but he was standing right beside it. How had he crept in so quietly? There was no other way out of the house. The blood was surging round her body, making her feel even more light-headed.

'What're you doing in my house?' she hissed at him. Rage filled her veins, while to her annoyance, at the same time, her whole body had started to shake.

'Your 'ouse?' he said mockingly. 'T'ain't your 'ouse, is it, Ellen Butler?' Without his hat she could see the unkempt mop of his hair, greasy lumps of it round his hairy ears. He shifted his weight forward and flipped the hat on to the table as if he owned the place. It landed almost on top of her chopped onions. 'You're just a visitor – for as long as you can pay yer rent.'

Her mouth twisted with revulsion and her heart was pounding. But all she had to do was shout – wasn't it? If she could get to the yard door before him, cry out so that the other women would come running . . . Surely they'd hear her, even over the crackle of the fires, the bellows' whoosh and the clang of hammers?

'No need to mither yerself, wench.' Seth slouched against the door frame. He was showing her he could come and go as he pleased, that he owned her – her body, her life – and there was not a thing she could do about it. He reached a stubby finger into his mouth to pick a shred of gristle from his teeth, before flicking it on to the floor.

'Get out of my house.' Ellen gripped the table. Stop shaking! Her mind clamoured to her body. The last thing she wanted was for this monster to understand that her heart was going like a piston and her knees were about to give way.

'That bank out there –' He moved his head lazily, to indicate the other side of the house, Hay Lane with the railway embankment beyond it, overshadowing them all. Mocking, he added, 'Or "bonk" as you lot call it over 'ere – it must get a lot of fires there, come summer.'

Bank fires, sparks from the train. He knew there were fires. Sometimes they had all rushed out with buckets. What the hell was he on about?

'Be a pity if any of them fires was to spread, now wouldn't it? Whole row of houses gone, tenants with nowhere to go.' He started on his teeth again and she saw the flabby cushion of his tongue. All these stupid threats – he was just saying things to make her feel small, as if he could do anything to her if he chose. Crush her underfoot like a mouse.

'What d'yow want?' Ellen glared at him, pulling herself upright. 'I ay standing 'ere canting with yow – and yow've no right coming barging into other people's 'ouses.'

Seth Dawson's face changed. His eyes narrowed.

'Fierce little body, ain't yer? I like that. Yer ain't got much meat on yer bones, but yer've got spirit.' He gave a low laugh. He was so vile, with his pitted nose, his mouldy cheeks. 'That's summat a man likes to see . . . Gives a man thoughts . . .'

As he pushed himself away from the door frame, he stumbled and for a split second Ellen thought he might go down on his back, imagined the fat bastard down there, arms and legs wiggling. She'd crush him under *her* heel like the glossy black-bats that crawled into the house! But he righted himself and she backed away towards the stairs. If only she could get to the door . . .

'You being a widow woman now the old man's gone . . .' Seth Dawson's voice was low now, silky like the gloss of oil in a sump. ''Ard times for a mother. A few bob 'ere and there wouldn't go amiss, eh, wench?'

He crept towards her stooped like a lion tamer. In the dim light she saw his sludge-brown eyes full of a leering, lustful expression. She could hear the pull of his lungs, see the hairs on his face, his chest. Her body felt paralysed. She was no lioness, she knew; she could never be a match for him.

'A few bob, eh, wench? If you was to tend to my needs . . .' Ellen was pressed against the bottom of the stairs, leaning backwards so that she toppled on to the lowest few steps as Seth came up close, breathing the stink of rotten teeth into her face. 'A man 'as needs that only a wench can tek care of . . .'

'Mom?'

Seth Dawson froze, a hand raised ready to grab hold of her.

Lucy was sitting on the top step, a shawl wrapped round her shoulders, her one foot bare.

'You touch me and I'll send her shouting into the yard,' Ellen hissed.

'What – that cripple?' he mocked. 'What's 'er doing 'ere?' He nodded up at Lucy as if trying to befriend her all of a sudden. 'Not at school then, eh? Playing the wag, am we?'

Lucy stared down at him. Ellen felt a flicker of pride at the stony expression in her daughter's blue eyes. The child was shivering, her cheeks a feverish pink, but her fierce little spirit was unmistakeable in the hostility that streamed from her gaze.

'Huh, chip off the old block, I see,' Seth said.

'Mr Dawson was just on his way out,' Ellen said, looking into his eyes. 'Door's that way.'

Seth swallowed as if there was something nasty caught in his mouth, and reached over to pick up his hat. Coming up close to Ellen again, he said in a rasping whisper, 'Don't think I won't be back, wench.'

The dull afternoon light appeared for a moment as he opened the door to pass through it, his bulky form filling the doorway.

'Right –' Ellen dashed across the room and shot the bolt. 'That's the last time we *ever* leave that undone.' Trying not to show how much she was shaking, she turned back to her daughter, forcing a smile.

'Why was he here?' Lucy had bumped her way almost to the bottom of the staircase and sat huddled up.

'Oh,' Ellen said, looking away. ''E was just poking his snout in as usual.'

'Mom,' Lucy said. 'Your finger.'

50

It was only then Ellen remembered that she was still bleeding from cutting the swede. There was blood spotted down her front.

'Stay there, babby,' she said. She felt light with relief. 'I'll get summat to bind it and then we'll get yow back into bed.'

Once she had helped Lucy up the stairs again and back on to her mattress, she sat with her for a moment.

'I don't like that mon,' Lucy said. She looked disturbed by what had happened. ''E's bad.'

'I know, bab,' Ellen said. With her good hand she stroked the little girl's forehead. Inside, she could feel the day's pressure building: she must get back to work, time was slipping by . . .

'Shall I sing a song?'

Lucy nodded.

Ellen sat by her, singing softly in her sweet voice, '*Cherry ripe, cherry ripe, ripe I cry . . .*'

'What's a cherry?' Lucy murmured sleepily.

'It's a kind of fruit,' Ellen told her gently. 'Red and juicy. We'll 'ave to find yow one to try one of these days.'

Lucy's eyes were closing. Ellen sat on with her for a few more moments, looking down lovingly into her little girl's face, so sweet and serious. Then quietly, she made herself get up. She had to get to work.

Seven

Lucy pulled herself slowly along the street. She was feeling better now and back at school. On her way home, she always kept in as close to the walls of the shops and houses as she could so as not to trip anyone, or have her crutches knocked away from her. Every few yards she stopped for a breather. She was warm from the exertion, even though the weather was icy cold.

All the other children from the yard would have been back long before. John and Clem no longer felt the need to drag along with her as they had at the beginning and, as so often, she was left alone.

It was already almost dark in the winter afternoon, some shops with their gas lamps on inside which cheered the dreary street a fraction. Lucy was used to fending for herself, being on the edge of everything, left out. But at least that felt better than being teased or mocked.

Mostly she kept cheerful, but now and then, sad feelings would drag at her little soul. Out here in the gritty air, with all the grown-up people hurrying on their errands, heads hunched down into their collars, amid the messenger-boys and carts and trams all moving about her, she felt very small and of no account – as if the great grey sky overhead was blind to her and nothing and nobody in this world had any care for her at all.

At last she reached Hay Lane and the yard. Everything was dank and filthy, the place cast in smoky gloom; the only light in the winter afternoon provided by glimpses, between the bars of the chain workshop windows, of the red glow from the hearths.

Over the chink of the hammers she heard Mrs Wilmott's belting voice break out with '*Rock of ages, cleft for me!*' And the other women joined in. Mari Gornall's voice, shrieky and out of tune, stood out above the others. Edna Wilmott was staunchly religious and knew her hymns off by heart, especially the more rousing ones.

When Lucy reached the door the four women were in full song and she could just make out her mother's soft voice among them. Amy Gornall was working the bellows at her mother's hearth. Seeing Lucy, her rat-like expression turned even sourer. Lucy ignored her. But Amy's little sister Margaret, who was nearly three, barefoot, with a rag of a dress hanging below her knees, was scrubbing about on the floor close to Lucy's own mother. She was playing with some of Ellen's finished chain.

''Ello, Maggie!' Lucy bent over her. Squatting was too difficult.

Margaret was too young to have learned the habit of Gornall spite. Straightening up, hungry for attention, she held out her arms for a cuddle.

'Oi, Maggie,' Amy called in the midst of the singing. 'Gerroff of 'er! Yow come over 'ere to me!'

But little Maggie ignored Amy and hugged Lucy. It made Lucy feel happy – the way it did when her brother George came up to her and wanted cuddles as well.

'*All for sin could not atone; Thou must save and Thou alone!*'

The women's voices soared around them. Sparks flew in the air like orange insects. Lucy brushed some out of little Maggie's mousey wisps of hair.

'Yow can give me a 'and, Luce,' her mother said, turning

to her as the verse of the hymn finished. 'Goo in and get yower piece first – it's on the table.'

She stopped work for a few seconds and followed Lucy to the door. Her eyes flicked nervously across the yard before she went back to the hearth again. Mom was uneasy. Edgy. Lucy could feel it all the time now – ever since that day a couple of weeks back when she was poorly and she'd come down to find Mr Dawson in the house. His rancid stink had lingered afterwards. She didn't know why he'd been there, or what he'd wanted, but Mom had said, 'Thanks to you we got shot of 'im, Luce.' And she had seemed so relieved.

Lucy went into the house to find a lump of bread on a plate on the table and a cup of tea, black and sweet but almost cold, beside it.

She ate it standing in the doorway, entertained by the Hipkiss boys who had erupted out into the yard, little Freddie also still chewing his piece. John and Clem headed for the wall and scrambled up it, standing on the top and running back and forth, Clem filling his face at the same time.

As the bread slid down into her belly, Lucy began to feel better. She thought about the new teacher who had just arrived at school, who seemed a nice, kind lady, and who had looked right at her and smiled today. And now she was home, and little Margaret had come and given her a cuddle. These two moments in her day had made every-thing better.

When Lucy first went to school, it had made her feel absolutely tired out. Mom said that to save her having to come back and forth twice, at dinnertime, she'd send her in with a piece and Lucy was allowed to eat it at school – in the playground if it was fine, or she had to huddle in the porch of the school if it was a bad day. There was a tap outside, a metal cup hanging nearby on a chain if she wanted water.

She was used to it all now and had always done well in her lessons, being quick in learning to read and write.

'Yow can do more than me already,' Mom said when she showed her she could write her name and a few simple sentences.

Some of the children teased her in the beginning, but mostly they were too busy with their games, running and jumping, playing leapfrog and skipping, chanting out the rhymes.

There was a little girl called Gertie who would struggle over and sit with her at the side of the playground. Gertie wore a caliper on each of her legs. She had a big head with her thick brown hair cut short round her ears, thick eyebrows and bulbous eyes. She never said much. Lucy felt badly because she was glad Gertie was there, that *someone* wanted to sit next to her, but in truth Gertie was not much company and she wanted someone she could talk to.

As girls in the class gradually realized that Lucy was clever and learned to read as fast as anyone, they started talking to her. And because she was a pretty girl with big blue eyes, a sweet expression and ready smile, they tried to include her in the games and to stop the boys teasing her and running off with her crutches. She could only join in chanting rhymes and be asked to stand and turn the skipping rope. But even that was being in the game, being part of things, and she was happy to be asked.

Soon she had a little friend called Abigail, who had long, thin brown hair in plaits and smiled a lot.

'D'yow want to be friends?' Abigail asked one day as they lurked at the playground's edge amid the roiling boys.

'Yes!' Lucy said, beaming.

They held hands and talked about their brothers and sisters – Abigail had two of each. Abigail said that she helped her mother, early every morning. They heated up a copper full of beer for the miners to come and fill their bottle and take to the pit, their boots ringing on the dawn streets. Sometimes, Abigail ran off and joined in with the games, but Lucy knew she would always come back, so everything felt all right.

They were all sitting at their little desks, Lucy next to Abigail. Their teacher, an elderly lady called Miss Boyne, had been taken ill and they were to have a new one.

Miss Jones was a quaint young woman, barely five feet in height, bespectacled and with seemingly endless energy and cheer.

On her first day when she walked into the classroom, a little sparrow-like figure in a long brown dress and brown button boots, she came and stood before the class with her hands clasped neatly in front, her specs catching the light like full moons. She greeted them crisply and told them to get their slates ready.

Later she came round to each desk and it was then that Lucy saw her eyes properly for the first time and smelt the lavender scent that always hung round her. She leaned over, looking at her register – although she had already called it – and said, 'Now, what are your names?'

'Lucy Butler.'

'Abigail Hodges.'

She raised her eyes then and looked at each of them, really looked. Lucy saw grey-blue eyes full of life and amiability and interest and she liked Miss Jones straight away.

'Good,' she said, moving on to the next desk. 'I'll soon sort out who's who.'

They heard the whisper of her brown skirt as she moved away.

Miss Jones spoke differently from the people Lucy knew and she told them she had come down to Cradley Heath from somewhere called Warrington. She was kind to Lucy – especially kind. Lucy knew it was because of her leg but she soon also saw that Miss Jones could see something more than that.

'You fashion your letters very nicely,' she said that first day, looking down at her slate.

And as time went by, 'You're getting along exceptionally well with your reading,' she said another day. 'One of the very best in class. Clever girl.'

Their last teacher, Miss Boyne, was quite old and tight-lipped – never one to praise. Her shabby clothes and miserable face, the force with which she would slap their hands with a ruler as a punishment, meant that the children feared her, learned less from her and had no affection for her. With Miss Jones, her face would light up when you did something well.

Lucy found reading and writing easy. Her mind took lessons in hungrily. Abigail was a quick little girl as well and they learned together, usually finishing first in any task set to them in class.

If Miss Jones was out in the playground and saw Lucy to one side, leaning against the wall or trying to hobble after her little friends, sometimes she would come and talk to her. Lucy would find those kind, lively eyes twinkling at her from behind the spectacles.

'Are you in pain, dear?' she asked one day.

Lucy shook her head automatically. But she thought for a moment, then nodded.

'Sometimes,' she said, looking up shyly at her teacher. 'It gets sore. Mr Clark, he's our neighbour, he's made me a couple of false legs, wooden ones, with sort of straps, but they make it hurt worse.'

Miss Jones asked her very quietly one day what had happened to her leg.

'It were when . . .'

'It *was* when,' Miss Jones corrected.

'It was when I were a babby.'

When Lucy explained, Miss Jones's eyes filled with horror.

'You mean . . .?' She stopped herself, covering her mouth with her hand. Then she asked, 'Do your mother and father make chains?'

'I ay . . .'

'I haven't . . .' Miss Jones couldn't resist saying.

'I haven't got a father. It's just our mom.'

Miss Jones seemed to think for a moment and then she squatted down. Even outside, Lucy could smell her faint scent of lavender.

'You and your friends – Abigail, perhaps? – might like to come to our little Sunday school. There are games and stories and a little something to eat . . . It's at the church on Graingers Lane on Sunday afternoons. Do you go to church, Lucy?'

Lucy shook her head, then said, 'Mom 'as to make chains.'

Miss Jones looked faintly shocked.

'Well, you could come along, dear? You'd like it, I think. Why don't you bring one or two children from your neighbourhood with you? Who are your friends?'

'John and Clem Hipkiss,' Lucy said. 'They'm on our yard.'

Miss Jones stood up looking a bit doubtful, but then she smiled. 'Well – bring them too if they want to.' She was about to walk away and then turned back. 'Your reading and writing are really very good, Lucy. If you come on Sundays I might be able to give you a little extra to do – would you like that?'

Lucy nodded, her face lighting up.

Eight

She looked nervously about her as she stepped out into the yard, even though it was morning and there were people about. It was what she did all the time now, forever on the alert, the slightest thing making the hair raise on the back of her neck. Was *he* somewhere nearby?

The yard rang with the sound of hammering. Bunched in Ellen's raw, chapped hands were Lucy's wet clothes. The child would have to stay inside, wrapped in her shawl until they were dry, which in this cold weather could take all day. At least Lucy had a little book to read. Ellen felt a surge of pride and gratitude go through her. Despite the horror that had happened to her daughter, she was a quick, bright little girl.

'Ellen – what ails yow, wench?'

Bertha Hipkiss was leaning against the door frame of the workshop, arms folded, taking a moment's rest. She wore a black blouse with a brown woollen shawl crossed over at the front and tucked into her waist above the long skirt and scorched hessian apron. She righted herself and put her hands on her hips, a handsome, steely figure in her big men's boots, dark hair tucked in under the manly cap.

'All yow 'ave ter do is give us a shout, wench, and I'll come over and shove this in 'is loffer.'

She bunched her fist and Ellen saw the muscles contort in her forearm.

'I know yow will, Bertha.' Ellen smiled faintly, pegging out the little dress and pinafore. Spots swam in front of her eyes and she had to look down for a moment. 'Only I see 'im everywhere, these days. I cor 'elp myself.'

Ellen brought her fingers up to her temples.

'Every time 'e comes into the yard now, 'e's looking at me as if 'e's trying to pin me to the ground.'

A couple of days ago he had come over and rubbed his hand across her backside as if staking his claim. And he knew there was nothing any of them could do about it for fear of losing the few shillings they scraped by on every week.

''E's in my head. I cor seem to get 'im out.'

'It ay yower 'ead yow need to worry about,' Bertha said. Shaking her own, she turned back into the work-shop. 'Just mek sure there's always someone with yer,' she said. 'Dow go working out there on yower own.'

Ellen was soon back at the hearth beside Bertha. Holding her link in the fire she worked the bellows, bent and ham-mered the glowing curve of it, softened in the fire, and inserted it through the last one on the chain. Her actions were almost as familiar as breathing.

Mari Gornall, her mousey hair scraped into a bun, was working the other side of her. She was hindered by the fact that she had her latest babby tied on her at the front, at her breast. After the feed the baby would be bundled into the box cradle which they sometimes hung on a rod fixed from wall to wall, to be rocked to sleep.

Mari's face was swollen with toothache. She kept giving groans of pain, and only noticed little Maggie enough to curse at her. The child wandered about the workshop, picking at things, or sat amid the cinders making games out of any scrap she found while sparks dropped softly on her hair and shoulders.

'Gerrover 'ere, yow little brat!' Mari yelled at her. 'At least yow could be doing summat useful!'

Maggie toddled over to the handle of the bellows and leaned on it, trying desperately to work it like the bigger girls did.

'That's it, goo on, Maggie!' Ellen said, to encourage her. 'Yow'll soon be able to do it!' But she was a small waif and even standing her whole weight on the bellows, she could not make them work properly. Her little face puckered with misery.

'Yower all right, Maggie.' Ellen tugged her lips into a smile. 'Yow'll be big enough to help us one day.'

Maggie stared back uncertainly at her, but she seemed to drink in these words of kindness.

Ellen pulled the back of her hand across her sweating forehead, feeling the scrape of dirt and soot on her face. Her mouth tasted of metal, her gums burningly sore. Worries seethed in her mind. It was always this way – get on, get on, work, work, make more chain, morning until night and half the night if necessary . . . How to reach the end of the week with enough money for food, just something to fill their bellies, even if skilly was all. Lucy and George were never much trouble, but Albert . . .

Last night when her boy came in from work, shoving his way sullenly into the kitchen, she saw a hard-faced little man in his cap and jacket, filthy all over and almost dropping with weariness. But it was the way his gaze flicked round the back kitchen that chilled her soul. He seemed to take in the boiling pot, his mother, thin as a rod, bent weakly over the fire and dragging herself upright again when she heard him come in. And those eyes of his seemed brimful of despondency, even of hatred.

'Wha's to eat?' he demanded. Even his voice had

changed, deepened into a manly growl. He took his cap off and flung it on the hook at the back of the door.

'I got yow a bit of bacon,' Ellen said, eager to please. He was starting to frighten her, all that was coiled up in him. He really would be a man soon, tall and strong, and she was intimidated.

'Huh.' He sat down. 'Let's be 'aving it then.'

He always ate the best of any of them now, out of the half-crown he slaved for, turning the blast wheel hour after hour.

'Yow can get me some decent fittle after all that,' he'd demanded. 'A working man cor get by on slop.'

After shovelling down the best food that none of the rest of them would sample, he pushed his chair back without another word, and took his cap again.

'Where're yow going?' she dared to ask.

He turned on her.

'Why d'yow want to know?'

Ellen took courage. 'I've heard yer've been hanging about down Five Ways at the pub. With that'un.' She jerked her head.

For all Edna Wilmott doted on her middle-aged and simple-minded son, in everyone else's eyes, Sidney Wilmott was a bad lot. Like a big, black-haired child in his too-tight jacket and trousers, he could be seen tagging along with any gang, in any place where he could watch a fight. Sidney loved any kind of scrap: cock-fights, rats in a barrel, two men with ferrets tied to fight it out in their trousers or a clutch of blokes knocking each other about – Sidney would be there, rocking and gurning with delight.

'Huh,' Albert said contemptuously. He went to go to the door, but she dared to bar his way.

'Dow yow go marching out like that – yow tell me

where yow'm going!' She could feel any control she had of him slipping away and it wasn't right, a lad his age carrying on like this to his mother.

'Nowhere,' he protested petulantly. 'Move over, will yow, woman. I've been stuck in there all day like a rat in a cage – I wanna go out with my pals and yow ain't gunna stop me, *Mother*.'

He almost spat the word. It felt like a slap. Ellen stepped out of the way. Albert pulled his cap on and slammed out of the door into the yard, as Ellen sank down at the table. Her boy, once her soft, dark-eyed little sweetheart . . .

Albert was not the only trouble whirling in her mind. Since that day three weeks ago when Seth Dawson had appeared in her house, she had not felt safe anywhere. That vile creature – inside the house! She never needed to bolt the door normally. But he had come oozing in like a slug. The very thought made her shudder; the look and smell of him, so close to her.

Every time he came to the yard now – and it seemed to be more often – it was as though he was seeking her out. It felt as if he was pointing a gun and she was the rabbit.

At night, she certainly bolted that door now. But she kept waking with a start, frightened that there was someone else in the house, thinking she could hear feet creeping up the stairs until she would drive herself into such a state of terror that she would have to light a candle to have a look in every corner of the house. The man seemed to be taking over her life even when he was not there.

Nine

It lit up Lucy's day, knowing she was going to see her teacher's eyes smiling down on her, full of kindness and encouragement. To be told how well she was coming on at reading and writing gave her a glow of pride. When the children were all sitting down – so that she was then equal to them – she was often the one who was ahead.

She adored Miss Jones as if she was an angel sent from heaven.

And now, thanks to her beloved teacher, she had something else to do on a Sunday afternoon. That spring she started going to the Sunday school in Graingers Lane. Best of all, the first time she went, she told John and Clem they could come as well.

'Do *what*?' Clem said.

For once she had their attention as they all stood back in the yard. She had had no way of keeping up with them on the way back from school.

'Sunday school. Miss Jones said I was to ask yer. 'Er said there's stories and games and singing . . . Freddie could come with us.'

John and Clem Hipkiss were now eleven and ten years old. John, who still had his cap on, listened, pale and serious, head on one side. Clem, who was never still, was restlessly kicking a pebble about.

'Why'd us wanna do that?' Clem grinned at her. His face was so handsome, so full of mischief, that Lucy's heart pounded a little faster. Even having Clem take notice of her for a second made her bubble with happiness, as if she counted as someone – wasn't just a stupid girl and a cripple.

'Might be all right,' John said in his steady way.

'They give yer summat to eat,' she added.

Well, that persuaded them if nothing else would.

In the big hall, a crowd of children of all different ages were milling about. Lucy's heart picked up speed as she spotted Miss Jones on the other side of the room, wearing a dark green skirt and a white blouse. When Miss Jones's eyes fastened on Lucy, her lips turned up and as she came across the room Lucy felt herself squirming with happiness.

'Hello, Lucy!' Miss Jones smiled at the three Hipkiss boys who were more silent and biddable-looking than Lucy had ever seen them, especially Clem. 'I'm glad you boys could come – and your friend Gertie's here as well, Lucy.'

Miss Jones pointed to Gertie, from school, sitting at the side of the room, her calipers preventing her from running about. Lucy felt a pang of dread. Gertie was all right, but Lucy did not want to be stuck there sitting next to her, both of them ignored as usual. She felt a bit guilty though, as she turned away and moved a little closer to Clem.

'We're all about to have a song –'

A dark-eyed, serious-looking man with a little moustache stood before them. He clapped his hands for them to quieten and told them his name was Mr Henry. Soon they were all rowed up on the floor holding some tatty little hymnbooks.

Lucy kept watching Miss Jones, seated at the piano with her back to them, her thick brown hair pinned back with little tortoiseshell combs, her slender body moving with the music as she played 'All Things Bright and Beautiful'. Lucy loved the sight of her teacher. When she glanced away for a moment, she saw Mr Henry standing at the other end of the half-circle of children. His lips were moving to the words, and he did not seem to need to read from the hymnbook. Instead, his gaze also seemed to be fixed on Miss Jones.

Mr Henry and Miss Jones and their two lady Sunday school helpers read stories, and then they played some games. And Miss Jones told them, as if she was telling a fairy story, that when the first Methodists came to Cradley Heath, they were full of their passion to share the love of God with all the hard-working people there, but that at first they had no church to call their own.

She sat on a hard chair as she talked, her back very upright and her hands in her lap.

'God is at home in the humblest place,' she said. 'So those good people thought it no shame to conduct their worship in the nailmakers' forge – their daily place of toil!'

Lucy loved listening to her, her different accent and fervent manner. She was sitting between John and Clem. John listened, his eyes fixed on Miss Jones, but Clem kept his head down, his fingers prising at a stone stuck in the sole of his boot. Freddie sat still, seemingly bored and half-asleep.

Miss Jones explained that the church had been built later, with its clock tower. But with all the mining in the area there were huge holes under the ground like caves . . . In her mind Lucy pictured the ground beneath them, its gaping spaces, dark and watery . . .

'And the clock tower began to lean so that it wasn't straight and it was thought that one day it might fall! So the tower had to be taken down. And very soon, we'll have our new church – but for the moment we give praise to God in this very hall.' She beamed round at them as if this was the very best thing that could ever happen in all the world.

Eventually they were given a cup of milk – milk! – and an arrowroot biscuit.

'S'pose I might come again,' Clem said, apparently convinced by the biscuit he was cramming into his mouth. All three lads were wolfing them down while Lucy nibbled hers, savouring every delicious crumb. They sang some more songs before being released into the chilly afternoon.

Soon Mom got her to take six-year-old George as well, to get him out of her hair for the afternoon. It meant she could get a good stretch of work in and maybe even have a few minutes of that rarest thing of all – rest.

On Sunday afternoons, when Lucy walked home from Sunday school with all the boys, it felt different from the normal school days. She still existed for them because they had all done something together. They might even play with her afterwards in the yard – jackstones or marleys – instead of leaving her to play with George and the other little ones. And one Sunday, something happened that made the whole summer for her.

It was a lovely mellow afternoon in early July and they had been released out into the sunshine. When they got back to the yard the lads ran and scrambled up the wall in their casual way, astride, making believe the wall was a horse they could ride.

Lucy looked up at them, so high above her, like sailors in the rigging.

'I want to come up,' she said.

'Yow?' Clem looked down at her, amazed, as if the idea of her being able to do anything was beyond imagining.

'Goo on – course I can if yow get me up there.'

John hesitated, then twisted round, bringing one leg back over and scrambling to the ground.

'C'mon, Clem – give us a 'and!' John said. 'Luce – you get up on my back.'

Daring herself, she laid her crutches down by the wall. John hauled her into a piggyback and Lucy pulled herself up as high on him as she could manage, reaching her arms up for Clem to pull on them.

Clem, immediately wanting to show he was the strongest, reached down and hauled on her arms. John then twisted round to push from behind until Lucy was laid across the wall on her belly like a sack of corn across a saddle.

'Tha's it – now get yower leg over!' Clem said. He wanted to take charge. Lucy had noticed this lately – a new edge of competition between the boys.

Bit by bit, pushing on her arms, kicking her skirt out of the way, she managed to get her good leg over the wall and sit up, gripping with both thighs. As she did so she saw Amy Gornall across the yard, smirking at her. Lucy turned away, ignoring her.

John climbed up again behind her and suddenly they were adventurers, all riding the same fast galloping steed! Lucy was beaming, ecstatic. Amy could make all the nasty faces she liked, but at this moment she was the one up on the wall with John and Clem.

'Oh – look!' she cried.

The world opened for her like a book. At the end of Hay Lane, you could cut through into the fields next to the railway embankment, and the other children often went to gather bits of wood for the fire. But Lucy had never been – no one ever thought it worth the bother of taking her. So she had only ever caught glimpses of the fields behind, on a rare walk to the end of the road.

Now, in front of her, she saw fields of ripening corn edged by the sooty, grass-tufted sides of the railway embankment which stretched away endlessly into the distance. At the field margins, clouds of butterflies, yellow or white, hovered round the flowers. Two fields away, a man was leading a strong-looking black horse and beyond him rose the winding gear of Codsall Colliery. Beyond even them, in the far distance, were trees and the rise of Haden Hill, though she did not know its name.

The world was so big and stretched so far! In all her life she had never seen so much of what lay about her and she was entranced.

Mom had told her once that when she was very small, after they had taken off her leg, she had started walking with Lucy in her arms. She carried her out all the way to the sacred spring at Mousesweet, to bless her little stump with water and pray for a miracle. Did Mom hope her leg would grow back? Lucy did not know. She could not remember anything about it. But that was the furthest she had ever been in her life, cradled in her mother's arms.

Clem swung his leg over and dropped down into the field, running along the edge, so John felt bound to join him. They ran and jumped, shouting and laughing, so free and strong in their bodies.

Lucy sat silent, drinking everything in. The mellow afternoon sunlight warmed her face and picked out the stalks whose green was just beginning to lighten to gold. The sky was a delicate blue with thin streaks of cloud. The world was wide and new, and she must have more of it! She thought this was the happiest she had ever been, there up high in the warm as the boys wrestled and played below her, the hardness of the wall clutched between her thighs.

A voice came then, from the yard. Turning, she saw the tunky figure of Seth Dawson, his black, stained jacket and slouching legs, moving towards the entry. He had come out of the forge which, she now realized, was silent. Before, the *chink-chink* of the hammer had been going on, unnoticed as the pulse of her own blood. Now it had stopped.

A moment later her mother came out in her old grey dress and apron, her head down. No one else was outside, but then Lucy saw Mrs Hipkiss emerge from her cottage and the two of them exchanged quiet words, standing each side of the remaining bits of broken wall round the Hipkisses' cottage garden. Lucy saw her mother shake her head as her neighbour questioned her, but she never raised her face to look at her. Lucy wanted to call out to her, for Mom to see her up here sitting on the wall! But something stopped her. A moment later her mother disappeared into the house.

Ten

She closed the door and leaned against it, pressing her trembling hands over her face.

Sunday afternoon – she could not claim to be a religious person but even so, that vile monster carrying on in that foul, evil way on a Sunday seemed even more abhorrent.

It had not crossed her mind that she was not safe, Sunday afternoon in broad daylight. Now that Lucy and George were off at the Sunday school she'd seen it as a chance to get a few hours in at the hearth.

No one else was working.

'I'll sit with Jonno for a bit,' Bertha had said. Heaven knew there was little enough time the rest of the week and that poor soul of a man sat sick and blind, hour after hour.

Edna Wilmott was round at her sister's and Mari Gornall – well, everyone knew how she and Victor spent Sunday afternoon since they took no trouble to be quiet about it. As night followed day, another babby would be on the way next year.

But for her it was a chance to try and make the week ahead a fraction easier. Albert, her boy who she hardly recognized these days, had started refusing to hand over his wages. Where was the money going – on the fights and mucky goings-on with Sidney Wilmott? But she could not make him give it to her even though she could weep just thinking of it.

'Son – I need yower wages to get the food yow like,' she pleaded with him.

But, hard-faced, all Albert would say was, 'I'm the one sweating for it – it's mine.'

It was as if Albert had no heart these days. If only he still had a father to keep him in order, a good man to show him the way in life – things would be different then.

She stood at the hearth, leaning on the bellows, heating, twisting, taking the heavy hammer to the links, her mind fretting . . . Minutes went by, an hour . . .

A shadow filled the doorway. She turned, jumping violently, then furious with herself for showing how much he frightened her. But she was alone. She must never be alone with this vile creature . . . Sunday afternoon – he never usually came around on a Sunday . . .

Seth Dawson leaned against the door frame in that leering way of his, seemingly comfortable in the knowledge that there was no one in the yard to see him. He stared at her, then opened his mouth wide and stuck two fingers in to tug at something. It was as if he was forever biting into some carcass and ending up with bits jammed between his teeth. No doubt he'd had a good plate of meat for his Sunday dinner – not like his slaving out-workers who could hardly afford a booster to eat. She caught the stench of him, the greasy foulness laced with ale. No wonder the man had no wife – who could ever live with *that*?

Ellen did not want to turn her back on him. She stood half-turned away, trying to go on working with one eye on him, there, blocking the doorway.

He slouched over to her and immediately she was trapped next to her hearth with him barring the way. He came so close that she could not move for fear of leaning any further into the fire.

Shout – get help! her mind insisted, but she was paralysed, her spine curved back, the brick edge of the hearth pressing into her buttocks.

'Well, wench – 'ard at work, I see.'

His foul breath forced itself into her nostrils. Those sludgy eyes looked down into hers. He had dark brows with a bristle of hair joining them in the middle. The face was heavy, baggy and pockmarked, with its shading of bristles which merged into his greasy black hair. The smell of him turned her stomach.

He stood staring into her face and then, sudden as a snake, he grabbed her hips, yanking her in close to his groin, kneading at her backside. Ellen whimpered with shock.

'I've 'ad my eye on yer, wench.' She turned her head to try and avoid the blast of his putrid breath in her face. 'Don't look away when I'm talking to yer! Yer ent got much meat on yer bones but I've a fancy for yer all the same . . .'

'Get off of me,' she hissed at him. 'Loose me – or I'll scream . . .'

But his hands tightened on her, bruising her backside, and he moved his face right up close.

'Oh – that Bertha 'Ipkiss, are it? Thinking of calling 'er? You're a fool to yerself, Ellen Butler, d'yer know that? Slaving away for every farthing when yer could be doing better for yerself.'

Ellen squirmed, trying to get out of his grip, but he was bigger and stronger, better fed. He would always win.

''Ow much is it worth to yer, giving me what I want? A shilling, two? You 'ere without a man of yer own – yer could do with a good seein'-to, wench.' He thrust his groin against her. 'Where d'yer want it? In 'ere? In the privy? Or what about that bed of yours?'

His breath whistled fast and heavy through his bristly nose. He removed his hands and went to grab at her breasts.

'No!' Ellen found the strength to push against him and Seth, caught off balance, was forced to step back. In a second Ellen reached for her hammer. 'Get away from me, you foul animal!'

'Oh-ho!' He held his hands up, laughing, pretending to surrender. 'So – you've some fire in yer belly after all!'

'Get out!' With all speed she turned, grabbed the shovel and scooped up a heap of hot coals, making to throw them at him. 'You foul Brumagen bastard!'

'All right – I'm going.' He lingered by the door, smirking at her anger. 'I'll be back though, wench – so yow'd best be ready for me.'

He made a lewd gesture, thrusting his hands between his legs, and then slouched away and out of the yard.

As the heat of summer grew, the fetid stench of the yard privies and alleys intensified, flies preying on the filth, and the forge workshops were almost unbearably hot to work in. Ellen grew more and more tense. There were days when she stood at the hearth feeling as if her head was going to burst open.

She was on guard at all times against being alone with Seth Dawson, who turned up regularly, leering at her, biding his time. And there was Albert. Her feelings had grown more and more angry and bitter at what was becoming of her son. His already clouded nature was not improved in the least by his hanging around with that halfwit Sidney. He was being ruined, turning against his family so that she could not reach him no matter what plea she put to him.

One baking afternoon, they were all in the workshop – Mari and Edna, Ellen and Bertha. Ellen's head ached. The tools were almost too hot to touch and with every blow of the hammer her heart seemed to lurch, her whole being ragged with anger and worry. In the baking, smoky air, she was struggling to breathe.

Edna started to sing, as she often did, her belting voice rising into 'Just a Song at Twilight' and the others began to join in, Mari's toneless yowling rising beside Ellen, despite the fact that her youngest, the baby, was crying. Mari carried on working, ignoring the screams.

Ellen, nerves already frayed, reached boiling point. All her fury rose up in her and she flung her hammer down.

'For the love of God!' she shrieked. 'See to that child of yowers, screaming its cowing head off all day!'

'Dow yow go telling me what to do . . .!' Mari started, turning on her, her white face tense with spite.

But Ellen was already striding over to Edna Wilmott.

'And it's all very well yow singing and carrying on as if there was nowt amiss! What about that yampy great son of yowers and what he's doing to mine?'

Edna turned, slow like a cow caught by surprise.

'My Albert's turned into a devil since 'e's been with that idle lad of yowers and . . . Yow want to keep him in order, not 'ave him going about getting young lads into trouble! Ever since my boy's had anything to do wi' yowers 'e ain't the same . . . 'E's horrible . . . A bully . . . I don't even know 'im no more . . .' She was so over-wrought she could not get the words out and instead, burst into tears.

'Ooh – listen to 'er!' she heard Mari say. 'Anyone'd think the sun shone out of 'er son's back end!'

'Come on, wench.' Ellen found Bertha at her side. She put one of her powerful arms round Ellen's shoulders and steered her out of the forge. 'Come out of 'ere and get yerself cooled down.'

Ellen found herself marched over to the pump.

'Goo on – get yower 'ead under there, wench!'

Ellen bent and Bertha pumped the tepid water over her head until she stood up, gasping, the water pouring in rivulets down into her clothes and between her flat little breasts. She found she was crying and laughing at the same time.

'It ent no good going on at 'er about Sidney,' Bertha said. 'Yow know what 'er's like – a fool for that boy. Not that he's a boy any more – but 'e's a simpleton and Edna ain't gunna mek 'im change 'is ways. Yower gunna 'ave to tek Albert in hand yowerself, bab – it ain't gunna sort itself out.'

'Can you help me, Bertha?' Ellen asked. 'You've got lads – you know what to do. He's bigger'un me – I can't handle him.'

''E needs a good hiding, that's what,' Bertha said, considering the problem. 'And if yower James were still alive no doubt the lad'd get it. 'E's far too young to be carrying on like that. We'll 'ave a think, see if we can come up with summat.'

Two days later, after going to the High Street for some bits of groceries, Ellen hurried back towards the yard. She had left going out to the shops until she had put in a good stint of work, but even so, her head seethed with worries and calculations. How much more chain did she need to get done today . . .? All the time she felt at the end of her strength, as if she was falling behind. And her worries about Albert still occupied half her mind.

She turned into the entry. She could hear some children playing – the Gornall and Hipkiss kids, and George would be out there too. There was a smell of boiling onions: the other women took a break from the chains at this time to start cooking for their husbands and children.

Tonight, she'd tackle Albert. She didn't want him to be beaten – not by someone else's man, if that was what Bertha had in mind. It didn't seem right. Bertha never needed to lay a finger on her own – they were in awe of her without that. Maybe she could sit Albert down, talk to him like the man he now seemed to think he was . . .

Her mind was so taken up that she didn't hear the furtive steps behind her as she walked along the yard and in through her back door. Immediately, he was inside with her, shoving her out of the way and against the table as he turned and bolted the door.

Ellen yelped as her hip bone crashed against the hard wood, tears of pain stinging her eyes. It took a second for the shock of the pain to subside before she felt the true horror of her situation. Seth Dawson, following her, trapping her in here with him . . . There was no one in the house – not even Lucy.

'So,' Seth said. There was no grin now. His face was set and full of purpose, his fingers digging into her arms.

'What d'yow want?' She could not pretend to be brave. He had her, she knew full well. Her voice came out high and terrified.

'What d'yer think I want?'

It only took seconds for her naive idea that she might somehow get away from him to be torn to tatters. He stuck his face right up close to hers.

'Best give me what I want, wench, or I'll tek it, whichever way. Get upstairs. I've bin patient wi' you but now my time's come.'

'No!' She tried to fight him, clinging to the door frame as he started to drag her. He rounded on her and slapped her so hard across the face that she tasted blood from the wound erupting on her lip. She was so jarred she could hardly stand, and clutched at the door. Her teeth on that side felt wrong, as if he had dislodged them. Moaning with pain, she sank to the floor, trying to scream, but all that came out was a pathetic little shred of noise. No one would ever hear her.

'Get up, yer stupid bitch.'

He hauled her to her feet and as if he had lost patience with the thought of dragging her all the way up the staircase, he pulled her behind the table, shoving it so that it rammed up against the door and forced her down on her back. The only thing between her and the brick floor was the grubby bodged rug.

'Get yer legs apart, wench . . . Yower gunna 'ave me whether yer like it or not. Should've said yes when I asked nicer, shouldn't yer?'

Seth was yanking at his clothes and to her horror she saw a glimpse of his thickened cock in the dark opening of his britches, before he bent over and started tearing at her clothes. Nothing took him long – she had so few things to wear and those were in tatters. His fingers forced her skinny thighs apart.

The stink of him – grease and sweat and piss – seemed to wrap itself round her, so rank and overpowering that afterwards, she thought that as he'd moved on top of her to carry out his vile forcing, she must have fainted. She came to in pain, the top of her spine and her pelvis grating against the floor, with a wet, violated ache between her legs.

But he was gone.

Eleven

1903

'Luce – go and get Mrs Hipkiss.'

Lucy had only been home from school for a few moments when her mother came hurrying across from the forge. She could hear shouts from the yard where her brother George was playing tip-cat with Freddie Hipkiss and some of the others.

She was about to tell Mom that Miss Jones had said she was the best at her letters in the class that day. But one look at her mother and Lucy could see she was not going to hear a word of it. Mom seized hold of the edge of the rickety table and leaned over it, gasping. Lucy could see something was hurting her.

''Ave yer burned your hand again?' she asked, trying to be helpful. Mom's hands were a mass of scars and wounds.

Ellen shook her head, her face all screwed up. As the pain eased, she sank on to the nearest chair. In a tight voice, she said,

'Goo on – hurry up.'

Bertha Hipkiss, still in her sacking apron, took one look at Lucy's mother and said,

'Yower getting close, ain't yer, El?' She hurried to open the door and bawl across the yard. 'George Butler – get yowerself over 'ere!'

Startled half out of his wits, Lucy's young brother George ran over, looking up at Bertha with fearful blue eyes. Lucy stood with a shrinking feeling as Bertha ordered, 'Right – yow can run for Mrs Heath along at number thirty. Yower mother needs 'er. Mek haste, lad!'

As George scurried away, another bout of pain seized Mom and Bertha stood over her.

'I don't know how'll I'll pay 'er,' Lucy heard her moan.

'Don't dwell on that now, wench. We'll see to it. Come on, let's get yow to bed. Yow'll be all right. Luce – mek sure there's a pan of water on the fire.' As the pain passed, Bertha Hipkiss helped Mom to her feet. 'Dear God, Ellen –' Bertha frowned in horror, feeling Ellen's arm and looking at her as if she had never seen her before. 'There's nowt to yow but skin and bone!'

As they shuffled towards the stairs, Lucy heard Bertha Hipkiss say something she did not understand then, or for a long time.

'That'un'll burn in hell for this . . .'

Mom clutched at the newel post, groaning. 'All those foggers'll burn. But I'm the one's burning now . . .'

Mrs Sarah Heath, who came to help birth the child, had started her working life at Netherton, as a 'pit bonk wench'. They were the girls out in all weathers in their long skirts and bonnets who scrambled over the ground around the pits, gathering pails of coal nubs to sell back to the pit masters for a pittance so that not a scrap should be wasted.

She was a strong, vigorous woman who by middle age had six of her own surviving children and had long left behind her pit-bank wench's garb for a rather dashing brown hat with a brim, topping off a black bombazine dress, gauzy from years of wear, and black button boots. Her face was rough and weather-beaten. Any mention of her former employers at the pit and her features would contort with loathing. There was not a good word to be said and she described them as 'filthy louses'. 'Treated us like dogs, they did – they was the death of my poor dear mother.'

Mrs Heath told this story, over and over, to anyone who would listen.

'Only reason they'm couldn't 'ave us slaving down the pit was the '42 act,' she would say. 'Or I'd've bin down there hauling with the pit ponies the way my poor mother did. That were the finish of 'er, God rest her soul. Dead at thirty, 'er was.'

The 1842 Mining Act had forbidden employment underground of women and of children under ten years old.

When it came to giving aid to birthing women, Sarah Heath was rough and ready but kind enough. She took the side of the women she cared for and was trusted in the neighbourhood. Only an emergency would send anyone running for a doctor who charged more than double Mrs H's two shillings.

When she waddled along the yard and into the house, a diminutive woman on rickety legs, carrying her carpet bag of things, Lucy was in the back watching over the fire.

'All right, little wench?' she panted chestily. 'Got me some water on the boil, 'ave yow?'

Lucy nodded. She was perched on a chair, rubbing her hand over her sore stump through her skirt. Her stomach clenched with dread every time she heard one of Mom's terrible moans from upstairs. She was so glad Mrs Hipkiss was in the house and she could stay down here.

'Mek us a sup o' tea, bab, and we'll get started.'

Mrs Heath's heavy tread made its way up the stairs, and then through the floorboards Lucy heard her voice, almost as low as a man's, talking to Mom.

Time passed. Lucy made the tea and managed to get it upstairs going up backwards on her bottom and holding on to the cup for dear life. She had hoped Mrs Heath would come to the door to get it but everyone in the room seemed very taken up.

'Mrs Hipkiss?' she called.

The door swung open and Bertha appeared.

'Oh – is that for Mrs H?' she said, taking the cup.

Lucy's stomach curdled as she saw into the room. Mom was on the bed, her hair drenched in sweat and all rat's tails, her shift barely covering her privates and the great mound of her belly like a growth on her. Her bare legs, thin as sticks, were bent up and on full show. Lucy had never seen so much of her mother's body before and it was only then that she took in how thin Mom was and how she had shrunk.

Mom was passing through one of her pains and her face was all screwed up, the veins standing out on her neck. Mrs Heath was bent over the bed, a dark figure against Mom's white shift, like a bird over a piece of carrion.

Bertha Hipkiss went to close the door. 'Can yow bring me one up, bab? Oh, no . . .' She saw Bertha realize what a struggle it had been for her to bring one cup of tea upstairs let alone two. 'I'll come and get it.'

She led Lucy downstairs, moving quickly ahead of her. In the kitchen she helped herself to water from the kettle.

'You'll need to put more water in 'ere. And I need to go over and tell our Pauline to feed the others.' She was talking half to herself.

83

Don't go . . . Lucy pleaded in her mind. The thought of being left here with no one but Mrs Heath and this terrible ordeal Mom was passing through was so terrible that she nearly burst into tears.

'I'll go,' she said hastily.

'All right, bab – ta.'

Lucy wanted Mrs Hipkiss to say that everything was going to be all right and that Mom would stop moaning and would soon be up and about as usual.

But Mrs Hipkiss did not say that. Her face wore a dark expression as she took her tea and went back upstairs again.

When Albert came in later, Lucy and George were at the table. George had had a heel of bread soaked into a slop with a drop of cold tea but Lucy felt sick and her body was jangled with nerves. All they could do was wait, hearing the movement of feet above, the faint sounds from their mother, high and thin now, like a cat left out in the rain.

'What's gooin' on?' Albert demanded.

His face was dark with filth and his mood not much better, but in a second, he took in that things were not normal.

'Mom's having the babby,' Lucy said.

'It's teking . . .' George ran out of words, holding out his arms to convey a time more endless than he could understand. His blue eyes were round and frightened.

Albert's face twitched with an emotion Lucy could not read. Then he said, 'What's to eat?'

She shrugged. She knew her brother's temper, how he flared up, angry, expecting to be treated like a man of the house who had the best treatment in everything. But for once he did not do that. He stood listening for a second. They heard sounds, the women talking.

'Well, there's nowt I can do about it!' Albert said eventually, slamming his way out of the house again.

There was nothing any of them could do. Lucy felt exhausted, her body aching, but her mind was wired tight with tension. Pauline Hipkiss put her head round the door to ask if they were all right and was her mom coming home soon? Lucy could only stare up at her and say she didn't know. Everything felt horrible and unreal, like a nightmare.

Pauline, who was nineteen, was a handsome, dark-eyed young woman like her mother.

'All right, Georgie?' She ruffled his hair, brown and straight like Lucy's. 'Don't get mithered – it'll all be over soon and you'll have a new babby in the house.' George leaned his head against her as he stood beside her, hungry for reassurance, and Lucy wished she could do the same.

Pauline stayed a while, talking to them, and before long her mother appeared, hurrying down the stairs. She looked sterner and more worried than Lucy had ever seen her.

'Pauline,' she said abruptly. 'Run for the doctor – and quick!'

The doctor, short and bespectacled, arrived and thumped his way upstairs. Albert did not come back. Lucy sent George up to his bed and she herself fell asleep eventually with her head on her arms on the table.

Then someone was shaking her. She jerked awake.

'Come up with me.' Bertha Hipkiss was pulling her chair back. 'Where's little'un?'

'Asleep,' Lucy said.

'Yow need to come and see yer mother,' Bertha said. Lucy did not take in her expression, her tone, just yet.

'Is the babby here?' Lucy asked, suddenly excited.

Bertha hesitated. 'No, Luce – the babby's gone to the Lord.'

In the bedroom Mrs Heath, a spare part since the doctor had arrived, was bundling up some bloody rags. The doctor was bending gravely over Lucy's mother. She lay covered by a sheet and Lucy could see how thin she was, like a pole in the bed.

'Ellen – your Lucy's 'ere.'

To Lucy's horror she heard Bertha's voice crack. And this, the idea of Bertha Hipkiss shedding tears, was more alarming even than the sight of her mother, so pale and still.

'This is all that filthy fogger's doing,' Bertha wept to Mrs Heath as they stood together in the corner. 'We all know who it was – but there wor no one else to see what happened. When's 'e gunna get what's coming to him, that's what I want to know!'

Mrs Heath shook her head. 'Even if this poor wench'd survived – the word of that filthy mon'd always count over her.'

Lucy could make no sense of what they were saying. She stood gazing down at her mother and the doctor moved away, saying, 'You'd best take your mother's hand, child. She won't be with us much longer.'

His words felt like stones sliding down inside Lucy's body. Not with us? What did he mean?

'Mom?' Her voice wavered. She dared to reach out for Mom's bony hand. It was so cold that she almost recoiled. But then she slid her own underneath it, seeking reassurance, holding it tight and longing for a reply.

There was nothing, not at first. Then she saw a flicker

of her mother's eyelids and Ellen managed to turn her head a fraction and open her eyes.

'Luce?' Lucy had to lean close to hear, even in the quiet of the room. 'I dow want . . .' She gathered herself and for a second Lucy felt her mother's fingers press down on her own, just a pulse of pressure. 'I'm sorry. I want to stay with you . . . My girl . . . You're my girl . . .'

Her eyes closed. It was the last thing she ever said on this earth.

II

1904

Twelve

The book, with its scuffed, deep red cover, lay in her lap as she sat in the Hipkisses' cramped kitchen.

It was a warm day, the door open on to the yard. Broken remnants of the old garden wall stuck up like blackened teeth, stubbornly remaining despite all the kickings the boys gave them. You could still see the scrubby rectangles of its patches of garden, this little house that had once stood alone on Hay Lane, a quiet country track before the industrial boom began in the Black Country and the railway arrived to nestle at its side.

Sunlight filtered through the grimy window, tracing a bright oblong on the bleached table. Beside Lucy, in his horsehair-stuffed chair, its leather worn through on the arms where his hands rested, sat Jonno Hipkiss. Except for times when he needed to be helped to his feet to carry out his bodily functions, he stayed in that chair beside the fire day and night, swathed in quilts and a blanket even on a summer day like today.

'Thank you, girlie.' He heaved in a rattling breath. 'Think I'll have a little rest now.'

Lucy closed the book with its rubbed gold lettering on the spine: *Little Dorrit, Charles Dickens*.

She watched the suffering man beside her for a moment. When she had first started reading to Jonno Hipkiss, she had felt a shock of distress every time she looked at him. Jonno had been their neighbour all her life. She could remember the energetic, laughing Welshman who had worked the face of local pits until his lungs got so bad that he was forced to look for a job above the ground. Two years later, as he was working in the lime pits on a day of high winds, a gust had hurled powdered lime into his eyes, scalding them into blindness.

The Jonno of today was a living skeleton. She could see his collar bones jutting in the neck of his shirt. His skin was yellow, his hair, once dark and abundant like Clem's, was now white and wispy thin. His frame tensed with the strain of every breath he took, with each cough, when his chest curdled up the tarry phlegm he spat out into a little tin can. When he reached out for this, he often knocked it flying, since those once laughing eyes were now puckered closed for ever. Instead of cursing in frustration as he might once have done, he would sit hunched over, defeated, holding the gob in his mouth until someone picked the tin up and placed it gently in his hand.

He was a beautiful man, a loving man. Everyone liked Jonno, and Lucy, hungry for a father, had quickly grown to love him when the family took her in. He always spoke to her with gentle kindness, would try to raise a smile to lift her from her sadness where he could, even though it was a smile he would never see.

And in turn, she would sit beside him hour by hour – she being the one who could read by far the best and who had the time. Clem had never had much truck with learning and the others who could read a little – Pauline and John – seemed seldom to have the time or patience to read to their father. Nor could they read anything like as well as she could.

Lucy sat for a moment. The children's voices echoed off the brick walls of the yard. Pauline Hipkiss was out courting with her latest young man and Bertha and the other women were in the forge, *tap-tap, chink-chink-*

chink . . . Every so often smoke wafted past the open door, some of it stealing into the room. She saw a robin alight in the old garden, hop about, then take off again.

The book was warm under Lucy's palms. Miss Jones had lent it to them.

'Read, Lucy,' she instructed her. 'Everything you can and as often as you can. You're a natural reader and you'll come on in leaps and bounds if you keep at it. And when they get that library built that they're talking about putting up in the High Street – well, you'll have all the books you could need then, lass!'

There were no books in the house except a Bible and Jonno soon tired of that. Miss Jones had lent them Walter Scott and Wilkie Collins, books that Jonno had sat through with pleasure – but his favourite was Dickens.

'Living inside a *prison* . . .' He spoke in gasps, his ringing, Welsh voice now ground down to a whisper. 'And his family . . . all that time . . . you'd think . . . that Dorrit fella'd get himself . . . out of there . . .'

They would laugh together at Dickens's jokes and characters and while Lucy was keeping Jonno amused, the stories helped to distract her from her own aching heart.

There was an added reason why she felt so low today. It was 20 June – her eleventh birthday. No one had thought of this last year, when she turned ten. Back then, everything was too raw with the grief of her mother's death and Albert's disappearance, and then George, what had happened to George . . . And today again, no one said a word. Mom would have remembered. She always did. 'The day my one girl came into the world,' she would say. 'I ay gunna forget that, ar I?'

Now though, as she sat hearing Jonno's rasping breaths, she felt sunk in woe. She was of no importance to anyone:

she was just another mouth to feed. Bertha was kind of course, in her rough and ready way, when she had a moment even to think of it. But Lucy knew that in truth she was just an extra child Bertha had had foisted on her.

What Lucy really yearned for was attention from Clem. However much she pined for him to take notice of her, he was a big man these days at thirteen years old and he only ever looked at her in passing. He and John had already left school to go to work.

Clem had grown even more handsome as he got older; sallow-skinned, brown-eyed and with his head of dark curls, he was popular and full of energy as Jonno had once been. He would come into the house like a whirl-wind, laughing and joking, his restless body seeming to be too big for the tiny rooms, and he only stayed inside long enough to shovel something in his mouth before taking off again.

John, at fourteen, still looked out for her sometimes, but because it was Clem's attention she craved, she took scant notice of his quieter brother. Most often she had ended up playing with little Freddie, their younger brother who was almost a year younger than she was. Freddie was amiable enough, a paler, less vivid version of Clem in looks – but she did not like being left with the little ones, always feeling excluded.

The air in the room was thick with the smell of coal dust and Jonno's stale bodily smells. Sometimes he would bend his scrawny neck and sniff at himself like a dog and it was terrible to see.

'Oh – I'm gone to the bad. Rotten . . .' He would groan to himself. 'A rotten old beast – I'm done for . . .' Sometimes he forgot anyone else was there, because he did not usually give way to despair unless he was alone.

Bertha worked as hard as anything to keep him clean,

but he had his own smell, that of a body in combat with itself, a pungent, fruit-drop smell. At least now, for a while, he was sleeping as peacefully as he ever did, his face sunken and lungs heaving.

Lucy sat, listening to the rhythms of Jonno's breath and of the hammer blows in the forge. She closed her eyes and dreamt that Mom was still here. She was out there with Bertha and the other women and any minute, she would walk in with her tired smile and wish her a happy birthday. Lucy's chest ached. Even in this crowded neighbourhood, she now felt so very alone in the world and so useless. The orphan, the cripple. Tears fell, the drops darkening the grey of her skirt.

That evening, Bertha had cooked a pot of scrag end. She would help Jonno to eat the small amount that he could get down him these days. Then the rest of them squeezed round the table, apart from Freddie who ate on the bottom step of the stairs. Lucy always felt bad that she had taken Freddie's chair, though he did not seem to mind.

But today there was someone missing from the table.

'Where's our John?' Bertha frowned through the steam from the boiling spuds. 'It ay like 'im to be late.'

'Out cooting,' Clem said with a grin.

'Nah,' Freddie smirked from the step. 'Not our John!'

'And why not our John?' Pauline cast on her brothers the forbidding gaze she had inherited from their mother. 'What would yow two know, eh?'

''Ere yow am – get that down yow,' Bertha said, passing Clem his tea.

John, unlike Clem who was apprenticed to a chain works, had a job in a hardware shop on the High Street, something Bertha was immensely proud of. Thanks to his regular attendance at Sunday school and church (unlike

Clem who had not lasted beyond a few weeks) and his genuine interest in the Word, he had thrived in the Methodist Church. He was even talking about becoming a lay preacher.

A member of the congregation, a Mr Hunt, ran a hardware business at the bottom end of the High Street. He saw in John a reliable and able boy and suggested that he come to work for him. He had taken a shine to John and was teaching him every element of the business. It wasn't clean work exactly, but cleaner than the chain works and all of them could see at once that it was work John was more suited to.

Bertha handed the rest of them a plate with the runny stew on it and a boiled potato. Lucy could appreciate the difference in a household with three wages coming into it – not like her mother struggling by on hers alone, since Albert had wanted to keep his hard-earned wage to himself.

They were just about to tuck in when they heard boots hurrying across the yard.

John was panting hard, as if he'd run for miles. He came to the doorway and stopped, flushed and suddenly horrified, realizing that the eyes of all the family were on him. In his hand was a little posy of flowers. He seemed to throw himself forward before he lost courage.

'Sorry I'm late, Mom. I was just . . . Here, Luce . . .' He came to her and handed them over, almost offhandedly because he was embarrassed. A pretty spray came into her hands: cow parsley and red and white campions, dog roses and cornflowers. She had never seen anything so lovely.

'It's yower birthday, in't it? So I went and picked 'em for yow.'

'Oh – is it? So it is!' Bertha exclaimed. 'I'd've sent one

96

of this lot down the Outdoor for a jug of ale if I'd thought!'

'See – 'e *is* cooting!' Clem cried, baiting John. Lucy heard Freddie let out a chortle from his seat on the step.

'Well, our John,' Pauline chuckled. 'That were a nice thought. And happy birthday, Lucy.'

John was all blushes.

''Er looks sad, is all,' he said. 'I wanted to mek 'er look happy.'

Lucy's heart lit up. She was so touched and grateful that John had remembered! Smiling, despite the tears in her eyes, she took the precious posy, stared at the delicate-coloured petals and smelt their scent. Finally, she dared to look up at John, her cheeks all blushes.

'They're pretty,' she said. 'Ta, John.'

Thirteen

That terrible night, more than a year ago now, the last time Lucy ever felt the touch of her mother's hand, Albert came back late from wherever he had been. That night when the baby should have been born and Mom should still have been with them, holding it in her arms.

Lucy knew she would never forget the expression on Albert's face. Instead of having a mom and a new brother or sister – whose origins they were too innocent to question – they were suddenly alone in the world. He walked in to find Bertha there instead of Mom and his world hollowed out.

She went over to him, wanting him to cuddle her; for them to be in this nightmare together and him to be her big brother. But Albert's face hardened into a furious, flinty expression and he would not look at any of them. He showed no feeling – not to her or anyone.

'I can't have yower brothers as well.' Bertha said this right from that first day, straightforward and direct as she always was. 'Not for good, any road.'

But the three of them stayed that first night in the Hipkisses' cottage. Lucy slept on a straw mattress on the floor of the upstairs room where Bertha and Pauline shared the bed. The boys, Albert and George, were in the next-door room, squeezed in with the three Hipkiss lads.

That night, as Lucy lay on the strange, lumpy mattress, the world seeming to whirl too fast and she, lost and dizzy with it, she heard someone get up and go creeping down the stairs. She knew, by instinct, that it was Albert.

Pushing back the old quilt – a tiny comfort brought from her own bed at home – she struggled up on to her one good leg. Leaving her crutches behind and using the wall as a support, she hopped barefoot, as quietly as she could, to the stairs. Sitting down, she shuffled her way to the bottom. By the time she reached the downstairs room, Albert had already gone out of the back door. She could hear Jonno's sleeping breaths from his chair.

She slipped out into the cold yard, sharp grit digging into her foot as she hopped. A sound came from down where the lavs were. Lucy scarcely knew why she was following him, except for a craving to be close. She and Albert had once been playmates of a sort – and he was the only one she had to look up to now. They were the ones who had lost everything.

Making her way with one hand on the wall she hopped along, stifling a cry of pain as a sharp cinder dug into her foot. One of the lavatory doors was left swinging open but the other was closed. From inside she could already hear sobbing: her brother, unable to hold back, in there crying and wailing like a little child.

She stood nearby, her own eyes overflowing with tears as she and Albert, even though he did not know she was there, wept for the loss of their mother. She knew she would not go to the door and knock, that he would not let her into his own bereft loneliness. Silently, she hopped her way back to the house.

The next day Albert spoke to no one. Then he disappeared. Leaving the house in the morning, supposedly to go to work, he never came home. None of them had heard anything of him from that day to this.

'That lad'll come running back when 'e's 'ad enough of

wherever 'e is,' Bertha said at first. Lucy thought she was the only one who knew where Albert had gone: he had run away to sea, that was what she thought. She said that to Bertha once.

'Dow talk saft.' Bertha turned, startled from the fire where she was cooking. 'That'un'd never get that far. 'E'll be in some chain works in Netherton or the other side of town. Yow'll see – 'e'll turn up.'

But the months passed, over a year now, and he had not come.

He had not even stayed long enough to bury their mother.

Lucy had hobbled through the graveyard, after the long, long walk to get there. Her stump ached in the cold, even though she had wrapped it carefully as she did in winter, in a special muslin bag with a drawstring tied under her bloomers.

With her spare hand, she held George's. He was seven, going on eight. Every night since Albert left, George had come creeping in and curled up next to her, burrowing into her like a little animal. But he was warm and familiar – a remnant of family – and she clung to him in return, comforted by him being there. He kept asking when Mom was coming back.

The two of them followed Bertha through Cradley Cemetery, the sooty red tower of the church rising awesome and austere close by. It was a day of April squalls blowing the wet into their faces, a day she had decided to try never to think about again. That gusty, sombre morning, the long yawning space of earth broken open and her mother's pauper coffin being lowered into it, were memories she had tried to bury deep in herself.

Bertha knew she could not manage two extra children to feed and clothe. In terms of wages she was a widow, for all her poor husband was still in this world, and while Pauline and John brought in a sum now, she had more than enough to contend with. She asked around the neighbourhood and announced, a few days after Ellen's funeral, that George was to go and live with a couple in Plant Street. They only had one daughter, and they craved a son.

On hearing this news, George let out heartbroken cries. Lucy watched his little face crumple, feeling as if her own heart was being torn into shreds. They couldn't take George away – her little brother, her companion – he was all she had!

'I do' wanna go and live with another lady!' George howled. 'Don't mek me – I wanna stay 'ere with you, Luce!'

At first he clung to Lucy but then he started punching her. When Bertha tried to pull him under control, seizing hold of his fists, he yelled even louder and flung himself on the floor, beating about so wildly that Lucy thought he was having a fit. She was sobbing her heart out as well. Bertha scooped George up in her strong arms and took him, writhing, out into the yard while Lucy stood sobbing in the doorway.

'You'll have a nice new home with Mrs Thorne,' Bertha said, when she finally managed to get him under control. She stood hands clamped on her hips as if having deliberately to harden herself against giving in. 'You'll have a bed all to yerself, yower sister can come and see yer and yow can come 'ere when you want. But for living day to day, yower going to Mr and Mrs Thorne and that's that.'

Half an hour later, Bertha Hipkiss set off with George, carrying his tiny bundle of possessions. He was still crying and dragging his feet, but Bertha tugged him along.

'C'm'on, yer gotta be brave, lad. It'll all be all right'. Mrs Thorne wants yer, so we're going.'

Lucy could only stand propped on her crutches and watch as Mrs Hipkiss dragged him out along the entry. She heard his sobs echoing even after she could no longer see him. And there was nothing she could do. She knew Mrs Hipkiss couldn't help it, but it was as if her whole world was being rubbed out, so fast that she could hardly take it in.

She felt terrible without her little brother, the one person left who had been her kin. Now she was a cuckoo in the Hipkiss family nest. It was bad enough being an orphan in this world without her brothers both disappearing as well.

Bertha came back from delivering George and reported that Mrs Thorne was a nice lady and he would be well cared for. She sank down at the table and it was only then that Lucy realized, seeing the drained look on her handsome face, just how exhausted and upset she was at what she had just done.

'That's a bad do, Jonno,' she said. 'I've let Ellen down.'

'You're doing . . . your best for 'em,' Jonno said. 'For all of us, girlie.'

Lucy crept closer to the table.

'Mrs Hipkiss?' she dared ask. 'When've I got to go?'

'Oh, bab – no!' Bertha looked horrified. 'No, no – that ay 'ow it is, Luce. I made a promise to yower mother I'd look after yow above all of 'em – what with yower leg and the world being the way it is. I just cor tek all of yow, not at my time of life. So you'll stop 'ere, long as yow give us a bit of help now and then. We can put yow to the hearth before long and yow can earn yower keep. I know yow'll be no trouble – yow've always been a good little wench.'

It was all very well Bertha Hipkiss saying that Lucy and George could visit each other, but Plant Street was a long walk for Lucy – all the way up and along Spinners Lane. And George was little and not used to going so far on his own. Lucy never saw him at school at Lomey Town any more either so Mrs Thorne must have moved him to a different one.

He came back just once. During the first week after he was taken to Plant Street, he turned up at the door one afternoon after school.

'Is it all right?' Lucy asked him. She wanted to give him a love but, standing there in the Hipkisses' downstairs room, he looked so bewildered and hard-faced that he was hardly like her little brother any more, even though he had only left a few days before.

'Is that . . .?' Jonno began, but interrupted himself with coughing. 'Our Freddie?'

'It's George,' Lucy said.

'Oh – George, is it? Come by 'ere for a visit?' She heard Jonno add, 'Poor little soul.'

She repeated her question to George.

'Tell 'er I want to come back.' He came up close, his eyes hard, but begging. 'I want to come back and stop 'ere with you.'

'I cor.' This conversation took place in fierce whispers.

'You *gotta*!' His little face was tight and fierce, fists clenched. 'I 'ate that cowing woman!'

'All right,' she said. 'But you best go now, George, or they'll be cross with yer.'

She watched him walk out of the yard, so little and lost-looking that her innards twisted at the sight. But she could not ask Bertha Hipkiss to bring him back. She knew what the answer would be and that she should expect nothing, not from anyone. She saw him only once after that, when she made the effort to lug herself on her crutches all the way to Plant Street.

Mrs Thorne was a chainmaker and was busy in the forge in the yard. Lucy knew better than to interrupt. When she asked George what his new 'mother' was like he just shrugged. His clothes looked all right and he said he got enough to eat. But she could get nothing else out of him and he was just as silent and surly as Albert had been.

She stopped feeling like making the huge effort it took her to go there. There was nothing she could do. She came away telling herself that it would be better to forget that she had once had brothers of her own. That it might be better for George as well. She got more out of Freddie Hipkiss these days, a jolly, round-faced little lad who quite liked having another older sister.

But one Saturday a few weeks later, she couldn't stop thinking about George. She ached with missing him and felt guilty that she had not been to see him again. She forgot how angry he had been when she last visited him and her mind filled with tender memories of him, her sweet, round-eyed little brother she had known and played with since he was a baby.

'All right, go and see 'im,' Bertha said. 'I think it's a good thing you've not gone too often. He needs to settle. But if yow want to visit him, bab, you do that.'

Eventually, shoulders aching, she was standing outside the door of Mrs Thorne's, a soot-encrusted front house on Plant Street. She tried knocking but there was no reply, so she swung herself on her crutches along the entry to the yard. It was a cheerless place. As ever, the chainmakers were busy in the forge. There were a few children in the yard and a woman turning the handle of her mangle, but she could not see George.

Hostile eyes fastened on her round the yard – she, a stranger. What did she want up their end?

'Are you Mrs Thorne?' she asked the woman working the mangle.

'No, I ay – who wants 'er?' Without waiting for an answer, the woman shouted into the workshop. 'Mabel – there's a cripple girl 'ere, asking for yow!'

Mabel Thorne appeared out of the forge, rubbing her blackened hands on her apron and squinting in the bright light. She was a gaunt woman, with an angular face and pebble-like eyes.

'Who're yow and what d'yow want?' she said with no more ado.

'My brother – George.' Lucy spoke very politely. 'I came to see him.'

'Huh,' Mrs Thorne said dismissively. 'That little brat – 'e ay 'ere no more. 'E ay not good to me. I dunno what sort of family yow both come from but 'e was wild as a dog. I 'ad them tek 'im off me 'ands and good riddance.'

She disappeared back inside, unwilling to be asked anything else. Lucy stood, stunned, trying to take in what Mrs Thorne had meant.

'Er took 'im to the orphanage,' the other woman said. More kindly now, seeing Lucy's distraught expression, she tried to soften the impact of her words by adding, ''E'll be all right, bab. They'll tek care of 'im. There's nowt yow can do about it now.'

Fourteen

'There – 'ad enough now, bab?'

Bertha was perched on a chair opposite her husband, helping him eat the few morsels of Sunday dinner that he could manage.

'Ta. Lovely that.' Jonno sank back, exhausted at the effort. 'Good bit of beef.'

Both knew it was stringy, though Bertha had done the best she could with it. And they'd had a sup of her pea-pod wine, which as well as making both of them mellow and muzzy in the warm July afternoon also helped the cheap cut of beef to seem much finer than it really was.

'Your spuds . . . food of the gods . . .' Jonno seemed about to fall into a doze.

'Oh – yower all flannel,' Bertha laughed. She could roast a potato with the best of them but Jonno had always praised anything she cooked to the skies.

'Sit with me,' he urged her, perking up again. 'Don't go back to work . . . Not for a bit.'

Bertha relaxed into her chair. The children had already eaten. John and Lucy had set off for the Sunday school and the rest were out and about in the summer warmth. Now there were other wages coming in as well as hers, a woman struggling alone, she could sit back for a bit. And this was the only time in the week when Bertha and Jonno had any quiet time together.

The worst of it was no longer sharing a bed. That had always brought them together. Whatever else had gone on in the daytime, the two of them always tucked up together, Jonno's strong body curving round hers and warming her on winter nights, as often as not quickening into lovemaking. They had always found time for that, even when they were both worn out.

Looking at her husband's devastated body, the scorched eyes and limp, old man's hair, Bertha's mind, try as she might to stop it, started to wander down the pathways of the past. Images forced themselves into her memory of her vigorous, loving Jonno as a young husband thirty years ago, striding about full of life, the children being born, the endless, gruelling richness of it all. And the thought that always followed hard on it – of all they had lost in between then and now . . .

She pulled herself up. It was no good wallowing. This was the trouble with stopping and giving your mind a chance to roam . . . That was when the sadness set in, the realization of being heartbroken and exhausted to the marrow of your bones. And what good could that ever do her?

'Eh . . . my girlie.' Jonno's voice held a certain tone of the old days, wooing, seductive. 'C'm'ere, my beauty.'

He held out a hand.

Bertha felt herself flood with longing.

'Let me put the wood in the 'ole . . .' She got up and closed the door to the yard, then turned to him. 'No more babbies, Jonno. You know I said I can't – not after that last one . . .'

'No, no . . . I'm not . . . up to it.' He wheezed and coughed. 'Just . . . come by 'ere, eh?'

The phrase touched her heart even more deeply. She had always loved his voice, the Welsh sing-song phrases.

She untied her house apron – made of thick cotton, not sacking – and folded it to make an extra pad for her knees.

She tugged the old bodged rug over from by the fire and put that down first, then the apron, and knelt in front of her husband's chair. Jonno widened his knees.

'There's my lovely,' he said.

'Oh, Jonno,' she said tenderly, as they eased, very carefully, into each other's arms.

He was like a bird in hers, so frail, the lungs rustling like paper and his ceaseless quiver as if everything in him was on alert. The feel of him made her want to weep, his ribcage like a washboard, arms thin as sapling trunks. But she did not want to weep. He was here. Now. And as long as he was still with them, her man, she wanted times to be happy, not to dwell on death and loss while he remained living, however much of what they'd once had together had already been taken from them.

Now and again, Jonno could perk up remarkably for a short time.

'You've always been the best medicine for me, girlie,' he would say. 'Like a tonic, you are.'

And now, his lips close to her ear, 'Oh – you're my girl . . . all I've ever wanted . . . magnificent, you are . . .'

His hands moved over her body, lingering tenderly on her breasts which hung, heavy and unbound, under the thin cotton of her frock. Jonno made a small sound of longing.

'Oh . . . I wish . . .'

'I know . . .' His touch had awoken all her old desire for him. 'But no, love . . . No.' It would be the death of him now, she thought. And it was all over for her anyway, the way her innards felt. Since that last babby she was having to bind herself underneath because everything in her seemed to have come loose and dropped.

He lay his thin, stubbly cheek alongside hers, contenting himself with caressing her, her hips, her breasts, and she held him in her arms, gently rocking and stroking him in return.

So many times in the past he had said, 'I'm sorry . . . so sorry . . . I'm no man for you any more . . .' Sometimes wept at what he had become. But now he was past even that.

These times were the brief crumbs of all that remained. In the lingering smell of roasted meat and coal dust, in the familiar closeness of their bodies, they held and caressed mostly in silence, knowing without words, the depths of love each of them held for the other.

Later, they snoozed, Bertha on the upright wooden chair. She could fall asleep anywhere. Head bowed, legs stretched out in front, covered almost to the ankles by her old dark grey dress, she allowed an afternoon muzziness to wrap itself round her.

There were voices, people calling out, the crash of something falling. She jumped, startled out of a deep slumber.

'What's going on?' Jonno stirred, sat forward, coughing.

Bertha hauled herself up, frowning, jarred out of her little sleep. She had long been the gaffer of this yard among the women – and on the whole the men too. If there was anything going on, she expected to be consulted. She opened the back door to find a tall, gangly man outside, bawling along the entry.

'I'm gunna 'ave ter tek the cowin' legs off of it!'

Seeing her appear, he raised his cap amiably and his face, long, wide-mouthed and with big tombstone teeth, an almost comical face, creased into a smile.

'Sorry, missus – only we cor get the table through the entry!' He moved closer, holding out his hand. 'I'm Wally

Shaw. We'm moving in over there.' He jerked his head towards number two, Ellen Butler's old house.

'Oh ar?' Bertha folded her arms and nodded. She wanted to assert herself, let this newcomer realize who he had to defer to round here.

'This is my missus,' he added with seeming delight as a young woman appeared out of the entry, a baby of about a year old in her arms.

Bertha found herself face to face with a person of the sort who somehow stood out. She caught your eye in a direct way and even on first sight, she had a force to her.

The young woman was of small stature – in contrast to her soaringly tall husband – but curvaceous. She wore a dark blue skirt topped by a bird's-egg blue blouse and from beneath the skirt peeped brown boots, neat and almost stylish, not like the heavy, hard-wearing men's boots many of the women resorted to. Her dark chestnut hair was fastened back in a simple knot, but even that, arranged slightly to one side at the back, had a jaunty air about it. Her blue eyes, and a frank, fearless gaze, had been passed on to the little one riding on her left hip, who was staring at Bertha as well.

'Rose Shaw.' For a moment Bertha thought she was going to shake hands, but she moved her spare hand round to support the child, rocking gently from foot to foot. She nodded at the child. 'This is Gracie.'

Though Rose Shaw was polite, there was something challenging about her that immediately put Bertha on her mettle. She drew herself up, hands on hips.

'I'm Bertha Hipkiss. I wondered when someone else'd come to tek that house. It's about time. Well – if yow want to know anything about this yard, yow come to me.'

Wally began to make some polite noises in the background, but Rose was on to that straight away.

'There's a spare hearth going in the forge, by all accounts?'

Bertha felt herself shrink inside for a moment. After Ellen died, thanks to that vile turd Seth Dawson, a couple moved into the house for a time, but neither had been chainmakers. The house had then fallen empty again. Lucy was to start work at the fifth hearth as soon as school finished for the summer. No point in her lingering on in the classroom when she could be bringing in a wage. She knew she'd upset the wench telling her she was to leave school, but she'd soon get used to it. What was the use of staying on now? She was tall enough to reach the block – and she could already read and write better than most. It was just wasted time.

Lucy had said that when she started work, she would prefer the other hearth.

'I thought yow'd want to work yower mother's?' Bertha said, surprised.

'No.' Lucy's little face clouded even more. 'I think it'd just make me sad.'

The thought of anyone taking Ellen's empty place filled Bertha with dread. But she knew she was being saft. She couldn't go on like that.

'There is 'un going spare,' she admitted. 'Where've yow come from then?'

'We come from Old Hill,' Rose said. 'I was at Harry Stevens, but now I'm looking for outwork. I'm good.' She spoke matter-of-factly, with neither pride nor modesty. 'I'm a fast worker.'

'Is there anyone'd give us a 'and?' Wally said. 'It's a job getting our things along the entry.'

'Well, my ole man cor 'elp yer,' Bertha said. 'Yow want to try Victor Gornall – number three. You're to be next-door neighbours so they might as well start right.'

'Oh ar – ta, Mrs Hipkiss,' Wally said respectfully, heading towards number three.

Victor Gornall was going to be overjoyed to be dragged away from his Sunday afternoon nuptials, Bertha thought, trying to suppress a smirk. After all, Mari was well out at the front with another of Victor's spawn already, so the wench deserved a rest.

Rose Shaw was still standing there, so she said brusquely, 'Yow'd best get on then, eh?'

Rose looked back at her, so uncowed by the matriarchal gaffer of the yard that Bertha decided she might be well advised to start off on a better footing with her – teach her some respect and good neighbourliness.

'D'yow want me to tek the babby off of yer for a bit?' she offered.

'Oh, ta,' Rose said, seeming surprised. 'That's very good of yer – it'd be a help, Mrs Hipkiss.'

She seemed happy to hand her little girl over and Bertha softened at the feel of the child's warm body in her arms. She had a cap of pale brown hair and that penetrating gaze. Her blue eyes fixed on Bertha's face, her brows settling into a slight, puzzled frown.

'I s'pose we'll be seeing you in the forge,' Bertha said to the little one as Rose took off purposefully, her boots ringing along the entry.

Well, Bertha thought, turning into the house with baby Grace in her arms, it was obvious who was going to be wearing the trousers in that household. And why had she suddenly offered to look after the child? She felt rubbed up the wrong way by Rose Shaw, and yet she had somehow wanted to get on the right side of her. She could not really sort out the whys and wherefores of how she felt about any of it.

*

The banging and shouting of removals went on, with the help of Victor Gornall, a weedy, ferret-faced man who seemed less resentful about it than Bertha had predicted. Perhaps Wally Shaw had promised him a skinful after, she thought.

But in the middle of it all she heard another sound, of the children coming back from Sunday school and something unusual – someone was crying.

'Oh dear – sounds like trouble,' Jonno said. He had good hearing, if nothing else.

A moment later she saw John emerge from the entry with Lucy. As they came to the door, John looked really stricken, and Lucy, who was usually so quiet and uncomplaining, was loping along on her crutches, sobbing as if her heart would break. It was the first time she had seen the child really give way, despite all that had happened.

Holding little Grace Shaw, she went to the door and demanded, 'What in 'eaven's name's up with 'er?'

Fifteen

Towards the end of the Sunday school session that afternoon, as they all sat, fidgety and ready to be dismissed, something terrible had happened.

They were in rows on the floor of the hall, light filtering dustily through the windows.

Lucy could just about manage to sit cross-legged like the other children. Miss Jones had asked her from the beginning whether she needed a chair, but she did not want to sit aside like Gertie, be one of the 'cripples' who everyone stared at or ignored. Sometimes she felt a pang of guilt at leaving Gertie there alone. But Gertie never said a word to her even when she did stay with her, and Lucy wanted to be like the other children and sit giggling and nudging with her pal Abigail.

On the other side of her, always, was John. There were not many fourteen-year-old lads who still came to the Sunday school. Clem, who had only lasted a few weeks of the first summer – mainly for the biscuits – taunted John about it.

'Yower a proper Holy Joe these days, ay yer? What d'yer wanna go there for?' Clem would tease him, baffled by all this. As the boys got older the difference between them showed up more. 'Sunday mornings – *and* the afternoon! Must be off yer 'ead! It's worse than school!'

John never said anything back. He was softer and slower, not good at coming back at you the way Clem was.

Lucy liked going to Sunday school because of Miss

Jones, even though she was in a higher class now, so Miss Jones was no longer her form teacher at school. She enjoyed the stories and songs – and yes, the biscuits. And she liked seeing Abigail. But even though he did not say much, she knew that John had found something else there.

When they sat on the hard boards, Mr Henry or one of the other helpers reading them stories from the Bible, Lucy and Abigail would exchange secret looks and jokes with their eyes and Lucy never really listened to anything that was said.

But John sat with his eyes raised to whoever was reading, seeming to drink it all in. And he had started going to the services, held here in the hall, on a Sunday morning.

Lucy was torn. She still adored Clem. Even though they lived in the same house and she knew she was just like a part of the furniture to him, she still felt her heart begin to thump harder if Clem even glanced at her. The crush she had long had on him never seemed to die away.

He seldom took much notice of her. With every year he grew more handsome and he was popular with the other lads, always game to go out on adventures and get up to something, whereas John was more often inclined to sit in. Sometimes he asked Lucy to help him with his reading.

And the fact that John also kept attending Sunday school made it much easier for her to come as well and see her beloved Miss Jones. Sunday school was a bubble of happiness in which she could take refuge every week.

Until this week, when she had a terrible shock.

'Now, children.' Miss Jones was standing beside the piano. Her face looked flushed, and she seemed excited about something, Lucy thought, a shimmer of emotion in her that was not usually there. 'We're going to sing our final hymn for this afternoon. It's a lovely hymn written by that blessed man, Charles Wesley.'

She sat down and started pressing on the keys with great vigour. Mr Henry beamed at the back of her head, his little moustache twitching. He gestured with his hands that they should get up. It took Lucy longer than everyone else to scramble to her feet and John and Abigail helped pull her up, handing her the crutches.

'*O servants of God!*' they all began.

John had quite a good voice and he sang with real enthusiasm beside her. Everyone joined in. Even the children forced there by mothers and fathers to get them out of the way for the afternoon enjoyed singing, especially as this was the last hymn which meant they were soon to be released into the sunshine.

The final chords rang out. Mr Henry extended his arms the way Jesus did sometimes in the pictures.

'Now . . . No, no – settle down. Before we have our last blessing, Miss Jones has a little announcement to make.'

Once more, he beamed as Miss Jones got up from the piano. She stood before them in her soft green dress, her cheeks now obviously full of blushes and her eyes, behind her spectacles, seeming alight with emotion.

'Well, children,' she began, bringing her palms together in front of her chest as if trying to contain her excitement. 'I have something very joyful to tell you. As you know, next week, the school term ends for the summer. The sad part is that I shall be leaving the school in Lomey Town, where I have enjoyed teaching a great deal. And you will also have two new Sunday school teachers who I know will do a very good job. Because . . .'

And here she cast a look of adoration at her moustachioed colleague in his dusty black suit.

116

'Mr Henry and I will be returning to settle in the north of England at the place to which the Lord has called us to continue his work. And –' her blush deepened – 'in two weeks' time we are to be married.' She looked round at them. 'I shall miss you all, children – and I shall remember all of you in my prayers.'

Lucy stood amid the murmur that followed this, most of the other children hurrying to get out. Miss Jones had moved over to the door to say goodbye to the children as they left and she heard a few of the older ones congratulating Mr Henry and Miss Jones.

She could not take it in. How could Miss Jones be *leaving*? How could she find it in her to leave *her*? Hadn't she been a special pupil? How could this be happening? Somehow, she had believed that Miss Jones would just be there for always.

Because if Miss Jones was not there . . . what would be left for her? When Bertha had told Lucy she expected her to stop going to school at the end of this year, Lucy had scarcely been able to hold back a cry of protest.

'I know yow could do summat else, with all yower reading,' Bertha said. 'But yower best off 'ere with us that knows yer, and with a job to do.'

Lucy knew what all this meant. *You, the cripple, who a man will never look at twice, who will be subject to all sorts of unkindness – you'd best stick close where we know you and can keep you safe.*

But how she longed to howl, *No! Please don't make me – let me stay on a bit longer, where there are things to do and to learn, not just the hammering of chains, day in day out!* But she was eleven years old now, older than both her mother and Bertha had been when they started making chains.

Lucy knew she could not beg. She was an extra burden

on the Hipkiss family and she must bring in her keep. But at least, she had thought, she would be able to go to Sunday school. Miss Jones would carry on helping her with her reading from time to time, would tell her how good at it she was getting through reading to Jonno. There would be light and learning and encouragement.

But no. At least not from her beloved Miss Jones. She stared ahead of her, her chest tight and full of a terrible ache.

'Come on, Luce,' John said, nudging her.

She tried to hold back her tears as she trailed behind John to the little queue filing out of the hall. There were three children in front of Lucy, then two, then one. She looked up at her teacher, feeling as if the dismay and hurt she felt must be flooding out from her eyes. Miss Jones smiled at her.

'There we are, Lucy. I expect I'll see you at school before the end of term, so this is not really a goodbye.'

And then she looked away and Lucy had to go out on to the muggy street, the stinking air and the light and everything about the day feeling cursed and spoilt. She hardly even noticed saying goodbye to Abigail, who set off in the opposite direction towards where she lived.

She felt something she had never experienced before, not even when Mom died and Albert left; even when Mrs Thorne gave George away to the orphanage as if he was nothing more than a parcel. It was as if all these losses reached their peak in this one, breaking open like a boil. Her whole body felt tight and bursting, as if she was about to explode with emotion.

Along the road, she stopped and leaned her head against a wall.

'What's up? John said, a bit impatient.

Lucy could not answer. Sobs burst out of her and there was no stopping them.

The thought of Miss Jones going, Miss Jones who Lucy thought had loved her, who had been an anchor that she held on to, made her feel as if everything in her life had shattered. There was no one in this world who really loved her, no one who would stay and be there for her and her alone. Once again, she felt like a little speck, a loveless flea, tiny and of no importance, who could be stamped on and no one would notice. A torrent of grief that she could not control poured out of her.

'Luce!' John said, really alarmed. 'What's up with yow?'

She shook her head, so overwrought that she could not speak. All the way home she cried and cried and John, awkward and not knowing what to do, finally put his hand on her shoulder and helped steer her along because her eyes were so blinded by tears.

Sixteen

Chink-chink-chink . . . tap-tap-tap.

The four of them stood working side by side in the forge. It was only a couple of days since Rose and Wally Shaw had moved in at number two and a muggy day of summer drizzle. The smoke curled out lazily through the chimneys and windows. The children, some too small for school and others now on holiday, wandered in and out of the forge or pottered about the yard with their games, oblivious to the wet morning.

On the far left was the hearth which was to be Lucy's and beside it, Mari Gornall working at hers. Her youngest, Jo, a pale little scrap who had at last learned to walk on bowed legs, was now tottering about with the wavering gait of a drunk. He managed to get in just about everyone's way, gazing with rapt eyes at the glowing fires as if he was thinking of jumping into each of them.

Mari had had a bad time with the child she was carrying this time round. She had been even sicker than usual in the early days, hurrying out to the lavs or heaving over a pail and even now, she kept feeling faint. Many were the curses she brought down on Victor Gornall's head, not to mention various other items of his anatomy. Gornall number six was on its way and for Mari, the novelty was definitely wearing off.

'It were all very well at the beginning,' she would moan. 'But I've 'ad more'n enough of 'im!'

Bertha was next to her, then Rose Shaw, and Edna

Wilmott at the end, in the place where she had now stood hammering chain for more than fifty years, day in, day out.

Edna's voice burst out suddenly, '*Guide me, O Thou Great Jehovah!*'

The other women's voices lifted to join with hers. Bertha heard Rose's voice, clear and strong at the climax of the final verse: '*Songs of praises, songs of praises, I will ever give to thee! I will ever give to thee.*'

Bertha felt a swell of annoyance, which only increased when Mari called over to her, 'Yow can sing nice, cor yer, Rose!'

Rose gave her a quick glance without a moment lost to hammering. 'Ta. Does yer heart good, a good sing-song. Give us another one, eh, Mrs Wilmott?'

Bertha seethed inside. She'd barely arrived and here was Madam, giving out orders! She even had Mari, the mardy cow, sucking up to her as if she was the Big I Am.

Edna began singing, '*Praise Him, Praise Him, Jesus Our Blessed Redeemer . . .*'

Rose joined in, and by the end of the long hymn to which she seemed to know all the words, whereas Edna and Mari had to stop and let her fill them in, they were all laughing. Bertha held back from singing.

'You all right, Bertha?' Edna called over. 'Yower quiet today.'

'I'm all right – got a head on me. I could do with a bit of quiet.'

She did not look up but could sense the others making '*Uh-oh, someone's in a mood*' faces behind her.

'I'm gunna brew a cuppa,' she said, downing tools before she said something she'd regret. 'Might pick me up.'

'What's ailing you, girlie?' Jonno said, starting as she came banging into the house.

'Nowt. I'll make us both a cuppa,' she said grumpily. What she really felt like was a nip of something much stronger.

'Doesn't sound . . . like nothing to me . . .' With a huge effort he pushed himself up in the chair, then started coughing agonizingly. Bertha softened, pouring water into the kettle. He looked so yellow, so frail. What on earth was she getting so mithered about – what did anything matter, set against this man, her Jonno?

'Oh, I'm just being ockered.' She settled the kettle over the fire. 'It's that new'un. Summat about 'er. Thinks 'er knows it all.'

'What – more than my missus?' Jonno teased her gently.

Bertha sank into a chair. It was true, she was the one used to being the boss of this yard, the senior woman to whom everyone deferred. It wasn't as if Rose Shaw had been rude to her – she just didn't seem to be the deferring type. And Bertha wanted to admire her for it, but instead it riled her. Who did the wench think she was?

'The way she went on at '*im*, though,' Bertha muttered.

'Who – Dawson?' Jonno said. It came out as a gasp. He was leaning forward, fighting for his breath.

''Er's got no idea how to handle a fogger like Dawson,' Bertha raged. 'One of the wust, 'e is – yow 'ave to play 'im, not get uppity with 'im . . .'

She broke off, seeing the struggle her husband was having. Sometimes she got so caught up in herself she forgot and thought she was talking to the old Jonno, her strong, able-bodied man who would have raged with her or teased her out of it all.

'I'll put some hot water in a bowl for yer,' she said quietly.

Sometimes it eased his breathing, inhaling the steam. She had to find ways to make something better, at least to try. And why was she even thinking about Rose Shaw – what was it about her?

But once she had drunk her tea and held the bowl of water in front of Jonno for a while until the steam abated, listening to the unmendable rattle of his lungs, she went back to work, still at odds with herself and seething about the newcomer in their midst.

Rose Shaw had immediately got herself added to the list of outworkers at Ridley & Son. In Ellen Butler's place – and indeed at her hearth. By Monday afternoon she had been at work and today, Tuesday, Seth Dawson turned up – to see what kind of new nanny-goat he had acquired to milk this time, the others said.

'Goose laying golden eggs more like,' Bertha commented.

There was a metallic crash from the yard, just outside the door, of a bundle of poles being dropped carelessly to the ground. Then his shadow fell over the doorway. He put on his usual performance of slouching against the door frame picking at his teeth. What could that lardy bugger have stuck in his teeth at this time of the morning? Bertha thought.

The women ignored him and kept working, backs to him, though Bertha knew that she, and every one of them standing there in a row, was primed for trouble the moment he made an appearance.

'I've brought you wenches some more work,' he said, as if he was doing them some great honour. 'Save yer fetching it.'

No one said anything. More work – what was new

about that? Were they supposed to kiss his stinking feet for it?

'Oi – you.' He pushed himself off the door frame, moving further into the shed. 'So yower the new'un?'

Rose finished what she was doing, then turned with an *'Are you talking to me?'* look on her face.

'They ain't told me – what's yower name then?' Seth Dawson stood with his legs wide, hands in his weskit pockets, which made him look ridiculous, like a hen, as his elbows stuck out.

'Rose Shaw.'

'So yower the new'un?' he repeated.

Rose looked round at the others, as if to say, *Well, I'd say that was obvious*, and gave a faint nod.

Bertha started to feel disquieted. This girl seemed to have a natural insolence and it was no good cheeking Seth Dawson. He could always get the upper hand and however loathsome his behaviour, it was better to play along. But her innards turned with hatred at the sight of him. The thought of what he had done to Ellen stopped her breath for a moment and her whole body clenched. God, how she longed to smash him down, see him bleeding on the floor! Poor Ellen, her friend – she hadn't stood a chance. She couldn't even have pinned what happened on Dawson: his word against hers – who would count anything she might say? And now this newcomer Rose had even taken over Ellen's hearth. She'd best not be about to cause them all trouble by being so uppity.

'Well, I 'ope yower a good worker?' Seth said.

'I am,' Rose declared, standing with her boots neatly side by side. Pert little cow, she was, Bertha decided. She almost gasped when Rose said, 'I know to 'ommer true.'

Seth seemed amused, in his usual sadistic way, like a cat that's met a mouse who can recite jokes.

'Well,' he said, rocking about on his feet, 'we'll see, won't us? And later, yow can lug some of this lot back to the works.' He looked at the coils of completed chains building up on one side of the forge. And you, Bertha – the two of yer are the only ones up to it around 'ere.'

He stared Rose up and down in a way that seemed to strip her naked. Rose stared back brazenly at him and Bertha felt her blood begin to boil. The stupid wench had a lesson or two to learn about how to go on!

'You got a mon?' Seth asked.

Bertha saw Mari Gornall grimace at the question. They knew all too well what this might lead to. Any woman on her own was prey to Dawson – and even a few who weren't if they got caught with him at the wrong moment.

'Yes. Ta,' Rose said. She managed somehow to be both civil and insolent at the same time. It was her eyes, Bertha decided. Brazen, the way she looked at people! She could not decide whether she felt more irritation or admiration.

'A good mon,' Rose added. And her tone so obviously implied a contrast with Seth Dawson that Bertha began to fear for her.

Seth, who could not be said to be quick-witted, could think of no reply to this.

'Ar – well, yow'd best get back to it.' He turned, jerking a thumb outside. 'There's a new load here so get cracking, wenches . . .' And off he went.

'Do we have to carry it back ourselves?' Rose asked.

'Ar,' Bertha said, turning away as she tried to swallow her annoyance with the girl. 'That one brings a dobbin for it when it takes his fancy – but today there ay no dobbin 'ere but us, wench.'

Later that afternoon, Bertha and Rose lugged two loads of chain along the road to Ridley's. They had to drape it round their shoulders, being careful not to get snarled up or trip over it, and Rose complained all the way as they dragged it along Corngreaves Road. It was time Ridley's entered the twentieth century and stopped using them as packhorses, she raged, and why didn't they all keep on about it until something was done?

What cowing world was she living in? Bertha fumed. She was very short with Rose Shaw, and walked back from the second delivery with her arms tightly folded, not saying a word to the woman – why encourage her?

Later on, when she had gone back into the house to see Jonno, she was startled by a tap on the back door. Amid all the racket of the children outside she had not heard any footsteps approaching.

Rose Shaw stood at her door as if her feet were somehow planted, not just placed side by side, but just far enough apart to seem challenging.

'Can I 'ave a word with yer, Mrs Hipkiss?'

Bertha found herself clamping her hands on her hips. This seemed to imply more than a quick cant on the step. Her annoyance on the walk back from Ridley's works must have been plain to see, she thought. She stood back and jerked her head. Letting the wench in would mean her seeing the state of her husband – but a dose of reality might be good for her.

Jonno was asleep, and Lucy, on the chair beside him, was just closing the book she had been reading to him.

'This is my mon – Jonno,' Bertha said. She did not succeed in keeping her voice free of bitterness.

She saw the shock and pity immediately in Rose Shaw's eyes. She looked questioningly at Bertha.

'The pit done for 'is chest and the lime works 'is eyes.'

Rose nodded slowly, humbly, in a way that softened

Bertha a fraction. At least she didn't offer cheap, meaningless words.

'Hello.' Rose nodded at Lucy, who quietly gave one of her sweet smiles. She was still learning who everyone was in the yard.

Bertha glanced at Lucy. 'Off you go, little'un.' To Rose, she added, 'That's our Lucy – 'er'll be starting in the forge this week.'

Lucy got up, adjusted her crutches and went to the stairs. Slowly, she made her way up them. Bertha saw Rose taking all this in as well.

'Very pretty – yower daughter,' she said.

''Er's my daughter now,' Bertha said. 'Only 'er ain't mine. Her mother's passed on.'

Again, Rose silently took this in and Bertha realized then that she already knew something of the situation.

'The other's've been saying things,' Rose began directly. 'Half saying, any road, about the woman who worked that hearth before me. And it feels to me as if there's bin summat amiss between you and me from the start.' She pulled her shoulders back and looked into Bertha's face with that frankness which again, both impressed and aggravated her. 'I don't want to start off on the wrong side of anyone 'ere, Mrs Hipkiss.'

Bertha looked back at her for a long moment. It pained her to talk about Ellen, but she knew that Rose Shaw was right, best to start off with the air clear. And she was gratified that Rose had had the guts to ask her and not one of the others.

'Sit down, wench.' She brought over the other chair that Lucy had been using. 'I'll tell yer – and why yow need to watch your step with that fogger – as with any other, as yer should've learned by now. But yower new to outwork, this is the way it is – that'un's one of the wust round about 'ere.'

She explained that the woman at the hearth previously had been Ellen Butler, a widow barely scraping by.

''Er were alone in the house one afternoon and that'un came for 'er. Walked right into her kitchen. 'E'd been trying it on before with 'er, like – more than we all knew.'

Rose sat forward, listening intently.

'Bringing that'un's spawn into the world were the end of 'er. The babby died with 'er.'

'Oh my Lord!' Rose sat up straight, horror dawning on her face.

'That little wench upstairs was Ellen's,' Bertha said. 'I promised her I'd look out for her. And I will. But you need to look out for that fogger, and not talk back . . .'

'But we'm on starvation wages,' Rose burst out. 'Yow said yower lucky to make five and six a week – and 'e's a divil, that mon!'

''E is that. But 'e's the devil that holds the keys to our wages – and it ay no good crossing him. There's foggers yow can 'ave a decent word with – but not Dawson. And there's plenty more women can take the place of the likes of us. So just watch yower step and don't get above yower-self.'

Bertha found herself getting heated, her already stored-up resentment of Rose bursting out.

'All right.' Rose stood up. 'Thanks, Mrs Hipkiss. I'm glad to know what's what.' She went to the door and paused, turning for a second as if to add something, but seeming to think the better of it. As she went out, how-ever, and the door closed, Bertha heard her muttering, 'But it's wrong – it's all wrong!'

Seventeen

It was not so hard leaving school in the end, now that Miss Jones had gone. The saddest thing was parting with Abigail, who was also about to start work in another chain forge. She lived such a distance away that they both knew they were unlikely to see each other much, if at all.

Soon after she had left school, and with it her childhood, Mr Clark stopped Lucy in the yard. Over the years he had always been very kind. He made her new crutches whenever hers got broken or she had grown taller. He always said hello to her when he was passing through. This time though, looking down at her with his gentle eyes, he said,

'Now, missy – I hear yower starting work. I think it's time we had another go at meking you a proper leg. Yower gunna be standing all day. And they'm long days, believe me. I've put a bit of thought into it and I think we can do better'un I did before.'

Lucy tried to look grateful, but her leg twinged at the thought of the peg Mr Clark had fixed on it for her all those years ago. It had been so uncomfortable and brought her stump up in awful sores. She always looked after her amputated leg, keeping it clean as Mom had taught her, and mostly she was all right. She dreaded to think what Mr Clark's new contraption might do to it. But she knew he was being kind.

A couple of days later, he came to the forge. It was early August and a heatwave. They were all down to the least amount of clothing they could manage. Sweat poured down Lucy's face and dripped off her nose. Her head was pounding from having to stand close to the fire on an already sweltering day and her hands were already sore with burn marks. She was still learning and it was so hard and humiliating. She spoilt a lot of iron, burning it in the fire, and she felt as if she would never learn. To make things even worse, the hip of her good leg felt as if it was going to disappear up into her body from standing for so many hours.

Mari, so heavily pregnant that she kept having to lean away, flexing her back, was in full squabble with Edna.

'That dirty whammel of a son of yours,' she shrieked, 'pissing up against the wall of our 'ouse last night. 'E were that kalied! It's disgusting – you tell the idle sod to do 'is business in the lav like anyone else!'

'Dow yow talk about my lad like that!' Edna was up and fighting. Lucy kept her head down, hoping no one else would weigh in – and then a welcome interruption arrived.

Mr Clark coughed in an embarrassed way at coming into this shed full of women, almost as if it was a boudoir where he should not venture.

'Er, all right?' he ventured.

'All right, Horace?' Edna called to him. 'What yow doing 'ere?'

Bertha and Rose both turned to look, their cheeks burning pink in the heat.

'Lucy – can I borrow yer for a few minutes?' Mr Clark said. 'I've got summat for yer.'

Lucy took her crutches and followed him.

'God, it's hot in there!' Mr Clark said, wiping his forehead on the back of his forearm. He had his sleeves rolled up to show a salt-and-pepper pelt of hairs. 'Dunno 'ow yow wenches stand it. Can you get along to my work-shop, d'yer think?'

Lucy nodded. It wasn't too far.

Mr Clark's workshop, a little brick building right at the far end of the road, was a cool haven of peace after the forge. He worked alone, a faint breeze blowing in through the open window from across the fields. And beside his workbench with the tools on it, she saw propped what was unmistakably her new leg.

The leg itself was a solid, rounded piece of wood about the thickness of her forearm. Fixed to the top was a lea-ther cuff and there were leather straps also attached to it. Most astonishing of all, at the bottom, another piece of wood had been set at an angle, a bit like a foot.

'I wanted to do the best for yer, wench,' Mr Clark said, seeming to be quietly excited. Picking the thing up he showed her. 'I need to measure you up proper now and make any adjustments. There's a bolt through there where the foot joins on, so it can move back and forth – I thought you might want to wear two boots for once, instead of just one!'

Lucy looked back at him, suddenly excited. What if the leg really worked? Might she really start to look more like other people, not be swinging along on crutches all her life?

'I dow know if it'll work,' he admitted. 'The foot might just drag. But in any case, I hope the leg'll be better than nowt for yer. Shall us give it a try for size?'

He indicated that she should sit on the chair by the bench.

'You dow need to fix the straps under yower clothes,' he said. 'Yow can do them up on the outside, just while we try it.'

Even though Mr Clark had seen her leg before she still

131

felt terribly embarrassed having to pull her skirt up and expose her stump, in its muslin wrap, so that they could try the false leg. Her already pink face seemed to pulse with heat as Mr Clark's skinny form squatted down in front of her with the contraption.

'I've made it as soft as I can inside,' he said. He showed her that the leather cup at the top of the wood was padded with more leather and what seemed like a little down-filled cushion. 'The wife stitched it for yer,' he smiled. 'Poll said, "That wench is a real good girl – always tries 'er best for everyone."'

Lucy felt a lump in her throat. Horace and Polly Clark were quiet people who kept themselves to themselves – but how kind they were! And she did try to please people – it was the least she could do, with her being foisted on the Hipkiss family by her circumstances.

He helped her stand with one crutch, as he gently fed her leg into the leather cuff and did up the straps round her waist, adjusting them so that they were tight enough. Lucy found she was trembling by the time he had finished, terrified at the idea of having to try and walk, at the pain, the feeling that she would fall. Nothing felt stable or easy.

'Well,' Mr Clark said, sounding pleased. 'The height seems about right! Can you stand on it for me?'

Very gingerly Lucy tried to stand on both legs. She swayed and gasped and he caught her spare arm.

'It's . . . just right!' To her surprise, it was. She felt evenly balanced.

'I'm gunna be right be'ind yow,' Mr Clark said. 'Try teking a step. You won't fall – I've got yer.'

The thing did not feel part of her at all. Its weight and height were both very well balanced, but it was an alien thing strapped on. It felt as if it might just fall off, and the 'foot' at the bottom was something she had no control over.

But she had to try. She managed a couple of stiff, shuffling steps, not daring to lift the foot yet, and she was sweating and shaking all over by the time she had finished. Mr Clark let her sit down again. He stood before her, frowning slightly.

'What d'yow reckon? We can fix the other boot on the bottom of it.'

Lucy was anxious not to disappoint him after all the work he had put in. The thing felt terrible – so alien and difficult. But she had to admit it was so much better than the last time. And maybe, just maybe if she kept practising . . .

'I can bring my spare boot . . . I think, if I was to do a little bit, keep on with it every day . . . If I use a stick, it might be all right,' she said, forcing herself to smile up at him.

Mr Clark's face cleared and he smiled back at her.

'Yower a brave little wench, yow are. I can see it's hard for yer. I'll help yer, bab – every day, until that thing's like second nature to yer – and where it ain't, we'll change it!'

A few days later while it was still stinking hot, Mari Gornall went into labour. It had all started in the night and that morning she was still at it. They couldn't hear her over the noise of the forge, but when Lucy went out to see Mr Clark, she heard a yowl of pain through the open window of number three that turned her stomach. As there was no school, Mari's younger children – Sid, Maggie and little Jo, were all milling about outside with Freddie Hipkiss. Amy, her eldest, was out at work now.

When she had had her session with Mr Clark – and

every time she did, the leg felt a little bit more familiar – and come back again, Mari's baby had clearly still not yet arrived.

Rose, red-cheeked, her hair damp with sweat, was at the door of the forge taking the air. She let Lucy in and came back to her hearth.

'Makes me feel funny, hearing someone else going through it,' she said.

'Just be glad it ay you,' Bertha said drily. She looked at Lucy. ''Ow're yow getting on?'

'All right,' Lucy said. 'It's getting a bit better.' But she was not ready to be let loose with the leg yet – was not sure she ever would be. It would be so much easier to carry on as she always had. But she felt indebted to Mr Clark, and she also wondered – could she? Could she really walk about with only a stick and a leg under her skirts which might make her look more like other people? It seemed almost too much to hope for.

Mari's baby arrived soon after four o'clock and the ending of the moans and groans was a great relief to them all. Later, to everyone's surprise, Mrs Heath – who, despite years of delivering babies, and to her annoyance, still got called 'that pit-bonk wench' – appeared in the door of the forge.

'Mrs Hipkiss – can I 'ave a word?' she said importantly.

'Ooh,' Edna said as Bertha followed the tough little woman out into the yard. 'What's going on there, d'yow think?'

Rose looked at Lucy and gave a shrug and a faint smile. Neither of them had any idea.

It was a long while before Bertha Hipkiss came back and when she did, her face was set, iron hard, so much so that no one dared say anything. She came into the forge, planted her feet and folded her arms.

'I've been in to see 'er,' she announced. 'And 'er dow want anyone seeing the babby.'

Lucy waited with the others, having no idea what Bertha was talking about. Soon after the mother had recovered a while, most of the babies born were brought out and everyone had a look and made admiring noises.

'What's up with it?' Edna said brutally.

Bertha swallowed. 'It's a girl. And 'er's a Mongol.'

Lucy was still none the wiser. It took a while to take in that Mari had had a child which, everyone seemed to think, had something wrong with it and was not to be shown about.

Later on, when Victor Gornall got in from work, he soon came slamming out again and disappeared. There was a quiet feeling through the yard, a sense of horror, as if a truly terrible thing had happened. It was not the sadness when a baby died – it was something more, and stranger, because it was not fully understood.

Lucy was one of the first people to see the baby the next day when Mari ventured out. Women often came back to the hearth only hours after they had their babies and Mari couldn't stay stuck in for ever. She had to earn. She came into the forge with the baby tied to her in a shawl. Lucy was on her own, working the bellows to get her fire going.

She felt a shock at the sight of Mari. Her face seemed to have changed in the last two days so that she barely recognized her. She was already haggard, as most of the women were, but now she looked gaunt, haunted, with dark circles under eyes which were red from crying. And she seemed subdued, almost frightened to be seen.

135

'Can I see the babby?' Lucy said. She still could not take in that there was anything wrong with her.

Mari flinched. 'I s'pose yow've heard – 'er's a . . . 'er's not normal.'

Lucy nodded. Her heart began to race. She was expecting something monstrous, perhaps two misshapen heads, or a horribly deformed face.

'What's her name?' she asked shyly.

'I dunno.' Mari started crying, her face crumpling. ''Er ain't got one. What's the use on giving 'er a name? 'Er won't know anything, won't be able to do anything . . .' She stood weeping. 'My Victor just ran out when he saw 'er – 'e won't 'ave anything to do with 'er – or me. It would've been better if 'er'd died, like the others!'

This all seemed so terrible. And not even giving the child a name! Lucy swung herself over to Mari. For a moment, Mari clung more tightly to the baby but then, as if to get it over with, she pulled back the shawl to show the little sleeping face.

Lucy braced herself. But all she could see was a baby. A round-faced, pink-skinned baby. There was something a fraction different about her that Lucy could not quite fathom, but it did not seem anything like the horror she had been expecting. She looked up at Mari, frowning.

'When 'er's awake you can see it,' Mari said, wiping her pale face. 'Mrs Heath saw straight away – 'er's seen it before.'

'She's got to have a name,' Lucy insisted. It all felt wrong. 'Or we won't be able to play with her.'

Mari gave her a sharp, disbelieving look. It seemed she had not thought that this child might ever play, that anyone might choose to play with her. Something seemed to soften in her, a tiny fraction.

'If 'er were a girl, I was gunna call 'er Dolly,' she said, sniffing. 'You know – short for Dorothy.'

'Dolly,' Lucy said. And she smiled.

It took Mari a long time to come to terms with everyone seeing Dolly. Lucy could see that her face was somehow different, but it was hard to understand quite what all the fuss was about.

'What does it mean?' she asked Bertha later that day when they were making tea, Jonno in his chair as usual. 'Being a Mongol? Why is Mari so upset about it?'

Bertha said she didn't quite know but that Mrs Heath had said the child would never be quite right.

'Is it because Mari did something wrong?' Lucy whispered. She could not make sense of the shame Mari seemed to carry now, as if she had been draped in some grim veil of wrongdoing.

'I dunno. No.' Bertha shrugged. 'No one knows, I dow think.'

'I knew . . . a couple of . . . little lads like that.' Jonno sat forward, gasping between each utterance. 'They looked . . . a bit different . . . bit slow, they were. Cheerful enough . . . the one, especially . . . Dai. Little Dai . . . his name was . . .'

Lucy kept her head down, her hands working at the potato she was peeling. After a while, without looking up, she said,

'Was my mother ashamed of me?'

She heard, rather than saw, Bertha's appalled reaction, her stiffening, a kind of suppressed gasp coming from her. Lucy looked up then.

'No, wench, 'er wasn't – *never*! All yower mother ever felt was guilt that 'er left you with that kalied sot Aggie Robinson because yower brother was poorly.' She brandished the knife she was holding to enforce her point. 'There's no shame in what happened – not for either of yer. It were an accident. Yow wasn't born like that and it were no fault of yower mother neither – and don't you ever forget it!'

III

1907

Eighteen

In the quiet morning, they could hear the distant tolling of the bell all along the street.

The coffin was eased gently along the entry to where the hearse was waiting in Hay Lane. John and Clem, strong lads of seventeen and sixteen now, managed it carefully along the narrow passage and were joined by Freddie – thirteen now and out at work – and Bertha's sons-in-law. Solemnly, ceremonially, they lifted it on to the hearse. They were not much burdened by the wasted body of the man inside the coffin. Neighbours stood round at a respectful distance, the curtains of their houses all pulled shut in sympathy.

Lucy, just fourteen now, followed behind Bertha and her other daughters – Susannah, Aggie and Pauline and their children.

Bertha, magnificent in black, stood in the road as they carried her man out – her husband of more than thirty years. Lucy could hardly bear to look at her face. Bertha was not weeping – not then. Her expression was stony. But behind it Lucy could hear the echo of Bertha's heartbroken weeping in her bed during these last nights.

There were four horses, black, with feathers jutting up jauntily from the bridles. A splendid show – nothing but the best for Jonno, Bertha had said. After all he had had to endure. With a husband in his state she had been saving, putting away a halfpenny a week for years now, at least when she could manage to, just in case. And the family and some of the neighbours chipped in as well, to make sure Bertha's man, loved by everyone, was properly honoured.

'Yower Jonno – 'e were the best,' Lucy had heard at the door, the week after he died, accompanied by the chink of ill-afforded coppers. 'I don't want yow to go short, bab.'

One of the horses scraped its hoof along the ground in the summer morning. It seemed too fair a day to be burying anyone. Smoke rose from the chimneys and forges of those working, not involved in this family's sadness. They could hear the distant tap of hammers in a nearby yard. No one spoke. Neighbours stood round in sorrowful respect. The cottage had black crêpe draped over the door.

With a creak and jingle of harnesses, the cortège set off. With hooves clashing on the cobbles ahead of them, everyone, dressed in the best they had, began to walk along the road to the church.

Lucy heard a sob from in front of her and saw Pauline, who was heavily pregnant with her second child, put her hands over her face. Lucy let the tears run quietly down her own cheeks. She felt terribly alone. If only she could see her brothers, have someone near who she could really call her own in this world! There had been not a word of Albert in all this time and she had never dared asked more about George. But she had come to love Jonno Hipkiss, that brave, kindly man, as if he was her real father. Hour after hour, she had sat reading to him and, in his halting way, he would say, 'Bless you, girlie . . . you're turning into . . . a real good little . . . reader, you are . . . You'll be . . . a professor . . . one day!'

He was one of the kindest and best people she had ever

known – but in the end she was not of his blood – and nor was anyone who she knew now in this world.

All through Jonno's funeral, she felt the agony both of his death and of her mother's. In her mind, she kept hearing Ellen's voice singing, high and sweet, *'Cherry ripe, cherry ripe, ripe I cry . . .'*

For the last weeks of his life, they had finally carried Jonno upstairs to the bed he had for so many years shared with Bertha.

'He needs to lie and rest proper like,' Bertha said.

Despite Jonno's protests that she would not get a wink of sleep with all his coughing, they wanted to be close for what both of them knew would be his last days. And Lucy, during that time, had slept on her little mattress downstairs.

They propped Jonno up in the bed to help him breathe the best he could. But he shrank away so fast that at the last, he lay with his eyes closed all the time and it felt as if he was hardly still there with them.

Afterwards, when it was over, Bertha said sadly, 'He seemed to go so quick – as if summat in 'im had given way, all of a sudden.'

Lucy would go up to see him sometimes. She had mastered her leg by now and could manage stairs without crutches. She hoped Jonno might be awake, that he would ask for another chapter of the latest book they were reading – or for his favourite of all, *David Copperfield.*

But it seemed she had read her last to Jonno. Standing by the bed, she stared at his shrunken skull, the dry, jaundiced skin and papery claws of hands. The rattle of his lungs was horrifying. But she was never horrified by him. All she could feel was an immense, loving sorrow for this man, once the vigorous young miner Bertha had described.

Last week, she had woken very early one morning to find Bertha also downstairs. It was her riddling the fire that woke Lucy. She lit it, poured water and put it on to boil. Lucy heard her moving about, the squeak of a stopper being pulled.

Lucy sat up sleepily. Bertha was swigging desperately from one of her bottles of home-brew. She replaced the bottle and sank on to the worn old leather chair that had been Jonno's resting place for all that time.

Bertha seemed weary to her bones and there was something odd about her, the way she was leaning forward, staring numbly down at the floor. After a moment she sat up and looked across at Lucy.

'Well,' she said. ''E's gone. My mon's gone. God rest 'is soul.'

Bertha had joined Edna Wilmott among the ranks of widows having to fend for a family. But at the younger end of the scale, over these past three years, new life had come to yard number three, Hay Lane.

Rose and Wally Shaw now had three children. Their little girl, Grace, now four, had been followed by a lad, Charlie, and another little girl, Ivy, who was now six months old.

Mari Gornall now had six living children, the last of these, little Dolly, a bitter pill that she had to come to terms with. She was in many ways a different woman from the one she had been before Dolly arrived. The noisy Sunday afternoons were a thing of the past. Victor Gornall never could accept the fact that Dolly was different and mostly ignored both the child and his wife. It was said that a child with his ferret-like features had been let loose on the lottery of survival in a nearby yard but of course people talk and no one could be *sure* it was his. But according to Mari, Victor was getting his oats elsewhere. He was like a cat with two homes, coming back to be fed but not much else. Mari cried at first, when she found out he was playing away, but soon became philosophical.

'Let some other poor cow 'ave 'im to deal with,' she said, eyes narrowed in loathing. 'That nogyead ent coming near me anyway – I've got enough on my plate without *'im*!'

She was still ready for a barny now and then, but Mari had grown up. She was especially grateful to Rose, because little Gracie Shaw took a shine to Dolly, who was in any case by far the most amiable of the Gornall family. Everyone liked Dolly, with her straight brown hair and round, often grinning face. Gracie was just over a year older than Dolly and she had taken her on and always looked out for her, even when they were very small. And now, everyone in the yard was long used to the little girl. Dolly was just Dolly and that was that.

Lucy had been working as a chainmaker long enough now to be quick and adept at it.

She had seen her 'hammer hands' become scarred like her mother's, had come to accept her lot. And she was now quite used to the leg Mr Clark had made for her. With adjustments over the years she could wear a boot over it and get along with a limping walk, usually using a stick if she was going any distance.

And working among the women who had ceased treating her like a child now she was fourteen years of age, she overheard all their commentaries on all sorts of ripe subjects. Working the hearth tucked away on the far left the other side of Mari, Lucy was often forgotten when these conversations began.

'I've told Wally,' Rose said, exasperated as baby Ivy cried once again to be picked up for a feed. 'I ain't giving 'im no more. Three's enough – I ain't a farm animal, to be birthing and milking all my life long.'

'What d'yow mean by that?'

Bertha stopped working and actually turned towards Rose, an ominous tone in her voice. Any sign of Rose saying something that seemed to challenge Bertha's way of looking at life, and she was on to it. Mari coming out with something like that was one thing – Bertha had always considered Victor a wastrel. But Rose was married to a good man and she had only three children, all healthy so far . . .

'I *mean*,' Rose insisted, 'I don't want babby after babby. Ivy's six months now and I don't want to catch for another. I ay an animal! And I want to be able to feed the ones I've birthed – not like some around 'ere!'

Lucy almost felt like ducking at the trouble she could see brewing. She was rather in awe of Rose Shaw and Rose was always kind to her – but why did she have to be so provoking? Many was the time now Lucy had heard arguments among the women since Rose had been there. Before, it had just been Mari saying something mean to get a rise out of someone. It was never over anything much. But Rose was one for throwing a cat in among the pigeons all right. She liked to think she had a mind of her own and she wound the others up. Of them all, Edna Wilmott was a placid sort and Mari grew quickly hot and cold. The one whose skin Rose really got under, time and again, was Bertha's.

'So yow mean –' Bertha stood with the hammer clenched

146

tightly in her right hand – 'yow think yow can just deny yower mon?'

Lucy felt worried by the tone of her voice. She knew Bertha often took refuge now in her bottles of home-made wine – pea-pod, elderberry, wild plum. She drank mostly at night, falling asleep in Jonno's chair. But had she been drinking now? She didn't sound quite steady in herself.

Rose glanced at Bertha, and then back at her work. She was never cowed by anyone, but it was only a fortnight or so after Jonno's funeral and even though she was sometimes hasty, Rose was not unkind. She did not want to say anything deliberately to upset Bertha.

'Come on – out wi' it!' Bertha was blazing now. 'Am yow saying yow dow think it's yower duty as a wife to give yower man what 'e needs?'

Rose turned, slowly. She seemed to be thinking. Sud-denly, unusually humble, she said,

'I just . . . Sometimes I think, Mrs Hipkiss, that there are too many babbies born into this world and there ay enough to feed 'em on. And a lot of women ruined into the bargain. But that's just my thinking – I ay not saying anyone has to agree with it.'

Bertha stood fuming. Lucy, young as she was, was beginning to understand that one of the proud prizes of Bertha's life had been that she had served her man, given him all he needed, birthed his children over and over again whether they lived or died, at cost to herself. And now he was gone – the very meaning of her life. She was not having some chit of a wench coming in naysaying all she had set her own pride in.

'Yower a married woman,' Bertha almost bellowed at her. 'And yower job is to be a wife to yower mon!'

'All I'm saying –' Rose could not help herself flaring

up – 'is I don't want a babby every year. There are ways and means . . .'

Lucy looked round to see Mari Gornall listening carefully to this, her eyes narrowed. Edna turned her head, placid as a heifer, then went back to her work.

'There may be "ways and means",' Bertha repeated mockingly. 'But they ay ways any good to man nor God and yow shouldn't be thinking of 'em. A mon needs a wife, not some uppity bit with ideas of her own!'

Lucy saw Rose's cheeks flare even pinker than they had already been made by the firelight. She actually bit her lip to stop herself saying anything. Turning back to her work, Lucy heard her mutter something. Things changing. Something about that. Rose was a great mutterer, always seeming to be having passionate conversations with someone even if she did not have them all out loud.

No one had ever explained the facts of life to Lucy but by now she had picked up plenty enough to make sense of this conversation, especially now she had stopped going to Sunday school.

The sounds from Mari and Victor Gornall's pleasant Sunday afternoons of the past had taught every young person in the yard a certain amount, although Lucy still had very little idea of the details of what actually went on. But the other thing that had, unknown to anyone else, seared through Lucy's mind, was that afternoon three years ago when Rose first arrived on their doorstep.

She had left the room as Bertha requested and slowly climbed the stairs. But then, not having much else to do, rather than with any real plan of eavesdropping, she had sat down on the top step. Her curiosity was about this new person Rose Shaw and her tall-as-a-poplar husband

Wally. But what she heard had frozen her to the spot and entered her soul like an iron spike.

Bertha talked to Rose about Seth Dawson. Then she heard her mother's name. And then,

'Bringing that'un's spawn into the world were the end of 'er. The babby died with 'er.'

The words floated like smoke up the stairs. Lucy sat completely still, hardly breathing. *Seth Dawson.* It was only then that Lucy learned what had happened, that Seth was responsible for her mother having a child, that he was the one to blame, in the end, for her mother's death.

Mom had not mentioned the baby to her, not in all the months she was expecting. And Lucy still had only the haziest idea of how a baby actually came about. She had an idea that it took a man and a woman, but even though her pa had been dead she had never really questioned how Mom came to be having that baby. But now . . . Her mind reeled. A man and a woman – in this case, a woman who was not willing but brutally forced by that filthy . . .

Seth Dawson.

Seth Dawson had forced . . . And Mom had had to have a baby and if he hadn't, she would still have her mother here with her now . . .

In those moments she felt herself change. Never before had she known the extent of loathing which entered her, like an iron thrust into the fire, seething and glowing with rage.

Nineteen

'What d'yer mean, dow go all the way?'

Rose could just see the glint of Wally's eyes looking down at her, adoring as ever. I like to *see* yer, Wally would say. They had the curtains open to let the faint light of the summer night into the bedroom – no need to waste a candle tonight.

He had been kissing her as they cuddled up close and Rose could tell from the feel of things that her husband was already properly keyed up and ready to make love with his usual enthusiasm.

But she held off, giving his nose a playful kiss to cover her prickling embarrassment at trying to put any of this into words. It wasn't something you talked about in the normal run of things.

'I just mean . . . When you get . . . you know, at the end, before you . . . Can you come out of me?'

'Come *out*?' Wally was horrified. '*Why*? That's the best bit! Don't yow want me?'

Rose felt almost as if she was going to cry. It came over her suddenly, how strongly, desperately she felt about this. And Wally just didn't understand.

'It's not you, Wal. I just don't want to catch for another babby – least, not yet. The others've come so quick and it's all I can do to get by, what with being so sick and tired at the beginning . . .'

'All right then . . .' But he was kissing her neck, eager

for her, and she could tell he was not really listening. 'Whatever yow say . . .'

He made love with his usual wiry vigour. She could feel the muscles in his lean back under her fingertips and all her loving instincts were to pull him closer and closer. Just as he was reaching the peak of his excitement she tried to say, 'Now . . . Wal, come out now – please!' But he was lost in his own feelings and there was no time to stop him letting go in her as usual, groaning and sighing with pleasure.

He had not heard a word she said. Wally rolled off her and snuggled up close again, still wanting to be all lovey-dovey. He stroked her belly, laid a hand on her breast for comfort and went to kiss her again but she moved her face aside, too angry and hurt to speak. Wally did not appear to notice.

She let several moments pass, fuming, as his breathing grew deeper. Typical – he had had everything he wanted and was falling asleep!

She jabbed an elbow forcefully into his ribcage.

'Oi!' He jerked awake with a curse. 'Watch it, woman! What're yer doing?'

'Be quiet!' she burst out in a furious hiss. 'Don't you *dare* go and wake the kids! And don't you just go to sleep, now yow've had your oats. I asked yer to do one thing for me and what did yer go and do – the opposite! Dain't you hear a flaming word I said to yer?'

'No . . . Well, yeah . . .' Wally lay down again, stroking her like a cat he was trying to pacify. 'Only once I get going . . . I mean, it's like – it's just heaven being in you, Rosie . . .'

She sat up furiously, pushing him away. He thought he could just give her flannel and she'd simply cave in every time! That her words, women's words, were like a little draught through the window – you could just let them pass by and take no notice.

'It's all very well . . .' She wanted to yell but the last thing they needed was Ivy waking up and screaming. 'Yow take what yow want and leave me with a babby – with months of feeling bad and hardly able to stand at the hearth – and then all the rest of it. Yow pay no heed to what I have to do . . .' She was almost in tears of frustration. 'Yow don't love me – all yow think about is yower flaming self, Wally Shaw.'

That hit home. Wally lay stunned for a moment, then sat up beside her.

'But that ay true, Rosie – you know 'ow much I love yer. I'd do anything for yer. I go out to work to keep us all every day, dow I? Like a mon should. But there are things a woman's got to do an' all.'

'And don't I do them?' she snapped. 'All of them? *And* work?'

'I mean, there are things a mon needs from a woman . . .' He spoke carefully, as if he knew he was venturing on to ground quite likely to give way under his feet.

'And I give yow them. I feed yow and keep the house clean and ay I given yow three kids?'

'Yeah?' This seemed obvious to him. 'And I thought yow was happy – *we* was happy?'

There was a gentleness beginning between them now, as if he had finally grasped that she was truly upset. Wally pulled her down beside him and held her, but the thoughts reeling round in her mind had not yet been expressed and she could not fully give in to him.

'I dow understand what you mean, Rosie. Yower a good wife and mother and I thought yow was happy.'

'I am, Wal.' She patted his hand. 'In the main, I am.

152

But . . .' She turned on her side, needing to let out the thoughts that had been building in her. 'I know it's difficult for yer to understand, but I feel as if – as if I could be *more* than this. As if I'm *meant* to be summat more in this life – that there are things I'm supposed to *do*.'

'Like what?' Wally sounded truly baffled.

'I don't know,' she said helplessly. She lay silent for a moment, then ventured to say, 'Only, last week, I saw . . .'

She trailed off, deciding to keep this thought to herself. The people she had seen were organizing with the union. There was a bearded man, but the other person really caught her eye: a determined-looking lady in a plain brown straw hat, talking to a small cluster of people in the street. The lady was gesturing with one hand and she seemed so strong and firm in her convictions. Rose had not stopped, feeling she would be barging in, perhaps didn't belong in that group of women, although they were working women just like she was. But she watched as she dawdled past with her shopping, her head turned to watch until the last moment.

'Wha'?' Wally said.

'I just mean – if I catch for babby after babby, there'll be nowt left of me bar a shadow, is all.'

Wally did not really understand, but he caught the feeling in her voice. He seemed to grasp, eventually, that his usually energetic and uncomplaining wife was saying something that was important to her.

'Know yower trouble, Rosie?' he said. 'Yow think too much about things.' Carefully, he added, 'It'd be a shame to stop at three.'

Rose nodded. 'But for a while, Wally – please?'

Sleepily he patted her leg. 'All right, my bab – I'll try.'

Rose listened to his breathing in the dark as he sank into sleep. Of the two of them she had always been the leader and Wally her devoted follower. In the end he would come round, she thought. And for these last moments, before sinking into sleep herself, she allowed the burning feelings that possessed her to have free rein.

Before she'd had baby Grace and they moved to Hay Lane, Rose had been employed at the chain works of Harry Stevens in Old Hill.

She knew about outworkers, of course. But becoming one herself, now a wife and mother, had been a shock. In the factory the pay was better. Nothing like as good as the men's, but more than the pittance she was slaving for now. The hours there were long, but once work was over, it was over. Here in the forges, dark and hidden away in backyards, she saw the women working every hour God sent, often from before first light until long after dark, barely able to find time to stop and boil a pan of spuds. They hammered away endlessly, making chain to scrape a living and only managing it by the most extreme toil. Worn out, haggard women, sick women, women surrounded by kids, underfed and often ailing, and so many babies buried after they were only a few days old . . . As for the women without a working husband or children – they were at the very bottom of the pile.

Edna Wilmott practically lived at her hearth, banging away, with seemingly no help from Sidney, that layabout simpleton of a son of hers – heaven only knew why he had not been put to the hearth at a young age to do something useful. But Bertha had told her that Edna had birthed child after child in her time and he was the only one lived past his second birthday. Sidney, black-haired, pale and pudgy, rolled in and out of the yard as he pleased. Now and again he managed to get a few delivery jobs – but he was apparently useless for anything else and Edna just kept on slogging, keeping him.

Bertha Hipkiss had sons working now, but out of habit she toiled and toiled – and that pretty little wench Lucy . . . Rose could see that Lucy was alone in the world. But she was a sweet girl, alert, could read better than any of them, even after leaving school so young. Rose had had some basic schooling, but she knew Lucy had been reading proper books, big fat books, to Jonno Hipkiss. Was the girl to spend her whole life doing nothing but hammer chain links? It had to be better than going into service, Rose thought. That was just like being a prisoner! But, like so many things, the more she thought about it, the more wrong it seemed.

The biggest shock of all, though, was the foggers. Again, she'd known about them, middlemen who squeezed and squeezed the chainmakers until the pips squeaked, to fatten their own bellies. Some you could reason with, but Seth Dawson was worse than any she had imagined.

Bertha Hipkiss had told Rose as soon as she arrived what happened to Ellen Butler, Lucy's mother. That Seth Dawson was responsible.

Over these three years, she had seen his leering, bullying behaviour, the power he had over these women so desperately dependent on their meagre wages. And from the moment she met the man, she wanted to make it clear he was not having any sway over her.

That first time when he came in and saw her at the hearth, he'd stood there, like he always did, legs apart as if to make room for his massive manhood, rocking back and forth on his heels. He'd said a few words and she had refused to be cowed. A few days later he came

155

back, almost seeming to have forgotten that he had already seen her.

'So – yower the new'un, then? I 'ope yow can keep up with all these other wenches of mine.'

Rose looked back at him, right into his eyes. She saw the rough, unshaven jowls and self-important stance of a bully. For a second, she held his gaze, then looked down with pretend demureness.

'I think so.' Her work was already in full swing by then, but she pretended to play along. 'I was at Harry Stevens.'

'Goo on then – yow'd better show us. Seems like Ridley's've teken yow on so let's 'ope yow can keep up. There's tools there for yow, left by the last wench.'

Bertha had told her she could take over Ellen Butler's tools and she had already made a start.

There were thin rods for making plough chains in a pile on the floor. Seth Dawson stood uncomfortably close to Rose as, prickling with loathing, she picked one of them up, gave the bellows a pump and thrust one end into the fire. Swiftly, well practised as she was, she shaped the link, hooked it on to the last one and hammered the ends together neatly and in record time, each blow true and accurate.

Without looking at Seth Dawson, who she pretended was not there – though by the overwhelming unwashed stink of him he clearly was – she kept working, starting on another link straight away.

'Seems like yow can do the job, wench,' he said, sounding almost disappointed.

'I know I can,' Rose couldn't help retorting pertly.

'It ay no good talking back to that'un,' Bertha Hipkiss reprimanded her once Seth had finally slouched away again. 'It only brings trouble.'

Rose worked on, fuming inwardly. She didn't argue with Bertha – not then. But it was the beginning of many set-to's.

Rose had great respect for Bertha Hipkiss. She was a good woman, strong as a carthorse, and the sight of Jonno had flooded Rose with sorrow for both of them. Bertha was a hard grafter, at the hearth every minute she was not working at something else. She had brought up a large and good family, taken Lucy in, provided counsel to any other woman in trouble. But mention to her how anything might change or be different – *better*, God forbid! – and she was immediately up in arms. This was how things were and how they would remain! She would try to make Rose feel like the greatest fool and upstart the world had ever seen.

Many was the time over the past three years, when Rose was not heaving over a pail or suckling a babby and had mustered the energy for thinking, that she had called things into question.

'Why don't they 'ave dobbin to pick up the chain? We ent cowing horses! Our wages are so low – and there ay no one to look out for us. In the factories they have a union!'

'Oh, not that old talk again,' Bertha would scoff. 'They ay never gunna give us outworkers a union – it's just the way it is. Yow 'ave to mek the best of it.'

Edna and Mari would nod knowingly as if to say that Rose, in asking such questions, was a deluded fool. All these women just accepted everything! Rose raged inwardly. The pay, the endless work, the crucifying toll on their bodies of child after child. Then they raised the little ones amid the smoke and sparks and fumes of the forge. And there was no one else in the yard who said different.

Rather, they sang hymns to God to thank him for the blessing of this life with its endless toil!

Rose sometimes looked around her and wondered if she was the one going mad. These women were exhausted and half clammed, unable to question anything for fear of starving . . . Sometimes they reminded her of beasts in a field, chewing endlessly, never thinking or questioning . . .

And yet this was not everyone's lot, was it? There were big houses in Cradley Heath and Old Hill and out in the countryside, where the rich lived in comfort and hardly lifted a finger.

Rose was beginning to feel there must be some answer to why the lot that fell to people in this world turned out so wide in its extremes between wealth and the very poorest. Were the rich just somehow more blessed? Did everything have to be accepted, however bad, as the will of God?

Twenty

'Aren't you coming, Luce?'

John Hipkiss stood at the door that Sunday morning, on his way out to church. He had nothing special to wear for Sunday best, but he had his cap on his carefully smoothed hair and had brushed his jacket down. The only other indicator that this was not a work day was the little Bible, with its black covers and wafer-thin pages, that he held in one hand.

Lucy usually went to church with him. Even though Miss Jones was long gone, she found comfort in the services – now in the brand-new church building in Graingers Lane. She liked a reason to get out of the yard, which was something she hardly ever did except when doing bits of shopping for Bertha. And the church gave her a feeling of peace, of a bigger life. That and the miracle of the brand-new library which had been completed in the High Street last year. Whenever she had the chance, she would go into the grand building with its echoing spaces and stone floor, to fetch herself something new to read.

But this morning she did not even feel like reading.

'No – not today.'

She sat on Jonno's old chair close to the fire in the October chill, trying not to show the boys she was in pain.

'You feeling bad?' As ever, John noticed her, showed concern for her. But today she prickled with irritation. She wanted him to go.

159

'No – not really.' Her cheeks flushed. She couldn't explain to John that her monthly had just come on. It was only the second time she had had it. She felt self-conscious about going anywhere, frightened she would be leaking blood and might smell bad. She had cramps in her stomach and the thought of walking all the way to church with her sore leg and chafing rag between her legs was too much.

'Yer'd best take the hint, mate,' Clem said. He was at the table, fiddling with his fishing rod. ''Er don't want to go.' He glanced up at his brother in a teasing, triumphant way. These days the two of them seemed to be in competition most of the time, like a couple of roiling dogs.

'All right,' John said, in a tight voice. 'I'd best be off, then.' His eyes met Lucy's for a second and he looked sad and disappointed with her. But she really couldn't face it and she looked away.

'Say one for me,' Clem said provokingly. 'And put the wood i' the 'ole as you go!'

John did not reply. He went out and the door closed on the cold of the yard.

To Lucy's surprise, Clem, instead of keeping his head down, looked over at her and winked, his face crinkling into a conspiratorial smile. Light flowed through her. Clem, whose attention she always craved, but who scarcely ever noticed her, was smiling at her! She beamed back at him. She didn't want to be mean about John – didn't intend to. But John was so stolid and sensible. Being alone here with Clem – having him smile at her! It made her feel as if something was happening in her life and she was of some importance.

'You all right, Luce?'

'Yes,' she said. 'I just feel like sitting quiet. What're you doing today, Clem?'

If only he would say he felt like staying in as well, that he would sit with her, maybe play a game of something . . . Or invite her to come fishing. However much it pained her to walk, however cold it was, she would do it, to be part of something Clem was doing.

'I'm going down the river and then Nance and I'll be out and about for a bit. But 'er's got to 'elp 'er mom this morning.'

The sun that had been rising in Lucy's heart immediately dipped back down again. Clem had a far more marked interest in the opposite sex than John had ever shown, even though John was the elder of the two. Clem was always about with some girl. The latest, Nancy, was lively and dark-haired, with flashing brown eyes and a quick tongue. Lucy felt like a dull, ugly little shadow next to her – Nancy who could dance and sing and was full of life whereas she was the cripple, forever sitting in the corner.

She sat watching Clem, willing him to look up at her again. These were precious moments – she and he alone, just for once! Clem's dark head of curls was bent over the rod he was mending. His sleeves were rolled back, showing his swarthy arms and dexterous fingers. They had lived side by side for all these years, brother and sister in all but blood, sometimes playmates. But all of a sudden, things felt different. Lucy's belly griped and there was an alarming, melting sensation in her innards. She felt a tiny trickle of blood leave her and the shame of it flushed her cheeks.

'So, yower a woman now,' Bertha told her when she whispered of blood on her mattress. 'We'll 'ave to tear up some rags for yer – and you need to keep out the way of the lads.'

Lucy knew, if only indirectly, what this meant. She

didn't feel like a woman – she still felt young and unformed. Being a woman meant babies, trouble – even though she still did not fully understand how the combination of a man and a woman managed to bring one about. And it meant having to bind yourself underneath like Bertha. She had shared a room with Bertha for years now. Only once or twice, when Bertha changed her clothes stealthily in the room, thinking Lucy asleep, had she caught sight of something bulging out of Bertha underneath, smooth and pale, like an egg.

'D'you think you'll catch any fish?' she said, wanting to keep Clem there, keep him talking, noticing her. She watched him, feeling she would do anything he asked to please him – anything at all.

'Hope so.' He grinned, pushing the chair back with his sudden energy. 'I'll bring us some tiddlers for our tea!' He grabbed his cap from the hook. 'Best be off – see yer, Luce!'

The room stilled. It felt so quiet and empty when he had gone. *Tap-tap, chink-chink* came from the forge.

Lucy folded her arms across her, hugging herself, and closed her eyes. She was hungry. Bertha had taken potatoes to lay in the fire for their dinner. If only they were ready to eat! She distracted herself by imagining that the arms around her were not her own but Clem's – those eyes looking down at her full of love, as if she was the only thing in the world that he wanted to see.

Twenty-One

The next day Lucy stood working at her hearth. Her arms were really muscular now, from all the lifting and hammering.

The smoke of the fires was tinged with the scent of autumn leaf smoke from outside, the light slanting lower in the afternoons. Rose was out for the moment. Bertha, Edna and Mari were exchanging remarks every now and then, but Lucy was not listening.

She felt strange, different all of a sudden. The horrible rag was tucked between her legs and the low grumble continued in her stomach. It was as if everything in her life had become heightened, colours brighter, her own feelings sharper and more sensitive, her body awakened as never before. She could feel a faint ache in her budding breasts. It was even as if she had grown taller, suddenly.

Hammering to close the link she was working on, again she saw her mother's hands in her own, the way hers were becoming scarred and rough with cuts and burns. A dizzy feeling filled her for a moment. Would she stand at this hearth now, all her life until she died, earning the pittance that Seth Dawson doled out when he had feathered his own nest? Seth Dawson . . . Her body tightened and she had to remind herself to breathe.

Was this to be her life, here for forty, fifty years like Edna Wilmott? Might she not go out and do something else – be like Miss Jones, teaching children? After all, she could read and write. Miss Jones had told her she was a clever girl . . .

Thrusting the end of the iron rod into the fire, she lost herself in a beautiful daydream of a new life in which she was whole and beautiful, without her ugly limp, and in which Clem was so much in love with her that he could not see any other girl but her . . .

She and Clem would go away and find a pretty little cottage in the country, somewhere in that wide expanse that lay over the wall, stretching away so far that she could no longer see it, its air clear and water pure. They would have a garden and grow cabbages and potatoes, have hens and a goose . . .

A whirlwind of energy entered the forge, breaking into her fantasy.

'Look at this!'

Rose Shaw came striding in, waving something in one hand. She was always energetic but now her cheeks were pink, her face lit up with excitement. She was holding some sort of magazine with a green cover, which she held up before them.

'I dunno how this came to be there – in the High Street! Someone must've dropped it or thrown it out. I've never seen anything like this before.'

Edna Wilmott turned her head, barely interested. Mari squinted across at Rose: her eyesight was not very good. Bertha took merely a glance.

'Oh ar, what's that then?' But she did not sound very interested.

'It's a magazine called *The Woman Worker*.'

Lucy made out that on the pale green cover there was a drawing of a woman holding a shield with writing on it.

'Have you ever heard of this?' Rose demanded of them all, breathless with excitement. 'It says, "Mag . . . a . . .

zine . . ." Oh, I'm no good – Lucy, come over 'ere, will yer? Have a go at reading it.'

Lucy hobbled over, feeling self-conscious.

' "Published by the National Federation of Women Workers",' Lucy read to them, nudged by Rose. ' "Union Buildings, Clerkenwell, London. Published Monthly. Edited by Mary R. Macarthur . . . CONTENTS, September 1907, No. 1." '

'A women's union!' Rose said. She was lit up with excitement. 'I never knew there was such a thing!'

'You want to get on with yower work, not go werriting over saft talk like that,' Bertha said. She had only paused in her hammering for a few seconds.

'What – you've heard about it before?' Rose demanded.

'Ar – there's one or two of 'em about, canting,' Bertha said with a dismissive gesture, before bending over, grunting slightly. She reached for a new rod to work on and turned away, thrusting the end into the fire. 'They'll only bring trouble down on us. What with *'im.*' She never uttered Seth Dawson's name. 'And there ay no mon'll put up with 'is woman being in a union.'

Rose frowned for a moment, but this discouragement did not dampen the excitement in her eyes for long.

'Look inside – read us some more, will yer, Luce? My reading's no good. See on the front, it says, "Something Bigger . . ." ' She read haltingly, like a small child.

' "Something Bigger Than Herself",' Lucy read, ' "by the Right Hon. Charles . . ." '

'Never mind that.' Rose seized it off her and turned the page. 'What else does it say?'

' "The Parable of the Bundle of Sticks, by Mary Macarthur . . ." '

'*What?*' Rose snatched it off her. 'What's that mean?

Oh, I wish I was better at reading! You're good, you are, Luce.'

Lucy beamed.

'Go on – read more!'

'"There have been many revolts on the part of women against those unjust terms of employment . . ."'

'Don't 'er read nice,' Edna commented.

'". . . which deprive the workers of all that makes life best worth living . . ."'

'Oh!' Rose clasped her hands together. Lucy could not really understand why she was so excited.

'We'm slaves working like this for these wages!' Rose cried. 'We should be asking for a rise from that Seth Dawson – 'e's nowt but a bloodsucker.'

'Yow'll do no such thing!' Bertha rounded on her. 'Get the whole lot of us the sack and then what'll us feed our families on? Ten a penny we am – they'll always find another outworker like you, Rose Shaw, so don't go getting above yowerself!'

Lucy saw Rose swallow down any retort she might have made, but her eyes were flaming. 'Read us a bit more,' she commanded Lucy, defiantly.

Bertha turned away again, saying nothing. Mari Gornall looked down her nose.

'Sounds dry as dust to me.'

'There's some recipes,' Lucy said.

'Ooh,' Mari commented. 'That's more like it.'

'Give it 'ere, Luce.' Rose was just reaching out to Lucy to take the magazine from her when a shadow fell across the door.

'Oi, oi – don't see much work goin' on in 'ere! What's that then?'

He came lolloping over towards Lucy. Suddenly, his gaze moved up and down her body. He never normally paid any attention to her, and Lucy was seized with panic. She looked wildly at Rose.

Rose grabbed the magazine out of Lucy's hand and tried to dodge past Seth Dawson's burly figure, but he grabbed her by the arm.

Rose held the magazine away from him, arm outstretched. She blazed with fury.

'Loose me, yow varmint – now!'

She lifted her leg, her knee heading towards such a dangerously low-hanging offering of Seth Dawson's anatomy that he stepped back, releasing her.

'Don't yow ever, *ever* touch me, you filthy . . .' she snarled, seemingly unable to think of a word bad enough. 'Yower never to lay a hand on me – or on any of us!'

And she tore out of the door, rescuing the dangerous union magazine from Seth Dawson's prying eyes.

She must have told her husband what happened because the next thing was Wally Shaw hanging about in the yard until Seth Dawson turned up.

Seth always breezed in at odd times, morning, noon and night, as if he was forever trying to catch them out. When he came into the yard at gone nine that evening, Bertha and Lucy were both in the forge, getting in another couple of hours' work.

He stood leaning against the doorpost. Bertha ignored him and kept working. Lucy did the same, but her body prickled all over with alarm at him being there. Loathing boiled in her belly.

'Oi!' They heard the slam of a door along the yard. 'Dawson!' Lucy paused. It was Wally Shaw and he sounded enraged.

Seth Dawson turned, in a languid way as if he knew no one could touch him.

'What d'yow think yower doing, laying yower 'ands on my missus?' Wally demanded. He came up close, towering over Seth Dawson. 'Yow wanna watch yower-self, mate, or yer'll 'ave me to answer to.'

Seth kept his hands in his jacket pockets as if Wally was no threat to him. He sneered up at Wally from under the brim of his greasy black homburg.

'You wanna get that wench of yours under control. The way er's carryin' on, yer don't know what 'er might get up to – or 'oo with.'

Wally's face creased with rage at what Seth was insinuating.

'Don't you talk about my missus like that!' Lucy saw Wally's spittle fly into Seth's face and she gasped. She and Bertha stood dumbly, side by side.

'My Rose is worth a hundred o' you, you . . .' Wally's hand flailed in the air. He was not naturally a fighter and words failed him.

Seth rocked insolently back and forth on his heels.

'If 'er wants work off of me 'er needs to watch 'er step,' Seth said. 'You tell 'er that from me. I ain't 'aving none o' that union talk from my workers. Any more of that and 'er'll be out – gorrit?'

Wally wilted. He didn't want Rose to lose her job – especially not on his account, for there'd be words about that, all right. He let out a frustrated sound and turned abruptly back to his own house.

'Huh,' Seth said, gloating. 'There yer go, see – yer all my wenches, so let's not be 'aving any nonsense from any of yer.'

He stood for a moment, his eyes moving over Lucy in the dim light. It was as if he was undressing her. She shud-dered, turning away as the longing rose in her to go and spit in his face.

IV

1909

Twenty-Two

Lucy and Bertha had just finished work, that chilly April night. It was gone half past nine and they were in the house. John was at a church meeting and Freddie out somewhere with his pals. Clem came slamming into the house from the dark yard.

'What's up with yow?' Bertha said, after jumping when the door flew open. 'Look at yower face – fit to curdle milk!'

'Is owt to eat?' Clem demanded. They'd had tea ages ago.

'See if there's a drop in the pot still,' Bertha said. 'And there's a heel of bread.'

Lucy could see she was trying to appease her son. It wasn't like Clem to be so stormy. He seized on the hard crust and chewed it, his strong jawbone moving under the skin. She glanced at him, trying not to stare. Because whenever Clem was in the room, staring was what she longed to do. He was almost eighteen now, a proper man; both he and John were.

It had taken a while for this change to come about. They had been playmates, kids, almost brothers and sisters. But now they were truly grown men and she was soon to be sixteen – and she was not their sister. Little by little, something had crept into the air that no one was sure what to do with, including her.

'Come on,' Bertha said. 'Spit it out, son.'

Clem sank down on the stool the other side of the fire from Lucy.

She pulled her skirt further down over her bad leg. She always wore her skirts as long as possible so that only her boot could be seen. Think about something else, she wanted to tell people. I'm *someone*, not just my leg. She almost felt she wanted to go about wearing a sign round her neck. 'Notice me! I'm not just a cripple!' But when would any lad ever look at her, limping about in that ugly way? Somehow John did not count. It was Clem she had always had eyes for.

She looked down at her hands, carefully folded and resting on her old brown work skirt, pocked with burn marks despite the apron she wore to protect it.

'It's Bett.' Clem sat forward on the stool, as if about to leap into action. He pounded his thigh with his fist. 'That'un's gone off and's walking out with . . . Well, I dunno who, but some other bloke!'

At the sound of Bett's name – Clem's latest girl – Lucy had felt her heart begin to sink. Now she raised her eyes to him in sympathy, even though she had never liked Bett. She seemed a spiteful little piece to Lucy. But Clem was not the sort who got let down in the normal run of things. He was so handsome, energetic and friendly that there was a queue of girls lining up for him.

'What did I do?' he demanded, full of indignation. 'That'un's fast, 'er is, putting 'erself about with any lad who comes along!'

'No need for that kind of talk,' Bertha said. She yanked the cork out of one of her bottles and poured herself another tot. ''Er weren't promised to yer.'

'It's not very nice though, is it?' Lucy said. 'Just going off like that.' She looked across at Clem and saw him notice her sympathetic, blue-eyed gaze, pouring all her feeling into him. For a second he looked disconcerted, then gave a reluctant little smile.

'Ta, Luce. Glad you think so. 'Er never said a word to me 'til it were too late.'

'Well, 'er's hurt yower pride, son,' Bertha said, sitting down wearily. 'And it ain't often that happens. Give the fire a poke while yower sat there, will yer?'

Clem reached out, poker in hand. To Lucy, every line of him was beautiful, the curve of his arm, his neck, the breadth of his shoulders. She felt her breath catch and had to remind herself to take in air.

'Knowing you, there'll be someone else along before many days have passed,' Bertha said.

'But I liked her,' Clem said indignantly. His mother was not taking him seriously enough. Lucy also felt indignant with her. How could she be so unkind to poor Clem?

'Well, yower gunna 'ave to find one that likes yer back!' Bertha laughed. She settled more comfortably and drained her cup.

Lucy and John had continued going to the church in Graingers Lane ever since Miss Jones invited them there as children. It was home from home.

John had always been kind to her and made sure she had help when she needed it. He had a maturity that Clem lacked, always had done. But he was so serious, that was the trouble. There was no lightness to him. Clem was careless, a laughing boy. He was fun, people took to him, but he did not automatically think of anyone else the way his more solemn brother did. Now though, with John, something had changed.

Lucy started to feel John's eyes on her more often, in a way that had not happened before, as if he was trying to get her to look back at him. And she did, because it was a nice feeling that anyone was looking at her at all.

173

That Sunday, a chilly day, but not raining, he turned to her on the way home from church as she limped along with her walking stick. Things were better than they used to be, but she was still very self-conscious about her ungainly walk.

'Lucy?'

Lucy, she noted, not 'Luce', which was what they normally called her.

'Umm?' She pulled her shawl closer about her, wondering what was coming.

'D'yer fancy going for a bit of a walk this afternoon?' He looked shyly at her. 'Get out into the country a bit, like?'

'I'm not the best at walking, John,' she reminded him.

'Oh. Course. I'd forgot.' He was really embarrassed but, she thought, how nice that he had forgotten, that her being a cripple was not the first thing he remembered about her.

'But if you don't mind taking it a bit slow . . .?'

He was suddenly in an agony of shyness, fiddling in his pockets. She wanted to laugh at how different he was from Clem. If only Clem would ask her to come out with him! Still, she told herself, it would be good to get out for a change. She had seldom been further than a short way down the road out of town, and never beyond the blast furnace.

'No – course not. If that's . . . I mean, if yer want?'

'Yes.' She smiled at him. 'All right.'

They headed out after dinner into the blustery afternoon.

'We'll go down here,' John said, in a commanding tone, pointing south along the road. 'There's a little chapel out near the old Shelton Forge – that'll be worth a look.'

'All right,' Lucy said. His bossy manner grated on her, but it didn't really matter to her what they did. It was a new experience to explore.

'Now you tell me if your leg hurts and we'll turn back,' John instructed.

'I will.' She made herself smile. There was no point telling him that her leg hurt on and off most of the time. She was not going to spoil an outing. She had half hoped that Clem might come along as well, but when John announced that they were going out, Clem looked bored at the thought.

'Dunno what yow think yow'll see in the countryside,' he said, grinning at them. ''Cept a sheep or two.'

They walked down Corngreaves Road, past the towering chimneys of the blast furnace. When John offered Lucy his arm to lean on, she refused at first. It felt too intimate, here in town. And something about him needled her now she was alone with him. Every now and then she glanced at him, his straight brown hair under the cap, his pale face and straight back. There was something rigid about John. He was quietly so sure of himself, of his rightness about everything. It was a rightness that reminded her of a pan of thick porridge with a skin on the top. An urge filled her to stick a great long spoon in and stir it all up.

But walking was hard. Once they had left the town streets behind and the eyes that might be staring at them, she finally took his arm. Seeing a blush rise in John's cheek, she almost snatched it away again. Suddenly she saw they were not just pals, almost brother and sister, but a man and a woman walking arm in arm, and that John had something else in mind. Was he becoming sweet on her? She had wondered about this before, a little, because she often looked up to find him watching her and he would blush and look away, seeing her notice him. But until now he had never done anything about it. She was not sure what to do now because she did not want to pull away and hurt his feelings.

Clouds moved across the sky, covering and then uncovering the sun. The road was muddy and the air still laden with smoke. They passed the carriage works. A train rumbled along the line to their left.

'See, the river's over there.' John pointed ahead of them. 'And that over there, behind the trees – that's Corngreaves Hall. The big 'ouse. Them's the ones started the Corngreaves works.'

Lucy knew this but she did not say so. John liked to tell her things.

'Course – t'ain't what it was,' he said. 'Be nice to go and see the house, wouldn't it? Inside I mean.'

'It would,' she agreed, laughing. 'But I don't see them asking us in for tea, do you?'

John smiled at her. She knew he was a good man, even if he was a bit stuffy. She told herself to appreciate him.

'Wish I could tek you somewhere for tea,' he said. 'I don't think there is anywhere.'

'We don't need to go for tea,' she said. 'It's just nice to be out in the air.'

He turned to look at her then. 'You're a good girlie, you are.'

'What d'you mean by that?' she said, startled.

'Well . . .' They walked on. 'You're . . . calm. Never one to make a fuss. Get mithered about things.'

Something in his tone infuriated her. There was a complacency, his idea that he knew who she was, or what she felt. That he saw her as some kind of symbol of virtue created in his own mind.

'What good would mithering ever do me?' she said, so sharply that he looked at her, taken aback.

'I just meant . . .' he began.

But she felt something give in her, like the wrenching open of a rusty hinge, unexpectedly releasing a host of feelings. She pulled her arm away from his.

'Don't you think I feel things? That every day I miss my mom, my brothers? When we're all sat round the table, with you all a family, don't you think I think about how *my* family used to be? *I* had a family and now they've been taken from me, every one of them.' Her voice was rising. 'How d'you think I feel at Christmas when there's no one there of my flesh and blood? When my little brother was handed over like a parcel and I don't know even where he is and I don't dare ask? Don't you think I look for him, every time I'm out, wondering if any of those lads in the street is him? And whether he's all right, how they're treating him . . .? Yes, I'm calm. As much as I can be – good little Lucy who sits in the corner with her wooden leg and no care in the world. Oh, she never makes a fuss! But don't think I don't *feel* things, 'cause I *do* – all right?'

John looked shocked to the core. 'Sorry, Luce . . .' He was blushing furiously, not knowing quite what had hit him. 'I never meant . . .'

She turned away to wipe her eyes.

'Never mind,' she said abruptly, embarrassed now. She'd needed so badly to say those things, but now she felt guilty for having come out with them. 'Come on – we're s'posed to be out for a walk.'

They went on in silence for a bit, trying to get over the awkwardness, but in the end they walked only about a mile because her going was slow. But they got as far as the little primitive Methodist chapel and row of brick cottages built for workers at the forge, before turning back again.

For a while they had talked about safe things: the church and John's ambition to be a preacher. But John seemed tense, as if there were things he wanted to say. It was as if her outburst had opened things. On the way back, he suddenly said, with great awkwardness,

'Our mother – she's . . . I don't like the way she's . . . Have you noticed?'

'What d'you mean?'

But Lucy knew what he was getting at. In the Methodist Church drinking was frowned upon and neither she nor John ever touched a drop. Both of them had signed the pledge. She could understand John's unease. At first, seeing Bertha drinking more after the death of her husband, Lucy had thought it was just a temporary salve. But she seemed to be taking comfort in drink more and more these days.

John was looking down, very uncomfortable.

'Maybe it's not doing any harm,' Lucy said quickly. After all, Bertha worked hard, as usual. All she was doing was falling asleep in a chair at night, and if she had the odd nip during the day, did it really matter? She was not comfortable with the demon drink herself and there had been times when she felt uncomfortable with how much Bertha was putting away, but she certainly did not want to criticize her.

John didn't say any more about his mother, but he walked on quietly beside her for a moment, frowning. He seemed to have a lot on his mind.

'Luce – I want to ask you summat else. That woman at number two . . .'

'Mrs Shaw?'

'Yeah. What d'you reckon on 'er?'

'She's all right,' Lucy said. 'Yes – she's nice.' Bertha and the other women seemed to be down on Rose Shaw in some ways, for her ideas about things. But Rose was always very kind to Lucy. 'Why?'

'I just wondered. Seems a bit on the wild side to me.'

'*Wild?* What d'you mean?' The barbed note came back into her voice. She couldn't seem to help it.

'Oh, I dunno.' He seemed uneasy discussing it. 'Talks a lot. A lot of opinions. You know – that sort.'

'Opinions?' Lucy found herself boiling with annoyance all over again on hearing these words spoken in John's rather prissy way. 'What's wrong with having an opinion?'

'Nothing. When you're . . .'

She stopped, forcing him to stop as well.

'When you're what, John? A man? Is that it?'

All that energetic life in Rose Shaw, her flashing eyes and passion for things. What was wrong with that? And what about Miss Jones? Was this ability to learn and think about things a little, like some of the things she read in her books – was that not allowed if you wore skirts?

He shook his head, shamefaced. But then, after thinking for a moment, he admitted, 'Well – yes. I s'pose.'

'So what exactly d'you think God gave women a mind for as well as a body?' she demanded, voice rising again. 'Is it only men who're allowed to think about anything? Do anything, *be* anything?'

John looked really taken aback at what he had started here – he seemed to be offering a red rag to every bull in town today. He wasn't used to women speaking back in this reasoned sort of way.

'I'm just trying to . . .' he stuttered. She could feel him retreating from her, wary. For a second, she wanted to laugh at his flustered expression. 'I mean, it says in the Bible . . . But let's not talk about it any more, Luce – not if yower gunna get cross with me again.'

179

'I'm *not* cross!' But she was. In fact, she was quite unusually steamed up. He was right to change the subject.

When they finally walked into the house, to Lucy's surprise Clem, who was hardly ever home, was sitting at the table. Seeing them come in together he looked at one and then the other, as if noticing something for the first time.

'Where've you two been then?'

'Out,' John said, walking past him. He seemed sulky now, as if things had not gone his way. He sat down and opened his Bible like a shield.

'Bit of a walk.' Lucy smiled at Clem. It was suddenly so nice to see him. She had a guilty feeling – John was kind to her, but so provoking. And she had annoyed him, speaking up like that. How much nicer it would have been to go for a walk with Clem instead! And she felt Clem's eyes following her as she moved across the room.

Twenty-Three

Rose hurried along the High Street, her old basket hung over her arm containing a few bits of shopping.

It was August, and so warm she had no need to bring a shawl out with her. She luxuriated in feeling the warmth on her face and in being able to go out in just her dark green frock and summer straw bonnet. Even if it was only to fetch a few groceries, it was nice to be out on the streets, smelling the fresh bread and mouthwatering aroma of cooked meats permeating through the smells of smoke and horse muck.

The shops had all the summer vegetables, and the green tips of spring onions and a bunch of parsley peeped over the edge of her basket.

I'll make Wally his favourite, she thought, stepping into the road for a moment to avoid a knot of people on the pavement, watching where she trod with all the muck and mess in the gutter. Kidney pudding. Summer or winter, Wally would wolf that down. She smiled at the thought of his long, amiable face, feeling a wave of gratitude to him. He brought in a decent wage, which hers only added to. They were hard workers both of them, young and vigorous, so they were not in the desperate straits of some.

And she did seem finally to be getting through to her husband that if she just kept bearing child after child, things would get ever harder and there would be less to go round for each of them. Not to mention the state she might be in if she spent her whole life with one in her belly and one at the breast . . . The very thought gave her a crazed, explosive feeling inside.

It was a tough message for Wally to hear – and live up to. She knew he loved her though, not like some men who only ever considered their own lusts, Rose thought acerbically. Like Victor Gornall. Since little Dolly's birth, Rose had seen Mari become thinner, quieter.

Turning into Graingers Lane she was thinking about when she was going to get any cooking done that day. She was so lost in thought that she almost collided with two women crossing the pavement to go into the church hall. They were both working women, Rose could see, scuttling along, heads down, as if they were not sure quite what they were doing there. One was an older lady, thin and pinched-looking. She stalled outside the door.

'Ooh, I dunno. D'yow think it'll go on long?' she said nervously to the younger woman. 'I'm gunna get be'ind myself. And if yower father 'ears of it . . . I dow think I shoulda come . . .'

'Come on, Mom – you're 'ere now. Just for a few minutes,' the younger one urged her. Rose made out the same pointed nose and sharp cheekbones mirrored in her daughter. 'You gotta 'ear what 'er 'as to say about us and our wages – I ay never 'eard anyone like 'er!'

Rose paused, curious. She saw a few other women, also chainmakers by the look of them. When another lady, rather genteel-looking, hovered outside for a moment she found the courage to speak to her.

'What's going on in there? Is it open to anyone?'

'Certainly, to all women,' the lady said. She was a neat, softly spoken person with gentle brown eyes, hair taken back under a dove-grey hat. She pointed to a poster on the wall. Rose could just make out the words 'Public Meeting'.

'It's Miss Varley – she's here to encourage women to join the women's union – the NFWW. Have you not heard of it before?'

'Yes,' Rose said uncertainly. 'I think so. Only, I wasn't sure . . .'

'I know a good many women are worried about what the men will think,' the lady said kindly. 'Are you a working woman?'

'I do outwork for Ridley's,' Rose said.

'Then you are very much someone who needs to hear Miss Varley.' She smiled. 'Do come on in.'

'What do you do?' Rose asked, as they turned inside. The lady was friendly, but she wondered if she would be considered rude for asking.

'Oh, I'm a housewife,' she said. 'My name is Jane Chisholm. And yours?'

'Rose Shaw.' It felt very strange that this lady seemed to be talking to her as if she was an equal.

'I feel very strongly about the way women have to work. The condition of sweated labour in this country is quite disgraceful. Of course, the exhibition brought it to all our attention . . .'

'The what?' Rose said, feeling foolish.

'Did you not hear about it? My goodness, it was . . . Well, it was in London – three years ago now, arranged by the *Daily News* – all about the sweated industries. I live in Dudley, and I can tell you, I learned a great deal about the condition of workers here, almost under my nose – and the women especially!' She continued heatedly. 'There *must* be reform – a minimum wage! And these factory owners *have* to be forced to comply, one way or the other. My husband thinks the same,' she added. 'The union has a marvellous magazine called *The Woman Worker* – you must have seen it?'

'Oh – yes,' Rose said, feeling rather overcome. 'I have – once or twice, at least.'

She felt more and more foolish. For all her big talk and fine intentions, she had done nothing in all this time! She had been only vaguely aware that there were things going on, meetings from time to time. A woman had appeared in their yard one afternoon, talking about the union, but Bertha and the others had given her short shrift and Rose had hardly got a look in. It was hard to be courageous and hold your ground when you were the only one. And what with work and looking after her young ones, she had not found the time herself . . .

But now, excitement tingled through her.

They stepped inside the church hall to find a gaggle of women, some clearly outworkers. There was a sprinkling of others who seemed more well-to-do. At the front stood a sturdy little woman wearing a severe brown dress with a high collar. Her hair was pinned back carelessly from a round, gentle-looking face. It was her eyes that drew Rose: dark and full of a strength and determination.

'That's Miss Varley,' Jane Chisholm said. 'A very impressive person – she was a mill girl. Comes from Bradford. She has done a truly marvellous amount of work in the Trade Union movement – and she is a suffragist.'

Rose seemed to feel Julia Varley's personality reaching out across the room as she looked about her, watching to see who was coming in. For some reason Rose felt rather afraid of meeting her eye, yet she could not stop looking at her.

Soon Miss Varley stepped forward and began to speak. Her clipped, energetic way of talking, her Lancashire accent and simple, determined energy, held Rose spell-bound. A tingle went up her spine.

'The National Federation of Women Workers is *your* trade union!' she said. 'It is run by women, for women. For *you*.' She looked across the modest group of women who were gazing wonderingly up at her.

'I was invited to come to Bournville by Mr Edward Cadbury, to set up a union among the workers in his factory. Mr Cadbury has expressed his *disgust* with the condition of sweated labourers – the women who toil on starvation wages, the seamstresses and lace makers, the box makers and jute workers – and those of you here in Cradley Heath who make chains as outworkers. All of these workers – *these women workers* – are the worst paid in the whole of this country! You know the wages better than I – the starvation levels at which you are expected to work, at which you have no choice *but* to work long, gruelling hours!'

There was scattered, timid applause. Jane Chisholm clapped her hands and at the last minute, Rose joined in as well. She felt ashamed of her complacent thoughts earlier. Being glad for her pittance earned to make up Wally's, even though she worked fourteen hours on most days? Should she be content with this? Why was she not being paid properly for all her pains?

'When you are working in your forges, in your back-yards, you may feel alone and powerless to act against the indignities of your situation. But know this – you are not alone, nor need you be from now on! The union is here to represent you in your struggle, against the daily oppression and injustice of starvation wages on which you can't even meet your families' most basic needs. Do not be deceived! Such conditions are not ordained by

Almighty God – they are arranged by the avarice of less than mighty Man!'

More applause followed this. Rose hung on her every word. There had been a strike of jute workers in Dundee – they had not yet won the day because they needed more unity among them as union members . . .

'Join the union and you are part of something bigger than your own hearth and yard, bigger than your street, your neighbourhood! You are part of a movement – a movement of women fighting for justice and for a fair wage to feed our families. And together, we *will* win!'

Rose listened to all of the speech, growing more and more inspired, but, even so, time was pressing on her and she did not join up there and then, despite Jane Chisholm urging her.

'I will . . . I expect,' Rose said, feeling like a coward. She picked up her basket and hurried away. 'Very nice to meet yer . . . I must get back to work . . .'

Out in the ordinary day again, hurrying along the street, she felt as if she had woken from a troubling but wonderful dream. She must join the union – mustn't she? Why had she run off – and why did she suddenly feel so afraid of the idea?

Hurrying now, to get home, her thoughts were interrupted by two familiar figures standing across the street outside the Bee Hive pub. She narrowed her eyes. Two people who did not normally belong together. Seth Dawson, in conversation with Edna's son, Sidney Wilmott.

Don't let him see me was Rose's first thought, turning her head away to slink past Seth Dawson. And then, with a flame still lit from Julia Varley's speeches, her spirit rebelled.

Why the hell shouldn't I be seen going out to buy food for my family – food bought with his slave wages? He doesn't own me! But she had to fight the feeling. All of them felt owned by the foggers – life if not soul.

She straightened her back, looked ahead and marched on past towards the Hay Lane yard, but it was still with a prickling at her back, as if Seth Dawson might be spying on her.

Going along the entry, knowing that Bertha, Edna and the others were all in the forge, she cursed herself. What would Julia Varley say about such cowardice? First of all, not having the guts to join a union in all this time and then slinking past that fogger as if she'd done something wrong. Julia Varley, who that Jane Chisholm woman had gone on to tell her had been a sweeper in a mill, an organizer on committees at a very young age. She wanted working women themselves to fight this battle, not just have do-gooders stepping in to do it over their heads.

Discontented and impatient with herself, she went into her house to put her shopping away. But she found herself standing by the range, breathing hard, not getting anything done.

She *had* to do it – to say something. No one else would, and if she could not even begin by talking to the women in her own yard – well, how were any of them ever going to get anywhere?

Twenty-Four

Bertha felt thick in the head that morning, a pain drumming at her temples. The August heat of the forge was too much for her. Her body felt dragged down, as if something was pulling on her innards as she stood shaping and hammering the chain links. She pressed a secret hand up between her legs.

Shrieks from the children in the yard raked through her head, corns burned on her feet and she was full of a terrible stifling feeling, as if she might be about to burst out of her own skin.

Pausing for a second, she wiped sweat from her forehead with her arm which felt gritty and she knew she was trailing muck across her forehead.

'What's ailing yow, Bertha?' Edna said. 'Yower quiet this morning.'

'Oh, I dunno.' Bertha picked her hammer up again. 'Just one of them days, I s'pose.'

'Yow 'ad a drop too much again, I s'pect,' Edna said complacently, hammering away.

The words, coming from Edna, were not loaded in any way, but they stung Bertha to the quick.

'What d'yow mean?' she snapped. 'I don't like what yower saying to me, Edna, poking yower nose in where it ain't wanted.'

Edna gave her one of her mild looks.

'Well, yow seem to be knocking it back a bit these days, is all I meant.'

Bertha could sense Lucy and Mari keeping their heads down while they listened to this and fury almost choked her – at least that uppity Rose Shaw wasn't around! She wrestled away the desire to erupt with fury and struggled to make light of it.

'It's nobbut age,' she said. 'Comes to us all in the end.'

Edna, who was a good ten years older than Bertha, gave a chuckle.

'Yow've gorra way to go yet, bab! I dunno what yower werriting about.'

It relieved the tension. The others smiled as well.

Bertha went back to her work but the desire, sharp and immediate, for a drink, forced its way through her. It wasn't true that she was 'knocking it back' – was it? But my God, it was a comfort, since Jonno had gone. For a good few months she had had no need to go sneaking down the Outdoor to get herself a tipple, because she had built up such a stash of her home-made brews – elderberry, pea-pod, rosehip, and even damson wine from one summer glut of tiny wild fruits. She had had energy for that sort of thing back then. Those bottles, stashed in the pantry and the bottom of the cupboard, had not gone bad. They had matured into dark red and amber liquids, pungent and comforting. It was only lately, every last drop gone, that she had had to go out and buy stuff. The longing swept through her now.

A moment later, *that one* came sweeping in. She always thought of Rose Shaw now as *that one*, the uppity bit. Bertha didn't turn around, determinedly ignoring her, because Rose was talking almost before she got through the door.

'I've just seen the most marvellous thing . . . at the church hall!'

Out of the corner of her eye, Bertha could see Lucy

turning to listen. She wanted to tell the girl to get back to work, but Lucy managed to keep hammering away while obviously paying Rose attention.

'What's that then?' Mari Gornall said, as if hoping for gossip.

'This woman. 'Er name's Julia Varley . . . 'er used to be a mill girl . . .' Rose sounded uncertain, even Bertha could hear that – almost as if she was having to force the words out. Maybe she wasn't quite as cocksure as she seemed! 'And she's trying to get women to join the union. The union for *women*.'

Oh, here we go, Bertha thought, anger curdling in her belly – and something else, a kind of dread. That little madam was off on this again. She thought she'd managed to shut her up after she first arrived, coming here making trouble. Rose had seemed to quieten down for a bit and get on with her work and raising her kids – things a woman was *supposed* to do.

They hadn't had any of this union talk over the last few months. But something had obviously set her off again. Bertha felt as if her head would explode if she had to cope with anything else. Well, she'd soon show that one what was what.

Bertha kept on working, trying to pretend she was not listening to a word Rose was saying. She didn't want to give the little upstart any encouragement. She had seen some of these union types come sniffing round, thinking they could tell you what to do. Where were they going to be when all of them lost their jobs through joining a union? The foggers would soon get shot of anyone trying that caper and all their families would go hungry – or even hungrier, she should say. Seething at Rose's stupidity she hammered a link so hard that she hit her own finger into the bargain and gasped with pain.

'Miss Varley said that every woman ought to join – that's the only way we're ever going to get anything changed!'

She was getting warmed up now, on her soapbox good and proper! When she was in a bad mood, Bertha found everything about Rose aggravating. She was a good worker, it was true, and fast with it. But she thought too much of herself. These modern ideas would only bring trouble and there were things about the girl that grated against everything Bertha believed in.

For a start, how long was it the woman had gone now without producing another child – what was going on there? Was she the sort to deny her own husband so that she could live in her own selfish way – and get all caught up with these modern ideas that would just bring trouble down on all of them?

Hearing Rose talking on and on, seeming to gain courage and momentum as she did so, Bertha found that she was actually starting to shake with anger.

Steady, she said to herself. Her heart was going like a piston.

'I saw her in the Sunday school hall – where you used to go,' Rose was saying.

Bertha glanced over to see that she had moved closer to Lucy and was speaking more to her than anyone else. Lucy had stopped work now and was looking up at Rose with shining eyes.

'Next time there's a meeting, you could come with me. What Miss Varley were talking about was getting the law changed so that all of us who work for a pittance would get a minimum wage! Just think how much better that'd be!'

'It would,' Lucy agreed. 'Wouldn't it, Auntie?' she

said, turning to Bertha, trying to draw her on to their side.

'Huh,' Bertha muttered, pressing her lips together. The blood was banging in her ears and she closed her eyes. Was she having some sort of turn?

'But if we want that we all have to get involved,' Rose went on passionately. 'If we don't all join the union – the National Federation of Women Workers, it's called – nothing will ever be done! We'll be cowed by the foggers and things will go on just as they always have – with us as slaves, sweating for thugs like Dawson!'

'Well, that's a true word,' Mari Gornall said, though she didn't sound certain about it all.

'You can try it,' Edna chipped in. 'But they allus win in the end. They don't care about us! They ay gunna hand out another farthing unless they'm forced to. But who's gunna be able to force 'em? Feathering their own nests – that's all they're interested in.'

'Mrs Hipkiss?' Suddenly Rose was addressing her. 'You've always been the voice of this yard – of all the women 'ere. Why don't *you* lead the way – join the union? People would listen to you – they respect you.'

That was the limit. Bertha's blood boiled. She flung down her hammer and went across to Rose Shaw, looming over her with her hands on her hips, eyes aflame.

'Respect me, do they? Well, I'll tell yow summat – they may respect me but they ay gunna respect me if I go about touting that union talk. You go . . .' She pointed, as if shooing Rose out of the door. 'Join the cowing union and see what 'appens. It's all right, you with a mon bringing in a wage, but some of us 'ave ter shift on our own with mouths to feed – and we'll be left with no wage at all!'

She looked round the forge. Lucy was staring at her, her sweet face looking stricken at what had developed.

Mari was lapping it up as the latest entertainment and Edna stood with her weight on one leg, a hand to her waist, with no sign of any emotion on her face.

'I'll tell you summat.' Bertha moved her face even closer to Rose's and to her satisfaction she saw the young woman shrink back. 'There'll be no union in this yard – not while I'm 'ere and I 'ave breath in my body. So yow can shut yer trap and stop spreading this talk about what'll only cause us all grief.'

Rose's cheeks flushed. She may have sounded uncertain at first, but she was a fighter, and now she pulled herself upright and stared back brazenly at Bertha.

'You may want our respect,' she said, her voice tight with emotion. 'And I do my best to give it yer. But yower living in the past – and trying to keep everyone else there with yer!' She looked round at the other women. 'Someone's got to make a stand – to start somewhere. And yes – I'm with a mon who earns better'un I do. But *why* does he? Most days I work more hours than he does – and keep a house and kids. Why's 'is work worth more than mine – that's what I want to know!'

'Because he's a mon!' Bertha roared at her, feeling as if her head might be about to fly off. 'They'm stronger and they're the head of their families – that's just how it is.'

'But look at the pittance we're paid!' Rose came back at her. 'How can that be right? You've been keeping a family with no mon to 'elp yer and you should've had a better wage!' She stopped for a second to draw breath.

'And maybe, since I'm the one has a mon earning, I can take the risk. Because, Mrs Hipkiss –' her words slowed into caution – 'someone's got to lead the way. And I ay 'aving you telling me whether or not I can join a union – I'll make my own decisions, ta very much.'

The slap rang round the workshop. Bertha hardly

knew she was going to do it, until her palm was stinging and Rose, startled and in pain, was reeling back, her own hand to her cheek. Lucy gasped. A stunned silence followed.

Rose straightened up, still holding her face. Her eyes bored into Bertha's; she refused to be cowed by the older woman.

'I see,' she said. Her voice was quiet, but they could all hear the force of disgust in her words. 'That's how it is, is it? That's how you go on as gaffer of this yard. Well, I'd rather throw my lot in with someone I can respect. I'll be seeing Julia Varley, soon as 'er's speaking to us in Cradley Heath again – and anyone who wants can come with me.'

She headed for her hearth and pressed vigorously on the bellows to raise the fire again.

'I'm not going to be frightened out of my rights by that fogger – or anyone else,' she announced, before reaching for her first rod and thrusting it in the fire as if it was Seth Dawson's head.

Bertha stood in the middle of the forge, still breathing hard, hardly able to contain her feelings.

'Oh – and by the way,' Rose said, looking across at Edna, 'I saw your Sidney with Dawson – outside the pub, thick as thieves. Thought you'd want to know.'

Bertha marched across the yard, weaving between the bits of washing hanging limply on the lines. In the house she went straight to the cupboard where she kept the latest open bottle – the cheapest of whisky, rank and pungent. Hands shaking, she poured a tot into a cup and sank on to Jonno's old chair, taking a big gulp. The liquid burned down into her stomach and a shudder went through her.

Tears came then, making runnels through the dust on

her cheeks, tears of rage, of bewilderment. All these years she had been the strong one – borne everything on her capable shoulders, hammered and pulled at the bellows, borne and nursed her children, her invalid husband, taken everything that was thrown at her – and others had always come to her for her strength and know-how, her advice. But now, all the things she had lived for seemed to be slipping away.

'Oh Jonno,' she sobbed, cradling the cup in her hands. 'I dow know what's up with me. I wish yow was 'ere – God I do, my love – I need yow 'ere with me. Everything's changing and I dow know what to do – about any of it.'

Twenty-Five

'All right, Luce?' Clem came breezing into the house the next evening. As he passed behind her, where she was sitting at the table, he touched her on the shoulder, let his hand linger there for a moment. She sat quite still. That second's touch, so careless by him – wasn't it? – did make her at least feel that he saw her, counted her as a person. And it made the blood rush round her body.

'Yes, ta.' She looked up, startled. Since her walk with John, she had noticed, Clem suddenly seemed to be taking notice of her.

Clem halted, as if stopped in his tracks, and smiled down at her. Her own lips curved upwards in response.

'D'you know, Luce – that smile of yours looks prettier every day.'

He glanced across the table to where John was sitting, as if to make sure he had heard, then back at Lucy.

'Oh, don't be saft.' She looked down, her cheeks pulsing with heat.

If Bertha had been in there she would have said, 'Listen to 'im, all flannel!' But she was in the forge and there was no one else to break the mood.

''Ere –' Clem perched beside her at the table – 'look what I found.' He put his hand in his pocket and opened his palm. Resting on his grubby skin, she saw something pink, flecked with grime but with a warm glister to it.

'D'yer want it? Found it on my way 'ome – just lying there in the muck.'

196

Lucy reached for the oval stone that lay in his hand and rubbed it on her skirt until it shone. It was a lovely colour, a soft pink with thin veins in paler pink snaking across it.

'It's lovely,' she said, tingling with pleasure just at the sight of the colour and even more that Clem was sitting beside her. 'But someone must've lost it – it looks like summat out of a brooch.' She looked up into Clem's lively eyes – but in that second became aware of John, at the other side of the table, watching them intently. 'D'yer think we should tell someone? I dunno who . . .'

'Nah,' Clem said, standing up again. 'You keep it, Luce. It's nothing all that precious, not like rubies or summat.'

'But that's dishonest,' John said.

Lucy felt a tightening in her belly. Whenever the two brothers were in the same room now there was a tension between them.

'Well,' Clem said carelessly, 'do as yer like, Luce – but I brung it back specially for yer.'

She tightened her own fingers round it. Clem, bringing it for her? She could never, ever, give it away, even if John did not think it was right.

'What's to eat?' Clem lifted the lid of the pot which was simmering on the stove. He lowered his nose to it for a second. 'Umm. I'm clammed.'

He disappeared into the scullery.

Lucy slipped her hand with the rosy stone clutched tightly in it under the table and into her pocket. She could feel John watching, and their eyes met for a second until he looked down, blushing.

John kept trying, in his quiet, restrained way, to show Lucy he was sweet on her. She was surprised, after the way she had lost her temper with him. But John had started being very attentive, helping her if he saw she needed it, asking her to go out with him for little walks. Nothing more, except that almost whenever she looked up when they were together in the room, she saw John's eyes fixed on her.

And it was gratifying, having someone care about her and pay her attention. John had always been good to her. She hardly asked herself whether she was sweet on him in return. It was surprising enough that anyone seemed interested in her. Although – and she felt unkind thinking it – she did wonder whether John's conversation would ever become a bit more interesting. His life revolved round his job at the hardware shop and the church. He was a good man, she knew, but somehow, whenever Clem came in and told them stories about things that had happened in the works, he made them all laugh and lit up the room.

'What's up with yow?' Clem called through from the scullery. She heard him pouring from the bucket of water into the stone sink. 'You're looking down in the mouth.'

'Who?' Lucy said. 'Me?'

'Yeah – you!' He poked his head out and grinned at her, so handsome that her heart fluttered. Having Clem fix on her was dazzling. 'T'ain't like you, Luce!'

'There was a bit of a scrap today. Yower mom and Rose. She hit her round the face.'

She had been upset by what happened between Bertha and Rose, because she could see Bertha was riled up, even if she did not really understand why. Any catfights did not usually involve Bertha – it was more Mari Gornall's sort of thing to be slapping and hair-pulling.

'What – Rose?' Clem gaped. 'Lamped our mom?

'No, the other way round.'

198

'You never said.' John sounded annoyed. 'What were all that about then?'

'Rose reckons us outworkers should be in the union . . .'

'What union?' Clem came out, rubbing his hands on a rag.

'The NFWW.' She straightened her spine.

'The what?'

She had the attention of both brothers now, as if she was a parrot who had suddenly started reciting Shakespeare.

'National Federation of Women Workers. It's a women's union.' She sat up even taller, feeling important in knowing this information. And Rose had been so lit up when she came in – Lucy was fascinated. 'They want to get a minimum wage, she says – Rose Shaw, I mean.'

'Blimey!' Clem burst out laughing. 'No wonder Mom lamped 'er one! 'Er's got no time for all that kind of talk. Going against the blokes and that – and if that wench is trying to get above her in the yard . . .! Our mom's the gaffer up this end and 'er won't 'ear otherwise.'

'But why shouldn't we get a minimum wage?' Lucy ventured. A cold feeling started to seep through her. She had thought for a little while that she and the boys were together, that they would see her point of view. But she could feel all that slipping away.

'It ay right, women carrying on like that,' John said, he and Clem allies again in their male certainty. 'T'ain't womanly. What next? They'll be going on strike – like them dockers, down London!'

Both brothers chortled at the thought of this. Lucy looked up at them, her cheeks burning. She was furious with herself that she had said anything, imagining they might agree with her.

But what Rose had said – and the look of her! She was so pretty and clever and she brought in fresh ideas, a new feeling of energy as if the world around them got a little bit bigger when she was about. And now John and Clem were both trampling all over any feelings she might have about it – she was just a stupid girl again, a cripple of no account.

You wait and see, she thought, looking up mutinously at them both. Things will change – I bet they will.

'We all have to accept the station in life that the Lord has given us,' John said gently. 'You know that, don't you, Lucy? We have to count our blessings and gather the harvest as best we can, not go stirring up discord.'

She looked back at him, horrified to discover in herself the desire to slap his face just as Bertha had done to Rose. Talking to her like that as if she was a halfwit! But her rage sputtered and died and she looked down again, deflated. Of course John was right. If anyone knew about accepting their station in life and not expecting more, it was her. For a second an agonizing image came to her of George. Little George, the last time she had seen him, and it brought her almost to tears. What power did she have – over anything?

Clem had gone to stand at the door. 'All right, Vic?' she heard him say to Victor Gornall. And then, 'Ay up – look who's 'ere! Brought a dobbin along for a change, 'ave yow!"

Lucy pricked up her ears. They'd brought a dobbin along to pick up the chain, so this time it would mean the women weren't going to have to drag it back to the works themselves. Some other factories had stopped expecting that now – Ridley's had taken their time.

'Oh – and look who's following 'im like a little whammel! Sidney Wilmott! Evenin', Mr Dawson,' Clem called with sarcastic charm. ''Ow're yer keeping? And you, Sid – gorra job at last, 'ave yer?' Over his shoulder he muttered, 'God, look at 'im. Looks like he's the dobbin for you wenches, Luce.'

Lucy went to the door. Sure enough, Seth Dawson and Sidney Wilmott were pushing one of the long, narrow carts, or dobbins, across the yard. They heard a grunting reply from Seth and something no more intelligible from Sidney, since that was his normal manner of communicating.

'About time,' she said, going to sit down again.

She felt a sudden, warm pressure on her hand, which was resting on the table. John had leaned across and put his hand over hers, and now their eyes met.

'Don't be cross, Luce.'

It was as if he was trying to reel her back towards him, away from the attention she was paying to Clem.

'I'm not.' But she pulled her hand away and, getting stiffly to her feet, went to the range to stir the pot.

'I'll go and see if Auntie wants me to put the spuds on,' she said, knowing without asking that that was what was needed, but wanting to get away – from both of them, damn them.

But she stalled in the middle of the yard: in front of her, blocking the door to the forge, were the two men she hated more than anyone in this world. Seth Dawson and Sidney Wilmott were loading chain noisily on to the dobbin. Rage rose in her. Sidney was the one who had led her brother Albert astray. As for Seth Dawson, if it were not for him she would still have a mother, her brothers . . .

But she pulled herself upright, steely, hatred like acid in her veins. She wasn't going to be cowed by these vile beasts. Slipping her hand into her pocket, she stroked the smooth stone Clem had given her, for courage. If she called Bertha out of the forge, she could give her an excuse to escape Seth Dawson as well.

''Scuse me.'

'Ooh – look 'oo's 'ere!' Seth said, dumping another length of chain with a clatter. 'Little 'Op-along!'

Sidney sniggered as if Seth had just told the funniest joke in the world. Neither of them moved either the cart or themselves out of the way. Lucy, even knowing that Bertha, Edna and Mari were close by in the forge, felt her courage seeping away. She would have done better after all to stay in the house.

A leer spread across Seth's fleshy features.

'This'un's coming on, yer know, Sid,' he said. ''Er may 'ave a leg missing but 'er's still a bit of all right.' He lunged forward suddenly, seizing hold of Lucy's right breast and squeezing so hard that she yelped. Rage and disgust lit in her and she stepped back, almost stumbling over. Her humiliation made her even more angry.

'Let me in!' she demanded. 'I need to speak to Mrs Hipkiss.'

'Ooh,' Seth mocked her, while Sidney sniggered like a fat, stupid five-year-old. 'You're a fierce little tiger, ain't yer? Mrs 'Ipkiss, eh? What're yer gunna give me, to let yer past?

Lucy stared at him, all her loathing showing on her face. *You killed my mother*, she wanted to scream in his face. *You with your evil, filthy, bullying ways!*

In that second it came to her fully, like a shaft of light breaking into her mind, that Rose was right. Of course they had to defeat these people! They were evil and wicked and everything about the way they worked was evil and wicked too, and Rose was the only one who would stand up and say so. Just as she was thinking this, feeling her spine straighten, rigid with rage and determination, a voice rang out behind her.

'Let her past!' Rose Shaw came striding out of her house. 'Move that thing out the road and let the wench in like you've been asked!'

Seth made his foolish noise again, mocking her. 'Oh – is that what 'er wants? Can't mek out what you yowm-yowms are on about half the time.'

'Let 'er in.' Another voice spoke quietly.

Lucy turned, startled, to see the tall figure of Wally Shaw behind them. He came no closer, but his tone was steely and forbidding. Then Lucy saw Victor Gornall come out of his house and stand just behind Wally.

'Both of yer – clear out the way. Now.'

Faced with two men fitter and wirier than themselves, Seth and Sidney shoved the dobbin along and stood aside, casually, as if they had been about to do just that in any case.

'There yer go, wenches,' Seth said with mock chivalry.

Lucy went inside and told Bertha she was wanted in the house, since that would get her away from the fogger and his mate. She was delivering her message when she heard Wally and Victor, by the door.

'Yow need to watch it,' Wally Shaw said. 'Any more nonsense around our women and yow might find yowerself not feeling so well as yer do today.'

Victor, not to be left out, added, 'Yow lay a hand on my wife and I'll 'ave yow – gorrit?'

Mari was standing by her hearth. Lucy saw an expression of amazed pleasure spread across her face at her husband's sudden defence of her. She suddenly looked as happy as a young bride.

'Oh, get out of it,' Seth said, not wanting to show he was cowed by the two of them. 'You wanna watch it – wouldn't want yer wenches out of work now, would yer? C'mon, Sid.'

The two of them pushed the dobbin away along the entry with a great rumble of wheels.

'Brummy bastard,' Wally said, spitting on the ground.

Rose looked in disgust at Edna, who had hurriedly turned back to her hearth, hiding her face.

'Yow want to get that lummux of a son of yours under control.'

Twenty-Six

'Hey – Luce?'

Lucy jumped, startled. She was standing at the table, washing up the tea things, humming to herself. The door was open, letting in the warm air of that September evening. Once the meal was finished John had gone to the church for one of his meetings and Freddie rushed out to meet a pal of his.

'Come out with us, eh?'

Clem was standing the other side of the table, hands thrust in his pockets, those lively, teasing eyes fixed on her. Just for once, he was the one left in for the evening.

'What – me?'

Clem laughed. 'Ain't no one else in the room!'

Bertha cleared her throat loudly. She turned and was frowning at Clem as if wondering what he was up to. Lucy was wondering much the same.

'Well, 'cept *you*, Mom, I know.' Clem kept his voice teasing. 'Come on, you dow wanna be stuck in – it's a nice evening.'

It was lovely, the summer waning and a warm, mellow light outside.

'What about . . .?' She struggled to remember the name of Clem's latest girlfriend.

'Ann? Nah – we ay walking out no more.'

'All right.' Lucy left the plates draining on the table and dried her hands on a rag. She was not sure how to feel. Was Clem playing with her because he had nothing better to do? The thought made her feel prickly, almost angry. Taking pity on the poor little cripple. And she suddenly felt very self-conscious because she had on her old work frock with its rents and holes stitched and re-stitched and just for once, in this moment, she felt not just an everyday chain outworker but a girl, doing something she never did – walking out with a boy. (Somehow John did not count.)

She longed to be able to dress up and go about looking nice. Should she go up and put on her Sunday frock? That was ancient enough, but it was in a soft blue instead of the dull brown she wore day in, day out and it was in better repair. But Clem seemed in a hurry to go.

'Come on.' He ushered her out of the door, striding ahead of her across the yard until he remembered who he was with and came back to her. 'Sorry.' He grinned. 'Forgot.'

He said it so nicely she could not be offended.

'Where d'you want to go?' she said uncertainly.

'Just along the lane – see the sun go down.'

Of course, she thought. Disappointment seeped through her. Just along Hay Lane. She told herself Clem was being considerate, thinking of her difficulty walking, but what she really felt was that he would not want to be seen with her about town – Clem with the cripple girl who limped along with a stick. That was not Clem's style – he went for the prettiest girls who danced and were full of fun. Tonight, she must remember, he was just filling in time . . .

They went out of the entry and along Hay Lane, Lucy trying to walk as straight and fast as she possibly could so as not to show Clem up. If only she could be normal, skip along like anyone else, just for a while!

At the end of the road, past Mr Clark's workshop,

they slipped through the gap next to the railway embankment and into the field. As they did so, Clem suddenly reached for her hand and took it in his big, strong paw, as she always thought of it.

'Watch yower step,' he said.

As if she wouldn't, she thought, smiling to herself. As if she didn't spend her whole life watching her step.

They walked a little way along the scrubby, cindery path that followed the bottom edge of the railway embankment. The sun was low in the sky and there was a smell of smoke – country smoke, not just the ever-present chimney and factory smoke. A plume of it, tinged with blue, rose in the far distance across the field.

'That's nice,' she said. 'Smells of the autumn.'

'Ar, it does,' Clem said, stopping. 'Nice, that. Shall us sit for a bit? Watch the sun go down?'

She thought he was being kind, giving her a rest from walking, and she was glad of it. Clem spread his jacket on the ground and helped her get down there, awkward as ever. She sat with her legs straight in front of her. Clem came down in a second and suddenly they were shoulder to shoulder, looking across the gentle slope of the golden field.

The lowering sun gave each blade of golden stubble a sharp shadow and lit the top of the chimney and winding gear of the pit. They could hear distant sounds: a voice, a rumbling sound from one of the yards behind them, of someone pushing a barrow. A bird sang in a tree to their left. Clem sat with his knees drawn up, arms resting on them in a relaxed way. Lucy felt the sun warm her face. She made sure her skirt was pulled well down, spread neatly along her legs.

'You always do that.' Clem turned to look at her.

'So would you.'

'What – if I wore a frock!'

His face crinkled up and they both laughed.

'You know what I mean.'

'You do well with it, Luce. It's only when you say that I remember yower leg.'

She doubted this somehow, but it was kindly meant and she nodded. Clem was still looking intently into her face and she found it all a bit overwhelming. The last person to look at her like that – really take her in – had been Miss Jones. She found herself blushing and staring at the ground in front of her, overcome once more by a defensive, prickly feeling. Was Clem playing with her?

Daring to look up again, in the silence, she found he was still gazing at her.

'Luce?' He smiled, a lovely, tender smile. 'You're so pretty, d'yow know that?'

She was burning now – at the compliment, at how she felt, which was uncertain and longing – but not trusting him. That was something she could not let herself fall into. She had seen Clem come and go with so many girls!

He leaned towards her and placed his two fingers under her chin, gently urging her to look up at him. Their eyes met and she saw Clem's face moving closer to hers. It seemed to take an age, as if in a dream where time has stretched in the odd way that dreams have. The strange trance continued and his lips met hers, little light kisses at first, then full on the lips, softly, tenderly . . . He drew back and was looking at her again so that she almost wondered if it had happened.

'D'yow know – you're the nicest girl I know,' he said.

'Well . . .' She smiled, keeping things a joke, though her heart was pounding and her mind whirling. Was this really happening? A kiss – Clem, kissing her! 'Yower the nicest boy I know.'

'Nicer than John? You know 'e's sweet on yer?'

Lucy frowned, mistrust seizing her again. She moved her head back. Was this what was going on – was it some kind of game between them and she was just a plaything for their amusement? A flush of anger went through her.

'If you know 'e's sweet on me, what're you playing at then?' she demanded. 'Are you just messing with me?'

'No!' Clem said. 'I'm not, Luce. I were just asking, that's all. I mean, John – well, 'e's my brother. But 'e's a bit . . . I dunno, lately – all that religion and that . . .'

She knew what he meant and it was true, but she was annoyed enough to say, 'John's always been good to me. 'E's kind. And he wouldn't muck me about.' She felt so stupid now. Why would handsome Clem Hipkiss, the lad all the girls wanted to be seen with, ever want to be with her, really and truly? He was just trying to get one up on his brother.

'Look, Clem . . .' She went to get up, inwardly cursing that she could not do it easily and with grace. Lurching to her feet, she had to accept the hand he held out to help her. As soon as she was upright she pulled away, hurt and angry with him. 'I know I'm in debt to your family.' It was hard to speak. There was an ache in her throat. 'Your mom took me in when I had no one. Even my brothers were taken from me – and I'm grateful and always will be. And I know I'll always be the girl who everyone looks down on and feels sorry for – "Oh, poor little Lucy – no one's ever going to want her, not with that peg-leg . . ."'

All her bitterness came flooding out, so much so that Clem looked startled.

'I don't look for much – I know not to. No man wants a woman like me on his arm and I ain't expecting it . . .'

'But Luce . . .' He tried to interrupt.

'No – don't give me any more of your flannel. I know you, Clem – I ought to by now. It's one girl one week and another the next. I know I'm nothing to you, 'cept like a kind of sister. So let's just . . . oh, I dunno . . .' She ran out of steam suddenly, looking away, embarrassed at all that had come flooding out of her mouth.

There was silence for a second. She could feel Clem staring at her.

'I never knew that's how you felt,' he said.

'Well – what did you expect?' she flared again.

'I never thought of you like that – honest.' He dared to step closer. 'Not just as a cripple. You're nice, you are – and you're pretty. A real looker.' He touched her arm for a moment. 'I never meant anything bad – not by coming out with yer.'

She nodded, unable to speak because she was so close to tears. Clem seemed to have no idea what it meant to be her: to be alone in the world, an imperfect, flawed person who nobody wanted. He had no idea about anything, had not meant anything – good or bad – and that was what made it worse. He was just passing the time.

'All right,' she said, managing to keep her voice under control. 'Let's go back now, eh?'

Twenty-Seven

They walked back along Hay Lane, changing the subject, talking about light-hearted things. But Lucy could see that what she'd said had affected Clem. He seemed quiet, awkward. Just as they got to the entry, he said,

'Hang on a tick, wait 'ere – or goo on in if yer want . . . I'm gunna get summat – for us . . .'

'What?' She laughed with surprise, touched that he seemed to want to make it up to her.

'Mrs Simms – 'er'll open up – 'er likes me! What's yower favourite? I know – wine gums!'

He took off along the street almost at a sprint and Lucy was left standing by the entry. She couldn't help laughing. Saft lad, running off on a whim to charm Mrs Simms into opening up shop for him, just so he could buy her a penn'orth of sweets! In that moment she had already almost forgiven him.

She was reluctant just to go back to the house and liked the idea of waiting for Clem. Leaning against the wall, she looked back down Hay Lane. The sun had nearly set and the east-facing lane was sunk almost in darkness.

She rested her head back and let herself slip deep into her thoughts, still feeling the press of Clem's lips on hers. Thinking of it now, her body throbbed with longing. Clem had kissed her! Actually kissed her – and all she had done was to push him away! Why had she been so sharp with him? But her doubts came back. She knew Clem – he flitted from girl to girl like a butterfly amid the flowers . . .

211

Someone grabbed her arm and yanked on it so violently that she almost fell over, stumbling on her bad leg which jerked at an angle so that she was forced to hop as she was dragged into the mouth of the entry.

'I've bin waiting for a chance to catch you on yer own, missy.'

Seth Dawson's weight shoved her hard up against the soot-encrusted wall, knocking the wind out of her. All she could do was let out a whimper.

'Yer can stop that racket,' Seth ordered. He clamped a hand over her mouth and pressed his body hard against her, forcing her against the wall. 'Turning into a right nice little bit you are – with more flesh on yer than that mother of yours 'ad.'

She turned her head to try and escape his putrid breath. His fingers were bruising her face and at any sound she made, he pressed even harder. *For God's sake, someone, come! Clem, get back here*, she was praying. Let him come around the corner now and rescue her . . . To her horror, Seth Dawson's other hand was already pawing at her breasts, hurting her. He began to yank up her skirt, in a huge hurry.

'Come on, wench – let's be 'aving yer . . .'

'Get off me!' she tried to say, but all was stifled under his hand.

'Yer can cut that out!' he ordered, rummaging in his clothing with his other hand. 'Shurrit and get yer legs apart, yer mardy little bitch . . .'

To her disgust and horror, she could feel Seth Dawson's hard prick jabbing against her. She moved her body this way and that, frantically trying to escape him. He was having trouble trying to adjust himself and both their clothing with just one hand and he took his other one from over her mouth.

'One word and I'll ring yer cowing neck, gorrit?'

As he grunted, pulling her skirt up, she did the only thing she could think of, which was to jab her finger as hard as possible into his eye.

'Aaagh!' He jerked back immediately, bent double with his hands over his face. 'You bitch! You evil little bitch!'

'What in hell's name's going on?' Clem appeared at the end of the dark entry. He paused for a second, then yelled at the top of his voice. 'What're yow doing, yow filthy bastard!'

He pushed past the cursing Seth Dawson to get to Lucy. Seth lumbered away and disappeared into the street, one hand still over his eye.

'You'll pay for this!' he shouted back down the entry. 'You evil cow!'

'Luce?' She could hear the rage in Clem's voice. 'What's 'e done? Come on – let's get you into the house.'

Shaking all over, Lucy adjusted her leg back into place. Her chest heaved and she could not help sobs of shock and terror breaking from her. When she straightened up, Clem took her arm.

'What's happened?' Bertha could see from the state of her and a moment later, Mari Gornall put her head round the door.

'What's all the shouting about?'

Lucy was not sure she wanted everyone in the yard to know of her vile experience but there was no stopping it.

'That bastard Dawson,' Clem burst out. 'Attacked 'er in the entry.'

Lucy saw Mari's mouth form an O.

'We ought to report 'im!' Clem said furiously. ''E'd get away with murder, that'un would!'

'Dow talk saft!' Bertha's expression was dark with rage.

Lucy had never seen her so worked up. 'We can look after our own without the Peelers interfering.' She came over to Lucy and guided her to the nearest chair and Lucy could feel a tremor in her hand, though nothing like as bad as the way Lucy was trembling herself now. Bertha bent over her. 'Well, out with it – what went on, wench?'

'Poor thing,' Mari said. 'Look at 'er.'

Lucy could tell from her tone that she was enjoying the gossip – but all the same, they all knew no one was safe with Seth Dawson roaming about.

'I never heard him coming,' she said, looking up at Bertha.

'So what happened – did 'e . . .' She trailed off in embarrassment. "Ow far did it go?'

Lucy lowered her head, shame washing through her as she thought of the vile pig Seth Dawson pawing at her skirt, the way he was thrusting at her, the stink of him . . .

'I stopped him.'

'How d'yow do that?' Mari asked, all agog.

When Lucy explained, Mari cackled with laughter.

'Well – I never've thought yow'd 'ave it in yer, Luce – you sorted 'im out good and proper!'

'But what's to do about 'im?' Clem asked, furious still. 'I wanna go and punch 'is lights out!'

'We do what we always do,' Bertha said. She spoke in a low, steely tone and her expression was hard and bitter. 'Nowt. It'd only come back on us if we start on anything. There's no harm done this time, thank the Lord – but by God, yow wenches need to be careful to keep out of that'un's way.'

By bedtime everyone knew what had happened to Lucy. A huddle of them stood in the yard after the lamplighter had been round. Rose listened, feeling more and more explosive with anger and frustration.

'If I could just get my 'ands on 'im!' Victor Gornall said dramatically.

'You'd what?' Mari said, though her voice was not as mocking as it once would have been. She and Victor seemed gradually to be making it up. ''E's twice the weight of yow. There ay nothing any of us can do with 'im . . .'

'What I wanna know,' Bertha said furiously, 'is what that saft lad of Edna's is doing knocking about with the likes of Dawson. 'Er wants to get 'im away or there'll be trouble for 'im.'

'It's that fogger wants seeing to,' Rose said grimly. 'He's the one went for Lucy.'

''Er's all right,' Bertha said. 'A bit shook up but 'e dain't – you know . . .'

'Well, that don't make anything all right!' Rose erupted.

She felt her temper boiling over and she turned and went slamming into her house. Why were they all like sheep? Why couldn't anything ever be *done* about anything?

'For the love of God!' Rose was still fizzing with rage at bedtime. 'Is there no end to it? The way 'e carries on. Someone should string the bastard up by 'is danglers!'

She and Wally were getting ready for bed and Rose removed her outer clothing, hurling things down in rage and frustration.

'It ay my fault!' Wally protested.

'I never said it was yower cowing fault!' Rose said, yanking her hair out of its pins and brushing it almost as if she was beating a carpet. 'Ouch!' She stared at the hairbrush as if it too was guilty of a crime.

215

'Well, if you go at it like that, no wonder it 'urts,' Wally said. 'And I s'pose that's my fault an' all?'

'Of course it ay your fault!' She was shouting and had to lower her voice quickly for fear of waking the children. Ivy, especially, was a light sleeper. 'Why would it be yower fault, you aydedaydy?'

'That Seth Dawson's a bastard and there's no more to be said,' Wally stated, hoping to be helpful.

Rose stood in her vest and bloomers, hands on hips, glaring at him. 'Oh – yow've only just noticed, ave yow? And I'd say there's a *lot* more to be said!'

'No, but . . .'

'He ought to be in prison – that's where he belongs, being hanged by the neck. Think about it, Wally – if it were me, and not poor little Lucy 'e were trying to poke 'isself into – what would yow say then – eh?'

'I'd *kill* 'im,' Wally said. 'Least – I'd want to kill 'im, any road.' He took his shirt off and stood naked from the waist up, pale and long-limbed. He stared at Rose and she could see he was sizing her up to work out whether she was still in a temper. Standing there in her undergarments, with her hair lying on her shoulders, those curvy hips and her nipples showing through the thin cotton, she was a sight to behold and maybe – if he struck lucky . . .

'I'm going to that meeting tomorrow if it's the last thing I do,' she announced. 'If we can't get 'im one way we'll 'ave to get 'im another.'

'What meeting?' Wally felt his chances of a good time receding.

'The union. And I'm flaming joining even if none of this lot round 'ere know what's good for 'em. I know it's time out of work, but I can make it up later. And I tell yer what . . .' She marched round the bed towards him.

'What?' Wally said cautiously.

'I'm gunna take that wench with me – Lucy. There's life in that one if it were just allowed to show itself.'

Wally nodded. What a bostin woman she was, his Rosie – especially when she was riled up. He felt a familiar, overwhelming sense of awe – combined with bafflement – at the fact that Rose had agreed to be his wife, even though she said he was the best man she knew. He felt a prickle of fear. Rose came from a better family than him and he knew they had thought she'd married beneath her. Now, powerful and headstrong as she was, she seemed to be heading away from him, past him. He was afraid he would not be able to keep up with her, his little firecracker of a missus!

'Good idea,' he offered humbly.

Rose came up close and smiled at him suddenly, her strong-boned face lighting up in a way that made his heart lift and sing.

'Yower a good'un, d'yow know that, Wally Shaw?'

'No – I'm just your saft old man, me.'

Wally grinned, relieved, and put his arms round her. They cuddled each other, he loving the generous curves of her body, the smell of her hair, impregnated as ever with smoke and the metallic perfume of the forge. He kissed her neck, feeling her give to him, leaning into him.

'Come on, wench,' he murmured, instantly aroused.

'All right . . .' She yielded to him. 'But don't you dare go and get me up the stick . . . I've got too much to do to be carrying another babby at the moment!'

Twenty-Eight

Chink-chink, tap-tap . . .

All five women stood at their hearths that morning. The light was November dull, the cold of winter closing in and the air full of smoke.

Everyone was quiet, even Edna who for once was not singing or humming.

Lucy had long grown used to all the standing, most of her weight resting on her good leg, and she could work as fast as anyone now – except for Rose, who was always the fastest, seeming to have more energy than all the others put together.

'Right – time to go.' Rose suddenly downed tools and started to untie her apron.

'Where're you off to then?' Edna asked.

'There's a meeting – along at the school again. Miss Varley's speaking and some others – and I'm going to hear her.'

Lucy suddenly found herself fixed by Rose's energetic gaze.

'You come with me, Luce, eh? Miss Varley's ever so interesting and you'll learn a thing or two.'

'No!' Bertha rounded on her before Lucy had time to say a word. Bertha had her cap pulled down hard over her hair and she looked truly formidable. 'Oh no – don't you go starting that. 'Er's not going anywhere. Our Lucy's a good wench and I ain't 'aving anyone turning 'er into any sort of . . .'

'Sort of what, Mrs Hipkiss?' Rose was truly riled up now. 'Sort of person who tries to make things better for other people, 'stead of staying stuck in the rut we're all in? Where the likes of that bastard fogger can . . .' She held out her arm towards Lucy. There was no need to say any more.

'Well, I'm going whether you lot like it or not.' She turned towards the door. 'And, Luce – one day maybe you'll be able to mek up yower own mind about whether you can go out or not without being bossed from pillar to post. All I can say is –' she turned back, full of passion – 'if we get things better round 'ere for yer, just remember it's the union you'll 'ave to thank for it even if you can't be bothered with joining it!'

And off she went.

Lucy kept her head down, her heart banging. She knew the others were rolling their eyes at each other. She didn't like fights and she certainly wasn't going to go against Bertha who had been the next thing to a mom to her. But her mind followed Rose Shaw along the street to the meeting in the hall in Graingers Lane and she wished she could be going too.

The union was something she did not fully understand, even though people kept talking about it. And Bertha was so sure that nothing you did ever made any difference to anything. But Lucy couldn't help wondering if someone shouldn't *try*, instead of just complaining but not doing anything – and if so, who should that someone be? Rose was an exciting person who had brought a new, lively sense into the forge – a feeling that things might be changed for the better. And surely that had to be good?

Lucy hammered away, her hands doing the work automatically, her mind in a daydream.

Clem's kiss still seemed to hover about her lips. Over

and again she kept reliving their little walk, that whole, magical evening, up until the moment when he left her beside the entry and . . .

Her mind shut down then, each time. Everything became evil, terrifying. She had not seen much of Clem since then, except in passing at home. Though she clung to the kiss in her dreams, she knew really not to trust it. Clem was a nice lad but he was like a child, running after every impulse – and she was afraid that one of those impulses was also to get one over on John. The thought made her feel sad and used.

Then her thoughts would turn to John. Did he really love her? Or was that just pretend as well? And even if he did, the thought of spending all her time with John, however good a man he was and however much they went to church together, made her feel deflated and dis-appointed. And then she felt guilty for feeling that . . . Round and round it all turned in her mind . . .

Until Rose Shaw came rushing back into the forge again later, all lit up and seeming completely to have for-gotten about the quarrel and the reality of her fearful stick-in-the-mud neighbours as she no doubt saw them.

'D'yow know what?' she burst out.

Lucy felt her heart pick up speed. This was the effect Rose always seemed to have, rushing about, full of excite-ment, her hair coming loose and her cheeks pink with the cold beneath her jaunty blue hat brim.

'What?' she dared to say. Mari and Edna turned to listen. Bertha kept her back emphatically turned on Rose.

'The government have been looking at the sweated trades – all of us who work for the lowest wages. And they've made an act, called the Trade Boards Act! It's just passed – Miss Varley told us!'

Everyone failed to look at all impressed by this, having

no idea what it meant. Lucy wanted to be as excited as Rose, but she could make no sense of it.

'Well, what's that then?' Mari asked, though half her attention was on little five-year-old Dolly who was playing in the cinders next to her feet, gazing up at her, longing to be noticed.

'It *means* –' Rose was tying her apron on, ready for work – 'they're picking out four of the worst-paid trades – well, that's us chainmakers for a start, the outworkers at least. There's the lace makers and box makers, the tailors and seamstresses and *us* . . . They're gunna . . .' She had to stop and think for a second. 'There'll be a board for each of them – not just with bosses on but *workers*. And they're gunna make sure we get a minimum wage!'

'O-oh,' Mari said, not really sounding as if she knew what that was.

'Well, that'd be all right, wouldn'it?' Edna agreed. 'If it ever happens.'

'It might happen.' Bertha turned, confronting Rose, her voice mocking. Lucy cringed on hearing her – did she imagine Bertha sounded slurred? 'It all sounds very clever – but you know what'll happen. If the bosses ever agree to a minimum wage – and yow wouldn't be wanting to 'old yower breath in while they do – next thing is that wage'll not just be the minimum but the maximum as well – so we'll lose whichever way they play it.'

'No, we won't!' Rose argued. 'Because if you all join the union you can fight it!'

'Oh yes, Miss Know-it-all?' Bertha was really spoiling for a fight now. Lucy cringed, hating all this.

'By going on strike!' Rose said.

'Strike! Oh yes – very likely that is. *Strike*, if yow please!' Scoffing, Bertha turned away again.

'You can mek fun if yow want.' Rose spoke more quietly now, and Lucy could see Mari and Edna listening to her. 'But you just think about it for a minute . . . Where we are 'ere, Cradley Heath, nearly all the chain made in the country is made by us – a lot of the chain in the world. And there's 'undreds of us. If we was to down tools, they'd 'ave to tek notice of us.'

Bertha made a dismissive sound. Lucy just could not understand why she was so angry.

'What – a few women with 'ommers? We ay never going to mek a difference to anything.'

Lucy heard Rose furiously muttering something to herself as she went back to work. She wanted to go to her, ask her questions about it all, but of course she did not dare, with Bertha there.

All afternoon she kept thinking about what Rose had said. Rose had this effect on you – disturbing, disquieting. Lucy was used to people who never believed that things could ever change, that anyone would take any notice of them or that they could affect the way things were. They thought anyone who said anything different was living in a dream world. In fact, until Rose Shaw had come along, she had never met anyone who thought so boldly and, what was more, tried to act on it.

Lucy longed to believe Rose but being at odds with Bertha was not what she wanted at all. She thought back to the night Seth Dawson tried to force himself on her. Her face twisted with disgust. Bertha had been good to her then – she was always good to her.

'Yow keep away from 'im. I've told yer, Luce – mek sure yower never alone with the brute.'

Lucy knew there was no point in arguing. *But I never even knew he was there. He just grabbed me.*

They had to accept Seth Dawson – that he could do

terrible things, the very worst, and nothing would happen. Just as they all accepted the fourteen or more hours at the hearth, day in, day out, the pain and sickness of so many of the women she saw, the slave wages when the men working in factories were on five times as much. And no one ever seemed to ask why. Not until now.

Now she was starting to see all this afresh, thanks to Rose Shaw. And she, too, wanted to know *why* Seth Dawson was the one with a fat belly and scraps of meat in his teeth while they were the ones scraping for a bowl of slop? *Why* was that? The thought made her feel burningly angry – and filled her with a bold sense of adventure.

But later that evening, when Lucy went back to the house from the forge where she had been working with Mari and Rose, she found Bertha in Jonno's old chair. John was the only other one there and as Lucy walked in, she saw a look of distaste, shame even, on his face as they both looked at Bertha.

Lucy could smell the drink even a yard or two from her. Her body was slack, legs splayed. She had a crushed look to her, laid out there in the chair, her hands turned palms upwards, head to one side and mouth half open, her rhythmic little snores scraping at the air.

'I've tried telling her. We had words,' John whispered, looking down at the table. He had his Bible open in front of him – his reading was gradually improving, with much toil.

Lucy went to the range and felt the teapot in its cosy. There was a measure of brewed tea still in it and she poured it into a cup. In the face of John's disapproval, she felt herself immediately on his mother's side.

In the daytime, Bertha always looked so tough with her hair pulled back under her cap and her big boots, always the strong one, in charge of the yard, everyone looking to her. But now, with her boots off and a pair of holey old woollen socks to warm her feet by the dying fire, her grizzled hair hanging down and her face slackened by sleep, she looked old and vulnerable and sad. It made Lucy's heart ache to see her like that.

She perched on a stool to drink her lukewarm tea.

'Let's not wake her,' she said gently. 'She looks all in.'

John nodded, but with an air of disapproval. She could tell what he was thinking: She's not just tired, she's *drunk* – my mother is *drunk*! And though she herself was beginning to be worried about Bertha, at that moment she really disliked John for being so superior and casting his pious judgements about.

'Where's Clem?' she whispered, and she knew she was partly doing it to rile John, prig that he was.

'How should I know?' He shrugged irritably. He looked down, then up at her again, and she could see he wanted to get on the right footing with her but did not know how.

'I'm going up the wooden hill,' she said, draining her cup and using the corner of the range to help pull herself to her feet.

On her awkward progress up the stairs, she felt the balance of her loyalties tipping away from her feelings earlier in the day. Rose Shaw was young and bold and Lucy would have loved to follow her into all sorts of new thoughts and adventures. But Bertha was the nearest she had to a mom. If there was to be trouble, she could not side with Rose – she had to make sure she looked after Bertha, the way Bertha had looked after her. She would have to keep her distance from Rose Shaw, however exciting she seemed.

V

1910

Twenty-Nine

It was Saturday, a freezing February night to end a day of quietly falling snow. She waited until dark, standing a moment at the back door, to check whether anyone was outside.

A man's slurred voice was shouting, arguing, in the next-door yard and she could hear someone coughing. But most people were inside their houses or, like John and Clem, out somewhere braving the cold for the pleasure of walking out with their latest wenches. The blanketing snow was wrapped about the neighbourhood, a couple of inches of it lying on the ground.

Lucy and Freddie were the only ones in, at the table with an old pack of cards. Lucy was a year older than Freddie and the two of them sometimes made good companions. Glancing back at them, Bertha left the house as if stepping out to go to the lav, muffled in her shawl, her fingers seeking out the little twist of rag which was tucked into her waistband, a few coppers secured inside. She slipped along the entry to the street, her boots sinking into the muffling layer of snow. A few flakes were still falling, half-heartedly now.

Toothache niggled at one side of her mouth and she gathered the shawl tightly around her head to stop the chill air sharpening the pain. In one hand she held a little brown bottle. 'Menthol and Eucalyptus', its label read. This was why she needed to go, she told herself. A medicinal dose to keep the pain at bay. Her head down, she hurried along to the Outdoor at the Plough and Harrow.

The street was dark apart from pools of brightness from widely spaced lamps, in whose glow she could see the slow descent of the flakes. The lights of the pub were not too far away and her heart buckled at the thought of its welcoming aspect. She and Jonno used to go often, of a Saturday night, sitting there snug together, toasting the end of the week. He'd become too sick for that in the end. She would never go without him, would not sit in there now, a woman on her own. She longed for those days with all her soul – but she forced herself to stop thinking about it. That was gone. Jonno was gone, and that was that. On she must go.

But a second later she was not going on but stopping abruptly, her heart thudding.

'Damn and blast it!' she muttered. 'Oh, *damn* you!'

All she wanted was to slip along, get her bottle at least half filled with the cheapest of whisky and get home again. But in the light of a lamp just beyond the pub, she saw them – the bulky, unmistakeable figures of two of the most hated foggers in the district. To the left, in the homburg, was Seth Dawson, his back tilted to balance the weight of his bow-window belly. Facing him, under her wide-brimmed hat, clothed in black like a walking tombstone, stood the monumental figure of Thirza Rudge.

Bertha narrowed her eyes. What were those two vermin canting about, their heads together? Some deal to skin us to the bone, knowing the pair of them, she thought.

Loathing filled her to the back of her throat. It was bad enough setting eyes on either one of them at a time. For a second, she prayed for a bolt of lightning to come down and strike them dead on the spot. The thought made her shiver with pleasure – by God, that'd be a sight to see!

And, she thought, enraged, why was she here, hiding in the shadows at the sight of them as if she had no right to live her life?

She marched towards the hatch where they served people coming for their drink to take home, realizing they had taken no notice of her in any case. Her hands were shaking as she pulled out the bottle, stamping snow off her boots. As soon as she had what she needed, she scurried back to Hay Lane and stopped in the entry, its darkness lightened a shade by the snow, almost frantic to get the top off the bottle. The liquor burned down into her and the pain in her jaw seemed to retreat a little. She took another deep swig.

'Ahh – that's better.'

The two of them looked up at her as she came in, Freddie only for a second. His eyes soon lowered to his hand of cards. But Lucy, opposite him, kept staring at her with those wide, innocent-looking eyes, her brow pulled into a frown. Bertha felt her hackles rise.

'So – what're yow gawping at?'

'Nothing.' Lucy looked down again, rearranging her cards. Bertha felt a strong urge to slap her. The girl seemed mardy most of the time these days. She barely said a word in the forge, and in the house she had her nose in a book nearly all the time. Flaming books, Bertha raged inwardly. What was the use of them? And the way that Lucy kept looking at her these days – it riled her. The wench should be grateful to have a roof over her head, that she should!

'Rummy!' Freddie cried gleefully.

'Oh!' Lucy groaned. 'You win every time. Right, I'm gunna deal this time and I'll beat you – just for once!'

Bertha sank down into Jonno's old chair and closed her eyes. Her face throbbed. So what if she needed a bit

of the hard stuff now and then – she had a raging toothache, didn't she?

But as she sat there, trying to shut them out behind her
eyelids, uncomfortable thoughts came to her. Her whole
life had been about hard labour – for Jonno and for her
children. But they were all moving on – her eldest daughters hardly showed their faces now they were married and
settled. And the boys would soon be gone . . . Nothing
felt right these days – nothing was as it used to be – and
if she could have admitted it, she knew she was not quite
right either.

Freddie glanced across at his mother and made a face at
Lucy. Both of them could smell the booze on her and
these days, drink was making her nasty. She'd never been
like this before.

'Go on then,' Freddie said. 'You deal.'

He handed over his pack of dog-eared cards and Lucy
dealt. She put the remaining pile in the middle, glancing
over at Bertha in her turn. Bertha was laid back in the
chair, eyes closed, her mouth sagging down at one corner.
Very often now, at night, when she dragged herself up to
the bedroom she flung herself down on the bed fully
clothed, snoring in a way she never used to and keeping
Lucy awake.

Lucy felt for her. She had seen much of what Bertha
had had to endure at first hand: Jonno's last years, his
death. All the babbies – dead ones too. The way she had
to bind herself, pulling rags up between her legs in the
bedroom when she thought Lucy was asleep. Lucy knew
Bertha and Jonno had loved each other like no other
couple she had ever seen. But Bertha had been changing
over the past few years – and none of it was for the better.

Lucy had done her best now for months, to show

Bertha the respect she deserved. Rose Shaw had asked her to come to meetings with her. She had returned full of excitement about one of the speeches she had heard: 'The lady's called Mary Macarthur and she's on the Trade Board for us chainmakers – she's the one trying to get us a decent wage. Oh Luce, you should've heard her!' But Lucy had dutifully refused, out of respect for Bertha. She did not want to offend her and cause trouble at home.

But trouble seemed to arrive in any case. Bertha was more quarrelsome with everyone. These days she seemed to want to fight with her own shadow.

And Lucy had her own pain to bear – something she did not want to talk about to anyone. Over the winter, Clem had got himself a new girlfriend called Jen, who he seemed to want to spend every second of his spare time with. Jen called in to the house sometimes. She was talkative, sucked up to Bertha no end and treated Lucy as if she didn't exist, or was some kind of skivvy. Jen's father ran one of the pubs Clem frequented.

After the kiss Clem had given her on that balmy evening, a kiss she had relived and treasured for ever after, Lucy had forced herself to expect nothing more. It had meant nothing to him. She had schooled herself in expecting nothing, after all. But that kiss, those moments when Clem had put his arms round her and his lips met hers – oh, how much she wished now that he had never done it! He was always the one she had had a soft spot for in her heart. Why did he play with her like that, waking something in her that she had tried to force herself never to feel? Because although she had always loved Clem, she had never really thought he could love her back. If only he had just left her alone.

On top of that, John, who had been pursuing her in his quiet way, glowering at Clem every time he came anywhere near her, came home one evening only a couple of weeks ago and announced that he was walking out with Maud. Lucy knew Maud; they all went to the same church. She was a nice enough girl, meek and down to earth. Lucy could immediately see that John and Maud went together like boiled beef and carrots. But even so, she couldn't help feeling hurt.

You never really wanted John, she kept telling herself. He was nice to you and you kept pushing him away because of Clem. So it serves you right! Even though she knew that deep down she did not really want John, she felt her nose pushed well out of joint. Because if the Hipkiss lads didn't want her, no one would. There was no one at the church for her and who else did she ever meet?

It felt as if everything was turning against her and everyone taking her for granted except for Freddie who was always good company, but he was just a playmate. Good little Lucy – she'll never want anything or get into any trouble. You can always count on her – she'll do as she's told. And she was getting heartily sick of it.

Thirty

Monday morning. Rose crept quietly down the curving staircase, her socks catching on the splintery wood. It was not yet light and the rest of the family were still asleep.

She lit the candle and started to get the fire going. The rough sound of the coal shovel seemed deafening and she was sure it must wake one of the children. She stopped and listened. There was no sound from upstairs. Grimacing, she rubbed a hand over her belly.

After putting the kettle on the fire, she sank on to a chair. The acid clenching in her belly became more insistent, and the dread in her mind even more so. She got up and poured a cup of water, drinking it down fast. A few moments later she had to run to the back and threw it all up again into the stone sink.

It was almost dark in the little scullery. She hung, panting, over the sink, resting her head in her hands.

'I'm gunna flaming murder you, Wally Shaw!'

The vague misgivings she had had were confirmed. Now there was no mistaking it. Her mind raced with calculations – tomorrow was the first day of March . . . She thought back. Yes, damn it, she knew when it had happened, roughly anyway. Child number four was on its way and there was nothing she could do about it.

She brewed a cup of tea, took a few sips which she managed to keep down for the moment, and took a cup up to Wally.

'Here.' She shook him, more brutally than usual. 'Get this down yer. I've got summat to tell yer.'

'Uh?' Wally pulled himself up like a large, startled dog and looked warily at his wife who was standing over him with an ominous air to her, hands on hips. 'Wha's the matter, Rosie?'

'I'm expecting again, Wally – that's what. I've been throwing my guts up downstairs – and this is just what I dain't want – not now and not for a long time. This is *yower* cowing fault, that it is!'

Wally's face went through various stages of not knowing what to say, fear of Rose's temper and, after a variety of contortions, ending up looking sheepishly pleased with himself.

'Another babby?' he said, dazed.

'Yes!' Rose hissed. 'Another cowing babby. It's all right for you, Wally – it might seem like you showing off your manhood but I'm the one has to feel like death every morning and all the rest of it. So do' yow sit there grinning and looking like a cat that's got the cream!'

'Oh, Rosie – do' be like that,' Wally said sorrowfully. 'It's a little babby – a new life, not summat to be ashamed of.'

'I'm not *ashamed*,' she said, fit to explode. 'I'm just *fed up to my back teeth* with yer!'

The dirty remains of snow still lay at the edges of the yard. She went striding into the forge and started slamming her tools about, having to let out her feelings in some way or another. The family had all been quiet, exchanging looks in the face of Mom's storming temper of that morning.

As she stood at her hearth, Rose could feel the other women exchanging '*What the hell's got into her?*' looks behind her back. She started pushing down furiously on the bellows, then had to stop, feeling suddenly weak and sick. She hung there for a moment, then turned to face them all.

'All right – if you must know, I'm expecting again. And I'm not best pleased.'

She knew she did not imagine the gleam she saw in Bertha Hipkiss's eyes and the *'And not before time'* sniff of satisfaction she gave.

'Oh,' Mari said. 'Well . . .' She shrugged, as if to say it was only to be expected. Rose felt her blood boil. She wasn't having her husband going about the yards like a goat, like Victor Gornall had done when Mari wouldn't let him near her! The two of them seemed to have patched things up somehow now. But was that the only choice? Birthing child after child, no matter what the cost or whether you could feed the infant – or expecting that your husband would get his oats elsewhere?

'You can't argue with nature,' Edna Wilmott said complacently.

'Yes!' Rose erupted. She threw her hammer down with a crack. What did Edna know – her husband had died young and she only had that idiot Sidney and no more children. 'I cowing well can!'

She stormed out again, over to her house, and sat on a kitchen chair where she burst into tears. The nausea in her belly was growing again. She rested her head on the table, between the cups and the teapot she had not yet cleared away, and sobbed. After she had relieved her feelings for a few moments, she sat up, drained.

What's the matter with me? she thought, staring out of the grimy window into the slushy yard. Why can't I just be like the others and accept everything? Just have baby after baby, give in to those bastard foggers and think, Oh well, that's just how things are. Slave wages are the will of God . . . She felt as if she might explode.

At least she knew there were others in Cradley Heath – those who turned out to hear Julia Varley or the other trade unionists. But there were many women who did not feel they could spare the time or dared not be seen for fear of the foggers turning on them. Her temper began to abate.

It wasn't simply that all these women were just like a field of dumb cows without a thought in their heads. They were frightened. Frightened of the likes of Seth Dawson – may he burn in hell – he at whom she should be directing her rage and frustration. Not the other women, the widows and mothers struggling for every crust. She began to feel foolish.

She wiped her sleeve over her face, dabbing at her eyes. She was going to have to climb off her high horse and try to talk properly to Bertha and the others, no matter how aggravating it was. After all, they were supposed to be on the same side. A bit of humble pie wouldn't come amiss; she could see that, now she had calmed down.

Rose was just about to get up when she heard a timid knock at the door.

'It's open,' she called wearily.

Lucy's face appeared round the door, looking quite scared.

'I just came to see if you're all right?'

Rose was really touched and her eyes filled with tears again.

'Oh, Luce – ta, that's really nice of yer. Come in . . .' She beckoned her.

The girl had her forge apron on over her old brown dress, a grey shawl crossed over at the front and tucked into her belt, the everyday look of all the women chainmakers. Her limp added an awkwardness to her appearance, but Rose thought how sweet and pretty she was.

'I shouldn't have lost my temper,' Rose said. 'It's just . . .' She found she was crying again, couldn't seem to help it. 'It's not that I don't love my babbies – course I do. But I just wanted not to have too many, so's we can look after 'em properly, like. I just want . . .' She shook her head, trying to find the right words. 'I dunno – I want *other things* – not just babbies and work.'

Lucy, leaning one hand on the table, was looking at her very seriously.

'I know,' she said. 'You want to make things better. And you're right. I know you are. I just . . .'

She looked away, seeming embarrassed.

'Yow dow want to go against Mrs Hipkiss?'

Lucy nodded.

'Well,' she added after a moment. 'Up 'til now I haven't. She's been good to me, after Mom . . . But she's not . . . I mean . . .' She seemed thrown into conflict, hardly able to bring the words out. 'Lately, she's got more *narrow*, sort of thing. Not wanting to budge in how she thinks. And angry about everything.' She hesitated, looking at Rose again, then said all in a rush, 'I think she just can't change but *I* want to and I want to come with you to one of those meetings – even if 'er gets cross with me.'

Rose felt herself flood with warmth. How much it meant even to have one person say they supported you, would come along and try at something with you. She was not on her own!

'Oh, Luce – that makes me feel ever so much better,' she said. She got up and hugged the girl briefly and saw a smile light up her usually serious little face. A sad face, Rose thought, for all she was pretty. 'Yower a brave wench, yow are – in lots of ways. We'll fight 'em, won't we?'

Lucy was suddenly radiant. 'Yes,' she said. 'All right.'

'Come on.' Rose linked arms with her. 'We'd best get back to work.'

Rose's bad temper came flaring again that afternoon, however. The sickness had worn off for the moment and she felt better. But what did not improve her mood was Sidney Wilmott, the idle sod, as she thought of him, turning up and hanging around at the door of the workshop. He just appeared and stood there, loafing about in the doorway.

'Can you move?' she snapped at him. 'Yower blocking out the light.'

'Move over, Sid,' Edna said to him. 'What're you doing 'ere?'

'Nothin'.' Sidney gave one of his foolish sniggers. 'Just looking, that's all.'

'Well, you can stop cowing well gawping at us and get out the road,' Rose said.

But instead of getting out, Sidney came into the forge to lurk. There wasn't a lot of room and everyone felt uncomfortable. Rose kept glancing at him and after a moment she saw him go over to Mari Gornall and peer over her shoulder.

''Ere – what the 'ell're yow playing at?' Mari turned on him, hands on hips. Since Dolly's arrival, she had become a fiercer person. And looking down she saw that Sidney was rummaging about in his flies. 'Oi – get away from me, yow filthy beast! Edna, look what yower son's doing – yow need to tell 'im!'

'Goo on, Sidney – push off,' Bertha shouted at him.

Sidney sniggered again and made the rudest of gestures round his groin area before slouching over to stand in the doorway again, playing with himself.

238

'Oh good God, Edna,' Bertha cried.

'It's that fogger I blame,' Edna said. 'Giving 'im ideas.'

'Look at 'im, the foul beast!' Mari shrieked. 'Just 'cause 'e's only just worked out what it's for don't mean 'e can come round 'ere carrying on like that! You're 'is mother – you tell 'im!'

For the second time that day, Rose threw her hammer down. Picking up the rod she had been heating in the fire, she advanced on Sidney Wilmott with it, the end of it glowing red-hot.

'Get away from 'ere, you filthy sod, or I'll stick this in there where yower hand is and you can see how yow like that!'

That got rid of him.

Rose caught sight of the grin on Lucy's face as she turned back to her work.

Thirty-One

Lucy always helped Bertha in the house, but this evening she was practically falling over herself to be of use.

'I'll peel the potatoes, Auntie,' she said. 'And shall I go and fill up all the pails?'

The trip to the pump at the end of the yard was arduous for her, trying to carry a full bucket back with her leg being the way it was. But they always needed to store water for use in the house and she wanted to show willing.

Bertha turned and looked at her, her gaze moving down meaningfully to Lucy's leg.

'No. I'll do it.' She spoke wearily, turning away and picking up the two pails. 'You get on with the spuds.'

Lucy did as she was told, standing at the table with the tin bowl of muddy water and potatoes. She was shrinking inside. Bertha was furious with her for following Rose over to her house this morning. It was as if Lucy had taken sides. And truth to tell, Lucy knew she had. Why would Bertha oppose something that would make things better for everyone? Unless it was just about being top dog in the yard and that seemed petty and not something to admire.

Standing at Rose's door, she had been a-flutter with fear. What happened after that still made her tremble inside. Rose Shaw, crying in front of her, being so kind and sweet, putting her arms around her! She had never known anything like it. It had made her feel grown up, as if Rose saw her as an equal. But it had also made her feel

240

honoured, loved. She who no one ever seemed to love, not truly. Hungrily, she turned all her devotion on to Rose, who was so brave and strong and kind. Whatever Bertha said, she felt she would follow Rose anywhere.

The three Hipkiss lads soon all came rolling in from work. Lucy could hardly look either of the older two in the eye for the hurt in her. She had never really wanted John, and he had soon moved on to Maud. But Clem – he was not constant, like a dandelion clock on the breeze when it came to feelings. He had played with her and that pain weighed in her, an ache in her chest.

The little pink gemstone he had once given her, which she had so treasured for a while like a lucky charm, now lay abandoned in a drawer upstairs, because she knew it meant nothing true. How could she have kidded herself for so long?

But today she had a cloak of protection round her – the cloak of Rose. Rose Shaw wanted her and treated her like a proper person even if they didn't.

'All right, Luce?' Clem said, as the three lads plonked themselves down at the table, waiting for food to be put in front of them, as usual. Lucy found her mind running an angry commentary. Like baby birds in a nest, they are! What if one day we just didn't cook? It's not as if we women are sat around on our backsides all day . . .

Blimey, she thought, what's coming over me? It was as if there was a cauldron of anger constantly steaming inside her.

'Yeah. Ta.' She was spooning out potato and didn't look up at him.

Freddie started talking excitedly about a fight he had seen outside the factory.

'There was blood all down 'im like a pinna!' He made

a spreading gesture with his hands. 'All down 'im – clots of it . . .!'

'Well, it seems to 'ave made yower day, any'ow,' Bertha said.

'I ay never seen anyone's snoz bleed that much before!'

'So you said,' Bertha snapped. 'We're all about to eat 'ere – all right? You going out tonight, John?'

John nodded earnestly. 'Maud and me're going to the Bible study . . .'

'Well, that sounds exciting, I must say.' Lucy heard the mocking tone in Bertha's voice. The drink was in already. She could tell, even though she had not seen Bertha tippling. She seemed to have a bottle hidden about her somewhere and took sips of it in secret.

John gave his mother a disdainful look. His air of superiority had grown lately, Lucy thought. He was going to heaven on a cloud while the rest of them burned below, that was how it felt. Bertha's drinking shamed him though he never dared confront her about it.

'Maud,' Freddie said, grinning. 'Yow gunna ask 'er to come into the garden with yer?'

Maud was a tiny, timid woman ('Looks like summat you'd set a mousetrap for,' Bertha commented when she first laid eyes on her) and not someone you could easily imagine any kind of romance with. Clem snorted.

'Don't you make fun of her!' John erupted. 'Maud's a good woman, I'll have you know!'

'Yeah,' Clem said, with a wink at Freddie and Lucy. 'I bet 'er is!'

Even though she was still also in a bad mood with Clem, Lucy couldn't help laughing along with the pair of them while John looked more and more huffy.

*

It was some time before Lucy and Rose managed to go to any sort of meeting. Rose was sickly with the latest babby on the way and both of them were working the usual long hours.

But one morning just before Easter, they had a visitor to the forge when all of them were working together. It was an overcast March day, the yard pooled with smoky gloom, the brightest and warmest sight the glow of the fires through the windows of the forge.

Mari's little girl Dolly was there. She was six now, a round-faced little girl, fringe cropped very straight over her eyes, wearing a ragged old dress cut down to fit her. Considered too simple to go to school, she was playing with Rose's little one, three-year-old Ivy, a dear little girl with a cap of brown hair.

A shadow fell across the door.

'Morning, ladies?' said a voice cautiously.

Lucy turned to see a woman of about forty in a dark coat, a felt hat pulled down over her ears, hovering in the doorway. She was round-faced and smiling nervously. 'Can yer spare me a moment for a word?'

Lucy thought Bertha would round on her and say that no, they couldn't. But all of them had stopped work and were looking at her.

The woman stepped properly inside, smiling at Dolly and Ivy who were squatting on the floor, looking up at her in wonder.

'My name is Madge Lunn. Like you, I've worked my hearth making chains for many a year. But now I'm doing some work with the union – the one set up especially for all o' yow.'

'They'm paying yow then, are they?' Bertha butted in. They had had a union person come round before but Bertha had not been there at the time.

'I get an allowance for the hours I put in,' Madge said, seemingly unbothered by Bertha's hostile tone. 'Yow have heard of the NFWW? The National Federation of Women Workers?'

Lucy saw Bertha fold her arms and waited for some outburst to begin. The rest of them stood quietly.

'I know some of yow're worried about being seen in the union,' the woman went on in her gentle voice. 'And I know why. I know yower worried about losing your jobs, about the foggers catching on that yow've joined the union. But the only way we can get past them is by working together. I've come to *implore* you to think about joining, all of yer.' She held her hands out in a beseeching way.

'What – yow think we can afford to hand out a penny a week for that!' Bertha burst out. 'A penny a week to lose our jobs – 'cause that's what'll 'appen, whatever yow might say about it.' She made a furious, dismissive noise and turned back to her hearth.

'But that *is* the only way we can beat them – all getting together!' Rose burst out. 'I'm a member of the union!'

The woman smiled at her. 'I'm glad to hear it, bab.' She cast a wary look at Bertha Hipkiss, seeing that she was not going to make easy headway with her. Mari was looking from one to another of them, not knowing who to believe. But Lucy could feel her own blood beating faster and faster until the words spilled over her lips.

'I'm gunna join!'

Bertha whipped round. 'Oh no, yower not!'

Lucy stared back at her defiantly. For the first time ever, she locked eyes with Bertha Hipkiss. It felt terrible, as if she was betraying her, Bertha who had taken her on when Mom died. But what about *me*? Lucy thought, explosive inside. I lost my mom, my brothers, I've got no one – and *I* earn the money I make, even though I give nearly all of it to her! I can decide if I spend a penny of it on the union!

Madge Lunn looked uncertain, obviously not wanting to get involved. She looked at Lucy and said gently,

'Well, I hope you do, dear. The more of us there are, the stronger we shall be – that's how we'll win, by bandying together.'

'Ho, yes – stronger than who?' Seth Dawson strode in, face like thunder. Lucy saw Sidney Wilmott, who seemed to be Seth's fat little shadow these days, lurking about outside the door.

'Who're you?' Seth said, sneering. 'And what're yer doing coming in 'ere, where yer've no business? You one of them union troublemakers? You work on the chains, do yer – who d'yer work for, then?'

'I am indeed a member of the union.' Madge Lunn's face pinked up, but she spoke back to Seth Dawson, not seeming intimidated. 'And so far as I know, speaking to someone is no crime.'

Seth Dawson stepped up and pushed his face right into hers. Madge Lunn recoiled.

'You wanna keep away from 'ere, you and yer meddling union talk. I ain't 'aving any of that 'ere – and my workers . . .' He stood back and swept a hand over them as if they were his private herd of cattle.

Lucy stared back at him, feeling as if her face had turned to stone.

'They ain't 'aving it with any o' this nonsense you people're peddling. They don't want a cut in their rate, do yer, ladies? Or to find there's someone else teken over your hearth when yer come into work one day? Because yer can be sure, if any of yer 'as any truck with all this union nonsense, that's what'll happen. Now you –' he made a sweeping notion at Madge Lunn – 'you clear off and don't come back!'

Sidney was still lounging in the doorway, probably hoping to watch a scrap. 'If you could ask your . . . friend to move out of my way,' Madge Lunn said, with dignity, 'then I can do as you ask.'

'Gerrout the road, Sid,' Seth ordered him contemptuously.

Once Madge Lunn had taken her leave, the fogger stood looking round at them all. Edna and Bertha had the wisdom to turn their backs and get on with their work. Lucy stared at him, as she could feel Rose doing, channelling the force of all her hatred towards him. Her body was quivering with the desire to go and stab each of his eyes out.

'Don't you look at me like that –' Seth came up close to her – 'yow mardy little bitch.'

Lucy spotted Rose in the background, signalling to her. She was carefully shaking her head. Don't get into anything. Make him think he's won.

Only then did Lucy lower her gaze, the loathing simmering inside her below the surface.

Thirty-Two

The first public meeting Lucy attended with Rose Shaw was in April. They did not announce where they were going – there just came a point in the morning, when they were at their hearths, when Rose looked over at her and gave a little tilt of her head towards the door. Bertha did not even look round, but Lucy felt like a traitor as she walked out of the forge following Rose.

'She'll be mithered when she knows where I've been,' Lucy said, wincing as she limped along beside Rose, trying to keep up with her. Her leg was troubling her that day.

''Er'll get over it.' Rose looked round at her. 'Oh, sorry, I forgot. I'll go a bit slower.' She was still looking sickly and Lucy could see it might suit her better to walk more slowly instead of charging about like she usually did. Smiling, Rose added, 'You know yower own mind though, don't yer, Luce?'

Lucy blushed. She wasn't sure whether she knew her own mind or not, but one thing she was certain of was that Rose had the right idea. And what the union people said made sense to her – their wages being so low while the bosses fattened on their work, and the men getting so much more.

But the meeting turned out to be a disappointment on that occasion. There was only a small gathering of people and Julia Varley announced that the negotiations of the Trade Board were not at present getting anywhere.

Looking up at her on the stage of the hall over a tired collection of hats and bonnets, Lucy could see that Miss Varley's face was tense. Her frustration was obvious and her voice was loaded with bitterness.

'The Chainmakers' Association,' she said, 'who before our union workers began to put pressure on them, didn't want to know about any negotiations or boards, have joined the discussions – and what's more, they have tried to take credit for them!'

A murmur went through the little gathering. *Typical*, was the sentiment, and there was laughter of bitter recognition.

'But despite this sudden outbreak of enthusiasm, we are getting nowhere. And why? Because, as our union comrade Thomas Sich has said, we all live in a fools' paradise, if we think these employers are eager to end the evils of sweated labour!'

There were more murmurs of agreement.

'But –' Julia Varley raised her hand – 'we will not give up the struggle! Chainmakers of Cradley Heath – we will continue the fight. We *will* make sure of winning a wage set higher than mere starvation level – a minimum wage, for all!'

There were scattered cheers and Lucy joined in when Rose shouted, 'Hurray! You tell 'em!' But she could not help thinking the crowd rather thin. And was Miss Varley right that they would win – that they could? It all felt very uncertain and she was suddenly full of doubt.

Bertha did not say anything to her when she got back. It was as if nothing had happened. Lucy knew she would have to work late into the evening to get enough chain made for the day. Rose was having to do the same and they were out there hammering away long after dark.

'Never mind,' Rose said to her, looking over at her

during the evening. Her face looked so pretty in the soft firelight. 'It'll be worth it – they'll soon have to pay us proper for all this toil.'

And Lucy smiled back. Even if it turned out not to be true, it felt nice – for the moment at least – to be able to believe in something better.

Things ground on for a while. Seth Dawson, who knew what was afoot, kept taunting them sarcastically.

'You women wanna settle down 'stead of meking trouble,' he'd say pompously, rocking back and to on his heels. 'All this union nonsense – if any o' yer's mixed up in that yer can work for someone else. We ain't 'aving any of that 'ere.'

'We wouldn't dream of it,' Mari said to him one day. Lucy looked round, startled at the pert sarcasm in her voice, which Seth seemed too dim to notice.

'Glad to 'ear it.' He stood there and Lucy could feel him staring, but she refused to react or turn round. She felt warmed by what Mari had said, though. Mari, who knew full well that she and Rose had been to a union meeting. Mari was changing, bit by bit.

It wasn't until May that they heard anything more. One morning, they had another visit from Madge Lunn, the lady from the NFWW. She arrived at the forge when they were all at work.

'Ladies,' she said, good and loud. 'May I have yower attention for a moment?'

The air suddenly emptied of the sound of hammers.

Lucy turned awkwardly on her good leg to see Madge Lunn's round face beaming at them.

'I've some very good news to tell yow. The Trade

Boards have agreed that yower wages are to be increased by seventy to as much as one hundred per cent.'

They all looked blankly at her. Lucy felt excitement start to bubble up inside her.

'If they was to increase by one hundred per cent,' she explained, 'you would be earning twice what you are earning now. But . . .'

She held her hand up as they all gasped with surprise and pleasure.

'Let me tell you that this is not as much as we would have hoped . . .'

'No,' Mari said, 'but *twice as much* – I mean, that ay bad!'

'But,' Madge Lunn went on, 'there are still a few things they've got to sort out.'

'Oh, here we go,' Bertha said, her voice thick with scorn for the possibility that anything might get any better.

'This agreement will not come into force for at least three months.'

They waited. Madge Lunn looked uncertain.

'And I believe there are some other things I'll need to come back and explain to yow, soon as I know . . .'

'What things?' Rose said. She had been listening with intense concentration.

'As I say, soon as I know . . .'

'Oh, don't bother yowerself,' Bertha said, turning away again. 'Yow know damn well them lot ay gunna pay us more unless someone puts a noose around their necks and that ay happened yet, not so far as I can see.'

Lucy felt all her excitement begin to subside and die away. Even if she didn't agree with Bertha, it did all sound far too good to be true.

*

Something had changed, though. They could all feel it in the air. Madge Lunn and the other NFWW workers made their way round the yards and to some of the remotest spots in the villages where there were isolated chainmakers, to tell them about the Trade Boards' agreement.

Though most of the women working in the forges kept mainly to their own yards, busy with their work, now when they went out, up the High Street to the shops and anywhere in the district, there were conversations going on. Women outworkers who did not know each other started striking up conversations in the street. Was it true what they were saying about a minimum wage? Had the union – a *women*'s union! – actually managed to pull it off and get something done for them?

Lucy realized that although no one was exactly sure what was going on or how it had turned out, what had changed was that they all felt more connected to each other, knowing someone had taken notice of their lives day to day. They were not just invisible. There was a feeling of excitement about something they were all in together. Something hopeful.

'D'you think they'll really do it?' Lucy asked Rose one day, soon after. 'It does seem a bit . . .'

'What?' Rose said. They were in the yard, Rose pumping water vigorously into a pail. She stopped, water splashing close to the top, and pulled it out of the way so that Lucy could fill hers. She was still striving to please Bertha at all times. 'Too good to be true?'

'Well – yes.' Lucy worked the pump. 'Them giving us more money when they don't have to,' she panted.

'Well, they *do* 'ave to,' Rose insisted. ''Ere – I'll carry that for yer.' She caught up the bucket with her strong arm and took it over to the cottage. 'I dow know 'ow you manage on that leg,' she said, setting it down.

Lucy shrugged and they smiled at each other.

'Thing is,' Rose said, with her usual force, 'that lot don't wanna pay us more – course they don't. But we 'ave to mek 'em, one way or another, see?'

Lucy watched Rose's curvaceous figure walk away, her blue skirt, sleeves rolled, a force to her as ever. She realized that for the first time in ages she felt truly excited and inspired by someone. Even her feelings for Clem were fading into unimportance now. Clem was all right really – but there was no future in fixing her feelings on him.

Now she saw that, for the first time since Miss Jones had left, there was someone else she could love, about whom she felt, *I want to be like her*.

Thirty-Three

Rose woke up in bed beside Wally. It must be early yet – there was only just a glimmer of light beginning at the window. It felt such a relief to start the day like this, without the sick clenching within her which tormented the early weeks of starting a baby.

She stroked a hand over her belly. It was June so she must be somewhere between four and five months now. She could feel the gentle swell of her belly, the little one making its presence felt.

Rose smiled. Oh, well. No going back now. She loved her children, every inch and every bone of them. She brought each of them to mind: Gracie, seven now, bossy and full of life; cheeky Charlie, who at five was the image of Wally and just as loveable, and little Ivy, always trying to keep up with the other two. How could she carry on being cross about carrying another? It was much easier to come to terms with now that the worst of the sickness had worn off as well.

Suddenly forgiving and affectionate, she turned over and snuggled up against Wally. He muttered sleepily and put his arm round her.

'Rosie . . .' And then he was breathing heavily once more.

She did not fall asleep again. After a time she extricated herself and went down to make tea. It was still not yet seven in the morning, but it was already light and she could hear a bird cheeping somewhere. When she at last brought the tea up, Wally's eyes were still closed.

'Come on, yow lazy brick.'

She climbed in beside him and once Wally had managed to prise his eyes open, they sat sipping the hot tea.

''Ello, wife,' Wally said, putting his tea down. He turned to her, wrapping his arm round her. 'Nice, you cuddling up like that.'

'Careful! You'll spill my tea! Now – none of that.' She could see what was on Wally's mind straight away. 'You've got me in enough trouble already!'

Rose's mind was already whirring busily. As Wally sheepishly withdrew his arm, she said,

'I wonder when they'll get this pay rise of ours sorted out.'

'D'yow think they will?' Wally gave a huge yawn. He sounded as if he didn't believe it for a moment.

'They said they would,' Rose said, irritated. Wally wasn't really listening, she could tell. He wasn't taking any of this seriously. 'There's no need to be like that – just 'cause yower pay's all sorted out for yer – some of us 'ave to struggle for it.'

'I know,' Wally said. 'I just can't see 'em taking no notice of a bunch of wenches, that's all.'

'Oh – is that it?' Rose put her cup down and jumped furiously out of bed. 'If a woman says summat there ay no need to pay attention – is that it?' She ignored his attempts to protest at this. 'That's cowing well you all over, ay it?' She marched to the bedroom door. 'Well, I've 'ad enough of it, that I 'ave!'

Her temper did not improve all morning.

Grace and Charlie went off to school. Ivy still had to hang about the yard and the forge.

As she began work, Rose could feel all her excitement about the unions and what they could achieve draining away. Although these promises had been made, where was there any real sign of them being carried out? She had come to realize that this struggle for betterment, being alongside other women in trying to bring it about, was becoming one of the most important things in her life.

Sidney Wilmott appeared late in the morning with a new supply of rods, which he dropped with a clatter in the yard.

Bertha strode across to the door.

'What're yow doing 'ere? Yow only brought us a load yesterday.'

'Mr Dawson said I was to bring yow this lot 'un all,' Sidney said importantly.

'Sidney?' Edna shouted to him, leaving her hearth and limping across to the door on her stiff hips. 'What's gooin' on? They'm piling the work on us like nobody's business.'

Rose kept working. She didn't want to tangle with Sidney Wilmott, the stupid fool. But it was true: there seemed to be more and more work all of a sudden, as if there was some grand emergency that suddenly demanded endless lengths of chain.

'I dunno,' Sidney said, giving his foolish giggle. 'An' if I knew I don't 'ave to tell *yow*.'

'Don't yow talk to yower mother like that!' Bertha erupted at him. 'Yow need to keep a civil tongue in yower 'ead.'

Rose and Lucy rolled their eyes at each other. Mari joined in as well. She even smiled at Lucy, Rose saw, taken by surprise.

And then Sidney was gone. There was no point expecting any sense out of him.

It was not until the late afternoon that Seth Dawson turned up. Afterwards, Rose thought, Yes, he came when he knew we'd all be tired, getting towards teatime. Edna had already gone to her house to cook. That bastard of a fogger knew what he was doing, all right.

Rose was working away, just thinking how she must stop and put the tea on as well. The kids were playing out in the yard, and she needed to get going before Wally came in . . .

Seth Dawson did not do his usual ploy of creeping up and standing in the doorway, watching them all like a guard dog. Today he came in in a rush, all self-important, a sheaf of papers in his hand.

'Right – down tools, wenches. There's summat yer need to do – won't take a minute. Come over 'ere . . .' He went to the end of the forge and brushed off a little space at the edge of the brick hearth. 'All yer need to do is put yer name under 'ere . . . Or yer fingerprint for those of yer can't write.'

The four of them gathered round.

'Where's the other one?' He glanced at Edna's hearth.

'I'll get 'er,' Mari said. ''Er cor read nor write, I know that much.'

A moment later they were all there.

'What's that then?' Bertha asked.

'Oh, it's just some paper or other from the firm,' Seth said casually. 'It's about some of the regulations, like. I've got one for each of yer to sign and then yer can get back to work. C'mon – just hurry up and get it done, will yer?'

'But what is it?' Rose said, immediately suspicious. 'Let's 'ave a look.'

'There ain't no need for that,' Seth said. 'Just stick yer name on and 'ave done with it. None of yer need to tek any notice – it's just factory business. I've been round some of the other yards and there's been no problem. Let's just get it over.'

'Well, we've got to know what it is to be able to sign it,' Rose said, making her voice as reasonable as possible, even though she was more certain by the second that the filthy so-and-so was up to something.

Seth handed the sheets of paper over. Rose saw a form with a space for a signature at the bottom. Bertha and the others were peering at theirs. Rose took the form over to the door to read it in the light, and Lucy did the same. It was all formal language and though Rose could make out the words she was not sure what it all added up to. Lucy seemed to be devouring the words, her face intent.

'Come on – Mrs Hipkiss, you sign 'ere,' Seth said.

'No,' Lucy hissed, looking at Rose with an urgent shake of her head. 'Don't sign! And don't let the others sign it . . .'

Rose could hear the force behind her words. She hesitated, but Seth was handing out forms to the others.

'Wait!' She turned to them hurriedly. 'All of yow – don't sign it. Wait for our Lucy to read it to yer and see what it is we're being asked to agree to!'

'I ain't got time for all this.' Seth was starting to lose his temper. 'Just get the thing signed and yer can get on with yer work. I'm not having any of this carry-on.'

'We ay signing this 'til we know what it is,' Rose said, 'no matter 'ow much of a hurry you're in, *Mr Dawson*. Come on, Luce – yower the one can read proper – let's 'ear it.'

Lucy stayed in the light by the door.

'"I hereby declare",' she read, '"that . . ."' She went

on to read the official-sounding words. They were being invited to opt out of the arrangement for a higher wage for six months – even though the new rate was supposed to be introduced in three months.

'"Opt out"!' Rose repeated. 'What – it means opt out of being paid a minimum rate?'

The full deviousness of Seth Dawson and the factory owners began to sink in. 'So you want us to sign it away – what, so that even when they say we can 'ave it, us won't get it?'

She felt Bertha, Mari and Edna all staring at her. None of them could read more than a few simple words.

'Is that what it says, Luce?' Mari asked.

Lucy looked at the paper again and then back up at them all. She looked really frightened.

'I think . . . Yes – it does.'

'We ay signing that,' Rose said. 'None of us. No, Edna – dow go signing it!'

Edna Wilmott was staring at the piece of paper as if she was really considering giving in.

'I can see what they'm playing at.' As Rose spoke she could feel rage rising more and more intensely in her, like a flame breaking out. 'They think they can get us all to say we won't 'ave it when the time comes – 'cause most of us cor read and they think we'm all ignorant and cor think for ourselves!' She turned on Seth Dawson. 'Yer can tek yower rotten papers away – we ay signing them!'

She flung her paper at Seth Dawson. It spiralled and fluttered to the floor.

''Cause unfortunately for you, our Lucy 'ere can read – and 'er can read much better'un you can an' all.'

Seth's eyes swivelled round and fastened on Lucy. He ran his gaze up and down her body and Rose saw Lucy

258

shiver. But there was a cold, dangerous light in her eyes which took even Rose by surprise.

'Yow can tek yower papers . . .' Rose went and seized hold of Lucy's paper and Mari's. When she went to Bertha she saw the woman's hackles had risen at being told what to do by her, for not being able to spot the problem herself. But she handed the form over, as did Edna. 'This is where they belong.' And she thrust them into the nearest hearth. They crumpled instantly, vanishing into the flames.

Seth watched her, an expression of disgust on his face. Then he gave a smile.

'It won't get you anywhere,' he sneered. 'All the other's'll sign – most of 'em already 'ave.'

As he went out of the forge, Rose saw him fix his eyes on Lucy once again, and the look of threat in them was clear.

Once he'd gone, Rose said, 'Well – that's all thanks to our Luce!'

They all made much of her until the girl was smiling and blushing and hardly knowing what to do with herself. But Bertha Hipkiss turned sullenly back to her hearth again, saying,

'It cor bring us any good, any of this. They know 'ow to get us – and they'll get us in the end. They always do.'

Thirty-Four

Miss Julia Varley called a meeting to warn the other chainmakers about the opt-out forms: the bosses trying to get them to give up what should rightfully be theirs.

Lucy was upset and annoyed when she set off with Rose that hazy morning, although she didn't want to show it. She had not hidden where she was going from Bertha. She wasn't going to lie. Bertha turned away, her face sour, saying nothing. Why did she act as if Rose Shaw was a bad influence into whose thrall she had fallen? Lucy thought angrily. Why be so resentful about someone who was always trying to make things better? But she knew she would never get anywhere if she tried to talk about it.

'I think Mom just likes to be top dog in the yard,' Freddie suggested last night, when Bertha had said crossly, 'I'm sure yow'll do just as yow please, like yow always do,' which was almost worse than her forbidding Lucy to go to the meeting at all. Bertha went stomping out of the house – to the Outdoor again, as they realized afterwards. ''Er thinks that Rose woman is teking over.'

'But she's *not*,' Lucy said. She didn't want to criticize Bertha to her son. 'Only – someone's got to stand up for things somewhere along the line.'

Freddie looked at her, eyes doubtful, but thinking about it. Even the chance that he might consider what she was saying and not discount it like the others cheered Lucy a little.

'Ar – I s'pose so,' he said.

260

Bertha did not forbid her to go out – she could not be sure enough of being obeyed. She just turned her back in displeasure any time anything like that was mentioned.

What Lucy also did not realize that morning, as she limped along beside Rose, was that that day was, in every way, going to be one full of events which would change everything in her life.

They all met on a cindery black patch of land called 'Lower Town Bonk'. This time, there were crowds gathering, not like the last meeting Lucy had gone to in the hall. She stood, craning to see over the mass of women, a few men who were obviously outworkers as well, and other curious passers-by for whom the presence of any speaker was a diversion.

The crowd was restless, questions shouted towards the front. Something was happening, that was certain, but no one could be quite sure what it was. People were confused and worried about what had been agreed by the Trade Boards and why they were being pressurized to opt out.

Julia Varley got up to speak first, balanced on a heap of slag which enabled her to see over the crowd. Standing beside Rose in the smoky air, the sun warming her face, Lucy strained to hear. Miss Varley, in her dark clothes and hat, looked energetic, angry. The firms and the middlemen, the foggers, were trying to cheat them all out of what was rightfully theirs. *Do not opt out!* That was her message.

Lucy turned and looked at Rose and for a moment they joined hands and squeezed them, smiling at each other. There was not much they could do, but at least between them they had stopped the women in their own yard from falling for Seth Dawson's tricks.

'Now,' Miss Varley called over the heads of the knot of

people, 'I'd like to introduce you to the person who has been negotiating on your behalf with the Trade Boards, who has worked with the Anti-Sweating League and who founded and leads our union, our *women*'s union, the NFWW.' She held her arm out: 'Miss Mary Macarthur.'

Lucy watched as Miss Varley vanished from sight and the top half of another woman stepped up into view, in a wide-brimmed straw hat with a black band round it, a high-collared white blouse under an elegant grey jacket. She saw tendrils of fair hair escaping from under the hat, framing a face that smiled round at all of them, a face brimful of energy and affection.

'Women of Cradley Heath!' she greeted them. There was a murmur of greeting in return. 'I first came to your town in 1906 and saw the conditions in which many of you have to work. I learned of the starvation wages inflicted upon you. There are many of you across this country, treated with unjust disdain by your employers, in dark, cramped rooms and workshops – the box makers and seamstresses of London, the jute workers of Dundee, and you, women of Cradley Heath!'

If there had been an explosion in the street just then, Lucy would likely not have noticed. This was something, a kind of person she had never in her life seen before. She listened with every grain of her attention as the woman's voice rose and fell, reaching her on the early summer breeze. Her arms swept from side to side to add even more strength to the points she was making. But though gentle, that voice was strong, her crisp Scots accent and her energy and passion making Lucy swell inside with enthusiasm, with love, for a woman she had only just set eyes on. Miss Mary Macarthur . . .!

'Let me remind you . . .' Miss Macarthur went on, 'that a Royal Commission and the Board of Trade have been debating this question of sweated labour since *1889*! It has taken these many years with no resolution. We are now living in a new century, one in which we have the opportunity to move forward to a fairer way of life for *all*, not just for a few!'

'Yes!' Rose exclaimed beside her. She was standing on her toes, seeming on the point of jumping up and down with excitement. Others in the crowd were clapping, crying out, 'That's right – that's 'ow it should be . . .'

'We will keep up this struggle and we *shall* succeed,' Mary Macarthur went on. 'But only together can we bring that about. In order to gather our strength, it is *vital* that we are all members of the union!' She leaned forward insistently sometimes while she was speaking, as if trying to encompass all of them in her words.

'A trade union is like a bundle of sticks. You, the workers, are bound together and have the strength of unity. No employer can do as he likes with them. They have the power of resistance. But a worker who is not in the union is like a single stick. She can be easily bent or broken to the will of her employer. She has not the *power* to resist a reduction in wages. If she is fined, she must pay without complaint. She dare not ask for a "rise". If she does, she will be told, "Your place is outside the gate: there are plenty to take your place." But make no mistake – your employers need you!'

Mary Macarthur drew herself up and with force, concluded,

'Without you, they are nothing and nobody – for it is on *all* of you that their prosperity depends!'

'I'm going to join the union now, I *am*,' Lucy said to Rose as they reluctantly returned to work. No one had much time to hang about as the meeting broke up – all the women were hurrying off to get back to their daily toil. But now, Lucy felt as if a fire was blazing in her.

'D'you keep any of yower own wages?' Rose asked, slowing herself a little, to keep her pace the same as Lucy's – to Lucy's relief.

'I give Mrs Hipkiss most of it,' Lucy said. 'Always have done, for my keep. But she lets me have a little bit of it – sixpence or so. So I can pay a penny a week.'

'Let's go and join you up now!' Rose said. 'Then we can 'ave another go at getting the others to do it an' all. If they'd only come and 'ear Miss Macarthur! But Mari's coming round, I think. 'Er can tek a penn'orth of drink money off of that idle mon of 'ers.'

And within a few minutes, as they passed the office on the way home, Lucy found herself to be a paid-up member of the National Federation of Women Workers.

The yard was strung across with washing lines on this warm day. Rose and Lucy ducked underneath them, but stopped in amazement.

'Oh, my word!' Rose said. 'What the 'ell's going on? They only brought a load of them yesterday!'

Outside the forge was piled the biggest heap of rods to work on that either of them had ever seen. Mari came out then.

'Oh – 'e's been again,' she said, rolling her eyes and tilting her head towards the inside.

'What?' Rose said. 'Sidney?'

'Seems to be that Dawson's dobbin these days,' Mari said, heading across the yard. 'And 'e ay getting paid for 'is trouble, or so Edna says.'

Rose and Lucy exchanged looks. Rose shrugged. Who cared if Sidney Wilmott was stupid enough to slave for Seth Dawson for nothing?

They went into the forge where Edna and Bertha were both hammering away.

'So – doubled our wages, 'ave yow?' Bertha said sarcastically.

Neither of them bothered to reply.

'Why's 'e bringing so much?' Rose indicated the heap of work waiting for them outside.

'Says orders is piling up,' Edna said.

'Is that what 'e said?' Rose went to her hearth and started pressing down on the bellows to get the fire going again, but she was frowning. Lucy wondered what she was thinking. Did it mean something, all this work piling up? She couldn't work it out, whether there was something going on and if so, what it was.

Lucy was in a daze all the rest of the day and nothing could shake her – not Bertha's sulks or the fact that she had so much work to catch up on which meant she'd be stuck in here almost all the rest of the day. But it was worth it! She had joined the union – Mary Macarthur's union!

All she could think of were Mary Macarthur's words which rang in her ears, and her smile and her voice like cool, pure water from the mountains, telling them all that life could be different, could be and *must* be better.

Thirty-Five

'Where'm yow off to, Luce?' Freddie asked that evening, as she went to open the door.

'Just need to get on.' She inclined her head towards the forge and disappeared across the yard.

Bertha stood up, taking Freddie's gravy-smeared plate with her own. ''Er was off gadding this morning,' she said bitterly, as Lucy disappeared. Lucy had not said anything while they were all eating about where she had been. The door closed behind her and Bertha added, 'That Rose Shaw's been putting ideas in her head.'

'Luce ought not to be going about with her,' John said, disapproving. ''Er's a bad influence.'

Clem got to his feet. 'I'm off out.'

John was going out too and they left together. Bertha poured from the kettle into a bowl to wash up, gradually becoming conscious as she did so that her youngest son was still sitting on his chair looking up at her.

Freddie was getting really handsome these days, she thought, moved by the sight of him. Of all of them he was the most like Jonno, dark-haired and big built – stronger now even than Clem. A pang went through her. She had not known Jonno when he was sixteen, like Freddie was now, but he must have looked much like that. God knew, she hoped life would treat her son better than it had her husband. The thought made her instantly crave a drink.

'All right, son?' she said, wondering why he was gawping at her like that.

'Mom?' He sounded hesitant, almost as if he was afraid of her. That was a terrible thought. She knew she was out of sorts these days, couldn't seem to get it together in her own head. Had her dark state lately even frightened her own son? The son of his father, her beloved man . . .? What was happening to her?

'What, son?' She softened her voice, looking across at him, relishing the feel of hot water on her stiff hands.

'I don't understand –' he spoke carefully – 'why yow keep coming down so hard on Luce. Where's 'er bin?'

'Oh – off with them union lot,' Bertha said. She looked down. Emotion rose up in her that she could barely even explain. 'They'm causing nobbut trouble. They'll get the lot of us the sack, the way they're carrying on.'

Freddie hesitated. He had heard his brothers going on at Lucy about all this, making out she didn't know what she was doing, as if she was a fool, saying it would all go wrong and the bosses would win again because they always did.

'Maybe 'er's right,' Freddie said slowly. He wasn't sure what he thought about it all. 'To try, I mean. They can't sack *all* of yer, can 'em? Who'd do the work?'

'Oh, there's always someone needs work.' Bertha laid the plates face down to drain on a piece of sacking, knives and forks next to them. She took the bowl into the scullery and tipped the water down the sink. 'That sort of carry-on always causes more trouble than not, in the end.'

'But this's never happened before, has it?' Freddie said. 'A union like this?' He got up and stood in the doorway to the scullery. 'What if yow could all beat that fogger at his game? What if yow *could* mek 'em pay more?'

Bertha stood for a second, feeling her inner discomfort rising to choke her. Fear – fear of the bosses and of Seth Dawson, her loathing for them – and the biggest terror of the lot, of them all being cast out, thrown into destitution.

'Out of my way, son.' She pushed past Freddie and headed for the door. A drink. She had to have a drink. 'I'm off out.'

Across the darkening yard she could see the orange glow from the fires through the iron bars of the forge windows and the shadows of the women still hammering away inside.

'The way yower all going, yow ay gunna 'ave any work soon,' she muttered furiously, as she set off along the entry.

Lucy stood by her hearth, resting most of her weight on her good leg. They worked by the light of the fires, she, Rose and Mari who had got behind that day as well. Tired at this end of the day, the three of them worked mostly in silence. But Lucy was anything but sleepy – she felt alight with all that she had seen and heard that morning.

Mary Macarthur's voice rang in her mind. She had never heard anything like it before! The lady looked so nice standing up there, so strong, Lucy thought and so certain of what she was saying! And she was smiling at us as if she liked us – as if she *cared* about us!

Her lips turned up as she hammered away, thinking about it.

'I wish Auntie would come and see that lady,' she called across to Rose. 'She might feel better about things if she did.'

'What lady?' Mari said.

'There was a lady from the union this morning, from

London,' Rose said. 'Spoke ever so nice, 'er did. Made yow feel we can do anything, day 'er, Luce? Yow should come and 'ear her if 'er comes again.'

'Oh, I don't think Victor'd like it,' Mari said.

''T ay 'im I'm asking to come,' Rose said pertly. She put her hammer down, wiped her forehead. 'And since when're yow still asking 'is say-so on anything, Mari?'

Mari stared at her. After a lot of ding-dongs, she and Victor seemed gradually to have patched things up well enough, though Sunday afternoons were a lot quieter in the yard these days. And so far, there was no sign of another child on the way. But it did not seem to have occurred to Mari that she could take charge over anything else.

Rose put her hammer down. 'Need the lav,' she said. 'Then I'll come and finish off – I'm nearly done for the day.'

She flexed her back to balance the weight of her own swollen belly, then yawning, she disappeared out towards the lavatories.

'You stopping here?' Lucy asked Mari.

'Yeah – for a bit, any'ow.'

Side by side, Lucy and Mari worked away. They were alone, then a moment later, they were not. Lucy didn't hear them coming. She jumped, horribly jarred by the rough, grating voice.

'Oh! Now – what 'ave we 'ere!'

Seth Dawson and Sidney Wilmott, both burly, both right inside the forge, blocking the door. It was as if the small building had filled up with men. Sidney had a stupid, leering expression on his face that filled Lucy with misgiving. She prayed that someone else was out in the yard to have seen them, but there was no sign of anyone.

'What d'yow want?' Mari stood with her hand on her hip, braving it out. 'What're yow doing, creeping about like that? We'm trying to get some work done in 'ere if yow dow mind.'

'Work, eh?' Seth said. He fixed his thumbs into his braces and rocked back and forth. Sidney sniggered as if something filthy had been said. 'Well, I always like to see wenches at work – 'specially from be'ind.'

He looked at Sidney and they both chortled. The drink was in, it was clear. Sidney was swaying from side to side.

Lucy froze with fear. She was trapped by this vile man who had attacked her mother, had sent her to an early grave . . . Even now, she only half understood what had happened to Mom. What did they want – what were they going to do? Even her mind was numb with terror. She wanted to shout for help, but her throat seemed to have closed up. And would anyone hear?

'Sid 'ere and me've been waiting for a chance like this,' Seth said. 'What d'yer think, Sid – fancy the skinny one or the one with the peg-leg?'

'Don't you talk about us like that,' Mari said, trying to bluff it out, but Lucy could hear the tremor in her voice. They were trapped, there was no doubt about it. *Never be alone with Seth Dawson . . .* But even now there were two of them, there was no more of a way out of it.

'Tell yer what – yow tek that'un,' Seth directed, pointing Sidney towards Mari. ''Er's a wench of some experience – likes 'er legs in the air, that'un. 'Er'll show yer what to do, won't yer, Mari?'

'Don't you come near me –' Mari seized the nearest thing she could find which unfortunately was only a short length of rod. Sidney grabbed hold of her and Mari started screeching.

'I'll 'ave this one,' Seth said.

As Seth Dawson started towards her, Lucy was only

dimly aware that Mari had somehow broken free of Sidney, got away from the hearth and been grabbed again. She was punching Sidney and screaming at him.

At the sight of Seth, something in Lucy began – an anger that began to thrum through her body, almost a feeling of ecstasy. She still had her hammer in her hand, and she held it behind her, gripping the handle with all her strength as she backed away and up against the hearth.

'It'll be like old times, won't it,' Seth was saying. The bulk of him swayed towards her, his black teeth, the foul cave of his mouth from which fumes of alcohol forced their way into her nostrils. 'Remind me of yower mother, yow do – only yower riper than 'er . . . Skinny rat, 'er was . . .'

'Don't you *touch* me,' she spat at him. God knew, if only she could run, but she knew, as he did, that she could not.

'Yow gunna stop me then?' Seth grabbed her by the waist, his stinking alcohol breath in her nostrils. He rammed himself against her like a rutting dog. This was what he did – she knew then – what he did to Mom, the way he finished her, killed her . . .

Her rage boiled in her. She brought her arm round and swung the hammer at his head. But the blow only knocked his hat to one side, barely touching him.

'Enough o' that, yer little bitch!'

He groped with his arm, trying to catch hers, but she managed swiftly to bring the hammer round again, and with all her force cracked it against the side of his head.

Seth yelled with pain. His grip on her slackened. He seemed stunned that she had fought back. Lucy was so full of panic and rage that she lifted the heavy hammer once more and brought it down again at the side of his skull. Seth staggered and she landed another blow at the top of his arm. He seemed incapable of fighting back.

She became aware of Mari, still fighting Sidney off, kicking and screaming. He was so kalied he couldn't seem to do anything except shove himself at her and be slapped and kicked in return.

'Oh, my Lord above!' she heard Rose's voice. Everything seemed unreal, slow and at a distance. Rose was hauling at Sidney Wilmott, trying to get him off Mari.

For a second Lucy wondered why Rose was not helping her, but she watched with astonishment as Seth Dawson, who no longer had a hold on her, stumbled towards the door. He looked round at them all for a moment, swaying on his feet, as if he had no idea what he was doing there, and lurched through the door, into the dying light.

Sidney Wilmott was far too caught up his own urges to notice what had happened.

'Get *off*, yow stinking varmint!' Mari was shrieking.

'Yow filthy beast!' Rose picked up a rod from the floor and drove the end of it into Sidney's backside as he pinned Mari against the hearth. He gave a roar of pain, like a cow.

Lucy picked up the length of rod she had left heating in the fire. Limping over with it, she shoved the burning tip up against Sidney's neck, under his left ear.

'Aaaargh!' He jumped back then, clutching at himself as Mari grabbed another length of rod. 'Yow bitch!' He whirled round, flies undone and it all hanging out. 'That 'urt me, that did!'

'You get out of 'ere or yow'll 'ave another one up yower backside!' Mari shrieked.

Faced with three furious women, two of them now brandishing iron rods and threats as to where various painful insertions might be made, Sidney decided to retreat. Cursing, rubbing his burned neck with one hand and clutching at his flies with the other, he took himself off as well.

Lucy leaned up against the hearth, trembling all over. The three of them stood silent for a moment, stunned.

'What . . .?' Rose began. She was still trying to make sense of all that had happened while she'd popped out to relieve herself. 'What the hell's gone on in 'ere? Mari – what 'appened? He never . . .?'

'Nah.' Mari looked shaken up, but she was straightening her clothes. ''E tried it on but 'e 'ardly knows what to do with it, that one.' She rubbed her back, grimacing. ''E dain't 'alf push me hard on them bricks, though – 'e flaming hurt me.'

'Lucy?' Rose's eyes were full of concern. 'Oh, babby . . .' She came over to Lucy, who was shaking so much she could hardly stay upright. She felt cold and shivery. Rose's comforting arms wrapped round her. 'How far did it go . . .? Did 'e hurt yow?'

Lucy shook her head. Her teeth were starting to chatter.

Rose looked even more confused. 'I s'pose I came in just in time.'

Lucy nodded, her forehead against Rose's shoulder. 'And . . . I hit him – with my hammer. On the head.' She looked up into Rose's face. 'He let go of me then.'

Rose was gaping at her in astonishment.

'And then you stuck Sid in the neck!' Mari said.

Lucy nodded. 'S'pose I did, yeah.' It was all starting to feel clearer now, what had happened. She felt released in some way as shattered, crazed impressions crowded in: Seth Dawson shoving himself against her, his stunned face as he reeled away, hat hanging over one ear; Sidney

273

Wilmott booming like a calf and staggering about with his flies gaping open. The shock of it all burst out of her in peals of laughter.

'Oh, my God,' Rose said, breaking out into wild cackling as well.

'D'you see 'is face when yow stuck it to 'im?' Mari cried.

Hysterical laughter overtook all of them, each feeding off the sight of the others, bent over, tears running down their faces. Lucy laughed and laughed, feeling as if something that had been building and boiling for years had burst, loosening everything inside her.

Bertha had made slow progress back from the Outdoor. Freddie was in and there was something about the way her son looked at her these days that made her hesitate to go home with her little medicine bottle and its burning, comforting contents. Freddie's gaze seemed to cut right through her.

She wandered back along the street, the bottle tucked into her waist, breathing in the warm summer air. There was always smoke, but because they were near the fields, she could make out scents of the countryside as well, the freshness of grass tinged with cow parsley and the herby smells of the weeds. Even these made her ache – for the past, for being young, courting with Jonno . . .

Turning into the entry in the dusky light, she stopped and lingered, taking her bottle from her waistband. She stared at it for a moment. Shame washed through her. What was she becoming? Drinking in secret in an alley like some disgusting old lag? What would Jonno say if her saw her?

But she could not stop herself. Tilting the bottle, she took in its warm, liquid kisses. The hot comfort of it burned through her. It was so hard ever to be alone even for a few minutes. Except for the lav, where you'd not want to linger, there was hardly a place to be and think your own thoughts. She leaned against the wall, took a few more swigs and drifted off into the past, which seemed a more reassuring place than the present day. Jonno, their youth when everything was full of hope . . .

She was jerked out of her reminiscences by a shriek from inside the forge. What was that? It sounded like Mari, Bertha thought, her thoughts befuddled. She righted herself and lurched along to the yard. Just as she reached the end of the entry, in the gloom she saw the outline of a horribly familiar figure emerge from the workshop.

So that bastard had been on the prowl. She stopped at the end of the entry, loathing rising in her. What was he doing – bringing them yet more rods? At least he was on his way out again, sod him.

Seth walked towards her and Bertha cursed not having managed to slip into her house without him seeing her. He came lumbering across the yard, but there was something so rambling about his walk, that she thought, 'E's proper kalied, that'un – he can hardly keep upright!

Standing at the corner of her house, near the entry, she waited for him to start on her – something rude, or mocking, as usual. Seth weaved up to her and, to Bertha's bafflement, he didn't even seem to notice her standing there.

He was passing her when the devilment got into her. He was so blind drunk he had not even seen her! On an impulse she stuck her leg out in front of him. Seth Dawson stumbled straight over it and measured his length on the ground, head sticking into the entry. A great grunt came from him as the wind was knocked out of him. Bertha waited, hand over her mouth and edging towards her door.

Dear God – what was going on? Why wasn't he getting up – he must be out cold?

She crept forward and peered round the corner, only dimly aware, as she did so, of more yells and shrieks going on inside the forge. It was eerie, seeing his lumpish form laid out, silent like that, a dark shape in the gloom of the entry.

Then Seth groaned. She saw his legs move very slowly and she drew back, peering round the corner as he staggered to his feet again, making noises like an old dog. At last she heard him lumbering along the entry and out into the street.

Thirty-Six

Everyone except the Wilmotts came hurrying out of their houses.

The three of them, Lucy, Rose and Mari, had been in helpless fits of laughter, but it had passed and suddenly they were shocked and angry as what had happened sunk in. Mari Gornall started yelling blue murder.

'It were that vile fogger – and *'im*!' Mari was soon shrieking to her husband, pointing at the Wilmotts' door. 'Come and attacked us while we was working!'

'I'll get that filthy bugger . . .' In seconds, Victor Gornall went striding over and was banging on the door of number one.

Rose stayed by Lucy's side. Soon, Wally Shaw had come outside and then Bertha, with Freddie.

'You all right, Luce?' Lucy felt Rose's arm comfortingly round her shoulders. Rose leaned down to look into Lucy's face and it was only then that Lucy burst into tears, all the shock of it starting to pour out. Shaking, she leaned on Rose, feeling as if her one good leg was about to give way.

'What's going on?' Bertha demanded. 'I saw that bastard coming out – 'e were so kalied 'e could 'ardly stand . . . What happened, Luce?' She looked at Rose. Even through her tears Lucy could see the horror and rage in her face. 'He never . . .?'

Rose shook her head. No. Not that. Not like her mother.

'That filthy bastard,' Bertha breathed. 'Wants stringing up, that 'e does.'

'What happened, Luce?' Freddie was asking.

She couldn't find the breath to reply to anyone and it all felt dirty and shameful. She buried her face in Rose's arm. Talk would get round soon enough without her having to explain to Freddie or anyone. In the background she heard Victor and Wally bashing on the Wilmotts' door.

'If 'e dow come out we'll come in and get 'im!' Victor Gornall was yelling.

'Yow leave 'im alone!' Edna's head appeared at the window. ''E's 'aving 'is tea!'

'I'll give 'im tea!' Victor shouted. 'Come on, Wal . . .' They started beating so hard at the door that it would soon have given way, but suddenly it opened.

The yard went quiet. Lucy looked up. Sidney Wilmott was peering round the edge of the door.

'Right,' Bertha ordered. 'Rose – you take our Lucy inside.'

'Wally – dow go and do anything stupid!' Rose shouted over to him. 'Come on, Luce.'

Lucy hobbled over to the cottage with Rose to the sound of Wally and Victor – and Freddie had gone to join in – dragging Sidney Wilmott into the yard.

'Yow ever touch any of our women again, yow filthy sod . . .!' Lucy heard Victor Gornall shouting, and the thuds of blows being administered were the last horrible things she heard before Rose shut the door behind them.

'I'll make us a cup of tea, shall I?' Rose said.

Lucy, sitting at the table, nodded mutely up at her. She didn't think Bertha would mind if Rose put the kettle on, but Bertha and Freddie themselves then came in.

'Wally and Victor's given 'im a right pastin'!' Freddie informed Rose cheerfully. 'That'un won't be bothering any of yow wenches again.'

Lucy saw Bertha taking in that Rose Shaw was with them.

'I put the kettle on, Mrs Hipkiss – I hope that's all right.' She spoke very deferentially to Bertha. 'I thought the wench might need a cuppa.'

'Ar – and the rest of us,' Bertha said. Lucy realized her voice was softer than it often was when she spoke to Rose. But she could also hear the drink slurring it. 'Ta – for looking after Lucy.' But she did not say anything more inviting.

'All right – see yer tomorrow,' Rose said, taking the hint.

A moment after she had gone, the door was flung open again and John and Clem came in, laughing together, an unusual thing in itself. They burst out with their news before taking in the state of Lucy.

'That fogger were coming along the road,' Clem said. 'John and me bumped into each other and then we saw 'im coming along. Dunno what 'e were doing heading off that way but anyroad, "Oh, 'ere we go," we said. " 'Ere comes trouble."'

'He never even saw us,' John put in. Lucy hadn't seen him looking so youthful and mischievous in a long time.

'Off 'is head, 'e was!' Clem chortled. 'As 'e came up I says to 'im, "Evenin', Mr Dawson, 'ow am yer?" sort of pretending to be friendly like. 'E never even heard us, did 'e, John?'

''E was staggering about,' John said. 'Must 'ave had a right skinful – 'e were like a statue walking along!'

'So when 'e'd gone past I gave 'im a bit of a push like,'

Clem said. 'I dow think I even pushed 'im all that hard – and 'e went straight down like a ninepin!'

The boys' laughter was so infectious that all the rest of them joined in. Even Bertha cracked her face and Lucy started to feel better. It felt as if everyone was on her side, and it was good to know that Seth Dawson could be pushed around as well as doling it out to other people. He had stunk of drink – he and Sidney must have been getting tanked up before they decided to come and prey on the women in their yard.

'When 'e got up 'e was looking round as if 'e day know what hit him!' John laughed. 'And off 'e went – never said a word!'

'Well, it weren't his first trip tonight.' Bertha waited a few seconds for the laughter to die down before she spoke. She explained briefly what had happened, the way the two men had come sneaking into the forge. 'Our Luce gave 'im a whack with a 'ommer. And I met 'im coming out of the yard and 'e never saw me out there by the wall, so I stick my leg out and down 'e went!'

'You never, Mom!' John said.

'The filthy sod!' Clem looked furious, fists clenched. 'If I'd've known I'd've done more'n trip 'im over, I can tell yer! You all right, Luce?'

She nodded, overcome by all the attention.

'Our Luce fought him off.' Bertha sounded emotional. 'Otherwise, heaven only knows . . .'

'Rose would have come back,' Lucy said. 'She helped us.'

'Ar,' Bertha had to acknowledge. 'That one helped see Sidney off, all right.'

But as she lay in bed that night, Bertha snoring gently, she couldn't stop reliving the moment when Seth grabbed her. Her arms hurt from the grip of his fingers on her.

The next morning, alone in the room once Bertha had

already gone down, Lucy sat up on her mattress and pulling her nightdress over her head, examined the tops of her arms. There were rings of bruising, oval-shaped finger marks the colour of a stormy sky. She had not even been alone when she was working out there and that had not stopped them.

Hugging her knees, she thought about her mother, trying to make herself face what had really happened to her. She remembered the horrible, confused feeling of that afternoon when she had been feverish in bed and had heard that voice from downstairs. His voice. The way she had slid down the stairs on her backside to find him there in the house. Was that how it was? Had he forced his way into the house again and . . . Her mind did not want to go down the path of what must have happened next to her poor mother, something she knew, yet at the same time did not know. Hatred surged through her, the same blind rage that had thrummed in her when she landed the heavy weight of the hammer on Seth Dawson's head.

At least I hit him. Her body was beginning to vibrate with energy as she relived the moment. I hit him three times – and he didn't get me!

Sidney Wilmott, with two black eyes and swollen cheeks and lips where the men had set about him, went limping out of the yard, obviously feeling very sorry for himself.

''E can't say 'e dain't ask for it,' Bertha said as they all set to work that morning. 'And don't you go canting and complaining about it, Edna.' Edna, with a sulky expression, was keeping her head down and banging away. 'That lad of yowers 'ad it coming a long time, carrying on like that.'

''E cor 'elp the way 'e is,' Edna said, finally raising her

head. ''E never meant any harm – it's that fogger, paying 'im attention, leading 'im astray.'

'Ar, well, that's a true word,' Bertha said. Everyone else was keeping quiet except Mari.

'I dow care who led 'im astray – 'e attacked me, like an animal!' she burst out. ''E should be locked up and the key thrown away!'

'No!' Edna begged, looking really frightened now. 'It won't happen again. It ay no good going blabbing to the Peelers – not when we dow need to. 'E's been dealt with. Leave 'im be. 'E's all I've got, my boy – I'm begging yow.'

Lucy found it terrible to see the pain and fear in Edna's eyes and she looked away.

'Well, I 'ope that lummox of a lad of yours's learned a lesson,' Bertha said, asserting herself as the person in charge. 'I ay gunna say anything this time, but 'e needs to keep well away from that *fogger*.' She almost spat out the word.

Edna gave Bertha a resentful, cringeing look but did not dare say any more.

There was such a heap of rods outside the forge that they had days' worth of work to do. And that next afternoon Rose went to another union meeting. Even at almost six months pregnant, she had energy when it came to the union. But she returned with such enraging information that it made everyone less eager to get through the work.

'What they're saying is,' she said, standing in the forge with her straw hat still on, 'that they're stockpiling chain supplies. What this is all in aid of –' she waved a hand towards the heap of rods outside – 'is that when the new wages're are supposed to come in, they'll say there's no demand and no orders. And then they'll blame it on us for asking for a proper wage!'

Her cheeks were pink from hurrying back along the road and she was speaking with her hands on her hips and leaning forward as if she was the one on a soapbox. With her rounded belly she looked rather awesome, Lucy thought.

'That way, they can say the new rate's to blame for everything and that we should scrap it or none of us'll 'ave jobs!'

'I said they'd never do it, dain't I?' Bertha said. But Lucy was surprised to hear that she wasn't crowing over Rose as she might once have done. 'They can always find a way to get out of it . . .' She turned back to her hearth and started pumping the bellows. 'Yow might just as well accept it, wench. Them's the ones with all the cards in their hands.'

Rose looked as if she wanted to argue back, but instead lowered her hands from her waist where they hung slack at her sides. Her face fell into beaten-looking lines which made Lucy feel truly miserable. If Rose was giving up, what hope was there for the rest of them?

'We've got to get them to do it somehow,' Rose said. She sounded close to tears. 'All these promises – they just trick us time after time. It's worse when . . .' Her face crumpled and she covered it with her hands for a moment. 'When you get a bit of hope things might change, and then they just throw it back at yer . . .' She gathered herself again, reaching for her anger instead of despair. 'It's all wrong, the way they get away with treating us, just because we'm women.'

'Well, what does the union say?' Mari asked. Unlike Rose and Lucy she had not joined the NFWW, saying she couldn't spare a penny a week with all her kids to feed.

'I dunno,' Rose said. She untied the string of her hat

and took it off, hanging it on a nail on the wall. 'They just keep saying we've got to hang on – to fight it and not sign any of them forms. But . . .' She tied her apron round her and went wearily to her own hearth. 'I dow really know.'

It was a few days before it was noticed that Seth Dawson had not been round, keeping on at them. And a few more to take in that he was nowhere to be seen. As a single man with no family, no one had missed him at home. None of the outworkers would be dismayed by his absence and it was only the factory employers who started to wonder why their fogger, who usually did the rounds of the out-workers, fattening his own belly as he did so, seemed to have completely disappeared.

VI

1910

Thirty-Seven

After ten days, a policeman came to the yard. Had anyone seen Seth Dawson? When had they last seen him? Everyone in the yard said, not for a couple of weeks. No one had much more to say. Only Bertha added another detail which was that the last time Dawson was seen in their yard, he had evidently had a skinful. The policeman even asked Sidney Wilmott, who gave one of his brainless sniggers and said no, he hadn't seen him, no, not in a good while.

Naturally, they began to wonder, after a time. But Seth Dawson had already brought such a great stack of rods and piled them in the yard, that they were not going short of something to do. And it was Sidney who was carting them back to Ridley's in the dobbin. But no, their fogger had not been round in a while.

Talk started, of course. If Seth Dawson had been drinking heavily that night, had he wandered off and passed out somewhere? Had the bang on the head Lucy gave him left him stunned? No one, Lucy included, could believe she had hit him with enough force to do any real damage. Not to mention the fact that Bertha had tripped him and sent him crashing headlong as, shortly afterwards, had John and Clem? He had seemed confused, but was it the drink? No one knew for sure, but so far as they were concerned, the longer he stayed away the better. The feeling was that he'd be back, like a bad smell.

After three weeks or more, fresh news was travelling

287

from yard to yard like a fire catching, leaping over walls, spreading everywhere. The young farm labourer who found Seth Dawson's body, in a field south of town, had spared no one the details over his next jar of ale. The news then migrated from pub to pub – and it was Clem who heard it first.

'Maggots – ugh!' Rose said, as they gathered in the yard and before realizing that little Gracie, Charlie and Ivy's ears were all flapping, their blue eyes turned up to Clem, drinking in the news. Seven-year-old Grace looked especially fascinated. Rose, now heavy with child, leaned down and whispered to them, 'Off yer go – go and play.' But there was no budging them from the source of these mesmerizing details.

Lucy listened, horror creeping through her. Lying in a field – for how long? Three weeks now since that night in the forge? Out in the hot sun, the rain, worms and maggots sliding into his flesh. The faces around her, of Mari and Bertha, Edna and Rose, all showed shock and revulsion.

'Seems like 'e was that kalied that night, 'e just wandered off, dain't know what 'e was doing,' Clem said.

Lucy watched him, handsome Clem, the boy she had loved so secretly and devotedly all those years. He was even more handsome now, but her bruised heart had cooled and turned away. It had been a relief to grow out of Clem.

'Well,' Edna said, with no shred of pity, 'that's got shot of that'un, any road. We ay gunna be seeing 'is fizzog round 'ere no more.'

There was a second's silence before everyone broke out into cheers and clapping.

Lucy found herself laughing along with the others. ''E's gone!'

'That bastard!'

'Coming round 'ere, preying on us women . . .'

'We wo' be going to 'is funeral!'

'Good cowing riddance!'

Sidney Wilmott had brought more rods from Ridley's when they had worked their way through the huge heap that Seth had brought before.

'I reckon my Sidney can get Dawson's job now,' Edna started saying over the next day or two.

'I cor see them teking on that simpleton,' Bertha said the next evening, when they were all inside the house. ''E'll be teking 'imself off to some cock-fight or summat in the middle of the job – 'e ay got no sense in 'im.'

Lucy's face crinkled with disgust at the thought.

'What's up wi' yow?' Clem said.

''E's dirty, 'e is,' she said. She looked down at her plate, cutting into a bit of potato, blushes rising in her face at the memory of Sidney, lurching his body into Mari's in the forge.

''E's a proper aydedaydy,' Freddie said. 'But at least if 'e was the fogger, yow women wo' let 'im get away with it.'

'Nah – 'e's not up to anything like that,' Bertha said.

'Edna'd have to keep him in line,' John said.

'Just for once.' Clem grinned, sitting back, his plate empty. 'He ain't as bad as Dawson, any road.'

'No one's as bad as Dawson,' Lucy said.

But they soon found out for sure that Sidney Wilmott was not to be the new fogger for Ridley's. The five of them were all at work the next morning, sweating in the rising August heat. None of them saw the wide-girthed figure turn into their entry and cross the yard, until it was planted in the doorway, blocking the light. Lucy turned.

289

'Right,' a deep, rasping voice said. 'Yow lot're working for me now.'

A silver-grey blouse fastened tightly high at the throat, black skirt, a hat with what looked like a whole dead bird arrayed across the brim and face like a hatchet: Thirza Rudge, the woman reckoned to be one of the very worst foggers in the district.

Rose wasn't having it, right from the start. She stood in front of Mrs Rudge, her belly protruding impressively, Lucy thought, looking straight into the woman's steely eyes.

'I hope you know the minimum rate of pay is due to come in the middle of this week – and there's union members in 'ere.'

'Huh.' Thirza Rudge made a dismissive sound. She folded her arms, her top lip curling with contempt. 'Union? What union?'

'The National Federation of Women Workers,' Rose said, hands on hips now.

'Look 'ere, wench,' Thirza Ridge said, her gimlet-like stare drilling into Rose in a way that made Lucy feel shrunken and terrified. 'I'm be'olden to Ridley's, it ay me sets the rate. Yow can work for them, at the rate yower at now, or yow can tek yowerself off and goo without. That's 'ow it is.'

Everyone else kept quiet, cowed by the very sight of Thirza Rudge, but Rose's temper was up.

'The Trade Boards've agreed to pay the rate – and they've got to pay it!' she raged.

Thirza Rudge looked back at her, seemingly indifferent.

'Who's gunna make 'em – yow? Tek the work or leave it – if yow dow want it there's plenty going 'ungry who will.'

She was about to go, then turned back.

'And yow can all do the fetching and carrying – I ay pushing no dobbin up and down.'

She took herself off across the yard. They all stood for a second looking at each other, aghast. Rose turned furiously back to her hearth. A few seconds later though, Lucy heard her gasp. Something was wrong. Rose collapsed on the floor, folding down on to her side and then sprawling on her back.

'Oh, Auntie – help her!' Lucy cried.

Bertha and the other women all hurried across.

'Get some water,' she ordered, kneeling beside Rose. Mari rushed out and returned with a cup of water. They soon had Rose sitting up again, looking groggy. Bertha supported her back with her strong arm as she sipped the water.

'What happened?' Rose seemed dazed. 'I saw all these lights at the sides of my eyes and then . . . it was all black.'

'You fainted,' Bertha said. 'Yow never fainted before?' Lucy was surprised by how kindly she spoke and to see her grudging admiration for Rose. It took real guts to speak up to Thirza Rudge like that. And everyone knew how passionately she felt, believing in it all so much more strongly than they had managed to.

'No – I've never 'ad that 'appen to me before,' Rose said. 'I don't half feel funny.'

'Just sit there for a bit – keep yer 'ead down and yow'll be all right,' Mari said. 'It was what that old cow said – got yow all mithered.'

'They said they'd pay the rate.' Rose looked up at them all. 'They'm just liars and cheats!'

All of a sudden, she lowered her head and broke down. The sound of her crying wrung Lucy's heart. Rose had believed so passionately in what they were trying to do – not just for herself but for all the women. And now they were being deceived and let down – again. But fiery Rose Shaw, crying! It made Lucy feel upset and frightened. Rose, who had always been the one who led the way.

'Eh, wench – no need for that,' Bertha said. She was still squatting beside Rose.

Rose lifted her head and her eyes met Bertha's. She was so cast down and upset after all her passion, her efforts, that she looked almost like a little girl.

'What're we gunna do, Mrs Hipkiss?'

Something changed in those seconds, in that moment of deference, in appealing to the older woman. Lucy saw Bertha straighten her back. Her opinion was being asked and she was the gaffer of the yard. Slowly, she got to her feet again.

'We're gunna 'ave to wait and see,' Bertha said. 'What's promised is promised – but there's many grown old waiting for them sort of promises to be kept. The date they set's not been and gone yet.'

'Mrs Hipkiss,' Rose said, still looking up from the floor, speaking with great respect. 'D'yow think you might join the union now? Everyone respects you. And if they was to decide on anything, you might be left out, else? It'd be better if we was all solid.'

Bertha considered. Edna and Mari, neither of whom had yet paid up to any union, were watching her, as if their decision was bound up with hers.

Lucy also watched Bertha. She could see her mind working, as if something in her was changing before her eyes. Bertha almost seemed to be growing taller. After a moment, she nodded, on her dignity. 'S'pose it might be for the best, the way things are,' she said.

*

A few days later, when the deadline passed and there had been no sign of the new rate being implemented, they had another visit from Madge Lunn, the union worker. She hurried into the forge, grim-faced.

'As yow will know, the date when yower employers were supposed to start paying yower proper, living wage, has come and gone with no sign of them doing what they agreed. They have already tricked a lot of the women round here into opting out. Did any of you . . .?'

'No!' Rose said fiercely. She had got some of her fight back now. 'We day sign the papers – and now all of us 'ere are in the union.'

Madge Lunn gave a faint smile. 'Well, that is summat. I came to tell you that the NFWW, led by Mary Macarthur, are drafting an agreement demanding that your employers start paying your proper wages immediately.' She wagged her finger. 'They will be sending it in today! I'll tell you as soon as I know anything.'

A day later, a dobbin came rumbling along the entry pushed by some bloke they'd never seen before, a sour, wizened old man with a dirty white beard, his hat perched on the back of his head. He drew it up close to the forge and started loading the rods piled outside.

Bertha, who seemed to be getting more of her energy back by the day, went out and confronted him. The rest of them peered through the doorway.

'Oi – what'm yow doing?'

'I'm teking yower rods,' he said.

'I'm not cowing blind,' Bertha said. 'What'm yow doing that for?'

The man straightened up, dumping another fistful of rods on the cart with a crash. He spoke looking across the yard and didn't meet Bertha's eye.

'I've been told to take yower materials.'

'What the hell d'yow mean, teking away our materials?' Rose pushed her way out of the forge. ''Ow're we supposed to get any work done?'

'Yow lot're part of that union trouble.' He obviously didn't want to look anyone in the eye and he stooped to gather up more rods. 'Mr Ridley says there'll be no work 'til yow all pack it in. So yower locked out – the lot of yer.'

Thirty-Eight

Rose stood by the bed, quietly buttoning up her best dress. It was already light, well before seven in the morning and she was raring to go. She went over to her chest of drawers, brushing her thick, nut-brown hair. The cornflower-blue dress – loose, fortunately, and fitting over her ripe belly – brought out the colour of her eyes, and the excitement bubbling inside her was evident in the face that was smiling back at her from the freckled old glass.

'Today's gunna be a *day*!' she whispered. She had seldom felt more alive.

Still looking in the mirror she saw Wally suddenly shoot up to a sitting position in the bed. He stared at her, bewildered.

'Blimey, Rosie – yow look *bostin*! What the 'ell're yow doing up this early?'

'I told yer.' She turned. 'We'm all going up the High Street – there's gunna be speeches and that by the Empire. That Mary Macarthur woman is gunna be there.'

Wally's brow wrinkled. 'You ent working?'

'Wally . . .' Containing her impatience with her loving but at times slow-to-catch-on husband, she went and perched on the edge of the bed. 'I told yow – we cor work. They've teken all the work away and locked us out. There's ay no work to be done.'

Wally gazed at her as if all this was a bit much when he was still half asleep. He reached out his hand.

'You look so nice when you're . . . yer know . . .' He nodded at her half-globe of a belly. 'C'm'ere . . .'

'No!' Rose laughed, quickly getting up. 'Yow know what that'll lead to! I ay rolling about with you in my best frock when I've spent an age ironing it!'

Wally lay back, looking at her. 'Looks like yow'll all get the sack.'

Everyone had been out in the yard last night, a lot of back-and-to about what was happening. Victor Gornall had been trying to lay the law down to Mari about all this union rubbish.

'Yow wenches're getting above yowerselves,' he was yelling. 'Thinking yow can just do as yow like – asking for money! Yow all need a good hiding, that's what!'

'It's too late to go on like that,' Mari shrieked at him. 'We cor work now even if us wanted to!'

'I dunno,' Rose said to Wally. 'There's some've signed those bits of paper saying they'd opt out of the new rate and most of them never even knew what they was signing – now they'm saying they wish they never 'ad. And the union's told 'em to pay us and now they've gone and locked us out. So what d'yow call that then? Am we sacked already?'

'A cowing mess and muddle is what I'd call it,' Wally said. He lifted his head. 'Are all yow wenches going to this meeting? None of the blokes'll stand for much more of it, yer know.'

'D'yow think I dow know that?' Rose rolled her eyes. 'I dunno who's going. And yower gunna 'ave to mek up your mind whose side yower on, Wally – yower wife's or the firm's and their starvation rates. I know one thing though – all them bosses, we've rattled their chains all right!' She grinned, her excitement returning. 'I'm gunna take Gracie and the others with me. 'They'm old enough to come and see what we'm doing.'

'C'mon, Grace, Ivy, let's get your hair done – that's it, Charlie – damp it down with a bit of water! You first, Gracie.'

Grace got up from the stool near the fireplace where she had been sitting, looking as if she was afraid to move. She and Ivy, standing solemnly waiting, were both wearing their best matching mauve frocks which Rose had stitched for them, with a pinner over the top.

'That's a good wench,' Rose panted. She started brushing Grace's hair vigorously.

'Ow – Mom!'

'Sorry, bab.'

'Where'm we going?' Grace said, as Rose hurriedly wove two plaits into her light brown hair. She could sense her mother's excitement, though she did not fully understand what all this was about.

'To hear a lady who's gunna help us get better pay.' Rose tied a little white ribbon at the end of each plait. 'Least, we hope so. Somehow. There yow go – all spick and span. Right – now you, Ivy.'

She worked deftly on the little girl's hair. Ivy was five, with Wally's long face. She was a quieter child than Grace.

'Yow've all 'ad yower piece, ay yer?' Rose said, bustling about when she had finished. 'Come on then – let's go and see what's going on with these other wenches.'

She was still half afraid that the others in the yard were getting cold feet and would refuse to come. And with Bertha Hipkiss, you never knew.

Lucy came to the door, beaming when she saw who was outside. She had also put on her best blue dress.

''Ello, Mrs Shaw!' She beamed at Rose and all the children. 'We'm getting ready.'

'Is yower auntie coming then?' Rose spoke barely above a whisper.

Lucy nodded, looking round, but the door was yanked wide open. Bertha Hipkiss stood there, looking so magnificent that Rose almost took a step backwards. Bertha, strong and upright as a ramrod, had on a brown dress patterned with white pinhead spots. She wore her heavy boots as usual, and her cap on her head, a long hatpin pushed through it, and to top off the outfit, round her neck hung a tatty fox fur, its now toothless head dangling over Bertha's sizeable chest. Her face was stern, as if to say, *I'm still the one in charge around here and you need to remember it.*

Rose's face broke into a delighted smile.

'Oh, Mrs Hipkiss, I'm *so* glad! If you come, it'll get everyone else out an' all.'

Bertha's face softened slightly. 'Not as if we can get any work done, ar it?'

'What about Mari and Edna?' Rose asked.

Bertha shrugged. 'Why do' yow ask them?'

'Come on, Luce,' Rose beckoned her and Lucy came hobbling out with her stick. 'Let's see if we can get 'em to come with us.'

'Is Miss Macarthur coming?' Lucy said eagerly.

'I think so. Mr Sitch – he's one of the other union people – said 'er was coming into the station about midday.'

'Mari?' Rose called in through the open door of number three. They heard squabbling children's voices, then Mari appeared. She kept her head down as she came to the door. 'Yow coming with us up the High Street? Hey – what's up with you?'

Mari had to raise her face then. Her left eye was so bruised and swollen she could hardly open it and her cheek looked puffy as well.

'Oh!' Rose erupted furiously. 'What'd 'e give yer that for – for saying you was coming out with the rest of us?'

Mari nodded miserably. 'Never get wed,' she said bitterly to Lucy. 'T'ain't cowing well worth it.'

'Yower coming though?' Rose said.

'I dunno.' Mari seemed really browbeaten. 'I said I ay going.'

To Rose's surprise, Lucy spoke up. 'Why doesn't he want you to have better wages?'

Mari shrugged again. She seemed to have no answer for this.

'My lot're coming,' Rose said, indicating the three children. 'Yow can bring Dolly and the others if yer want. Yow ay gunna earn any money today if yow stay in, are yer?'

Mari thought for a moment. 'All right. I 'ope Victor dow find out, that's all.'

Edna Wilmott shook her head.

'I ay going marching about. It ay gunna make no difference to anything.'

'All the yards are coming out you know, Edna,' Rose said. 'There'll be crowds there – and it's a nice day. Mek a change. Why don't yer just come and see?'

Edna folded her arms, leaning against the door frame. 'Oh – I dunno.'

Edna truly tried Rose's patience, but she managed to hold on to her temper. Edna did look older suddenly, and she seemed very weary.

'What am we gunna live on with no wages coming in – that's what I want to know,' Edna said. 'It's all right for yow with sons and 'usbands working.'

No one wanted to point out at that moment that her idle layabout of a son should have been put to bringing in a wage years ago.

'Well, the rest of us are going. We'll be leaving soon.'

Bertha stood looking out as Lucy and Rose, with the Shaw children trailing along behind, went to each of the houses along the side of the yard. Her dress was of a heavy weave and a fox fur really not the thing for the hot weather, but she was going to stand up with the rest of them and look her best.

She fingered the thick cotton of the dress which hung more loosely on her now. The last time she wore it, Jonno had still been alive. She'd been got up for one of his nephews' weddings. Pain sliced through her. It was a long time ago now – almost ten years. The dress had hung there, stinking of camphor all that time – but they had not had many occasions to get dolled up and go out since then.

For a moment her whole being cried out with the need for a drink. She clenched her fists, drawing in deep breaths. No. She knew she had been close, very close to going under with it. The drink may have been her saviour, but it would be her ruination if she kept on. It was time to take hold of herself, find some dignity. She was not having people saying she went about stinking of hard liquor.

As for all this union business – well, they'd see, wouldn't they? But she had joined, in the end. After all those tricks Ridley's played, through that filthy fogger, that had been the last straw.

Seth Dawson's face flashed through her mind. And the staggering figure she had seen that night, blind drunk. What exactly had finished him off? Surely not a quick tap on the head from that little wench who only came up to his chest? He'd left the yard all right – even after she'd met him and tripped him over. And none of them knew what happened after John and Clem sent him down like a ninepin as well. Had they all had a hand in finishing off Dawson? They never would know now. The Coroner brought about a verdict of 'accidental death'. So. No need to dig that filthy mon up again – they were all better off with him where he was. What was done was done and good riddance. There was not a single soul would miss him.

As for all this union business, it was too late to turn back now. They were locked out and there was no work, so she might as well go and see what these people had to say. This Miss Macarthur everyone was on about. A lot of the others around the yards were speaking up more and more these days, bold as brass. Enough was enough! She was just beginning to catch some of their fighting spirit.

She watched as Rose and Lucy went towards Edna's house. That Rose was a fighter, there was no doubt – and keeping up all of it when she was more than six months gone. Bertha had to give her credit for it.

Maybe 'er's right, Bertha thought. If there's enough of us, they can't ignore *all* of us – can they?

Thirty-Nine

At last they were ready, fluttering and laughing as they prepared themselves to leave the yard. Lucy thought, It feels as if we're having a day out somewhere! Which we are, I suppose. Any day not spent with a hammer in hand in the forge was a special occasion. The official time that the strike was to begin was two o'clock.

Mari had cheered up and put on a pink-and-white checked frock and her straw hat with a grubby yellow ribbon round it. Her children who were not out at work came along: Maggie, who was twelve now, looking after Dolly with Gracie and Ivy Shaw, and eight-year-old Jo, dashing up and down the yard with Charlie Shaw, both eager to be off.

'Yow gunna be all right, Luce?' Rose eyed her leg.

'Course!' Lucy looked eagerly up at her. She wouldn't have missed this for anything, even if she had to hop all the way there.

Just as she spoke, Edna Wilmott came out of her house. She had changed into a long black dress, an ancient coat over it with an astrakhan collar and a big black hat, looking for all the world as if she was off to a funeral. She was already pink and perspiring in the heat. Lucy watched in amazement. She had hardly ever seen Edna anywhere but at her hearth or criss-crossing the yard.

Bertha looked her up and down.

'So – yower coming then?'

'Might as well, mightn't I?' Edna said.

302

'Oh – hang on a tick!' Rose hurried over to the forge as fast as her heavy body would allow and came back with a couple of short lengths of chain. She hung one round her neck. 'Want one, Luce?'

She draped it round Lucy like a necklace and they both laughed.

'Us women in chains!' Rose said.

'Right,' Bertha said. 'Let's get going then. Oi – yow kids. If yower coming yow've gorra behave yourselves!'

The six children fell in line and they were all about to advance along the entry when a looming figure emerged out of the shadows into the yard. Thirza Rudge. Lucy's stomach clenched with fear at the sight of her.

'What's gooin' on?' she demanded. 'Where d'yow lot think yower off to?'

Rose stepped forward immediately. 'We're going to the meeting called by the union,' she said. 'As we 'ave a right to.'

Thirza Rudge seemed to swell up and her face darkened.

'It's them union troublemakers, coming 'ere, wrecking this industry for everyone!' she barked. 'And I ay 'aving it! Yow lot – get back in yower 'ouses. Yow signed up saying yow wasn't 'aving no cotter with them unions and yow'd work for the old rate . . .'

'No, we dain't!' Rose erupted. 'Not one woman in this yard signed – and even if we 'ad, we'd be cancelling 'em and throwing them back at yow for the dirty trick they played on us! But we *day* sign, *none* of us. And we're *all* going to our meeting!'

'Oh dear, oh dear,' Edna was muttering in the background. She kept her head down, hoping not to be noticed.

Thirza Rudge stepped closer to Rose. Lucy was

trembling – she found the woman utterly terrifying and could hardly believe the way Rose had spoken to her.

'If yow go out to join that rabble –' Thirza was puce in the face, completely unused to this kind of challenge to her fearful rule – 'yow can all be damned sure no one in this yard'll ever work for me again – or for Ridley's. Yow'll be blacklisted, the lot of yow!'

Bertha stepped forward then as the others murmured in fury against the fogger.

'Miss Macarthur's called us out and we'm going to our meeting.' She spoke quietly, looked Thirza right in the eyes. 'Like we said.'

She started walking, leading the way, and they all stepped round Thirza Rudge.

'If yow want to starve yower all going the right way about it!' she bawled after them.

Lucy felt a chill of fear. There was no work, no money coming in. What were they all going to do? Supposing they defied the fogger and went out to find there was no one else there?

But Bertha, head in the air, marched along the entry and they all followed, the children now quiet as quiet. Thirza Rudge was powerless to stop them and whatever their fears and worries, they all kept walking, in single file. A moment later they were out in the sunshine of Hay Lane.

There had been talk, catching like fire from yard to yard. The union organizers like Madge Lunn had kept coming round, encouraging everyone. They had to keep pressing for just wages, for what they needed. They mustn't let the Chainmakers' Association keep them on starvation wages for ever. The men in the factories earned a living wage and the women were entitled to it as well.

But it was only now, walking along Graingers Lane towards the High Street, that they all began to see what was happening. A good number of the chainmaking factories in the area had locked out their outworkers, most of them women. There was no work to be done and there was a battle to win.

Along the street, they saw groups of women emerging from backyards. And there were kids everywhere, all on summer holidays – boys in caps, little girls in bonnets. It was a few at first, but as they got closer to the High Street, the numbers grew until the pavements were a moving stream of hats and frocks, everyone dressed in their best for this momentous occasion, taking pride.

They were walking along their usual, day-to-day streets, seeing the shops where they bought their groceries. But today everything felt different, looked different in the summer sun. There was a holiday atmosphere, songs breaking out, dances even and Lucy heard the strains of the Sally Army band playing further along the street – yet it was all lifted beyond mere leisure and enjoyment. There was passion and defiance, a unity and determination.

As they were walking along, someone suddenly called out behind them.

'Luce! Lucy Butler!'

'Someone's calling you.' Rose elbowed her.

Lucy turned to see a smiling, almost forgotten face beaming at her.

'I knew it was yow!'

'Abigail! Well, my leg's a bit of a giveaway, eh?' She grinned at her old schoolfriend and they hugged. They had not set eyes on each other since leaving school. 'It's nice to see you. You all come out as well?'

'All of our yard's out,' Abigail said. 'I best go with them. But don't be a stranger – we're not that far away!'

She went back to her other workers, leaving Lucy glowing. When she'd last seen Abigail, it felt as if they lived half a world away from each other – especially with her bad leg making it so hard to get anywhere. But now she realized it wasn't so very far and everything was opening out. They had exchanged addresses and promised to meet another time.

Little Grace Shaw held Ivy's hand and walked close to their mother, each of them wide-eyed. Mari's kids followed on, more sober than usual. Even Jo Gornall and Charlie were well behaved because, exciting though it all was to be in the crowds and the holiday atmosphere, everyone could sense that this was momentous. It was a crux point. The women – and the few males – had no agreement that anything would be paid to them – and the factories now had no outworkers. What was going to happen?

Bertha was silent, as if she was now past commenting. She had committed to being here and she stood, iron-faced, as they joined the throng gathering outside the Empire Theatre.

Looking round, Lucy was filled with wonder. All the time, more and more were joining to swell the crowd. On the summer air, she caught the odours of mothballs and must from clothes seldom worn, added to the smoke from cigarettes, the whiffs of horse dung and coal smoke on the summer air and everything, in those moments, smelt of hope.

Voices round her chattered excitedly. What was going to happen? Would there be speeches? When was that Mary Macarthur going to put in an appearance? She *was* coming, wasn't she? She was good, that one. Bostin, that Mary Macarthur. Everyone wanted to hear her.

'What're they going to do?' Gracie asked, looking up at Rose. She was too small to see over the crowd.

'There's a lady coming,' Rose told her daughters. 'Yow might not be able to see much, but when 'er speaks yow need to pin yower lugholes back and listen to 'er.'

After a time, there was a ripple of excitement through the gathered crowd and people started shooshing. Lucy, who had settled herself to stand balanced between her good leg and the peg one, strained her ears and eyes.

'It's Miss Varley,' Rose said.

'Who?' Mari said, too loudly.

'Miss Varley,' Rose said impatiently. ''Er's one of the organizers round 'ere – and that's Mr Sitch with her.'

Lucy saw Julia Varley's stern face appear as she stepped up so everyone could see her. Close to her, Lucy could just make out the bearded face of Mr Charles Sitch, the man she had seen at some of the other meetings.

'That Miss Varley . . .' Rose said. Lucy could see she was speaking loudly enough so that Bertha, the other side of her, could hear. 'A lady told me – a while back, 'er went about sleeping in the workhouses.'

Bertha's head shot round. 'What? What'd 'er do that for?'

'To find out what it were like for women 'aving to stop in those places,' Rose said. 'So 'er could tell people about it. That was before 'er came 'ere and was involved with the union.'

Bertha looked back at Julia Varley as if seeing her with new eyes. Julia Varley's voice reached them.

'We have reached a crucial time in our dealings with the employers here in the hand-hammered chain industry.'

She was almost shouting, her voice carrying to them. 'This –' she swept her arm across to indicate the assembled crowd – 'is something that has never been seen before . . .'

Cheers and clapping broke out. Lucy turned her head and became aware of just how many women there were now, all around them. She had never been in a crowd of so many people! The street was crammed full of chain-makers of all ages: old women and young, some like herself barely more than children, others carrying babies and many with their children standing alongside them, some in the crowd waving little flags. Nearly everyone seemed to have put on their best frocks and hats and shawls. She looked at Bertha and Rose and even Mari. Their faces were rapt. This was like nothing any of them had ever seen before either.

'Now, just arrived from London to speak to you, we have our founder and the general secretary of the National Federation of Women Workers – Miss Mary Macarthur!'

Cheers and applause broke out even more loudly, echoing between the buildings in the narrow street. A hat appeared, broad-brimmed, a white blouse, the smiling face that Lucy remembered from the last time. She swelled inside, her eyes filling with tears as her feelings brimmed over. She wiped them away – she wanted to be able to see *everything*. Mary Macarthur! If anyone could help them, it was Mary! It felt to her as if an angel was appearing before them.

'I want to see,' Grace said, infected by the rising excitement in the crowd. Lucy bent over her.

'You'll have to go right round to the front if you want to see, Gracie. Just listen – you'll hear her.'

'Women of Cradley Heath . . .' Mary Macarthur's Scots voice came to them, clear on the breeze. 'There will be those of you who are wondering what right have I, a stranger among you, to be speaking to and on behalf of the women chainmakers . . .'

Lucy heard shouts of agreement at this: there were employers and foggers bristling with helpless rage at the edge of the crowd. They all sounded absolutely furious. Lucy caught a glimpse of Thirza Rudge among the fist-shaking men, her face flint hard and angry.

'Oh, shurrit, yow cheating bastards . . .' voices around them shouted. 'It's us 'er's come to speak to – not yow!'

Lucy wondered if either of the Ridleys, senior or junior, were there. In all these years she had never know-ingly set eyes on either of them. It was Seth Dawson who had always done their business for them round the yards. The horror of that night filled her again for a moment and she shuddered at the memory of him looming close to her, grabbing her. But at least he was gone, she thought, her lip curling with satisfaction.

But to her these domineering male voices sounded so much louder and more powerful than Miss Macarthur's that they filled her with dread. How could the lady go on speaking in the face of that? But Miss Macarthur ignored them completely and just kept on going.

'I hope you will come to believe me when I say it is the sense of injustice and unfairness that drives me to use all the resources at my disposal to help these women and their families. For making one yard of chain, you get one penny! One penny for a yard of chain struck to last a lifetime!'

'Yes!' she heard Rose burst out beside her. 'You tell 'em, Mary!' She was chewing on her thumb, her eyes never leaving Mary Macarthur's face.

'For the past three months,' Mary Macarthur went on, 'I have been engaged in negotiations with the Trade Boards. Having agreed on a rate at which a minimum wage should be set, you will know with what reluctance they have bestirred themselves to pay it. I have seen that reluctance first hand. Some of you were instructed to sign papers opting out of receiving your rightful earnings . . .'

'We was tricked into it!' Murmuring and booing broke out across the crowd of women, drowning out the rough jeering of the foggers.

'Such a request, to rob you of your rightful wage, should never have been made. On the twenty-third of this month, I drafted a letter from our union – to which now, more than four hundred of you belong . . .'

Lucy and Rose cheered even more loudly, beaming at each other. Rose raised her arm. Young Grace, seeming to think this a good idea, raised hers as well and Ivy followed. Both were wide-eyed and amazed at all they were seeing.

'In my letter I requested that the agreed minimum wage come into force immediately. Instead of complying, your employers, most of whom live in the green, leafy outliers of our industrial towns – not as you do, amid the smoke and toil of their industries – have seen fit to lock you out, thus denying you the basic means of earning your living . . .'

'They can lock us out – we ay opting out!' Voices rose all about them.

Close to Lucy, an elderly lady thrust her skinny arm into the sky. 'I'll drop dead before I sign them papers!' she shrieked. 'More'n fifty years I've slaved for 'em, for starvation wages. No more!'

To Lucy's astonishment, Edna Wilmott suddenly yelled, 'Ar – and I've worked their hearths since I were ten year old!'

Lucy caught sight of Bertha Hipkiss's face just then. She was watching the scrawny old lady who had shouted and Lucy saw something in her expression: that Bertha was deeply moved. Were those tears in Bertha's eyes?

The cheering and shouting gathered pace. Lucy and Rose joined in and saw Mari and Bertha doing the same – even Edna. All of them were lit up by being among so many others, at hearing someone outline their cause, the struggles of their daily lives. Things were wrong – they had been overlooked, cheated, ground into the earth for long enough and now someone had raised her voice to say so. *No more!*

Lucy listened to the excited voices, the anger, the hope. All those years of toil at the hearth. Her emotions rose up and tears were pouring down her cheeks as well.

'What's up, Luce?' Rose called to her.

'I just wish my mom was here,' she sobbed. 'I wish 'er'd lived to see this.'

'Oh, bab –' Rose put her arm round her for a moment – 'I wish 'er was too. We're doing it for her – for everyone.'

'A struggle faces us all, the like of which none of us has faced before,' Mary Macarthur went on, her voice rising so that it felt as if it carried them all on wings. Lucy quickly rubbed away her tears, straining to see and to hear every word.

'We will all fight this injustice together – and you will be strongest if you are all together, as members of the union.' Mary Macarthur paused, gazing round over the crowd. And seeing the way she looked, the way she appeared to gather them all in, it seemed to Lucy that she loved them, every last one of the women standing around her, and her own heart swelled with love in return. Mary Macarthur seemed to her like a beautiful creature who had come from another realm!

'Just remember this – an employer can do without one

worker,' her voice rose as she concluded. 'But he cannot do without *all* his workers!'

'We're out!' someone started shouting. Others joined in. 'We're with you, Mary!' 'All of us – we're out to stay!'

The cheering and clapping rang around the streets and singing broke out. 'Rouse ye women . . .' All of them from their yard turned to look each other, excited, happy – and in some ways appalled. What was happening? Whatever it was, they were all in this together.

Because it seemed they were now on strike.

Forty

As the crowd broke up and they all made their way back to their own yards that afternoon, everyone was buoyed up by the emotions of the rally and of Miss Macarthur's words. She had come to their streets as someone so strange, foreign almost, well dressed, with her soft Scots accent, like someone from another world, standing raised up just high enough so that they could see her, people shushing so that everyone could hear her voice carry across the bonnets and caps of the gathered crowd. And she had changed their lives.

As they turned into Hay Lane, Edna Wilmott, who seemed like a different woman from the one who had left that morning, striding along as if she had lost ten years in the last few hours, led them singing 'Guide me, O Thou Great Redeemer', and as they turned into the entry, their voices rose, echoing in the confined space:

'*Strong deliverer, strong deliverer, be Thou still my strength and shield!*'

They were laughing as they emerged into the yard. Lucy looked around her. Bertha, Edna and Mari, all as she had never seen them before: determined, passionate, full of fire. And a lot of it was thanks to Rose Shaw, she knew that. Grace Shaw and Mari's children scrambled up the wall, helping little Dolly to get up as well. Lucy's heart buckled for a moment, remembering John and Clem hauling her up there that day. Bittersweet feelings filled her. How she had worshipped them both! And they had toyed with her for a while. For a long time she had felt especially sad and bitter towards Clem. But now she knew better than to invest her heart in either of them. They had, in their way, replaced her lost brothers – and it was as brothers they would remain.

Now, her heart was full of Mary Macarthur. *Miss* Macarthur. She was not married, that lovely young woman. Maybe if she had been, her husband would have stopped her doing what she was doing. And what an inspiration she was! There were other things in life, things to do apart from marrying. Lucy's heart swelled. The way her life was, she was never going to meet a man. But what did it matter, when there was someone in the world like Mary Macarthur?

There had never been such a day. The children all sensed the excitement and roared about.

'I 'ardly know what to do with myself,' Edna Wilmott said.

They made tea and brought chairs out into the yard, claiming an interval before the men came home, to sit in a ring in the remaining corner of sunlight, talking over and over what had happened. But gradually the excitement started to wane and a chill reality made itself felt.

'A strike,' Bertha said, as if she could hardly comprehend the meaning of the word. For a second, they were all silent, taking in the enormity of what had happened.

'How long're we gunna be like this?' Mari said. Everything suddenly felt even more uncertain. What did it mean?

'I cor be staying out for long,' Edna said. 'I ay got money to live on – not like you with all yower men folk.'

'Victor's not gunna like it,' Mari said. Her face was shrinking back to its normal pinched, harried look.

Lucy heard Rose mutter something which was clearly not complimentary about Victor Gornall.

'It's all right for you, Rose,' Mari said. 'Yow can tell yours what to do!'

'Well, you can an' all,' Rose retorted. 'Just dow let 'im get away with it!'

Mari had certainly gained the upper hand when it came to satisfying Victor's lusts, even if at times she had to call on the help of a heavy frying pan. No more kids – that was that. She was past caring where her husband got his oats these days so long as he left her well alone. Some of the time they seemed to have reached a truce – even a harmonious one. At others they were both capable of knocking lumps off each other. And Victor still had a hell of a temper on him and wanted to rule the roost.

'Yow need to send that lad of yours out to earn a wage,' Bertha was saying to Edna. 'It's high time 'e were teking care of you at yower age.'

Edna looked away, with a shameful expression. Sidney was not a son who had ever made her proud, but he was all she had.

'What's yower Wally gunna say?' Mari asked Rose.

'Oh, 'e'll be all right,' she said.

Lucy saw Mari and Bertha exchange looks, as if to say, *He won't dare be anything else . . .*

'Yow've got all yower lads at 'oom,' Edna said to Bertha, in a desperate tone.

'Look, Edna – we ay gunna let yow starve,' Bertha said with an air of impatience. 'But it's true – it's more than time yower Sidney was bringing in a wage instead of knocking about getting into trouble.'

'What do we *do* all day, when we're on strike?' Mari asked.

It was a question everyone was at a loss to answer.

'I s'pose . . .' Rose was starting to say before being interrupted by the sound of footsteps pounding along the entry.

'Yow lot needn't think yow can sit about canting all day long!' Thirza Rudge appeared at full speed to stop in front of them, her fleshy cheeks pulled into a furious scowl. Lucy's very skin came up in goose pimples at the sight of her.

'What would yow like us to do?' Rose said, with mock politeness.

'We'm locked out, if yow remember,' Bertha added. 'So if yow want yower chains made yow'll 'ave to bring us the rods. We can't mek chains without the rods,' she added, as if explaining to a child.

'Yow lot'll never be able to keep this up!' Thirza raged at them. 'Who d'you think yow are? You'll starve and it'll serve yow all right!'

Rose stood up. She walked closer to Thirza Rudge, hands on her hips.

'We ay gunna starve,' she said. 'Not 'cause of yow.'

'Yow think yower very clever, dow yow? Well, let me tell yow – yow may 'ave men in yower houses, working for the other firms . . .' Thirza leaned towards Rose, wagging a stubby finger in her face. 'But that ay gunna save yer. I'll get them blacklisted in every works round 'ere and then what're yow gunna do?' She took a couple of steps backwards before turning to leave.

'Blacklisted for what?' Rose shouted after her. But her voice held a note of uncertainty. 'What does 'er mean?' she asked the others. 'Can they do anything to our men? They'm all in their own unions, ay they?'

They all looked at each other. Bertha, who was never keen to admit she did not know something, just shook her head.

'I dow like it,' Mari said, sounding frightened now. 'That mardy cow can do anything 'er wants. What's 'er gunna do to us? They always win, them people with their tricks and their money – one way or another. 'Er's right – if our men're let go or whatever 'er's planning, we'm done for – we might as well call it off now.'

'No!' Lucy found the word bursting out of her mouth before she even had time to think about it. 'We can't call it off. We haven't got any work anyway if they won't give it us.' All the others were looking round at her in astonishment. Belief swelled in her even as she spoke. 'We can't call it off!' she repeated firmly. 'Miss Macarthur said she'd help us and if she said it, she will. She'll know what to do!'

'Yower *what*?'

Clem was in the scullery, washing his hands after coming in from work. John was already home and Bertha, who was at the fire cooking up a stew with kidneys, had not yet said anything, but Lucy felt a kind of devilment rise in her. Today had made her feel different about everything.

'We're on strike – all of us.'

'On strike?' Clem said it in a scoffing tone. 'What d'yow mean?'

Freddie came through the door then. Lucy and Clem were either side of the table.

'What's going on?' he asked.

'We're on strike,' Lucy said. 'All us outworkers.'

'Dow be saft,' Clem scoffed. Lucy could see John watching them, his face hard to read. 'Yow cor go on strike!'

'What d'yow mean?' Lucy felt her temper rising. She didn't know what had come over her – she seemed to be unable to contain herself these days. 'They've already locked us out – and we ay going back, not 'til they pay us our proper rate, like the unions've said.'

Clem was laughing, a mocking, dismissive sort of laugh, and turning away. 'That'll be the day when they listen to a bunch of women.' He turned back. 'You ay on strike, are yow – not really?'

'Seems we are,' Bertha said. 'We'm locked out and they won't pay us. They won't give in.'

'It dow seem right,' John said in his stiff, constipated way which increasingly made Lucy want to scream at him. It had got a lot worse since he'd started walking out with Maud, who Lucy had concluded was a prissy little thing. 'Women, carrying on like that.'

'Like what?' Lucy flared up. 'Carrying on doing the work all day as well as all the work in the house, and having babbies and doing all the work for that an' all – and for pay that's nothing to what you men get for doing a lot less!'

Clem and John stared at her as if she had just grown another head.

'Well – I s'pect yow'll be glad of our men's wages if yow wenches ain't gunna be bringing any in,' Clem said nastily.

Bertha suddenly stepped in front of him.

'That's enough,' she said. 'If yow get paid more than us it's only because that's how things've been fixed, not because yow've done anything to deserve it – so don't yow go canting at Lucy like that.'

'Are you saying women should be paid the same as the men?' John said incredulously. 'When the men do heavier work?'

Lucy saw Freddie's head moving back and to, following this argument.

'What, because they make bigger chains?' Lucy said.

'We're all making chains! And what about you, standing there behind a shop counter with yer clean fingernails, earning a fat wage to what we get! There ay nothing heavy about yower work, John, so far as I can see!'

'We get a pittance and we've all put up with it for too long,' Bertha said. 'That Miss Macarthur's right – it's a wrong and it needs righting. And I ay being told by lads whose noses and arses I've wiped about 'ow much pay I get and whether I ask for more! Yow can both shurrup and sit down and eat yower tea – unless yow want to cook yower own, that is?'

The stunned, rather sulky silence that followed this lasted through most of the meal, the boys not liking to be spoken to like children but still in awe of their mother. John and Clem took themselves off as soon as they could, grunting their thanks.

Lucy sat with a mutinous feeling inside her. The men were so used to telling everyone what was what – all of them! Even if it was only John and Clem she was arguing with, it made her feel stronger and it'd do them good to have someone take issue with them for once.

To her surprise though, before he got up, Freddie leaned towards her and said quietly, 'What them two said – I dow agree with 'em – yow know that, dow yer, Luce?'

Startled, she looked into his face, this little playmate of hers now a tall man, and their eyes met.

'That's good of you,' she said. 'Ta, Freddie.'

Forty-One

'Well, what're yow gunna do all day then, if yow ay working?' Wally said that night.

Rose, who was hustling the children into the house for tea which she was also in the middle of cooking, and so big with child she had to be careful how she put her feet down, stopped in front of her husband, stared hard at him for a moment, then started laughing.

'What's so funny?' Wally asked indignantly.

'I s'pose yow think I spend my time sitting staring out the winder, don't yow, yow noddleyead! I've got quite enough to do in a day without working – but since you ask, I'm gunna go and give the union people a hand – if it's needed.'

As they crammed round the table to eat, Wally said, 'So what d'yow think's gunna 'appen, Rosie? I mean, we'm gunna be a bit short with none of your wages coming in.'

'Miss Macarthur said we'm gunna get strike pay,' Rose said, chewing ravenously on a slice of bread.

'Strike pay?' Wally knew better than to argue but Rose could see he looked disbelieving. 'Well – I 'ope 'er's right but where's all that gunna come from? I can't see the union 'aving enough to keep paying out – there's quite a few of yer.'

'Miss Macarthur's so nice,' Gracie said dreamily. 'I want to be like her when I'm bigger.'

'Oh, Lord 'elp us,' Wally said.

But Rose looked proudly at her. It had been quite

something, being there with her daughters – letting them see something like that, someone who had fire in their belly – a woman no less – who could make things different, and show them that life could be bigger than the one they all knew.

'Good for you, Gracie.' Rose shifted uncomfortably on the chair. 'Oh – I'll be glad when this babby's born, that I will. I feel bigger than I've ever been before.'

Wally gave her a soppy smile.

'You look nice, Rosie.'

'That'd suit yow, wouldn't it?' she scolded him fondly. 'Me just 'aving babbies 'til there was no room to move in 'ere – like a tin of sardines!'

Everyone was anxious. How would things be? Had they been locked out and now gone on strike only to be left to starve?

But very few who had heard Mary Macarthur speak went along with that. That was what their employers wanted: to see them shattered, defeated so thoroughly that they would give in to working at any price as they always had.

Rose, and most of the other women she talked to, felt a strong trust in this woman who had come to lead them. She could see that she and Mary Macarthur were about the same age, yet Mary felt so much older in a certain kind of confidence and experience. She made them believe that they could do it, that they were all worth the trouble, knowing that she, a fine lady who did not have to come here or to work so hard, believed in their cause.

Stepping out into the yard the next morning, Rose saw Mari at the tap filling her pails. The door of the cottage was open and she could see Bertha Hipkiss moving about inside. But the forge, like all the other backyard forges in the area, was silent. There was no smoke wafting out through the window bars, no tapping of hammers, and the floors were dusted with the cold white ash of yesterday. It was a sunny day – and everything felt very strange.

When she went to the union offices, she found Miss Varley and Mr Sitch and the other workers in a fever of activity. Gaggles of women were arriving to join the union, there were letters to write, volunteers to be sent round the yards to see all the outworkers and keep them informed about what was going on. Groups of striking women were in the offices trying to find out what was going on or volunteering to help. The place was a-buzz.

The bundle of sticks, Rose thought, looking round the large room where people were bent over desks or scurrying back and forth with messages. We are the bundle of sticks and we have to keep everyone together. The thought made her swell with pride.

But she also felt self-conscious. No one else she could see was expecting a baby, or at least no one was visibly jutting out at the front quite the way she was. She was about seven months gone. Doubt seized her for a moment. Maybe she should just go home. But she couldn't miss this! Among the busy workers she spotted Madge Lunn, who had come several times to their yard. She went over to her.

'I'm Rose Shaw – I'm from one of the yards in Hay Lane,' she said.

'Yes, I remember you.' Madge Lunn beamed at her. Though her face seemed dragged down with tiredness, her dark eyes glowed back at Rose. 'Well, if you want to make yowerself useful yer can keep yower yard and the others along Hay Lane up with news about what's happening? We want to get everyone out on the streets, keeping us together and keeping morale up – and raising money.'

Rose nodded. 'I can do that.' Her face broke into a broad smile. 'Course I can.'

She found Bertha Hipkiss and Lucy spring cleaning. Bertha was sweeping out the house vigorously, dust flying into the yard.

'Not that it's spring,' she said. 'Only I dow know what else to do with myself and the house needs a good going-over.'

'Oh – there ay gunna be much time for cleaning!' Rose said. She felt very important suddenly. 'If you come out I'll tell all of yow what Miss Lunn said.'

'Oh ar,' Bertha said. Rose could hear the old resentment in her voice – *I'm in charge here, not you.*

'It won't take more than a minute or two,' Rose said politely. 'Only it saves me going round every house. I've been asked to tell the other yards an' all. They want us out on the streets, not staying in our yards.'

Everyone gathered round. I'm a union worker! Rose thought, looking at their expectant faces. I'm doing something useful and good!

'Miss Varley said to tell yow,' she announced at the top of her voice.

'There ain't no need to shout,' she heard Bertha mumble. 'Yow ain't on a soapbox – or was yow talking to the next-door yard an' all?'

Rose felt her cheeks turn red. She was rather hoping they would regard her as their own, local Mary Macarthur. But Lucy was smiling adoringly at her, pretty little thing, and that made her feel better.

'Any road,' she went on. 'According to Miss Varley,

Miss Macarthur went straight to London after speaking to us . . .'

'Ooh,' Mari said. 'Straight to London!'

'And er's doing everything 'er can to make sure people know about what's going on 'ere in Cradley Heath.'

They waited, looking doubtfully at each other.

'Is that all?' Edna Wilmott said. 'What about our strike pay?'

Rose felt affronted. 'Well, that's all for now,' she said, walking away irritably. 'I mean, 'er only went yesterday. Give 'er a chance! And we can't just leave it up to 'er. There's gunna be marches – and us out with collecting boxes. We've got to help raise the money ourselves – so it's no good just sitting on our backsides!'

Rose would never forget the next few days as long as she lived.

The union offices were alive with activity and later the next morning she made sure she took Gracie, Charlie and Ivy in to see for themselves.

They arrived to be met by an extraordinary sight. Suddenly everyone seemed to be interested in Cradley Heath!

Outside, a crowd had gathered. There were reporters with notebooks and photographers with their cameras set up, much to the interest of passers-by who had stopped to stand and look on. At this moment all these cameras were pointed at a gathering of about twenty women who must have been some of the oldest female chainmakers in the region. She stopped and watched for a moment in an amazement which only grew greater when she saw Edna Wilmott among them, standing proud and wearing a hat which must have dated from when the old Queen was a girl.

One row of women stood behind a line of chairs on

which the others were seated. Some wore their working caps, others fine bonnets of all kinds and their best clothes. A few had lengths of chain draped about their necks. Some of them were holding wooden collecting boxes in their laps and on the ground at their feet were two placards.

'WHITE SLAVES OF ENGLAND!' read the first.
'HELP THE WOMEN CHAINMAKERS WHO
ARE FIGHTING FOR 2½ D AN HOUR!'

And:

'ENGLAND'S DISGRACE! LOCKED OUT
AFTER 67 YEARS CHAINMAKING,
FIGHT FOR 2½ D AN HOUR!'

Rose watched the women, standing so strong and upright as their pictures were taken. She saw that Edna's old face had a worn beauty to it. Tears filled her eyes, thinking of all Edna's dead babies, of just how many hours of all those women's lives they had stood at their chain hearths, sick and exhausted, half clammed and heavy with child, like she was now, or suckling the latest arrival.

All this while their bosses ate their fill and slept between soft sheets. It was all wrong: they had to win this fight, *had* to!

Forty-Two

News came in: articles were spreading all over the region, and then the country, about the striking women of Cradley Heath.

'It sounds as if Miss Macarthur has told the whole world about us!' Lucy said. Each day when they set out, there were more people on the streets, more newspaper articles about the strike.

'I know!' Rose laughed excitedly. 'It seems as if 'er knows *everyone*! And even some of the papers that dow normally tek any notice of the likes of us – they're on our side an' all!'

More and more women outworkers poured out on to the streets. There was an atmosphere of party, of celebration. Lucy managed to march – nothing would have stopped her! – despite her leg. She walked with Rose and Mari and the children, with Bertha and Edna who linked arms and sailed along the street together. They sang songs, they rattled the collecting boxes which the union had handed out. A few women took along saucepans, and coins went clinking into them.

They split into groups, some marching round Cradley Heath – Lucy stayed with them – others walking further out to Old Hill and Quarry Bank. They sang and danced as they went and nearly everyone was prepared to put something in the collecting boxes, no matter how small.

'Support the chainmakers!' Lucy had learned to call out, saying it every time with more conviction.

'Good luck to yow, bab,' other women said when Lucy held out her box. 'It's high time summat was done about yower pay – it's a disgrace.'

But still, amid all the excitement, there remained a niggling worry. They were on strike, and that was right – but could they really keep going? Were they going to be able to get by?

This worry was short-lived. On the Saturday, only four days after the strike had begun, Lucy was crossing the yard after taking her turn cleaning the lavs and hanging cut-up squares of newspaper on the strings inside. Rose came dashing back along the entry as fast as her heavy condition would allow and burst into the yard.

'All of yow – get out 'ere!'

Her voice was so urgent that no one argued, not even Bertha who emerged wiping her hands on her apron.

'What's gooin' on?' Her face looked stern, as if expecting bad news. Until she saw Rose, panting hard and looking as if she was about to explode with excitement.

'You wanna tek care,' Mari said, 'or you'll 'ave that babby 'ere and now!'

'They've agreed the strike pay!' Rose said.

'What?' Edna gaped. 'Yow mean – for all of us?'

'Six shillings a week if you're in the union,' Rose announced. 'And four shillings if yower not.' She looked round at them. 'For each striking worker!'

'But . . .' It was the first time Lucy had seen Bertha Hipkiss almost speechless. 'That's . . . I mean, that's about what we'd get for a full week's work!'

'Six bob if yower in the union,' Mari murmured. 'God – it's time we joined, Edna!'

'Well . . .' Rose pulled her shoulders back. Lucy could see she was on fire with pride. It was astonishing – it was a relief, a miracle. And how pleased Wally and the other men were going to be – they could hardly complain now! 'That's what happens when you join the union. We're all in this together and we're going to win!'

News poured in. The papers published story after story. Some about people they knew. Sometimes Rose would bring Lucy a cutting to read to them.

'"It is now seventy-six years since Mrs Round, as a young girl, started on her long career of chainmaking."' Lucy stumbled through the *Daily Express*'s description. She had not been reading much lately and was out of practice.

'"Since that day, her world has been the forge in her backyard. The great happenings in the world outside have never pierced the smoke-begrimed walls of her home, where day after day and year after year, she has ceaselessly beaten the glowing iron into shape and worked the bellows until her figure has become bent and her hands indented with the marks of the chains she has forged."'

All the others were listening avidly as the reporter described the life of seventy-nine-year-old Mrs Patience Round. It was the only time any of them had ever heard the only lives that most of them had known described in print. Lucy felt a sort of chill go through her as she looked up at them. Her own hands were as scarred and pitted as Mom's had been.

For a second, she saw her life stretch before her – this life, endlessly, and nothing else . . . Her eyes met Rose's and she could tell she was thinking something similar.

They marched and sang. Songs were composed for the strike. Thanks to Mary Macarthur and the other union organizers, good news continued to pour in.

George Cadbury pledged to give £5 a week for as long

as the strike lasted. Neville Chamberlain donated £50 – Lady Beauchamp £200! Gifts of food and money poured in from the other unions and from businesses.

No one in their yard felt able to travel far, but soon, other striking women were going to football matches, holding out sheets at the end of the game, and people poured money into them, so much that it was almost too heavy to carry.

John, Clem and the other men in the yard had stopped making any critical comments in the face of this wave of power and sympathy which was engulfing their little town – a place almost unknown before, even if it had been producing most of the world's chains. Wally Shaw wore an almost permanent grin of pride from ear to ear. And even Victor Gornall had to admit that maybe, after all, the wenches had a bit of a point.

Forty-Three

'Mary Macarthur's coming up from London tomorrow!' Rose announced the next week.

'Our Mary,' Bertha said, in awed tones.

'Shall us go and meet 'er at Cradley station?' Rose was frustrated, Lucy knew. She would have liked to be one of the ones going to collect money at the football matches or sent with one of the delegations to London. But she was too much in the family way, too tired and heavy to do anything more than local work, which she did with a passion. How wonderful Rose was! She was the one who always made Lucy believe that there could be something more than the forge and this life.

'I'll come!' she said. She could manage to walk to the railway station, couldn't she?

By the time the group of women had got down to Cradley station, they had grown into quite a sizeable crowd. They came trotting out of yards along the way in twos and threes, tying on bonnets and calling out, 'Wait for me!' Their clothes may have been threadbare, re-made from other frocks, turned and stitched, but everyone wanted to look their very best.

There were a few banners, one from the union, another strip of sheeting which just read, 'WELCOME OUR MARY!'

Lucy had never been to the railway station before. It seemed like an exciting sort of a place, somewhere where there were comings and goings, and a route out to the world beyond, about which she knew only fragments from books she had read.

They sang as they walked along in the sunny, smoky morning, a song which everyone knew now, to the tune of 'Men of Harlech'.

> *'Rouse, ye women, long enduring,*
> *Beat no iron, blow no bellows*
> *Till ye win the fight, ensuring*
> *Pay that is your due.'*

Lucy and Rose beamed at each other as they all launched into the chorus:

> *'Through years uncomplaining,*
> *Hope and strength were waning,*
> *Your industry*
> *A beggar's fee*
> *And meagre fare was gaining.*
> *Now a Trade Board is created,*
> *See your pain and dearth abated,*
> *And the Sweater's wiles checkmated*
> *Parliament's decree!'*

As they approached the station, their words rang off the walls of the buildings. Lucy saw a couple of lads in railway uniforms who were standing, smoking, to one side of the entrance, turn and look in astonishment.

The gaggle slowed down.

'D'yow think we'm better waiting out 'ere 'til the train gets in?' someone asked.

They hesitated outside. Someone went in to find out exactly when the train from London was due to arrive.

'You all right?' Lucy said to Rose. She was bending

over as if in pain. Lucy felt panic rise in her. 'The babby's not coming, is it?'

'No, t'ain't that. It's just, walking fast like that gives me a bit of cramp. I'll be all right.' She straightened up again, grimacing.

'D'you want to sit down a bit? Look – there's a seat over there.'

To one side of the station there was an iron bench.

'All right then. Just for a tick.'

Other women started to enquire after her, but Rose waved them away. 'I'll be all right . . .'

Lucy took Rose's arm, feeling how solid and strong it felt against her own. As they got to the bench, she felt the two lads watching them. Perhaps they think she's about to have the baby, Lucy thought. It made her want to giggle and when she and Rose had sat down, she looked across at them, still smiling.

There was a little while before the train was due in. Rose sat breathing heavily and Lucy was so caught up with keeping an eye on her that she did not see the lad coming over to her until he was close in front of her and she looked up into his face.

'Lucy?'

His face came into focus. Her heart began to pound before her mind had fully taken in who it was standing there.

'George?' she breathed. 'Oh – is it you, Georgie?'

She leapt up, sure already that it was her little brother! He was a head taller than she was now, his hair still curly under his cap. It was his smile which told her, the way his lips moved, and his big eyes a bit like their mom's.

'Oh, George – c'me'ere!'

They flung their arms around each other and Lucy found tears pouring down her face in seconds. After a moment she realized George was sobbing too as they clung together.

'Oh – let me look at you!' She drew back, gazing on her brother. Last time she'd seen him he'd still been a little boy – and now he must be fourteen! 'Oh, Georgie, you look all right! I was so frightened when that lady said you'd been given away and I dain't know where you'd gone. And I felt terrible – have felt it ever since.'

He smiled down at her, bashfully wiping away his tears. 'I'm all right, sis,' he said. 'It weren't yower fault. I'm not in the orphanage no more – I work on the railway, just started. They'm training me on the signals.'

She gazed at him. There was too much to say. She had forgotten about Rose, about everything. 'Oh, my word, oh, look at you, George!'

'What about you, Luce?'

'Oh, I'm all right. I stayed with Mrs Hipkiss. And now,' she added proudly, 'we're all on strike. This is my friend – Rose. She lives in the yard.'

Rose smiled up at George and said hello, seeming unsure what else to say. Lucy never talked about her brothers – Rose had never even realized she had had any.

'This is my pal, Sam,' George said.

'All right?' Sam said shyly. He was a solid-looking lad, an inch or two taller than George and several years older, with dark brown hair and smiling eyes. Lucy tried to stop crying in order to say hello.

'Honestly – look at me!' She wiped her face and the lad's smile widened. He seemed encouraged and came a little closer.

'Sam,' George said, swelling with pride, 'this is my sister, Lucy.'

Sam seemed a bit confused by this, but he nodded and said hello.

'Sam and me – we work together,' George said. 'Least, 'e's sort of my boss – the one teaching me the work.'

'I try not to be too hard on 'im,' Sam said amiably.

He seemed so nice, with kind eyes and little waves of hair emerging from his cap. But Lucy was so overwhelmed with meeting George she scarcely noticed. Family – a little bit of her own, real family appearing before her eyes!

'Oh, George – it *is* nice to see you! Come and see us, won't you? Why've you never come? You knew where I was.'

'I dunno.' He looked awkward, ashamed. 'I dain't know if you was still there. It all seemed like another world to me by then. And I was ... I s'pose I was fed up at being sent off ... Dain't know if you'd want to see me. I thought everything'd have changed.'

'It hasn't – hardly at all! And *course* I want to see you! *Promise* me you'll come – soon? Have you seen ... I mean, there's no sign of Albert?'

George shook his head. 'He'd've come to you, if anything.'

Lucy could feel Rose watching them both.

'You will come?' Lucy felt tearful again. 'I don't want to lose you again, George.'

'I will – I'll come soon!' George grinned. 'Sis.'

'Auntie!' Lucy spotted Bertha at the edge of the crowd. 'It's George!'

Bertha came over, frowning slightly, and looked carefully into the lad's face.

'Yow'm little George? 'Er brother?' Her suspicion died and she smiled, showing all the gaps in her teeth. 'My word – so it is! Where've yow bin all this time, lad?'

'The train's coming in!' someone shouted.

'Come and see us?' Lucy pleaded again. She didn't

Forty-Four

Never had she known such a day.

Bertha and the others came back to the yard in Hay Lane, still singing and buoyed up with the excitement of it all. The unions told them that there were over eight hundred chainmakers on strike, now that the outworkers from Old Hill had come in with them as well. Some were members of the union and some not, but the strike was solid. They now had such abundant funds from donations from all quarters – even from people abroad! – that at the moment it seemed they could keep up the strike indefinitely.

Bertha had stood there in the High Street with the other women in her yard, all togged up to look their best, amid the crush of excited women, the banners and flags, the band playing, the songs and sudden outbreaks of dancing. She felt as if she was living in a dream.

Edna, beside her, gave her a look early on and Bertha could see she was thinking exactly the same. Both of them had been set to the hearth when their ages were barely in double figures; their mothers were chainmakers and there was very little more of the world that they had seen. All Bertha had known for almost two decades of her life was the harsh filth of Anvil Yard – until Jonno came along. They had had no idea that things could be different, that change could be made, *forced*, by anyone, least of all by women, least of all *them*! That they had any power to make things happen at all. And now . . .

A wave of cheering passed through the crowd. She saw Mari Gornall, in front of her, her mouth stretched in a shout. Little Mari, who had never known anything else either. Some of the kids were back at school now but Rose and Mari had their younger ones with them.

Edna leaned towards her.

'My Sidney's gone and got 'isself a job.'

'I saw 'im going out this morning,' Bertha shouted down Edna's ear.

A wave of cheers blocked out whatever Edna said next and outbreaks of singing:

> 'Rouse, ye women, long enduring,
> Beat no iron, blow no bellows
> Till ye win the fight, ensuring
> Pay that is your due!'

Edna looked fit to burst with pride. 'They've took 'im on as a carter at Higgins,' she repeated. ''E's ever so pleased!'

About cowing time that idle lump worked for a living, Bertha thought. She winked at Edna.

'That'll keep 'im out of trouble.'

Edna pulled her mouth down and rolled her eyes. Then she nudged Bertha.

''Ere 'er comes.'

And they saw Mary Macarthur step up to the make-shift stage and everyone broke into a great roar of cheering.

That evening, when all her lads were home, she said to Freddie,

''Ere's two bob, son. Go down the Outdoor and get us a jug of ale to 'ave with our tea.'

'George? Oh yeah, little Georgie!' Clem looked amazed. 'I felt bad when 'e got sent away.'

Bertha felt herself buckle with shame inside. What a terrible time that had been, walking away with her friend's young son, handing him over to a stranger. But she just hadn't known what else to do.

'Least 'e's come back now,' she said quietly.

Forty-Five

George came the very next evening, as if he could no longer bear to keep away. They had just finished tea when he rapped on the door.

Lucy looked round and there he was!

'George!' She got carefully to her feet. 'Oh, you came!'

'Come in, son,' Bertha said. The kindness in her voice brought tears to Lucy's eyes.

George stood with his cap in his hand, looking quite overcome. He was fourteen now and had not seen any of them for more than six years. To Lucy it felt longer than her whole lifetime.

'George!' Clem cried. 'Come in, pal – come and sit down.'

'You look almost the same,' John said, laughing.

Freddie quietly gave up his chair. ''Ere – you sit 'ere,' he said and perched on the stool.

Lucy felt flooded with happiness at the warm greeting offered to him by the whole family.

'Yow 'ungry, lad?' Bertha asked.

'Clammed,' George laughed. 'Always am, me, even if I've already 'ad summat!'

Lucy sat quietly, gazing at him, taking in this moment. All of them round the table like a family – a family in which now, at last, she had one blood relation present in the room.

'You still in the orphanage?' Bertha asked, laying a plate in front of him with a few potatoes and the last of the stew.

342

'Ta, Mrs Hipkiss . . .' George tucked in, shaking his head. 'No – I left there when I got taken on by the railway. I've got a room – share it with another lad, up Lomey Town. It's all right.'

There was a silence suddenly, none of them sure what to say or ask. Lucy found her mind full of questions. *Why did that lady make you go to the orphanage? And what was it like? What were the other children like? All these days, these years . . . were you unhappy? Did you miss our mom every hour of every day the way I did?*

'Sam was in the orphanage with me,' George volunteered. 'I mean, 'e's older and 'e was there when I got there and 'e left before me – but 'e was always nice to me when we was there. 'E's the one got me the job.'

Lucy found herself listening with even more intense interest. She wanted to ask how old Sam was, but decided against it. Her pride stopped her showing how curious she was about Sam in front of all the Hipkiss boys – or George, for that matter.

''Ere, lad . . .' Bertha put a cup of tea on the table for him. Lucy could see Bertha wanted to do everything she could for him, as if to make up for not being able to bring him up, her friend's son, for having let their mother down. She wanted to tell Bertha it was all right, that she understood how much she had had to bear, with Jonno and doing all the work, but she did not know how to begin.

That evening, George sat with them and they all asked each other questions, trying to fill in the intervening years. It was hard at first. They had not shared time together, the remainder of their childhoods which had begun in this yard. George did not seem eager to talk about any of it and the conversation stopped and started like a faltering engine.

'I best be on my way,' he said after only an hour or so. 'My landlady'll be after me, else – bit of a tartar 'er is!'

'You will come again, won't you?' Lucy said anxiously. 'And tell me where you live?'

She got up then and followed him out into the smoky half-light of the yard.

'It's very nice to see you, Georgie,' she said softly.

'You too, sis.' He glanced down at her. 'You been all right – your leg and that? I see you've got a . . . a false leg?'

'Mr Clark, from round the Lane.' She nodded her head. 'He's been ever so good to me. Everyone has.' Her throat ached. 'But I missed you, Georgie. Every day.' Tears rushed to her eyes then. This was true, so achingly true, all that she had felt for him. She saw him nod, then look away, as if he could not begin on what he had felt.

'D'you think . . .' She hesitated. George met her gaze once more. 'We'll ever see Albert again?'

'Dunno.' He shrugged. 'I doubt it.'

There was a silence – sad, helpless. George was turning to go, then looked back at her.

'Oh – I nearly forgot . . .' Lucy experienced a moment of inner dread, afraid that he might be about to tell her awful things that had happened to him. But instead, he laughed.

'Thing is – Sam, who you met. I know it were only for a minute or two, but he took a real shine to you, Luce. He asked me how old you are and I had to think about it for a bit. I felt bad that I could hardly remember.' He smiled, but now she could see tears in his own eyes. 'Yower ever so pretty, yer know, sis . . .'

Lucy felt a blush rising in her cheeks though George would not be able to see it in the dusky evening. She looked down, dabbing at her eyes.

344

'He said he'd like to see you again and that I was to ask you for 'im?'

Her head jerked up, her heart thumping. She had so liked the look of the boy with the kindly smile, his shape, his voice . . . Just *him*. Even just seeing him – there had been something so appealing, so right about him.

'He said you was the prettiest girl he's ever met and he wants to come and see you – if you'll let him.'

'But . . .' She looked down. The old dread of her difference rose in her, of being rejected for not being a whole person, a proper woman. 'My leg.' She looked up at George. 'Does he know?'

'I told 'im,' George nodded. 'And d'yow know what 'e said?'

She waited, her heart hoping.

''E said, "Well, what does that matter? 'Er's a smasher and that's all I need to know."'

Lucy just stared at him, silenced by the sweet kindness of this.

''E's a good bloke, Sam is – I've known 'im a long time. 'E's had a lonely life – like all of us in there – and 'e's never let me down. Will yow meet 'im, Luce?'

'Well – yes.' She found she was grinning, excitement rising in her. 'Yes, course I will!'

'I'll tell 'im. That's bostin. Shall I say Sunday afternoon?' George turned to go. 'And I'll come and see yer soon!'

'Wait – Georgie . . .! I mean, how old is he – Sam? And what's his other name?'

George turned in the mouth of the entry. There was laughter in his voice, as if he knew he had just done a good thing.

''E's nineteen. And 'is name's Ashmore – Sam Ashmore! Ta-ra-a-bit, sis – see yer soon!'

Forty-Six

After Georgie had gone that night, Lucy lay in bed, full to the brim with happiness. It was as if two ends of something had joined together, completing her. A little piece of her family, of what was left of it, come back to her at last.

And there was Sam. She lay on her side of the bed, Bertha's heavy, regular breaths coming from the other. In her mind she joyfully went over all that had happened that morning at the station: Sam Ashmore's handsome, kindly face, the dark waves of hair escaping at the edges of his cap, the way he had looked at her. A longing filled her. Something about Sam felt inevitable, fated, as if she had met him somewhere before but could not quite remember where . . .

She shifted in bed. The nights were chilly now and she pulled the musty old quilt up further to cover her. Curling up, she thought, I mustn't wish for this, mustn't put myself in his hands – not this time . . .

All those years she had hungered for Clem's attention – even for John's. All that love and need she had for someone – a person who had eyes only for her, who would love her as their own. But John and Clem had toyed with her and passed by. She knew they were not bad lads – they were just learning at life the way she was. Although the hurt she had felt after Clem, her beloved Clem, had faded as time passed, she was still on guard against feeling such pain again. She fell asleep with this dampening thought at the forefront of her mind.

The days were busy with the strike. There was another meeting at the hall in Graingers Lane the next day and she went with Rose. Lucy was even more in awe of Rose now she was heavily pregnant – not just because she was different and determined about everything, but because of this mysterious miracle she was bringing about, of producing a new human life.

A chair was found for Rose in the school hall and for Lucy too. They sat at the side and Lucy cast shy glances at Rose before the speeches started.

'What's up?' Rose smiled wearily at her. 'Yow looking at my big belly?'

Lucy blushed, nodding. 'Does it hurt?'

'What, now? No. My back aches though. Everyone's a bit different, it seems. I get it in my back. I'll be glad when it's over – it gets to that stage. I s'pose nature meks yer ready.'

Lucy returned her smile, suddenly feeling grown up, the way Rose was talking to her as if she was a woman and an equal.

'I don't know if I want to do that,' she said. All of it seemed strange and frightening.

'I wouldn't be without my babbies,' Rose said, as both of them hauled themselves to their feet as clapping and singing broke out. 'Only I don't want one a year 'til we cor get in the door!'

Everyone was belting out a song based on the tune of the 'Marseillaise' but with the words adapted to their cause – the 'Strike Marseillaise' it was called: *'Fall in and follow me!'* The atmosphere was electric. They had started this strike in fear and hope and they were still not defeated!

Julia Varley went up to the stage at the front and signalled that she wanted quiet. Lucy was always quelled by her flinty expression. This was a woman who had been a trade union officer when she was *fifteen*. And Mr Edward Cadbury had invited her specially to come to Bournville and start a union for women there in the Cadburys' chocolate factory! She filled Lucy with awe.

'Comrades!' she called over their heads. 'Chainmakers of Cradley Heath!' Clapping and cheers broke out.

Lucy looked at the faces around her, mostly of women – a few male outworkers as well, a lot of them elderly. The hall stank of sweat and of the ragged, soot- and metal-impregnated clothes of the chainmakers. Many of the faces were gaunt and worn – but today, once again, they were lit up with passion and excitement seldom seen before this summer. She and Rose were clapping and cheering along with them all.

'We are now entering the fourth week of the strike for a decent living wage – a fight we are more determined than ever to win!'

Lucy looked round at Rose who was listening avidly. She felt a wave of love for her. Ever since Rose Shaw had come to their yard, things had changed. Thank heavens for someone like her who believed that such things were possible!

Miss Varley was explaining that the Chainmakers' Association, to which many of the chain works' employers belonged, were horrified by the publicity their strike was generating and the bad light in which it cast them.

'They are now talking about creating a "White List" of employers – and those who sign will be those who agree to pay you your rightful minimum wage . . .'

Cheering and shouted questions criss-crossed the hall in waves.

'Our bosses'll never sign that!'

'What about the foggers? Make 'em sign an' all!'

'What about the ones not in the association?'

Julia Varley held up her hand sternly for quiet.

'Yesterday, a delegation from your number travelled to Sheffield to the Trade Union Congress. They spoke to Congress – they held up their chains and told them of the poverty wages they are paid to make them!' She paused. 'Yesterday, the TUC pledged its support, the support of the whole Trade Union movement, for our cause – they are solidly behind us!'

Through more cheers, she added, 'And the money for our funds is still pouring in – we shall win this fight!'

The two of them filed slowly out of the hall at the end of the meeting. Two queues formed – one of people trying to get out, the other of those waiting to be signed up for the NFWW.

As soon as they stepped outside, standing to one side, face sour as a jug of milk in a heatwave, stood Thirza Rudge.

Lucy nudged Rose. 'D'yer think she was in there?'

'Likely,' Rose said. 'Spying on us, the evil old cow.' She stuck out her chin. 'Afternoon, Mrs Rudge! Enjoyed the speeches, did yow?'

Thirza Rudge seemed to swell up with rage, but she turned away as if she had not heard what Rose said.

Rose and Lucy looked at each other and laughed, gleefully.

'Ain't nowt 'er can do about it!' Rose chuckled joyfully. 'Oh, that's a sight I never thought I'd see.'

'Almost makes me wish Seth Dawson was still here,' Lucy said. Though the minute she'd opened her mouth she started to wish she hadn't. Digging Seth Dawson up, in any way whatsoever, was never a good idea.

'Well, 'e might be if you ent lamped 'im over the head!'
Rose said.

Lucy felt as if her blood was turning cold. There it
was again – someone thinking that it was she who had
been behind Seth's death. She put her head down and
said nothing. At the time, when he had taken himself
off, she had hardly given it a thought. And she knew
Bertha was right – that a number of things had happened
to Seth Dawson that night and they might not even know
the half of them. But if Rose was thinking it might be her
fault . . .

'Hey . . .' Rose bent to look at her. 'Luce? What's up?
I were only joking!'

'But it might've been me – mightn't it?' she said.

'Oh, I dow s'pose so, little thing like you – you cor 've
hit 'im very 'ard on that wooden nut of 'is. Look, Luce –
we'll never know now, will us?' Rose went on briskly.
'And whatever the case – 'e was in there up to no good as
usual. 'E was the one attacked yow – remember? Yow
was just defending yowerself. 'E was like an animal, that
man, and he got no more than he deserved. Dow go wast-
ing any more time thinking about it.' She stopped,
looking earnest. 'When I think what 'e did to yower
mother – and then to yow . . . He deserved to rot. And
now,' she finished cheerfully, 'that's just what 'e's doing –
six feet under!'

Lucy smiled, thinking, Well, only God knows what
happened. And she would have to hope that God could
forgive her.

They went back to the yard to report on the meeting
to the others. Mari Gornall was out in the yard hanging washing with little Dolly. Bertha was still at the
maiding tub, vigorously turning the wooden dolly this
way and that to bash the filth out of the clothes.

'So – what did 'er say?' Mari said.

And Lucy, for the first time, felt a warm sense of liking for her.

She helped Bertha that afternoon, hanging out the clothes and later gathering them in again, still slightly damp. Her mind was occupied with George, to seeing him like that, all of a sudden at the railway station. Inevitably then, her thoughts strayed on to Sam.

He'd like to see you again, George had said. But did he? Or was it just another of those honeyed things lads seemed to say so easily, without necessarily meaning them? Or kissing you, the way Clem did – because he had nothing better to do . . . Bitterness still rose in her when she remembered that night. It had meant nothing. How could anyone hold such an action so cheap? In the church she had learned that your words and actions should be true and should be used carefully . . .

She hauled Bertha's thick winter dress, which she had taken it into her head to wash today, down from the line. It was a tricky business for her, reaching up to the line, and she almost lost her balance as she did so.

'Eh – steady on,' a voice said behind her and she found her arm grasped strongly, catching her before she tilted over on to the ground. Lucy gasped, and looking round, found herself meeting the smiling eyes of Sam Ashmore.

Forty-Seven

She felt caught completely unawares: scruffy and flustered and on top of that almost falling flat on her back in the yard under the awkward weight of Bertha's frock!

'Ta,' she said, her tone tarter than she had intended. As soon as she had her balance back, she pulled her arm away from his. The handle of her stick was looped over the washing line and she reached for it, the laundry draped over her other arm. *What're you doing here?* she wanted to say.

'Can I give yow a 'and with that?' Sam said, obviously eager to please, as she set off towards the house.

Lucy started to feel ashamed of herself. What was he doing here? He knew no one except her, so he had come to see her, not Clem or John or any of the others. Her. And she had been rude and unwelcoming. She stopped.

'It's nice of you to come,' she said shyly, her cheeks flaming now. 'Sorry I was a bit short with you.'

They were standing face to face outside the Hipkisses' cottage. Lucy could feel eyes all around her, the kids in the yard, neighbours like Mari perhaps having a good nose out of the kitchen window. She looked up at Sam and he smiled. His cheeks looked rather pink and flustered as well and there was a humility about him which disarmed her.

'You coming in?' she said. 'I've got to put this lot down.'

For the moment only Bertha was in because the boys

were not back from work. She was sitting in Jonno's old chair. These days of the strike had meant something quite unaccustomed for some of the women – time to rest.

'Auntie,' Lucy said, as Bertha's stern face looked up at them both. 'This is Sam. 'E works with Georgie – on the railways.'

'Afternoon, Mrs . . .' He looked at Lucy.

'Hipkiss,' Bertha said. For the moment her voice was neither friendly nor unfriendly. 'All right, lad? There's a drop of tea in the pot if yer want.'

'Oh, no ta, Mrs Hipkiss,' Sam said earnestly.

Poor Sam, Lucy thought. She could see he did not know what to say now. She quickly folded the washing at the table ready for ironing. It was going to be up to her to say something and put him out of his misery.

'Was there some reason you came?' she asked, as she folded Clem's spare shirt.

'Well –' His cheeks flushed even more. Lucy wished very strongly that Bertha had not been in the room. It would be so nice, just once in a while, to have some privacy. 'I was wondering if you'd like to walk out with me – just for a little while.'

Lucy stared at him. Best get this over.

'You do know about my leg? I'm not the best at walking.'

'Oh . . .' Sam looked even more awkward. 'I dain't mean . . . But I thought . . . I mean, yow was at the railway station that day . . .'

'I can *walk*,' she interrupted, rather harshly. 'I'm slow going, that's all.' She smiled then, trying to soften things, the way she had spoken to him. Because she liked him already, liked him so much and it would be better to be let down now, for him to know the worst and her not to have to deal with another bitter blow later.

353

'That's all right!' Sam beamed. 'I don't mind how slow we walk! I'd walk anywhere with . . . I mean, it'd just be nice to go out a bit, that's all.'

She put the shirt on the pile. 'Now?'

Sam's smile took over his whole face. 'Well – yeah!'

It was another mellow, late summer evening. Lucy took her stick and led Sam Ashmore out along the entry. All the way she was terribly aware of the lurching ugliness of her walk.

But you decided to come here, she thought defiantly. You knew, so this is how it is. She was prickly with nerves.

'If we go this way,' she said, turning right along Hay Lane, 'there's a little walk at the edge of the fields.'

It was strange, she found herself realizing very quickly, that with Sam she did not feel timid, or like some kind of supplicant. It felt right just to be able to speak her mind, to lead the way, even.

'Sounds nice,' Sam said. He measured his walk against hers, taking small steps, but not as if it was a bother for him.

'It was quite a sight,' he said, 'all of you at the station the other day. I've never seen anything like it round 'ere before.'

'We've never had anyone like Mary Macarthur before,' Lucy said. She heard the reverence in her own voice as she said it. 'She's like a miracle. I know it's not just her – there's Miss Varley and all the others have put the work in here. But Miss Macarthur – well, when she comes, she makes you feel we can do *anything*, so long as we all stick together.' She was talking excitedly, unstoppable.

'And when she went back down to London she told everyone about us and so much money came in! Everyone was amazed! From her writing for the papers – they even made a film, to show at the pictures. Oh, there's no one quite like Miss Macarthur!'

Sam listened, almost with reverence, to her animated talking.

'I bet them foggers dow like what's going on.'

'They don't!' Lucy said. 'Our fogger's an old witch called Thirza Rudge. But there's nothing she can do about it!'

They had reached the end of the lane and they squeezed through the little gap into the field. It was always an awkward moment for Lucy and Sam offered a hand to help her balance as she squeezed round the little iron railing. She took it, smiling gratefully.

And they were in the fields. It was so like that evening when she had come here with Clem: still warm September, the air smoky, a hint of decaying leaves on the mellow breeze and the soft colours of the dying year.

Sam drew in a deep breath. He walked in the stubble at the edge of the field, leaving her the path to walk on. They ambled along slowly, side by side.

'It's nice 'ere. Have you always been 'ere?'

Lucy nodded. 'We used to come out and fetch wood for the fire as kids – well, the others did. I couldn't really go far in those days. And the boys – the Hipkiss boys, that is – would be up on the wall at the end of the yard and I could never get up. That was all I wanted – to get on there with them and look out. And then one day, I got them to pull me up.' She laughed. 'I thought I'd died and gone to heaven when I saw over the other side – even though I knew already what was there.'

'You don't half speak nicely, Lucy,' he said. 'How come?'

'I s'pose because I've always been to church,' she said.

'And Sunday school – in Graingers Lane. I had a teacher at the school . . .' She told him about Miss Jones. 'She would say, "Don't say 'ar it', say 'isn't it,' " – or, "There's an H at the beginning of that word, you know!" She taught me to read – that's one reason the foggers didn't get our yard to sign away our minimum wage, because I could read the form and tell everyone what it really said.'

She glowed with pride. Sam looked at her.

'Yower quite a wench, Lucy Hipkiss.'

'My name's Butler,' she said. 'Not Hipkiss.'

'Course,' he said. 'Same as George.'

'Tell me about yourself, Sam,' she said. Even as she spoke, she wondered at how confident she felt with him, how much at ease. 'What about your family?' For a moment she imagined a household of parents and loving sisters that, if things went well between them – well, maybe she could find herself a part of?

He gave her a puzzled look.

'I ay got no family – that's how I met George.'

It was her turn to look awkward.

'Sorry – I forgot,' she said. More delicately she added, 'You've really got no family? See, George had me, all the time. We've got another brother somewhere, our Albert. He took off when our mom died and we don't know where he is. But George did have someone, it's just we was separated.'

Sam looked down at the ground for a moment and there was such sadness in his face that she almost wished she had not asked.

'I dow think I've got anyone,' he said. 'I can't remember any of 'em. I was told my mom died having me – and then my dad died of summat else. That's all I know. I cor remember anything before the orphanage. To be honest,

I was scared when I had to leave and come out into the world. It was all I knew, being in there . . .'

'Oh – that's sad,' she said. She found her eyes were full of tears on his account. 'So sad.'

He looked at her and took in her emotion and she saw he was moved by it.

'Both of us orphans then,' he said huskily.

Lucy nodded. 'I can't remember my father. My grandfather was with us when I was young. But he died, and then Mom . . .' She felt her features twist bitterly for a moment. This was not the moment to start on Seth Dawson and all that had happened. 'She died when I was quite young. Mrs Hipkiss was Mom's friend – she took me in. She's always been good to me but, what with her husband being sick and everything else, she couldn't manage George as well.'

For a moment they both stood still, looking out across the field at the distant winding gear of the mine. In a corner of her mind, she realized they were close to the spot where Clem had kissed her. It felt so long ago. A piece of history. And it didn't matter now – not at all.

'I can remember her, though,' she said, wiping her eyes. 'That's summat.'

'It is,' Sam said quietly and then she felt bad for saying it because he had no one to remember.

She looked round at him. He was staring ahead, his dark brows frowning slightly, blue eyes taking in the distant view. And she felt a warmth spread in her chest. She loved his face, the way he stood, feet placed firmly apart, sleeves rolled to show strong forearms which hung loosely at his sides. He was just nice, and right – it was as simple as that. She had never felt anything quite like this before.

'Sorry,' she said.

'What d'yow mean?'

'Well – you can't do that. Remember, I mean.'

'Don't be saft.'

She felt him take her hand and the last thing she wanted, she realized, was to pull away. Their fingers settled round each other's, gently, in a careful, understanding way. We both need someone, she thought. Both of us – we're starved of family.

'George must be angry,' she said. 'Because he was sent away and I wasn't. Did he say he was angry at us?'

Sam shrugged. 'No. I dunno what he feels. It's no good having feelings when yower in there. There's no real use in feelings, if no one teks any notice of them, is there?'

She took this in silently, shifting her weight carefully, trying to stay comfortable on her leg. She did not realize Sam had noticed, but he must have done.

'There was a lad in the orphanage, had his leg crushed by a cart,' he said. 'It was his right leg – they took it off below the knee. 'E was only a year younger than me and we were pals.' He looked at her, into her eyes. 'It's not a sight that's strange to me, is all I'm saying.'

Again, tears slid into her eyes as she looked up at him, her throat tightening so she could not speak. She had to look away.

'Lucy . . .' Very gently he reached out and turned her face towards him, then drew back, as if he was afraid he had overstepped the mark. But there was so much feeling in his eyes and she knew that her own were giving back the same, because that was how she felt. 'When I saw you that first time, at the station – with all the others, all bold and knowing what you was all about – I was . . . Well, I were bowled over. I thought, that's the one for me. Just like that. Cheek of it really because I dain't know if you already have someone . . .'

'I don't,' she said simply. Smiling, though still tearful, she added, 'Or I didn't – up until now.'

'Well – thank goodness for that,' Sam said.

Holding out his arms, he drew her gently to him. They stood, in the soft air of the evening, sheltered in each other's embrace.

Forty-Eight

The urgent clatter of knuckles on the door woke her with a start.

'Mrs Hipkiss?' Rose Shaw came steaming into the room that afternoon like a liner with a full cargo, her face flushed. Bertha, who had been snoozing in the chair, pushed herself up, dazed.

'There's a meeting tonight – at the school. Mary Macarthur'll be there, and everyone. It's over – they've all caved in!'

'They've all . . .?'

'Even Thirza Rudge's had to sign up. The Chainmakers' Association ay gunna deal with any of the firms or the foggers who won't sign up to the White List. They dow like the bad publicity they've been getting.'

Rose grinned gleefully. Her face was plumper than usual, puffed up by the last weeks of carrying a baby, the hem of her skirt hitched up high at the front by the jut of her belly.

'D'yow want to sit down a minute?' Bertha said.

'Oh, no – I've got to go and tell the other yards about the meeting . . . Hopping mad, old Rudgie is. So we won! Eleven and threepence they've got to pay us.'

Bertha just kept staring at her. Eleven and three – more than twice the amount she had been slaving for for all these years. It was hard to believe even after the long weeks of the strike, of asking for it.

'Still not a patch on what the men get,' Rose said, her

face darkening for a moment. 'But it's a start, eh? And they cor get out of it without trouble. It'll mean other workers can ask for it for themselves. So – up the school hall again tonight?'

Bertha nodded. 'I'll be there.' Course she would – wouldn't miss it for the world.

As Rose lumbered off again to spread the word, Bertha sat in the astonishing quiet of her house. These days she was getting into the habit of having a little snooze in the early afternoon. That was going to have to stop, she thought. Back to work again . . . But God in Heaven – eleven and three a week!

For a moment she remembered the morning when Rose and Wally Shaw had arrived in the yard. She looked back with a certain amount of shame. How much she had resented Rose at the start – how nasty and closed in on herself she had been. Jonno was so poorly and she wasn't really herself at the time – and it was even worse after he died. Her face flushed at the thought of all that tippling and sneaking about. Those nights she'd drunk until all she did was pass out in the chair. What a cowing disgrace!

I s'pose I was all ripped to shreds with Jonno going, she thought, finding a drop of kindness for herself. All those years they'd had together – she'd had to find out who 'she' was on her own; to go on, somehow, without him.

What an uppity little bit Rose had seemed back then. A threat to how things had been for a long time, to her place as gaffer in this yard. Even now she had her moments with her. But in the end, she had to admit, Rose had led them – dragged them to begin with – into this strike. And she had been right. They'd had to stop thinking they could never do anything, had to get together, join forces. And now, by God, they had won. They had actually got something by demanding it of the bosses – and won! She still could hardly take it in.

'Oh, I don't think there'll be room for *you* in here,' Lucy said later, to all the Hipkiss boys. 'There won't be room for the people who *ought* to be there, else.'

Word had got round about the meeting in Graingers Lane and now, as the chainmakers' strike and Mary Macarthur were famous – there'd even been a Pathé film about it in the cinema! – a lot of people wanted to come and see for themselves.

John, Clem and Freddie all nodded obediently to the new Lucy who stood before them, telling them what was what.

'We can hang about outside – and we might be able to hear a bit,' John said.

'We can come in if there's room, can't us?' Clem said.

'There won't be,' Lucy said decisively. 'There were at least eight hundred of us on strike and we all want to hear our Mary. So don't you go crowding the place out.'

'We won't, Luce,' Freddie said. Cautiously, he added, 'What about George – and Sam?'

No one could have failed to notice that Lucy and Sam Ashmore had been almost inseparable since the day they met.

'They'll have to stay outside like everyone else,' Lucy said. But a blush stole through her cheeks. In fact, she felt fit to burst with happiness. All this – the strike, Mary Macarthur, her heroine, coming back to Cradley Heath today *and* Sam. Her lovely, loving Sam! How could life get any better?

As they all set off, Freddie nudged her, grinning. 'Yow look ever so pretty, Luce.'

She smiled at him. Of all of them, he had never hurt her feelings.

'Ta, Fred,' she said.

The women were all coming out of their houses: Mari and Edna, Rose, Bertha pulling on her cap with her shawl wrapped round her.

'Mek sure you get them to bed,' Rose called to Wally. 'I dow want to come back and find 'em all still milling about.'

'All right, bab,' Lucy heard from a resigned Wally.

This was the women's big night – absolutely nothing was going to get in their way.

Even walking up the road to the school hall with the women of her yard felt like a triumphal procession to Lucy. It was already dark and cold, but women were emerging from other yards and streets, all chatting excitedly.

Sam appeared suddenly at her side, George with him as well.

'I know you said we had to stay outside,' Sam said. 'And we will, but I wanted to see yer!'

Lucy laughed. 'Sorry – there won't be room, I don't think. But it's nice you came.' They linked arms and he supported her along the street. George walked behind with the Hipkiss lads. Lucy had been surprised and secretly pleased that even they wanted to be able to say they had set eyes on the famous Mary Macarthur.

'See you later,' Lucy said outside, squeezing Sam's arm before they had to separate.

'I s'pose we might pop into the boozer while it's all going on,' he said.

'Oh, I s'pect you will,' she laughed. 'Ta-ra!'

The hall was filling up fast.

'Yow gunna be all right?' Lucy heard Mari asking Rose. 'D'yow need a seat?'

'Oh, I'll be all right,' Rose said. 'I dow think there's much room to sit and I want to be able to see!'

On the stage at the front they could already see Miss Varley and Mr Sitch.

'Who's that?' Mari asked, pointing at another man.

'That's Mr Mallon – up from London,' Rose said.

'Well, where's Miss Macarthur then?' Bertha said. ''Er ought to be up there.'

They could hear others asking the same question. Had she not yet arrived? Everyone wanted more than anything to see their saviour, Mary Macarthur.

But soon there was a stir at the back and someone called out, 'Ooh, it's 'er – our Mary's 'ere!'

Lucy saw Mary Macarthur's beaming face, topped by a black hat, move along the side of the hall. It was as if she created a wave of movement as she went along, everyone drawing back to let her pass. The packed room burst into applause as she made her way to take her place on the stage.

''Er's no age,' Bertha said wonderingly.

Suddenly everyone burst out into singing the 'Chainmakers' Marseillaise', some stamping their feet, and the song finished with more clapping and cheering before Julia Varley stood and held up her hand, smiling, for quiet.

'That's the happiest I've ever seen 'er looking,' Rose murmured.

The other trade unionists spoke. They all thanked the chain outworkers for their strength, their faith in the struggle. They talked about the funds that had poured in, the solidarity they had had from others in the Trade Union movement, the great achievement of this strike paving the way for others to claim their own rights.

Lucy sensed Rose fidgeting beside her after a while. She was flexing forwards at the waist and at one point she turned and grimaced at Lucy.

'You all right?' Lucy asked.

'It's doing my back in a bit,' she said. 'I'll be all right. Let's just hear our Mary.'

Finally, the moment came for Mary Macarthur to speak. Lucy thought of Sam and the others. Were they all outside, listening? Could they hear anything? She swelled with pride at the thought of them hearing any of her words.

But as Mary Macarthur got up and stepped forwards, Lucy forgot everything else, because everyone was crying out and clapping wildly for all they were worth. Her emotions spilled over and she and many of the others had tears running down her cheeks. This wonderful person, this kind, lovely woman who had come to them like an angel from heaven and shown them all how they might be strong together!

Mary Macarthur stood for a moment, her smile turned on everyone in the room and at last they quietened to let her speak.

'So,' she cried, above their heads. 'We have the victory – for freedom and the right!'

More applause followed this, and it took some time to settle down again. Lucy drank in the sight of her, of all that was happening. What an amazing, miraculous day this was! Mary's now familiar, well-spoken voice rang about them.

'Your story has been told the length and breadth of this country. I say to you, women of Cradley Heath, your names will go down in history as the brave women who stood up against poverty wages for sweated labour. And this is just a first step. Who knows what you can go on to achieve as an army of women workers!'

She paused again, her face alight with joy as they all cheered and clapped.

'You cannot win such victories alone,' she went on. 'And I would urge any of you here, who are not yet part of the union, to join, to be part of the whole, where we can find strength and resolution together. For if we remain together, we will prevail!'

'Oof . . .' Rose groaned, bending over, and even amid all the pandemonium of clapping, Lucy heard her moan, 'Oh Lord, no!'

Looking down, she saw with a shock of horror that the floor around Rose's feet was all wet. Rose was looking up at her with a desperate expression.

'The babby's coming – and I reckon it's coming quick!'

Forty-Nine

Her bloomers were saturated and she could feel it running down her legs, but even so, the expression of utter horror on Lucy's face made Rose want to laugh.

'I ay wet meself,' she said. 'It's the waters – it's what happens, bab.'

Pain snatched her breath, doubling her up, so overwhelming that she knew things were not going to go slowly. Dear God, how the hell was she going to make it home in this state? Would she even get out of here with all these crowds, never mind along the street? She couldn't have a baby in front of all these people!

'Oh, Lor.' She heard Bertha Hipkiss's voice. 'Rose – 'old on to me, bab. Luce, Mari – we've got to get 'er back 'ome. Mari – get the lads to fetch Wally. If they ay out there, run and drag 'em out of the pub!'

Lucy watched, feeling completely helpless as Rose panted out the pain, as quietly as she could. At last she was able to stand upright again.

'I'll walk ahead of you,' Lucy said. Her stick and her limp encouraged people to move back as Rose, supported by Bertha and Mari, with Edna Wilmott behind, managed, like a convoy, to push their way through the crowd. People stepped aside to let them pass but they were so entranced by Mary Macarthur that they scarcely took their eyes off the stage, so they all escaped the hall without too much bother.

'Thank God for that,' Mari said as they stood in the cold darkness. 'Yow all right, Rose?'

Rose was bent over again, in the middle of a contraction, and all she could do was let out a moan of pain.

Sam was hovering outside with John and Freddie. Lucy was so happy to see him, even though he would have no more idea what to do than she did. At least all the other women were here: they were the ones who knew!

'Clem's gone for 'er husband,' Sam said. 'Ooh, dear – that dow look too good! Is 'er gunna be all right?'

Rose was leaning against the front of the building, huffing and puffing again.

''Er will be,' Bertha said. 'We just need to get 'er back 'ome. Has someone gone for Mrs Heath?'

'I'll go.' Freddie, seeming glad to escape, shot off along the road as Bertha shouted, 'Cokeland Place – number four!'

'Can yow walk now, Rose?' Mari bawled down her ear.

'Ar, I can – and I've not gone deaf, neither,' Rose said, straightening up.

Lucy gratefully threaded her arm through Sam's. They were all making gradual, agonizing progress along the street, when they heard a metallic rumbling sound on the cobbles ahead. Lucy narrowed her eyes, seeing someone come hurtling into view, and after a moment they all made out the frantic figure of Wally Shaw, loping along and pushing a huge, rusty wheelbarrow.

'Oh – there you are!' he panted, jerking to a halt in front of them.

Rose was just in the midst of recovering from another bout of pain, leaning against a wall again.

'What the hell's that for?' Mari Gornall shrieked.

'I thought 'er might need it . . .'

'Wha' – put 'er in a wheelbarrow?' Mari seemed to find this very funny and was still cackling when Rose straightened up, took one look at the strange carriage her husband had thought to bring, and climbed in without hesitation.

'Oh, thank God,' she said. 'Just get me home – quick.'

'Well, I 'ope it's good and strong, is all,' Bertha said, seeming amused. 'Don't go and tip 'er out of that thing, for heaven's sake!'

But they were all relieved that the journey back to Hay Lane might now proceed a bit more speedily.

John Hipkiss and Wally each took a handle of the wheelbarrow and managed to keep it moving, if swervily, along the street, Rose clinging grimly to the sides. Mari got the giggles and the others followed on, hearing her snorting and gurgling most of the way. Lucy and Sam lagged behind as the men were hefting the barrow along at quite a rate.

'There's always summat going on whenever I'm with you,' Sam said. 'Is it always like this?'

Lucy grinned up at him in the gloom. 'Why – don't you like it?'

Sam laughed. 'I think I do. It's a bit more exciting than what I'm used to, I can tell yer.'

Freddie was already back at the yard when they came rolling in, Rose groaning loudly as she had to climb out of the wheelbarrow which Wally and John, arms shaking at the effort, tipped to one side to make it easier.

'There ay no sign of Mrs Heath!' Freddie said. 'I dain't know what else to do – who to ask for.'

'Never mind,' Rose said. She reached out and seized Bertha Hipkiss by the hand. 'You know what to do?'

Lucy saw the shock on Bertha's face at this.

'You can do it, Auntie,' she said. 'You know all about babbies.'

'That's all very well . . .' Bertha was saying.

'We'll get the water boiling,' Mari said. 'Victor!' she yelled. 'We need water. Get yowerself out 'ere and mek yowerself useful for once!'

'Right,' Bertha said, catching hold of Rose's arm. 'In we go. Mari – I'll need yow. Everyone else – keep out the road.'

Lucy stayed out in the yard with the lads and Edna. Wally, John and Freddie fetched pails of water. Victor Gornall eventually came out of his house looking dishevelled, peered about him as if to say, *What the hell do they need me for?* and retreated inside again.

'I'm gunna mek a cup of tea,' Edna said, disappearing into her house.

'Should we go inside?' Lucy said to Sam. The two of them and Freddie were left as rather spare parts in the yard. Then she added, 'I don't want to though, some'ow.'

Sam shrugged. 'T'ain't that cold yet. 'Ere – c'mere, Lucy.' Shyly, he reached out and put his arm around her and she snuggled close to him. It was one of the best feelings, standing close with Sam like that. They stood outside Rose's house. The door was not quite shut and she could hear Rose's groans, which made her legs turn to jelly.

'Gracie – you get back upstairs!' she heard Bertha say to the girl. 'Yower mother's busy and she dow need anyone else hanging about. Goo on – yow'll 'ave a new sister or brother very soon.'

'They haven't even managed to get her up the stairs,' Lucy said. 'Poor Rose!'

'D'yow think that woman'll come – the midwife?' Sam said.

'It didn't sound as if she were at home.'

After not much time at all there was a loud, shrieking cry from inside the house which made Lucy dig her nails into Sam's arm.

'Blimey,' he said. 'That sounds bad.'

'Oh,' Lucy gasped. 'Oh dear, poor Rose!'

A moment later, after a deathly pause, they heard a quite different sound – the scraping cry of a new baby expressing its shock of arrival into the waiting world.

'It's here! Oh, Sam – it's here already!'

They flung their arms about each other just as Edna Wilmott came back with a cup in her hand.

'What's gooing on? 'Er ain't 'ad it already?'

'She has – we heard it!' Lucy cried. She found she had tears running down her cheeks again, hardly even knowing why. 'Oh, what a good thing we got her home!'

'Well, come on then,' Edna said. She went and rapped on the door. 'We've come to see the babby,' she announced, with a brusque lack of delicacy.

Since no one told her to go away, Lucy stepped forward, longing suddenly to see the new arrival. The lads hung back a bit.

Inside, the room was full of steam from the kettle and Rose was sitting by the fire, holding a wrapped little bundle in her arms. She beamed up at them all – Bertha and Mari, Lucy and Edna all crowding round. Wally, the proud father, was standing by Rose's chair looking stunned and bashful. Gracie had slipped back downstairs as well and was gazing with rapt attention over her mother's shoulder.

'Blimey,' Rose said. 'I've never 'ad one come quick as that before – 'er nearly joined in the meeting!' She looked well and hardly different as the birth had been so fast.

'Is it a girl?' Lucy whispered. She leaned down and saw a little crumpled face, still smeared with blood and the white paste of birth. Her eyes were closed and she looked peaceful, as if she felt that things were all well and that she already belonged here.

'Hello, little one,' Lucy whispered, her tears coming again. Hearing Rose's cries of pain had brought back the night Mom had the baby, the fear and horror of it. But now it was such a happy thing and the baby was so sweet that she was crying as much from happiness.

'Well,' Rose said, looking down into the baby's face, then up at her husband and at Gracie. 'What d'yow think? Seems there's only one name we can give this little'un since 'er was nearly born in front of Mary Macarthur!'

'Mary,' Gracie said. 'Hello, Mary Shaw!'

'Mary Julia,' Rose said. 'That's what we'll call 'er. And thanks to them, 'er'll never 'ave to collar for five bob a week!'

Everyone made welcoming noises to little Mary. When Lucy looked round, she saw all the lads in the doorway, shoving each other so that they could see in. But she could not see Sam.

She went over to the door. 'Let me out,' she said. She found Sam leaning up against the wall on the other side of the yard.

Lucy went over to him. 'Couldn't you get a look-in?' she said, joking.

'Oh, I did. I saw 'er – from the door, like.' He sounded strange and after a second she realized he was swallowing back tears. 'I've never seen anything like that.' He spoke very quietly because his voice was all choked up. 'A new baby – a family, like them. It's . . . Well, it's the best, ay it?'

A lump rose in Lucy's throat again and all she could do was nod. She had had a family once, had known something of that before it was all blown apart by death, and by the wicked actions of Seth Dawson. And at least she had found George, even if Albert was lost to them. But poor Sam had never even known it.

'Lucy.' He turned to her in deadly earnest and put his hands on her shoulders. 'I know we've not known each other long, like. But . . . you're the one for me. I know you are. All I want in this life is . . . that.' He jerked his head towards Rose and Wally's house. 'A family. A little home and people I can love and who'll love me back.'

Emotion twisted inside her. That longing – her longing, which met his.

'*I* love you, Sam,' she said. 'I do. It's all I want as well.'

'And I want it with you, Lucy. You and me and our own little place and kids and . . .' His voice broke. 'I know we're both young – but I love you so much – and I can't think of anything I want more.' He stepped closer and took her in his arms, gently, so as not to throw her off balance. 'Will you stay with me, Luce, and be my wife? You and me – and be family with me?'

He looked down into her eyes in the gloom of the yard, able to see her answer before she even had to say anything.

VII

10 June 1912

Fifty

The music from the band floated across the rooftops, creating a festive atmosphere before they had even arrived, all of them walking to the celebration along the sunny street.

Lucy, pushing her old perambulator, walked beside Sam and Rose. She loved being able to walk with the pram because she could do without her stick and feel, for once, as if she looked almost normal.

The other women from the Hay Lane yard followed on behind – Bertha Hipkiss and Edna, with Mari, who was very heavily pregnant, trailing along with them.

'I feel like an old woman,' she grumbled. 'I cor go any faster.' After quite a bit of shouting, off and on, some truce had been arranged with Victor and now there was another Gornall on the way.

Rose was also six months gone with a baby, despite her best intentions.

'I've told Wally, this is the very last one,' she said when the sickness all started again and she was dashing out to the lavs. Everyone knew they would believe it when they saw it.

Today was a very special day. Now, on what had previously been Lower Town Bonk, a building had been going up and was finished at last. Drawing closer they could all see the imposing brick bulk of it, a solid, attractive building, with a lot of rooms inside. A crowd was gathering. Lucy looked up at the wide, triangular-shaped frontage and the cast-iron sign fixed above two wide windows.

'THE WORKERS' INSTITUTE!' Rose said. 'I can read that, any road!' Her cheeks were pink and she looked happy and proud. 'Look at that – that's another thing 'er did for us, our Mary!'

The funds in support of the striking chainmakers had amounted to at least four thousand pounds. So much had been left over that it was enough to fund the building of this institute – a place for the people and the union work of Cradley Heath.

They had all followed news of Mary Macarthur avidly since the strike. Last year all those women in Bermondsey down in London had gone on strike during a boiling hot August. Mary seemed to be unstoppable.

Lucy stood beside Sam, gently moving the pram back and forth, hoping to get her little one to sleep. Sam ducked to look inside.

'No luck there,' he laughed. ''Er's wide awake, looking round! 'Ere – let me hold 'er for a bit.'

As he reached into the old pram, Lucy looked lovingly at the back of his neck, the little soft bits of hair that always wanted to twist into curls. She and Sam married in the January of last year, hell bent on it, despite Bertha asking what the rush was. Both of them wanted a home – and as soon as possible. They wanted each other. What was there to wait for when they were both so sure? It was a quiet, simple wedding at the Methodist church, with George, then fifteen, acting as Sam's best man.

And home was what they had – a little back house in a yard on Beehive Street, not too far from Hay Lane, where Lucy still worked her hearth with all the others. They both worked hard, and at the end of the day were delighted to see each other. Lucy felt a great surge of happiness every time Sam walked through the door in his railway uniform and immediately called, 'Luce?'

'Here!' She'd put down whatever she was doing and go to him, throwing her arms around him, Sam's eyes smiling gladly down into hers. She could still hardly believe how much love they had for each other – that life could be like this. That she had her precious little Ellen. Her sweetest joy of the day was getting her little one ready for bed, sitting beside her singing lullabies to her, and, softly as her eyes closed. *'Cherry ripe, cherry ripe, ripe I cry . . .'*

Bert lifted the child, now seven months old, her head covered by a soft down of pale brown hair. She was kicking her legs with delight at being able to see everything and when she caught sight of her mother she kicked even harder.

'Ooh, look at 'er,' Rose said, laughing. 'You ay gunna sleep, am yow, little Ellen?'

Bertha came up and tickled Ellen's cheek as well. 'All right, missy? Look at yow!' She treated the little girl as if she was one of her own grandchildren, even though John and Maud now had a little son and Clem was just married too. Only Freddie was left at home. Lucy could tell that Bertha missed them all – missed her, too.

But they were all together at work. Lucy kept Ellen outside the forge as much as possible, away from the fumes, but Ellen was happiest when she was with everyone and able to watch everything that went on.

''Er's a born chainmaker,' Rose said, with a roll of her eyes. Then she added with a grin, 'Over yower dead body, I s'pose?'

Rose still did what she could for the union, but she knew she would always be in the chain forge. She was determined that Gracie and her other children would stay on at school longer, have a chance at something else.

'I want 'er to be able to read – like you. Even better'un you, Luce!' And at nine years of age, Grace was already doing very well. ''Er can be summat else – not have all this toil and muck and mess we've had.'

Lucy still felt lucky to have had anything at all. But yes, when she looked at Ellen, so full of life and spirit already, she knew she didn't want her fed into the chain hearth, the back-breaking work, the heat and fumes and filth – not if she could better herself and do something else.

She steadied the handle of the pram and slid her other arm into Sam's as he held Ellen, jigging her in time with the music the band was playing. She looked up at the warm coloured bricks of the building. What a time that had been. The strike, the changes – better wages, it was true – but all the changes in themselves. The way they had learned that they could do things, achieve things, if they organized, insisted, found their own power together. And the way they all felt stronger for knowing they were part of a bigger world than just their own yard and their own little town.

The Workers' Institute. She smiled. Mary Macarthur, she thought. Our Mary – the angel of Cradley Heath, passing through here, changing us all with the powerful beating of her wings.

Black Country Glossary

ay am not
aydedaydy half-soaked person
black bat beetle
bonk bank
booster quarter loaf of bread
bostin fantastic, great
cant talk, gossip
clammed starved
collar work
cooting courting
cor cannot
cotter with dealings with, hassle with
darcent daren't
diper sanitary towel
dobbin handcart
dow don't
fittle food
fizzog face
frit frightened
foggers middlemen and -women between the chain-making
   factories and their outworkers
kalied drunk
loffer chin
lugholes ears
lummux clumsy oaf
'oss road horse road
mardy bad-tempered

381

marleys marbles, usually from the tops of bottles
miskin dustbin or ash-heap
mithered fretful, nagging, questioning
mollycoddle spoil, fuss over
mon man
noddleyead foolish person
noggin chunk of thick bread
nogyead thick, slow of thought
ockered awkward, bloody-minded
pinna pinafore, apron
pit bonk the bank of a coal pit
riffy dirty
skiddy anvil
skilly thin porridge or soup
snoz nose
sop bread softened in hot water, sometimes with a dribble
    from the teapot
squilt spot, blackhead
tat scrap
thowd mon your man
tunky fat, portly
um home
up the stick pregnant
werriting fretting
whammel dog
wust worst
yaller yellow
yampy mad, daft, eccentric
yowm you are
yowm-yowm – person from the Black Country with the
    'yow' pronunciation of 'you'

Acknowledgements

With special thanks for all help in researching this story – first of all to particular books: *Portrait of the Black Country*, Harold Parsons; *Breaking Their Chains: Mary Macarthur and the Chainmakers' Strike of 1910*, Tony Barnsley; *The White Slaves of England*, Robert Harborough Sherard; *Righting the Wrong: Mary Macarthur 1880–1921, The Working Woman's Champion*, Cathy Hunt; *Chain and Anchor Making in the Black Country*, Ron Moss; *A Fair Day's Wage for a Fair Day's Work?: Sweated Labour and the Origins of Minimum Wage Legislation in Britain*, Sheila Blackburn; *Cradley Heath, Old Hill & District*, Ron Moss and Bob Clarke; *No One But a Mother Knows: Stories of Motherhood Before the War*, Margaret Llewellyn Davis; *Life As We Have Known It: The Voices of Working-Class Women*, Margaret Llewellyn Davies; *A Capful O'Nails*, David Christie Murray; *Black Country Dialect*, Brendan Hawthorne.

To the invaluable Godfrey Edition old OS maps of Cradley Heath and Old Hill, 1901, which have made an understanding of the landscape in those times a great deal easier.

Also to the Black Country Museum, where the old Cradley Heath Institute has found a home, as well as a good deal of information about Mary Macarthur and sweated labourers involved in the strike and many other things of interest (including the best fish and chips in the world).

Thank you also to Pat Witherspoon, who welcomed me so warmly to her home to talk about her Black Country childhood and all sorts of other useful snippets of information.